MINOTAUR
MYSTERIES

GET A CLUE!

Be the first to hear the latest mystery book news…

With the St. Martin's Minotaur monthly newsletter, you'll learn about the hottest new Minotaur books, receive advance excerpts from newly published works, read exclusive original material from featured mystery writers, and be able to enter to win free books!

Sign up on the Minotaur Web site at:
www.minotaurbooks.com

Outstanding Praise for S. J. Rozan's Novels
Winter and Night

"Okay, listen up: this woman can write! With *Winter and Night*, S. J. Rozan paints with the full palate of the human heart, using depth, detail, and nuance of character that I haven't seen since Raymond Chandler. (Yes, I mean it.) Rozan delivers a wonderful mystery that is also a full-bodied novel about the pressures we place on ourselves and our loved ones, and how these pressures can crush us."

—Robert Crais, author of *Hostage*

"Featuring two of my favorite characters in crime fiction, Bill Smith and Lydia Chin, *Winter and Night* is a chilling and compelling look at the dark roots of violence among American teens. It is the most intense and topical work from one of the finest crime writers today. This is a writer—and a story—not to miss."

—Linda A. Fairstein, author of *The Deadhouse*

"The language bounces and bites and zips the tale along, offering rewards at every level in this tense thriller about children growing up amid adults who've never grown up themselves . . . Rozan does a terrific job of mixing football and family, past and present, old crimes and present police investigations. Her minor characters . . . are gems."

—*Washington Post*

"A powerfully moving tale told by Smith that not only covers several hot-button topics, from our natural obsession with winning at all costs to the horror of high school homicide, but also forces its usually enigmatic narrator to unlock many of his family secrets." —*Los Angeles Times*

"A compelling mystery about the roots of teen violence."
—*Library Journal*

More . . .

Also by S. J. Rozan

**Available from
St. Martin's/Minotaur Paperbacks**

winter and night

s. j. rozan

St. Martin's Paperbacks

WINTER AND NIGHT

Copyright © 2002 by S. J. Rozan.

Cover photo of houses © Don Spiro / Stone / Getty Images.
Cover photo of moon ©INC. 'L'Image Magic / FPG / Getty Images.

Library of Congress Catalog Card Number: 2001048659

ISBN: 0-312-98668-8
EAN: 80312-98668-1

Printed in the United States of America

St. Martin's Press hardcover edition / February 2002
St. Martin's Paperbacks edition / April 2003

St. Martin's Paperbacks are published by St. Martin's Press, 175 Fifth
Avenue, New York, NY 10010.

10 9 8 7 6 5 4 3

acknowledgments

Three cheers for:

Steve Axelrod, my agent
Keith Kahla, my editor
MVPs

Steve Blier, Hillary Brown, Monty Freeman, Max Rudin,
Jim Russell, and Amy Schatz
All-stars

Betsy Harding, Royal Huber, Barbara Martin,
Jamie Scott, and Keith Snyder
Coaches

Kim Dougherty, Corey Doviak, Pat Picciarelli,
and the team at Manhattan Sports Medicine
Trainers

NeverTooLate Basketball and the SKW Laser Beams
Teammates

David Dubal
for continuing education

Carl Stein
the car guy

Deborah Peters and Nancy Ennis
the home team

Helen Hester
traded to New Orleans

Peter Quijano
for the circus catch

and DL and GP
for raising the bar

Then come home my children
The Sun has gone down
The dews of evening arise.

Your spring and your day
Are wasted in play
Your winter and night in disguise.

—William Blake, *Songs of Experience*

one

When the phone rang I was asleep, and I was dreaming.

Alone in the shadowed corridors of an unfamiliar place, I heard, ahead, boisterous shouts, cheering. In the light, in the distance, figures moved with a fluid, purposeful grace. Cold fear followed me, something from the dark. I tried to call to the crowd ahead: my voice was weak, almost silent, but they stopped at the sound of it. Then, because the language I was speaking wasn't theirs, they turned their backs, took up their game again. The floor began to slant uphill, and my legs were leaden. I struggled to reach the others, called again, this time with no sound at all. A door swung shut in front of me, and I was trapped, longing before, fear behind, in the dark, alone.

The ringing tore through the dream; it went on awhile and I grabbed up the phone before I was fully awake. "Smith," I said, and my heart pounded because my voice was weak and I thought they couldn't hear me.

But there was an answer. "Bill Smith? Private investigator, Forty-seven Laight Street?"

I rubbed my eyes, looked at the clock. Nearly two-thirty. I coughed, said, "Yeah. Who the hell are you?" I groped by the bed for my cigarettes.

"Sorry about the hour. Detective Bert Hagstrom, Midtown South. You awake?"

I got a match to a cigarette, took in smoke, coughed again. My head cleared. "Yeah. Yeah, okay. What's up?"

"I got a kid here. Fourteen, maybe fifteen. Says he knows you."

"Who is he?"

"Won't say. No ID. Rolled a drunk on Thirty-third Street just up the block from two uniformed officers in a patrol car."

"Sounds pretty stupid."

"Green, I'd say. Young and big. I told him what happens to kids like him if we send them to Rikers."

"If he's fourteen, he's too young for Rikers."

"He doesn't know that. He's been stonewalling since they brought him in. Two hours I been shoveling it on about Rikers, finally he gives up your name. How about coming down here and giving us some help?"

Smoke twisted from the red tip of my cigarette, lost itself in the empty darkness. A November chill had invaded the room while I slept.

"Yeah," I said, throwing off the blanket. "Sure. Just put it in my file, I got out of bed at two in the morning as a favor to the NYPD."

"I've seen your file," Hagstrom said. "It won't help."

Fragments of stories I would never know appeared out of the night, receded again as the cab took me north. Two streetwalkers, one white, one black, both tall and thin, laughing uproariously together; a dented truck, no markings at all, rolling silently downtown; a basement door that opened and closed with no one going in or out. I sipped burnt coffee from a paper cup, watched fallen leaves and discarded scraps jump in the gutters as we drove by. The cab driver was African and his radio kept up a soft, unbroken stream of talk, words I couldn't understand. A few times he chuckled, so whatever was going on must have been funny. He let me out at the chipped stone steps of Midtown South. I overtipped him; I was thinking what it must be like to grow up in a sun-scorched African village and find yourself driving a cab through the night streets of New York.

Inside, the desk sergeant directed me through the glaring fluorescent lights and across the scuffed vinyl tile to the second floor, the detective squad room. Two men sat at steel desks, one on the phone, the other typing. A third man, at the room's far end, punched buttons on an unresponsive microwave.

"Ah, fuck this thing," the button-puncher said without rancor, trying another combination. "It's fucked."

"You break it again?" The typist, a bald-headed black man, spoke without looking up.

"Hagstrom?" I asked from the doorway.

The guy at the microwave turned, said, "Me. You're Smith?"

I nodded. He was a big, sloppy man in a pretty bad suit. He didn't have a lot of hair but what he had needed a trim. "You know how to work these things?" he asked me.

"Try fast forward."

The typist snorted.

"Screw it," Hagstrom said, abandoning the microwave, crossing the room with a long, loose-jointed stride. "Doctor says I should lay off the burritos anyway. Come with me."

I followed him into the corridor, around a corner, into a small, stale-smelling room. It was empty and dim. The only light came from the one-way mirror between this room and the next, where a big kid rested his head on his arms at a scarred and battered table. Two Coke cans, an empty Fritos bag, and a Ring Ding wrapper littered the tabletop.

Hagstrom flicked a switch, activated the speaker. "Sit up," he said.

The kid's head jerked up and he looked around, blinking. His dark hair was short; he wore jeans, sneakers, a maroon-and-white varsity jacket with lettering I couldn't make out on the back. They were all filthy. He rubbed a grubby hand down his face, squinted at the glass. That glass is carefully made: It will show you your own reflection, tell you what's behind you; it hides everything else.

Hagstrom switched the speaker off again. "Know him?"

"Yeah."

Hagstrom waited. "And?"

"Gary Russell," I said. "He's fifteen. Last I heard he lived in Sarasota, but that was a couple of years ago. What's he doing here?"

"You tell me."

"I don't know."

"What's he to you?"

I watched Gary shift uncomfortably in the folding chair they had him on. The knuckles on his left hand were skinned; his jacket had a rip in the sleeve. The dirt on his face didn't hide the bags under his eyes or the exhausted pallor of his skin. As he moved, his hand brushed the Fritos bag, knocked it to the floor. Conscientiously, automatically, he picked it up. I wondered how long it had been since he'd had real food.

"He's my sister's son," I said.

This small room was too close, too warm, nothing like the crisp fall night the cab had driven through. I unzipped my jacket, took out a cigarette. Hagstrom didn't stop me.

"Your sister's son, but you're not sure where he lives?" Hagstrom's eyes were on me. Mine were on Gary.

"We don't talk much."

Hagstrom held his stare a moment longer. "You want to talk to him?"

I nodded. He stepped into the corridor, pointed to a door a few feet away. He backed off, so that I was the only thing Gary saw when I opened the door.

Gary stood when I came in, so fast and clumsily his chair clattered over. "Hey," he greeted me, his fists clenching and opening, clenching and opening. "Uncle Bill. How's it going?"

He was almost as tall as I was. His eyes were blue, and under his skin you could still see a hint of softness, the child not yet giving way to the man. Otherwise we looked so much alike that all the mirrors I had seen that face in over the years rushed into my mind, all the houses I'd lived in, all the things I had seen in my own eyes; and I wanted to warn him, to tell him to start again, differently. But those were my troubles, not his. You could look at him and see he had his own.

I pulled out a chair, nodded at the one he'd dropped to the floor. He righted it and sank into it.

"It's going great, Gary," I said. "Nothing like getting up in the middle of the night to come see your nephew in a police station."

"I'm . . ." He swallowed. "I'm sorry."

"What are you doing here, Gary?"

He shrugged, said, "They say I tried to rob this guy."

I waved my hand, showed him the walls. "Not here. We'll get to that. What are you doing in New York?"

He picked at a dirty fingernail, shrugged again.

"Your folks here too?"

"No." Almost too low to hear.

"They know where you are?"

"No." He looked up suddenly. "I need to get out of here, Uncle Bill."

I dragged on my cigarette. "Most people in here say that. You run away?"

"Not really."

"But Helen and Scott don't know where you are."

He shook his head.

"You still live in Sarasota?"

Another shake.

"Where?"

No answer.

"I can find out, Gary."

He leaned forward. His blue eyes began to fill. With an effort so desperate I could see it, he pulled himself back under control: boys don't cry. "Please, Uncle Bill. It's important."

"What do you want me to do?"

"Get me out of here. I didn't hurt that guy. I didn't even take anything off him."

"No?"

He spread his hands; a corner of his mouth twisted up. "He didn't have anything."

"Why are you here?"

"Something I got to do."

"What?"

"Something important."

"What?"

He dropped his gaze to the table and was silent.

I sat with him until my cigarette was done. Once he looked up hopefully, like a kid wondering if you'd stopped being mad at him and were ready to play catch. His eyes found mine; he looked quickly down again.

Wordlessly I mashed out the cigarette, got up, opened the door. Hagstrom stepped out of the observation room at the same time, and I knew he'd been listening to what we'd said.

Back at his desk in the squad room, Hagstrom brought us both coffee in blue PBA mugs. "I checked you out," he said.

I drank coffee.

"Your sheet: five arrests, one conviction, misdemeanor; interference with an officer in the performance of his duties."

"You want to hear the story?"

"No. That officer was kicked off the Department the next year for excessive use of force. You also did six months twelve years ago on a misdemeanor in Nebraska." He shook his head. "Nebraska, for Christ's sake. Where is that?"

"In the middle."

"You think your sister still lives in Sarasota?"

"Even though the kid says no? Maybe. Helen and Scott Russell. Street has a strange name . . . Littlejohn. Littlejohn Trail."

Eyes on me, Hagstrom picked up his desk phone, dialed Florida information. I worked on the coffee. After a while he put down the phone again. "No Helen Russell, no Scott, no Gary, anywhere in the Sarasota area."

"They move around a lot."

"You got any ideas?"

I shook my head. "Sorry."

"This is your sister?"

I didn't answer.

"Christ," Hagstrom said. "My brother's an asshole, but I know where he lives." He finished his coffee. "I wondered why the kid wasn't afraid you'd call his folks."

I had nothing to say to that, so I just drank coffee.

"Mike Dougherty, lieutenant, Sixth Precinct?" Hagstrom said. "Says hello. Says he's a friend of yours."

"That's true."

"In fact, you seem to have a lot of friends on this Department. Especially for a guy who's been picked up half a dozen times."

"Five."

"Whatever. You're Captain Maguire's kid."

I took out another cigarette, lit it, dropped the match in a Coke can Hagstrom fished from his trash. I made myself meet Hagstrom's eyes. "That's true too."

"I never met him. Leopold did." He tipped his head toward the man who'd been typing when I first came in and was typing still. Leopold looked up, surveyed me silently, went back to work.

"What I'm saying, Smith, I hear you're okay."

I finished my coffee. "I never heard that."

That got a snort from Leopold. The third guy, off the phone now, looked up from the sports page of the *Post*, went back to it.

"This kid," Hagstrom said. "Your nephew. He's fifteen?"

"That's right."

"If I put him in the system now, he'll have a hell of a time getting out."

I nodded; I knew that was true.

"We'll find your sister, but Child Services will have to check them out. Wherever they live now, they'll contact the child protection agency there. There'll be an investigation. He'll be here, in Spofford, while that happens. Even if they send him home, they'll start keeping records. He have brothers or sisters?"

"Two sisters. Younger."

"Your sister and her husband—they abuse these kids? That why you don't speak to them, maybe?"

The question was asked with no change of manner. Hagstrom sipped his coffee and waited for the answer.

"No," I said.

"That the truth, Smith?"

"Yes."

"So why'd the kid run away?"

"You heard him. He says he's got something important to do. He also says he didn't run away."

"When I was his age, 'something important' only meant a girl. Or a football game."

"Could mean the same to him."

"Does he do drugs?"

"I haven't seen him in a while. But he doesn't look it."

"True."

Hagstrom studied me, making no effort to hide it. I finished my cigarette and shoved it in the Coke can. The cop with the paper flipped the pages. The other kept typing. Somewhere else a phone rang.

"I'll release him to you if you want him."

"All right."

"I never did the paperwork. What he said, he didn't take anything from that wino? It's true. I got no reason to hold him, except he's a green, underage kid who doesn't even know how to pick his targets. A wino on Thirty-third Street, jeez. Will he tell you where his parents are?"

"I don't know. But I can find them."

I took Gary in a cab to my place downtown. He slipped me worried sideways glances as we moved along near-empty streets. For most of the ride he said nothing, and I gave that to him. Then, as the cab made a left off the avenue, he shifted his large frame to face me on the vinyl seat. "Uncle Bill? Who's Captain Maguire?"

I looked out the window at streets I knew. "Dave Maguire. He was an NYPD captain. My uncle."

"My mom's uncle too?"

I nodded.

"I never heard about him. All these cops, it seemed like he was a big deal."

"He was." That was about as short an answer as I could give, but he didn't drop it.

"I heard them say you were Captain Maguire's kid. What does that mean?"

I turned to him, turned back to the window, wished for a cigarette. "When I was just about your age I moved in with Dave. For the next couple of years I kept getting in trouble and he kept getting me out. It got to be a joke around the NYPD. Dave was the only one who didn't think it was funny."

Gary gave a thoughtful, companionable nod; this was something he understood. After a moment he asked, "Did you?"

"Think it was funny?" I asked. "No, I didn't."

He was quiet for a while. As we turned onto my block he said, "You moved in with him, like you mean, instead of living with your folks?"

"That's right."

"Did my mom too?"

The cab pulled to a stop. "No," I said.

I paid the cabbie, unlocked the street door, had Gary go ahead of me up the two flights to my place. At this hour, on this street, there was no one else. Even Shorty's was closed, everyone home, sleeping it off, getting ready for another day.

Upstairs, I showed Gary where the shower was, gave him jeans and a tee shirt for when he was done. The kid in him had stared around a little as the cab stopped and he realized this street of warehouses and factory buildings was where I

lived. He gave the same wide eyes to my apartment above
the bar, and especially to the piano, but he said nothing, so
I didn't either.

I made a pot of coffee and scrambled four eggs, all I had
in the house. When he came out of the bathroom, dirt and
grease scrubbed off, he looked younger than before. He was
wiry, long-legged, and he didn't quite fill out my clothes,
but he came close. His shoulders were broad and the muscles in his arms had the sharp, cut look lifting weights will
give you.

I watched him as he crossed the living room. The circles
under his eyes seemed to have darkened; they looked as
though they'd be painful to the touch. He'd found Band-
Aids for his knuckles. I saw a bruise on his jaw.

"Hey," he said, his face lighting up at the smell of scrambled eggs and buttered toast. "I didn't know you could cook,
Uncle Bill."

"Sit down. You drink coffee?"

He shook his head. "Uh-uh. Coach doesn't like it."

I poured a cup of coffee for myself, asked, "Football?"

"Yeah." He dropped into a chair, shoveled half the eggs
onto a plate.

"What position?"

"Wide receiver," he said, his mouth already full. Then he
added, "I don't start yet," to be honest with me. "I'm just a
sophomore, and I'm new. This school, they're pretty serious
about football."

I looked at his broad shoulders, his muscled arms. "Next
year you'll start."

"Yeah, I guess. If we stay," he said, as if reminding himself not to get too sure of things, reminding himself how
many times he'd started over and how many times he'd have
to. I had done that too.

"You used to play football, Uncle Bill?" he asked, reaching for a piece of toast.

"No."

He glanced up, clearly surprised; this was probably
heresy, a big American man who hadn't played football.

"We left the U.S. when I was nine and didn't come back until I was fifteen," I said. "Your mom must have told you that?"

"Yeah, sure," he said offhandedly, but a brief pause before he said it made me wonder how much he did know about the childhood Helen and I had shared.

"The rest of the world plays soccer," I said. "Not football. I played some soccer, basketball when we came back, and I ran track."

"Track's cool," he said, seeming relieved to be back on familiar ground. "I run track in the spring. What events?"

"Longer distances. I started slow but I could last."

"Track's cool," he repeated. "But except when you're running relay—I mean, it's a team but it's not really a team. You know?"

"I think that was why I liked it." I brought a quart of milk and the coffee I was working on over to the table. "Take the rest," I said, pointing at the eggs. "It's all yours."

"You sure?"

"I don't eat breakfast at four in the morning. You look like you didn't get supper."

He ate like someone who hadn't eaten in a week; but he was fifteen, it might have been two hours. Between bites, he said, "Thanks, Uncle Bill. For getting me out of there."

"I've been in there myself," I said.

"Yeah." He started to grin, then stopped. He flushed, as though he'd said something he shouldn't. He bit into a piece of toast. "How come you don't come see us?" he suddenly asked.

"Hard when I don't know where you are."

He poured a glass of milk. "You and my mom . . ."

He didn't finish his sentence and I didn't finish it for him. I said, "It happens, Gary."

After that I waited until he was done: all the eggs, four pieces of toast, two glasses of milk, a banana.

"Feel better?" I asked when the action had subsided.

He sat back in his chair, smiled for the first time. "You got anything left?"

"You serious? I could dig up a can of tuna."

"Nah, just kidding. I'm good. Thanks, Uncle Bill. That was great."

"Okay, so now tell me. What's going on, Gary?"

The smile faded. He shook his head. "I can't."

"Don't bullshit me, Gary. A kid like you doesn't come to New York and start rolling drunks for no reason. Something wrong at home?"

"No," he said. "What, you mean Mom and Dad?"

"Or Jennifer? Paula?"

"They're kids," he said, seeming a little mystified at the question, as though nothing could be wrong with kids.

"Are you in trouble?" I kept pushing. "Drugs? You get some girl pregnant?"

His eyes widened. "Hell, no." He sounded shocked.

"Is it Scott?"

"Dad?" Under the pallor, he colored. "What do you mean?"

"I told Hagstrom it wasn't. That you wouldn't run away to get away from Scott. But guys like Scott can be tough to live with."

He didn't so much pause as seem caught up, blocked by the confusion of words. His shoulders moved, his hands twitched, as though they were trying to take over, to tell me something in the language he was used to using. "It's not like that, Uncle Bill," he said, his hands sliding apart, coming back together. "I told you, I need to do something. Dad, he gets on my case sometimes, I guess. Whatever. But he's cool." His hands were still working, so I waited. "I mean," he said, "this would be, like, cool with him. If he knew."

"Then let's call and tell him."

I hadn't expected anything from that, and all I got was another shrug.

"He gets on your mom's case, too, am I right?" I asked. "And your sisters'? That can be hard to take."

"I—" He shook his head, not looking at me. "This isn't that. That's not what it is."

"Then what?"

"I can't tell you."

"Christ, Gary." I put down my coffee. "How long since you left home?"

"Day before yesterday."

"Your mother must be worried."

"I left a note."

A note. "Saying what?"

"I said I had something to do and I'd be back as soon as I could. I said not to worry."

"I'm sure that helped." I was sorry about the sarcasm when I saw his eyes, but it was too late to take it back. "We have to call them, Gary."

He shook his head. "We can't."

"Why?"

Nothing.

"Where are you guys living now?"

"Uncle Bill. Uncle Bill, please." He was leaning forward the way he had in the police station, and his eyes looked the same. "You got to lend me a few bucks, let me go do what I got to do. I'll pay you back. Real soon. Please—"

"You left home without any money?"

He glanced away. "I had some when I got here. But some guys . . ."

I looked at the skinned knuckles, the bruise. "You got mugged."

"Three of them," he said quickly, making sure I knew. "If it was just one—"

"They don't play fair in that game, Gary."

"Yeah," he said, deflating. "Yeah, I know. Look, Uncle Bill." I waited, but all he said was, "Please."

"No," I said. "Not a chance. Not if I don't know what's going on."

He shrugged miserably, said nothing.

"Gary?" He looked up at me. I asked, "Did you know I had a daughter?"

He nodded. "She . . . she died, right?"

"In an accident, when she was nine. She'd be a little older than you are now, if she'd lived." I looked into my cup, drank coffee. "Her name was Annie," I said. "I never talk about her to anyone."

He said, "That's . . . I get that."

"Do you know why I'm telling you about her?"

"Yeah. But . . ."

"Why?"

"Because, like, you're telling me something important, so I'll tell you. But I can't."

"It's partly that," I said. "And it's partly, I want you to know kids are important to me." I spoke quietly. "Maybe I can help."

A quick light flashed in his eyes, a man who'd seen water in the desert. Then his eyes dulled again: the water was a mirage, everything as bad as before.

I waited, but I didn't think he'd answer me, and he didn't.

"All right," I said, getting up. "You look like you haven't slept in a long time. I have people who can find your folks, but I'm not going to wake them now. Take the back bedroom. I'm not going to sleep, Gary, we're three floors up, and I have an alarm system here, so don't even think about it. Just get some sleep."

"I—"

"You can sleep, or you can sit around here with me. Or you can tell me what's going on. That's it."

His eyes were desperate, trapped; they searched my face for a way out. What they found was not what he wanted. His shoulders slumped. "Okay," he said, and his voice was a small boy's, not a man's. "Where should I go?"

I showed him the bedroom in back, unused for so long. I brought him sheets for the bed, offered to help him make it up. "No, it's okay," he said, and he looked like someone who wanted to be alone, so I started out.

"Uncle Bill?" he said. I turned back. "Thanks. I'm sorry." He shut the door.

I cleaned up the dishes, put the milk away. I went through the clothes Gary had left neatly in the laundry basket, picked up the jacket—the word arched across the back was WAR-RIORS—from off my couch. I was hoping for something, a label, some scrap of paper, that could get me closer to finding where he'd come from, but there wasn't anything. Back in the living room, I put a CD on, kept the volume low. Gould playing Bach: complex construction, perfectly understood. I kicked off my shoes, lit a cigarette, stretched out on the couch, wondering how early I could call Vélez, the guy who does my skip traces. Wondering what it was that was so important to Gary, so impossible to talk about. Wondering where my sister lived now, whether everything was all right there, the way Gary had said.

The searing crash of breaking glass came a second before the alarm started howling. I yanked myself off the couch, raced to the back, but I wasn't in time. When I threw the door open I saw the shards, saw the pillow on the sill and the chair lying on the floor, and knew what had happened. Gary was a smart kid. He'd been afraid to mess with the catches, afraid the alarm would go off before he got the window open. So he smashed it. Held a pillow on the broken glass in the frame, lowered himself out, dropped to the alley. And was gone.

I charged down the stairs and around the block to where the alley came out, because I had to, but it was useless. I chose a direction, ran a couple more blocks calling Gary's name. A dog barked; a drunk in a doorway lifted his head, held out his hand. Nothing else. Finally I stopped, just stood, gazing around, like a man in a foreign place. Then I turned, headed back to the alley. I checked under my window, where the streetlights glittered off the broken glass. No sign of blood: I let out a breath. I straightened, looked up at the window. Light glowed into the empty alley and the alarm was still ringing.

I'm sorry, Gary had said, before he closed the door.

two

Back upstairs, I silenced the alarm, killed the music, called Vélez. I didn't give a damn what time it was.

"Better be fuckin' important," was how he answered the phone.

"It's Bill Smith," I said. "I need you to find someone."

"Oh, no shit?" he groaned. "*Dios mio,* man, they got to be found now?"

"Yeah," I said.

"*Ay, Chico—*"

"All you have to do is put on your underwear and go sit at your computer, Luigi. Come on, man, it's important."

"What I need my underwear for? Okay, okay, tell me."

"A family. Russell: father Scott, in his forties; mother Helen, thirty-nine. Three kids: Gary, fifteen; Jennifer, eleven; Paula, nine. Last known address, One-eighty-two Littlejohn Trail, Sarasota, Florida."

"When?"

"Three years ago. Could be more recent than that. I don't know when they left."

"What kind of work this guy do?"

"Trucking, shipping. He's management. In Sarasota he ran a trucking company."

"He owned it?"

"No."

"She work?"

"Last I heard, no."

"What else?"

"Before Sarasota, Kansas City. Before that, somewhere in Maryland. Gary plays football. Left behind a varsity jacket that says Warriors."

"What colors?" he interrupted.

"Maroon and white."

"What else?"

"Mother's maiden name is Smith." I gave him the date of her birthday.

"Hey, *chico*—"

"Yeah. So the sooner the better, okay?"

He hesitated, as though he was about to say something else, but all he did was ask, "*Chico*: These people. They looking to stay lost?"

"I don't think so."

"*Bueno*. Makes it easy."

We hung up. Luigi Vélez was a stick-skinny guy with curly hair and a scruffy goatee. His mother was Italian, his father Puerto Rican. He had a bloodhound's nose for the search, a predator's ability to track people through the data spoor they left behind. He almost never left his apartment. "Hey, you makin' wine, you don't go around chewin' chili peppers, *chico*," he told me once. "Real people, they just confuse me."

I smoked and waited for Vélez to call. I didn't know what the hell else to do while I waited so I cleaned up the mess in the bedroom, righting the chair with a vindictive roughness that made me stop, breathe, tell myself there were things that helped and things that didn't. More than once I thought about calling Lydia. She was my partner; I needed help. But I didn't call. I didn't know what she could do right now besides tell me this wasn't my fault, and I didn't want to hear it.

I left the room, closing the door behind me. I was making another pot of coffee when the phone rang. I grabbed it up before the second ring. "Smith."

"Luigi Vélez *el Fantastico*."

"You found them?"

"DMV, *chico*. You get in those databases, it's pig heaven."

"Give it to me."

"Five-sixty-two Hawthorne Circle, Warrenstown, New Jersey."

"Warrenstown?"

"High-class place, man. Fancy houses, trees and shit. Big football town, too. Warrenstown Warriors, division champs. Maybe you seen them in the papers."

"If you say so, Luigi. Phone?"

"973-424-3772."

"Sure this is right?"

"You got to ask?" He sounded hurt. "Here's how genius works, amigo: First I find Helen Russell, driver's license is new in the last three years. People move, they still got to drive. Then I—"

"Luigi—"

"—look at the birthdays for the one you said. Then Scott Russell—"

"Luigi!" He stopped. "Sorry I asked. The check's in the mail."

I wouldn't make conversation about Warrenstown's high school football team and I wasn't willing to listen to his explanation of his methods, which would have been interesting if you had that kind of time. I could hear Vélez's disappointment in me as a client and a student of human nature in his sigh. He said, "Better be double its usual size, *chico*. It ain't even six yet."

It wasn't, but I poured a cup of coffee, lit a cigarette, and called the number he'd given me.

The "Hello?" that answered was a woman's voice, high, soft. I spoke to her seldom, and if you'd asked me to describe her voice I wouldn't have been able to. But I'd know it, I suddenly realized, anywhere.

"Hello?" she said again, quick, anxious, weary but not

sleepy. I hadn't woken her. Maybe, since Gary left, she hadn't slept.

"It's Bill," I said.

She drew a breath; I'd caught her by surprise. "Bill? Bill, what are—?"

"Gary was here," I said.

"Gary? Oh, thank God." The relief that flooded her words made my stomach knot. "Thank God! Let me talk to him."

I said what I had to: "He was here. He's gone."

A small silence, a small voice. "Gone? Where? Where did he go?"

I told her: Midtown South, the silent cab ride, the broken window. "Why did he come here, Helen? What's he up to?"

"I . . . I don't know. He—" She broke off, said away from the phone, "It's my brother." Then she must have covered the phone. I heard nothing, stayed on the line, smoked, waited.

The next voice I heard was a man's, hot and loud. "Smith? What the hell's going on? Gary went to see you? What the hell for?"

I kept my voice even. "He didn't come to see me. He got himself arrested and the cops threw a scare into him, so he gave them my name so I could come get him."

"Arrested?" The word came out clenched. "What the hell do you mean he got arrested? My boy?"

"Why did he come here, Scott?"

"I have no goddamn idea! I—"

"He said it was something you'd approve of, if you knew."

"Approve of? I'll kill the stupid bastard! What do you mean, he got arrested? Where the hell is he? Helen says he ran away again—what does that mean? Why didn't you call us?"

"He wouldn't tell me where you were."

"I thought you're a fucking detective!" he exploded. "You can't find people? Where the hell is my son, Smith?"

I worked at not letting my tone match his; this was a man whose child had been missing for three days. "He broke a window and dropped three floors so he could go do what he came to do. You cool down and we figure out what that was, maybe we can find him."

"Oh, fuck you, buddy. Fuck you and fuck cool down! You can't keep your hands on a kid like that? You let him jump out a goddamn window? Fuck you."

I felt the heat rise in me. "Scott," I said, my words tight, "I need to know why he's here. I'll get the NYPD on it, I'll—"

"Get them? You haven't called them yet? What the hell are you doing, waiting until he turns up in the river?"

I heard a wordless sound from Helen when he said that, but Scott kept on. "Smith, if anything happens to that boy—"

I heard ice in my own voice now, felt my shoulders hard and locked. "What did his note say?"

"His note? His fucking *note* said, So long, Mom and Pop, see you later. His mother's falling apart here, Smith, she's been crying since Monday. I'll kill that bastard when I get him home! Shit, he came to you!"

"Scott, I'm doing—"

"No! No, you're not doing anything. I'm calling the police. I'll go to New York, I'll find my boy. You stay away. You stay out of it. He went to you; you fucked it up. No big surprise. Now you stay the fuck out of it."

I heard a rattling crash as he slammed his receiver down, left me holding a piece of plastic empty and dead. I hung up, sat staring at the phone. It took everything I had not to pick it up and throw it across the room.

I crushed out the cigarette I was smoking. A moment later I lit another one, called Lydia. "It's me," I said.

"Wow," she said. "This is early even for me. For you it must still be last night."

"In a way. Look, I need help."

The weight in my voice made hers lose its lightness. "Bill? Are you okay?"

"Can you come here?"

"You're home?"

"Yes."

"Is twenty minutes all right?"

"Sure, yeah."

"Are you okay?" she asked again.

"I'll tell you about it." Which meant no. But she knew that already.

While I waited I called Midtown South, got Hagstrom at the end of his shift. "The kid," I said. "I lost him."

"Lost him?" Hagstrom's tone was guarded. "What does that mean?"

"He jumped out the goddamn window, Hagstrom, before I could get to his folks. He's gone."

"What're you biting my ass for? He's your nephew."

I rubbed a hand over the back of my neck. "Yeah. Look, I'm sorry. I need to find him."

"I'll put the word out." Hagstrom spoke tiredly, a cop not surprised something he'd thought might be okay had, in the end, turned out badly.

"You take a photo when they brought him in?"

"No. I told you, I didn't book him. I was trying to give him a break." We'll give you a break, Gary, we'll call your uncle, he'll take care of you. "You don't have a photo?" Hagstrom asked.

I didn't answer.

"All right," he said. "I'll put out his description. It's the best I can do."

His description. "Jeans and a blue tee shirt, Hagstrom. Not the jacket. He left that here."

"Shit," Hagstrom said. "It's cold out there."

I went downstairs to wait for Lydia. Behind the street-lights and the black bulk of the buildings the sky was beginning to gray. Across the street a truck backed into a loading dock. The driver jumped down from the cab, took his paperwork to a guy who was waiting. The driver's day was over, the load in his truck no longer his problem. It belonged to the guy on the dock now, whose day was just beginning.

I spotted Lydia a block away, moving at a steady jog along the sidewalk. I headed toward her.

"Tell me you didn't run all the way," I said after I'd leaned down, kissed her cheek. Her hair was glossy and smelled of freesia.

"If I hadn't been coming here I'd have gone to the dojo. This way at least no one's yelling at me for doing it wrong. Aren't you cold?" She put a hand on my bare arm.

"Come on," I said. We walked together back to my place. The guy in the dock was unloading the truck as we started upstairs. The driver was gone.

Inside, I put water on to boil so she could have tea. "Want something to eat?"

"No, it's early for me. Bill, what's the matter?"

I dropped myself on the couch, suddenly drained, exhausted. Lydia came over and sat on the arm beside me; after a moment, she reached out, kneaded the muscles at the back of my neck. When I leaned forward to pick up my cigarettes from the coffee table, she stopped.

"There's a kid who's missing," I said, shaking out the match. "We need to find him."

"Okay," she said, and then because that clearly wasn't all, she waited.

"Gary Russell. He's fifteen. He left home Monday. He's here in New York." She was still waiting. "He's my sister's son."

The kettle started to whistle. I got up to turn it off. She followed me with her eyes.

"Your sister?" she said. "Your sister's son?"

I opened the cabinet, realized I didn't know what kind of tea she wanted. "My sister Helen," I said. "She's two years younger than I am."

"I didn't know you even had a sister," Lydia said slowly. "Why didn't you ever tell me that?" She got up, walked over and reached into the cabinet, took out a box of Yunnan tea she'd put there a week ago. She pulled open the drawer for the strainer. I felt useless and went back to the couch.

"When I was fifteen, she was thirteen, she ran away," I said.

She turned to me. "She was thirteen? Why?"

I shrugged. "It was tough at home."

Lydia considered me. "That was when you went to live with your uncle Dave, when you were fifteen."

"Helen ran away just before that." I didn't want to tell the whole story, not now. "She never came back. She called every now and then, just enough so we knew she was alive, not enough to be found."

"My God, what did your parents do?"

"Nobody could find her," I said, hoping she wouldn't notice how far that was from an answer to her question. "She spent most of the next ten years on the road with one man or another. When she met Scott, the guy she's married to, she settled down, and when Gary was born she called me. I went down to see them—they were in Atlanta then— and when the girls were born, too. But Scott—" I pressed my cigarette out. "Shit. I don't like him and he doesn't like me, and Helen and I . . ." I looked up at Lydia. She was standing, drinking her tea. "I never told you about her because she's been gone for twenty-five years. She's just not part of my life."

She could have said, Bullshit. She could have said, There's a lot more to this, I can hear it, and if you're going to hand me a line I don't need it. She could have demanded to know, walked out if I didn't tell her.

Instead she came and sat next to me again. She drank her tea and for a while there was silence.

She said, "And Gary's in New York now, and he's missing?" She said it the way she would have on any case, giving me back the information I'd given her, waiting for the rest. I turned to look at her, warm and solid and beside me, and I almost laughed, so strong was the sudden idea that we could go away somewhere, up to my cabin in the country, to China, to a farm in New Zealand, leave and start over and never come back.

Lydia returned my look, sipped her tea, waited for me to speak.

I said, "Yes. Gary's missing."

I told her the story, all the details, including the phone call with Helen and Scott. I showed her Gary's jacket, and the broken window in the back bedroom. The cold night air had filled the empty room; when I opened the door it pushed past us into the the rest of my place.

"Boy," she said, peering out the window into the alley. The streetlights were off now; the day had started. "I'm impressed."

"He's a football player," I said. "Strong and big. He didn't jump: he swung over the sill, held on, and then dropped. He took some time and thought about it, planned it before he broke the glass."

She was leaning out the window now, saying something I couldn't hear.

"What?" I asked.

She pulled her head back in. "I said, I'll bet it was exciting. Breaking the window, holding on like that, dropping. I'll bet it was a real rush. Even afraid you'd catch him. Even with whatever trouble he's in."

"If you say so," I said. "You're the athlete."

We closed the door, walked back into the living room. "And you were fifteen once," she said.

Yes, I thought, and when I was fifteen, I'd done a lot of things for the rush. Stupider things than dropping from a window. Worse things than running away. And the things I'd done, wild and bad, hadn't had reasons behind them, not the kind of reason Gary seemed to have.

"You think it's true he didn't just run away from home?" Lydia asked. I sat on the couch again, lit another cigarette. She took the big armchair, folded her legs up under her. "Your brother-in-law doesn't sound like any prize."

"He's a son of a bitch. I can see wanting to get away from him. But Gary said not. He said there's something important he has to do." I dropped the cigarette pack, empty now, on the table. "What was important to you when you were fifteen?"

She frowned as she thought. "Boys. Staying out late. Getting my brothers off my back. Getting good grades." She sipped some tea, said in a tone of confession, "But mostly, being cool."

I smiled in spite of myself. "I can't imagine you ever not being cool."

"I am totally cool, it's true," she said airily. "But what I mean, if you want to be serious, is making sure the kids *I* thought were cool thought I was cool, too."

"Did they?"

"Never enough."

"I'm going out to Warrenstown," I said. "Someone must have some idea why Gary came here. If not his parents, then his friends."

"Want me to come?"

"No. I want you to stay here and start looking."

"A needle in a haystack," she said. "My specialty."

I kept my gaze on her for a few moments, then got up and went to the desk, opened the bottom drawer. From an envelope in the back I took out a stack of old photos. I leafed through them, pulled one out: two guys in uniform, clowning around. I handed it to her. "The guy on the left," I said.

She looked from the photo in her hand to me, back to the photo again. "This is you," she said.

"I was seventeen, in the navy. Gary looks like that, except his eyes are blue."

After Lydia left, I showered, shaved, and went to get my car. Lydia would get the photo enlarged and copied and start handing it around; she'd get it to Midtown South and they'd fax it to the other precincts. Gary had said he needed money to go do what he had to do; he'd asked me for it and I hadn't given him any. Maybe he'd try to roll another drunk, get himself picked up again.

Or maybe he'd try something dumber.

"What about your brother-in-law?" Lydia had asked as

she'd pocketed the photo. "He said he was coming to New York to look for Gary."

"He may come," I'd answered. "And he may know something we don't, and find him. So maybe this is useless. But I can't sit here and do nothing."

Traffic headed out of New York was light and I was through the tunnel and rolling west on the Garden State ten minutes after I left the lot. Warrenstown was about an hour into New Jersey, one of those plump, prosperous places where three quarters of the working population commute into New York and the others keep the picture-postcard small-town home fires burning.

If Scott really had gone to New York, if we were passing each other somewhere on these roads, it would at least make talking to my sister easier. If he hadn't, it was still the professional thing to do: a kid runs away, talk to the family first.

Not that that had worked years ago, when Helen left. But there were other reasons for that.

For the first half hour, most of what I saw was strip mall: gas stations, garish fast-food joints, dull price club warehouses with an intense blue sky arching over them and the autumn hills in the distance behind. Then I switched roads and the hills came closer. It was mid-November, and some trees still held tightly to their leaves, glowed crimson and gold in the early morning sun. Some trees were bare.

I'd brought the Gould CD with me, Bach Inventions, put it in when I started, but I didn't get far. For the first time, the pieces seemed forced. I'd always heard them before as the result of equal parts exuberance and discipline; but now all I heard was necessity, and a hint of smugness in rising to the challenge. It irritated me, and I turned it off.

The Warrenstown exit brought me to tree-shaded streets lined with old houses with porches and fenced backyards, newer split-levels with wide lawns and shrubs. I stopped and asked directions in a downtown of two-story brick shops centered on a well-trimmed park. A banner across the main street reminded everyone that the Hamlin's game was Saturday, that the bus would leave at nine. I didn't understand about the bus, and I wasn't sure what the game could be. This late in the fall, the football season must be over, surely, and the basketball season not yet begun.

I drove on, found what I'd been directed to: a new subdivision of vaguely colonial homes on streets carefully curved to provide both interest and easy steering radiuses. In front of a house with pale gray siding and gray-blue shutters, different only in small details from the houses around it, I pulled up and parked. Chrysanthemums bristled along the concrete walk leading to the door; two carved pumpkins, staying beyond Halloween, stood on the low stoop. One grinned a lopsided grin. The other sneered.

I pressed the button and heard two tones ring inside. A dog barked. I waited and the door was pulled open. A brown-haired girl in glasses, jeans, and a blue Pokémon tee shirt stared at me a moment, seemed caught off guard. She had her hand on the collar of a black Doberman that glared and growled warningly. The girl, manners returning, said, "Yes?"

"Hi, Jennifer," I said. "You don't remember me, but I'm your uncle Bill. Is your mom home?"

Confusion washed over her face. "Oh," she said, then called over her shoulder, "Mom? It's Uncle Bill."

Another girl, smaller, dressed in corduroys and a flowered turtleneck shirt, came running to the door to have a look at me. For a moment, it was just the three of us. Then, coming down the stairs, pushing her hair back with her hand, her blue eyes unsure and unsmiling, was my sister Helen.

"Bill," she said, stopping behind her daughters. The girls looked from one of us to the other. Helen was wearing jeans and a white turtleneck with fall leaves embroidered on the collar. She was small, high-cheekboned, fair-skinned. Delicate and pretty. Her daughters both looked like that. It's the men in our family who are always big. Gary, my father.

Helen's husband Scott is a big man, too. And me.

Helen started to say something else, seemed undecided, stopped, settled on, "What are you doing here?"

"Can I come in?" I asked, not certain of the answer.

"Yes," she said after a moment, stepping aside at the door. "Yes, of course."

I moved past her into a vestibule lined with raincoats and rubber boots. A child's snow shovel leaned in the corner; umbrellas large and small stood, each in its own slot, in a rack with plenty of empty spaces for visitors and friends. From inside the house came the sweet smell of maple syrup: Breakfast had been pancakes, a hearty breakfast for a cool fall morning.

"Go on, get your things," Helen said to the girls. They skipped off with backward glances—whatever we were doing was more interesting than making sure they had all their homework and books for another school day.

Helen led me into her living room, a sunny, rose-carpeted place where the upholstered furniture looked used and comfortable, the slate fireplace ready for the chilly nights to come. Lined up on the mantel were family pictures: the three kids as babies; in Halloween costumes; on the floor in front of a Christmas tree surrounded by toys and torn wrapping paper and untied ribbons. One photo showed Gary in a football uniform, helmet under his arm, wide grin on his face. The black grease smeared on his cheekbones mocked the dark circles I'd seen last night under his eyes.

There were photos, too, of adults I didn't know, probably Scott's parents; and there was a small one, a snapshot really, of my mother, framed now behind glass, but bent and tattered. In the picture, my mother wore a sunhat, and she smiled, and she was younger than Helen was now. It struck me that Helen must have taken that picture with her twenty-five years ago, when she left.

"What are you doing here?" Helen asked me again. As it had at the door, it sounded like not quite the right question.

The answer was wrong, too, but I stuck to the narrow

path: "I want to find Gary," I said. "I need to know why he went to New York."

Helen hesitated. "Scott told you to leave it alone. He said he'd find him."

"Do you think he can?"

She looked away, not answering that.

"Forget everything else," I said. "I'm a detective. This is what I do. Gary's in trouble, Helen."

She looked at me swiftly, resentment in her eyes. "He's a good boy."

"A good boy in trouble. It can happen."

I let that wait, and the sounds of cars and children's voices from outside the windows seemed to surround but not penetrate the silence between us.

"Mom?" came tentatively from the wide doorway into the hall. Jennifer and Paula stood there, backpacks strapped on, sneakers tied. Jennifer said, "We better go."

Helen looked at me. "I have to walk the girls to school."

"I'll come along."

She nodded, put the dog on a leash, and lifted a jacket off a peg as we trooped through the vestibule. We went down the walk, past the Chevy Blazer in the driveway with the WARRENSTOWN WARRIORS sticker on the bumper, and made our way through the curving subdivision to the sidewalks of the older part of town. Here the streets were straight and the trees were large and old, their arching branches offering shelter from the full glare of the morning sun. The trees near Helen's house were too young to do that, yet.

"They could go on the bus," Helen said as we walked, the girls kicking at fallen leaves. "But I like to take them."

I wasn't sure why she told me that. It seemed to me she wasn't sure, either.

three

For a while we said nothing as we walked, Helen and I, and I let that be. Helen greeted kids and their mothers as we passed them, and girls called out the open windows of the school bus to Jennifer and Paula. They'd only been at this school, in this town, a couple of months. But the younger you were when you came to a new place, the easier it was to make friends, to belong. I remembered that. I also remembered that leaving again was just as hard.

We didn't speak, just strolled through the suburban streets as though this were something we'd done many times before, my sister and her children and I. Every now and then I caught Jennifer's dark eyes on me, though I pretended I didn't see. I wondered if it bothered her, how much I looked like her brother; I wondered what the girls had been told about Gary being gone.

We turned a corner and the school came into view, a group of long low brick buildings with big windows, set back on a broad lawn. WARRENSTOWN ELEMENTARY SCHOOL spread in bronze letters above the open glass doors. A walkway ran between young maple trees wearing their November burgundy, and the air was filled with sunlight and children's voices. Hastily dropped backpacks and jackets, some a smaller version of Gary's maroon-and-white one and reading JUNIOR WARRIORS, were piled on the lawn between the path and a pickup football game.

As soon as we crossed the street Jennifer and Paula patted the dog, politely told me, " 'Bye," waved to their mother, and hurried up the sidewalk to find their friends. That left Helen and me standing alone. She watched her children as they disappeared through the big glass doors, and I did, too. When they were gone there was nothing for her to do but look at me.

"Scott went to New York," she said.

"Does he know why Gary went?" I asked. "Where he might be?"

She looked down at the sidewalk, shaking her head. "We don't know. This just isn't like him."

"What is like him?"

"He's a good boy," she said, repeating that as though it could protect him.

I looked around, the quiet suburban street, the low brick building that sheltered the children of the people who belonged here. "All I want," I said carefully, "is to find him. Send him home. That's all."

Her eyes searched my face as though it were new to her. I wondered, suddenly, how much there was left in me of the brother she'd grown up with. I wondered, too, if that's what she was looking for.

She spoke suddenly, quickly, as though she wanted to get the words said before she could stop herself.

"It's mostly Scott. Because you were in jail. Because of what you do. Because . . ." She trailed off.

"It doesn't matter," I said. "That's not what this is about." It wasn't; this was about Gary. But I would have stopped her anyway. I didn't want to hear any more, didn't want to listen to her lying to me.

I pulled out my cigarettes, shook one from the pack.

"You're still smoking," she said.

I lit up, shook the match, dropped it on the walk. "If Scott doesn't know why Gary went," I said, "he won't have much luck. I can do better. I know how to do this, Helen.

Give me pictures of Gary, tell me who his friends are."

"The police talked to his friends already."

"I can ask different questions. Please," I said, and thought how much I sounded like Gary, asking me for help.

We stood on the sidewalk in front of the school and she looked at me for a long time. I turned away, watched the kids streaming up the walkway between the maples. The last of the stragglers was inside, the doors had closed, and the first bell had rung when Helen's eyes, without warning, filled with tears. She wiped them away and said, "Oh, God, yes. God, please. Can you really find him?"

Yellow leaves drifted at our feet as Helen and I walked beyond the school, down to where tall oaks shaded a street of shops. Most of the shops had GO WARRIORS! posters in their windows, in school colors, maroon and white like Gary's jacket.

We slipped the dog's leash over a parking meter, went into the bakery, sat over coffee while I asked Helen the questions I'd ask any client. Had Gary been depressed lately, distracted, different from usual? No, she said. He liked this new school, was excited to have made the varsity, looked forward to the school year, to the football games. His grades were good, and he'd played well when he'd gotten in, which wasn't often, of course. He was only a sophomore, and he was new.

Nothing he wouldn't talk about, nothing she or Scott had sensed? No, nothing. Was he involved with drugs, I asked casually, either that she knew about, or even just suspected? No, of course not, she answered firmly but without heat, making me think that though Gary might be hiding something from her, she was not hiding it from me.

I asked, how long had they lived in Warrenstown? Since June; they'd left Sarasota right after the school year ended. Scott had grown up here, she told me, though he left after high school and never came back. At "never came back" a pink flush crept onto her cheeks, and she looked at the table, out the window, anywhere but at me. She and I both knew

about people who left and never came back, though we saw
that picture from opposite sides.

I said nothing, drank my coffee. It was rich and fragrant,
hometown coffee served with hometown smiles by women
who knew most of their customers and called them by name.

Helen picked at the cinnamon bun in front of her and
went on with her story. When the firm Scott worked for was
bought by a bigger one, he was offered a promotion, given
a choice of three branch offices to relocate to. He'd chosen
Newark. He'd always talked about Warrenstown, what a
great place it was to grow up, and he'd been saying it was
time to come back. They'd packed up the family and moved.

Did she like it here? I asked, wondering why I was asking. It didn't matter to the job I was doing. But she answered
just as she had everything else I'd asked. I was the expert
she'd decided she needed, and my role seemed to give me
rights she didn't question. She wouldn't argue with the
plumber over which valve to repair, with the doctor over
which drug to prescribe. She wouldn't argue with Scott over
whether to uproot them all and move, over and over again,
and she wouldn't think to wonder how I chose my questions.
I felt my shoulders tighten, wanted a cigarette, settled for
getting up for another cup of coffee. Helen had barely
touched her first cup, didn't want more.

Yes, she did like it here, she told me when I sat again,
and she hoped they'd stay, and I tried to listen through my
new impatience, my need to be in motion. It would be nice
for the kids to be able to settle somewhere, she said. Of
course, that would depend on Scott's job. Each time they'd
moved it had been so Scott could do better, provide better
for his family, and he'd done well and she was proud of
him. It was nice, she added, it was a kind of relief, to be
where Scott had grown up, where it felt like the family had
some roots. Did I understand that? Although moving
around, well, it wasn't so bad, really, and it could even be
fun—we knew all about that, she and I.

She gave me a small smile when she said that, the first
I'd had from her. I smiled back automatically, the smile I

use to reassure a client. She glanced away uncertainly, and I didn't know if that was because of my smile or her own.

"Tell me who Gary's friends are, Helen." I took pen and paper from my pocket. "The ones the police already talked to, and anyone else you can think of. Any girls he's interested in?"

She sipped her coffee, though it must have been cold by now. "He was seeing a girl for a little while in the summer, but that stopped before school started. He's too young to really date, but they went for ice cream and things like that."

"What's her name?"

Her brow creased in thought. "Victoria," she finally said. "Such a lovely name, old-fashioned. They call her Tory."

"Last name?"

"I don't remember," she said. "He didn't see her for very long."

"Okay," I said. "What about other kids?"

She looked into the distance. "Gary always makes friends in a new place once the school year starts, especially once the boys start to play sports, but it takes me a while to know who they are," she said apologetically. "There's a tall boy named Morgan Reed—I think he's one of the quarterbacks—and there's one called Randy Macpherson. He plays in the same position as Gary, but he's a senior, so he always starts the games. And a boy near where we live. Paul Niebuhr." This she said in a more tentative way. "He's older than Gary, and he doesn't play football. I haven't seen him much since school started, but they were friendly during the summer—they went skateboarding together. Paul used to come over for dinner. I don't think his mother cooks much." Helen's voice held a note of disapproval. A good mother, her tone said, cooks for her children. "But some of the boys aren't around this week, you know."

"They're not?"

"It's Camp Week at the high school. The seniors from the football team are all at camp. And some of the other families go away, because the high school's closed."

"What's Camp Week?"

"In Warrenstown, the high school starts a week early. Before Labor Day. Then, if the football team makes the play-offs, they send the senior boys to football camp at the end of the season. For a reward, to help them get ready for playing in college."

"A reward? Camp at the end of the season?"

She looked at me blankly. "Why, is that strange?"

I shrugged. "I never played. But from what I remember, football players are pretty beat up by the end of the season. Camp's usually in the summer."

"I don't know," she said, and her voice rose and her hands started to twist a paper napkin, as though not knowing was a frightening thing.

"They close the whole school for Camp Week?" I asked, because that was something she did know, could tell me.

"So the boys won't have to miss classes and make up any work."

"What if they don't make the play-offs?"

"Everyone just stays in school and does a week of special projects."

I get it, I thought: You make the play-offs, you go to camp and everyone else gets the week off. You screw up, everyone stays in school. But no pressure.

"Intriguing place, Warrenstown," I said.

"Scott always said that," she agreed with me, either not hearing, or totally ignoring, my tone.

I asked her, "Where is this camp?"

She tilted her head in thought. "Hamlin Sports Camp," she finally said, not sounding entirely sure. "Somewhere on Long Island. The sophomores and juniors from the varsity team, plus some of the boys from the junior varsity, go up there on Saturday to play against the other boys. Gary's excited about that game." She bit her lip, looked away again. "Why?" I heard a whisper of hope in her voice. "Is it important?"

"I don't know. But New York's between here and Long Island. Maybe he's headed there."

"Why would he do that?"

"I have no idea. And I suppose the police already checked that."

"Well, if they talked to Randy, it would have to be there. I think they said they talked to him. Or maybe they talked to Morgan." She looked up at me with a hint of the same desperation in her blue eyes that I'd seen in Gary's, in my apartment, in the middle of the night. "I don't remember what they said—"

"It doesn't matter," I told her, trying not to grit my teeth at the tremor in her voice. "You don't have to. I'll talk to the police and I'll find whoever I need." I slipped a card from my wallet, handed it to my sister the way I do when I meet a new client. "Here's my office number, my cell phone. I want to look at Gary's room, and then I'll be in town for a few hours at least. I'll let you know what I find."

She held my card, studying it as though every piece of information on it was elusive and valuable. Maybe it was, now; but nothing on that card except the number of my cell phone was anything she hadn't had for years.

We walked in silence through the crisp morning air back to her house. I followed her upstairs; she showed me which room was Gary's. Standing just inside the door, looking around, I did it the way I was taught: start in front of you, back and forth, fanning out, nothing but your eyes until the place has lost its newness, is familiar. Then you can go inside.

The room was neat, but not so much you'd say this wasn't a normal kid. A plaid spread was stretched over a bed made dutifully if not overly well. The bookcase was full and more books sat in piles on the desk and floor. I looked them over: schoolbooks in the piles; thrillers, science fiction, and, from Gary's younger days, stories of knights and pirates in the bookcase. The top shelf held sports books, mostly football: training manuals, playbooks, athlete's biographies. On top of the bookcase trophies crowded each other, again mostly football, but also baseball and track:

school championships, summer league teams, division winners. A Jets poster hung on the wall above the bed, the entire
team in three rows, helmets under their arms, grease on their
cheekbones, fierce unsmiling faces.

"Was Gary always a Jets fan?" I asked Helen. "Or just
since you moved here?"

"No, in Florida he liked the Dolphins," she said. "And
when we lived in Kansas City it was the team there."

"The Chiefs."

"Chiefs, that's right. I don't always remember." She gave
an apologetic shrug. "I think it's part of how he makes himself belong. The way you used to learn the language every
place we moved to."

I turned to her, surprised. After a moment I said, "You
remember that?"

"Of course. I wanted to, too, but I couldn't. You were
smarter."

I shook my head. "Just older."

"Well, anyway," she said. "Besides, Dad didn't like it."

That stopped both of us. We looked at each other in this
bright room in this still-new house, the quiet suburban day
just outside the windows. Goddamn it, I thought: It's over
twenty years.

"I don't think he cared that I spoke the language," I said,
deliberately not giving it up. "What he didn't like was the
friends I made."

"No, you're wrong." She had looked away, but now she
brought her eyes back to mine. "He thought you didn't want
to be American, and that made him mad. You never understood. You never listened."

I felt my jaw tighten. I turned to the desk, pulled a cigarette from my pocket. I almost lit it, but I didn't know
which would be worse, if she asked me please to put it out,
or if she just stood there and said nothing. I crammed it
back in the pack and started going through the papers Gary
had left behind: an algebra quiz, research notes on the Iro-
quois. I knew exactly where Helen was, standing behind me.

"Bill—"

"Do you know how to work this thing?" I switched on the computer on Gary's desk.

First she was silent. Then she said, in a soft voice, "He has a password. I don't know it."

With Helen quiet behind me, I tried a few obvious things: Gary's name, his birthday, his sister's names. None of them worked, but they hadn't been likely to. He probably used the title of a hit song by some rock group I'd never heard of, or maybe the name of an NFL receiver he was modeling his game after. I tried *Jets, Dolphins*, and *Chiefs* and then gave up.

"I'll send someone out who's better at this than I am," I said. "Does he have e-mail?"

"Not his own." Helen spoke now in a quiet monotone, the voice I imagined she'd used when she'd answered questions from the police. "We have a computer in the family room that's online. The kids can all use it whenever they want, but we have only one account. Scott thinks they're too young for us not to monitor what they're doing. Because of what you hear."

"Did the police look at it?"

"One of the detectives did. But he said he didn't find anything. Things the kids needed for school, and some sports sites."

"NFL.com, that kind of thing?"

"That's right."

"The guy I send out here, can he look anyway?"

"I . . . I'm nervous about you sending someone."

"Why?"

"Scott won't like it."

"Scott's in New York."

"He'll know."

Meaning: The only things she'd ever successfully hidden from Scott were things he didn't give a damn about anyway.

I said, "If it helps find Gary, what's the difference what he knows?"

She didn't answer, and I took that to mean what I liked.

I asked her for the name of the local cop in charge and left it at that, for now.

Helen showed me the note Gary had left, but it didn't say anything other than what he'd told me: I have something important to do, I'll be back as soon as I can, don't worry. I stayed a little longer, looked through this and that, the pictures and papers, CDs and books and clothes that made up Gary's life, but I didn't turn up anything that would help me understand where he'd gone, what it was he had to do. I faced my sister, standing silent in the doorway.

"Is it Scott?" I asked quietly.

"What do you mean?"

"Did Gary leave to get away from Scott?"

She flushed. "Why would he?"

"Because Scott's not a nice man."

"You're wrong. He's not nice to *you*. He loves the kids. And me," she added. "He's very good to us."

"Gary has a bruise on his jaw."

"He does?" Her eyes grew anxious, worried about her baby; then she must have realized why I'd told her that. "You think Scott did that?" She drew herself up, her small chin thrust out, quick to rally to Scott's defense. Too quick, I thought; and this was not the first time I'd seen that posture, though the image that flashed in my mind was not of Helen.

"Tell me he doesn't hit the kids." My words were calm but it was clearly a challenge.

"No." Her voice matched my own. "When they were small he spanked them sometimes, we both did. We're strict with them. It's very important to Scott that they know right from wrong. But what you mean—no, he doesn't do that."

We both knew what I meant. I looked at her, standing in her son's room, the sixth or eighth or tenth place he'd tried to make his own in his fifteen years. When we were young, Helen never lied to me. But it had been a long time since either of us was young.

When I drove off, she stood at the curb and watched me. She stayed in my rearview mirror until a curve in the road

set someone's home between us. She didn't wave, but she
didn't turn away, either.

I headed into town, pulled into the lot behind the solid brick
building that held the mayor's office, the town council
chambers, the Warrenstown Police Department.

"I'm Bill Smith," I told the cop behind the counter. The
counter's brass rail gleamed under the old-fashioned ceiling
globes. A WARRENSTOWN WARRIORS banner hung on the
back wall, between a JUST SAY NO poster and one listing
ways to TAKE A BITE OUT OF CRIME. "I'm a private investigator from New York. I'd like to speak to Detective Sullivan."

"About what?" The cop, a muscled young guy with an
open, friendly face, turned my card over in his hand, found
nothing hidden on the back, looked at me again.

"Gary Russell."

He looked blank.

"Runaway," I said. "Hasn't been home since Monday."

"Oh, yeah. New kid in town. Sorry, now I remember."
The cop grinned. He didn't look any older than Gary himself. "Sullivan's in a meeting." He said *meeting* as though
having to be in one was one of the penalties of adulthood,
and something he wasn't looking forward to when he got
there.

"When can I get him?"

"Hour or two, probably."

"Okay. I'll try later. Meanwhile, I'm in town. I'm driving
a gray Acura." I gave him the license number. "My cell
phone number's on the card. In case anyone has a problem
with me."

"You're what, investigating? This Gary Russell thing?"

"That's right. Anything you can tell me?"

"Oh, no, sir. It's just," he grinned, "I never met a private
eye before."

I'd met a lot of cops, so I just shook his hand and left.

Helen had given me the addresses of kids she knew were

Gary's friends. I'd have liked to talk to the police before I tackled them, but I could do it the other way. As I drove I called Lydia.

"Anything?" I asked.

"No. I've spread the picture around, and I'm talking to people at youth hot lines and places like that. I'm about to go down to Times Square and the East Village and talk to some kids myself."

"Good. And do one more thing? There's a camp on Long Island, a sports camp called Hamlin's or something close. The Warrenstown varsity seniors are there for the week. It's a long shot, but Gary may be headed there."

"Why?"

"I don't know. But check it out, okay?"

"Sure. How's it going out there?" It was what she'd have asked any time, on any case, but now I heard behind the words a different question.

The answer to that one was long, though, and I didn't really know it. I said, "Nothing yet. I'll let you know."

Briefly, silence. Then, "Okay. Be careful."

"You, too." Something struck me. "Hey, Lydia? Speaking of careful: It seems my brother-in-law did go to New York. He may be covering the same territory you are."

"I'll consider myself warned. You be careful," she said again, and hung up.

The bright November sun and the quiet tree-lined streets brought me to a wood-frame house in the older part of town, yellow with white shutters, neatly trimmed hedge, red leaves spotting a clipped lawn. The door was answered by a short-haired woman about my own age, who didn't look happy when she read my card and I asked for her son.

"What's this about?"

"There's a boy missing, Mrs. Reed. Gary Russell. I'm working for the family. I'd like to ask Morgan a few questions."

"The police have already been here. Morgan doesn't know anything."

"I know they have. I won't be long."

In the end, because another mother's son was missing, she agreed, providing she could stay. Expecting a fifteen-year-old to reveal any secrets with his mother in the room was like expecting snow in July, but I wasn't necessarily looking for secrets. And if I got a sense from Morgan that he had more to say than he'd say in front of his mother, I'd find a way to hear it.

Mrs. Reed called up the stairs to her son. After the second call, "Yeah, awright!" floated from above, and after the third call a tall, broad-shouldered kid appeared at the top of the stairs. He loped down to the landing, where the staircase took a turn he didn't want to bother with; putting his hands on the railing, he swung over, landed a foot in front of me. He slapped his hands against each other as though the cleanliness of the railing hadn't been up to his standards.

"I wish you wouldn't, Morgan," his mother said, and it was clearly something she'd said before. "That banister is coming loose."

"Whatever." Morgan looked me over. He was a tall kid, with huge hands, weight-room muscles on his long arms. Even standing still, he held himself with the ease and unconscious grace of the natural athlete, someone who had always been at home in the world, never doubted he would land on his feet every time.

"Morgan, this is Mr. Smith. He's a detective and he wants to ask you some things about Gary Russell."

Morgan flashed his mother a look of annoyance, as though my intrusion into his day were her fault. To me, with a lift of the chin, a set of the shoulders, he said, "I talked to Sullivan already." He added, "I never saw you before," as though any Warrenstown cop Morgan Reed didn't know was an obvious impostor. At fifteen I'd known every cop in my Brooklyn neighborhood, too; I'd been picked up by most of them.

"I'm private," I said. "From New York."

"You mean you're a private eye?"

"That's right."

He snorted, and I got the feeling that the grown-ups had

just proved once again how ridiculous we were. He looked at his mother and then at me; then, maybe deciding the whole thing would be over faster if he went along with it, he said, "Whatever," crossed in front of me to the living room and dropped onto the sofa. He wore cargo pants, a plaid shirt over a tee, Nikes that he propped up on the coffee table, pointedly ignoring his mother's frown. He picked up a *Sports Illustrated*, flipped through it without interest while he waited for me to begin.

I took the armchair, resisted the urge to light a cigarette and to put my feet on the table, too, the way I would have if he'd been a man, to show I understood, to level the field.

"Gary Russell left home on Monday," I said. "I saw him in New York last night and he said he had something important to do. Do you know what he meant?"

"You saw him, how come you didn't ask him?"

"He wouldn't tell me."

"Well, I got no idea," he said, turning pages. "I don't know the guy that well."

"You're on the football team with him, right?"

"Yeah." He looked up from the magazine, talk of football sparking some interest. "But I mean, he's new here."

New here. I was getting the idea that that was a problem in Warrenstown. But I'd been new in a lot of places, and it was a problem everywhere.

"He seem to have anything on his mind, anything worrying him last time you saw him?"

"Nope."

"When was that?"

"What?"

"Last time you saw him."

I could have sworn Morgan hesitated a fraction of a second before he shrugged, said, "I don't know. Probably practice last Monday."

"You guys are still practicing? Isn't the season over?"

He looked at me as though I'd asked if he was still breathing. "Practice every afternoon, three o'clock. We got the Hamlin's game this Saturday." He added, "Coach'll be pissed if Gary doesn't show."

"Morgan, language," his mother said, and Morgan rolled his eyes.

Trying to connect, to keep Morgan with me, I went back to football. "Postseason game at Hamlin's?" I asked. "Is that big?"

"Yeah." Morgan's eyes shone. "Varsity juniors, sophomores, some guys from JV Coach thinks might be ready? We go up to Hamlin's, play the guys at the seniors' camp."

"There are enough seniors to field a full team?"

"Well, not from *here*," he said, as though anyone knew that. "Seniors' camp at Hamlin's, it's like . . . like an all-star thing. A bunch of schools, if their teams make the play-offs, they send the seniors to seniors' camp. Then Warrenstown comes up and plays."

"None of the other schools?"

"Nuh-uh."

"Why not?"

Morgan looked blankly at me, as though that question had never crossed his mind. Well, why should it have? When you're fifteen, the way the world is is the way the world works.

"All-star seniors," I said. "After a week at camp. You have a chance?"

"You kidding?" A stupid question, obviously, but what could you expect from a grown-up? "Whole thing is to lose by less than last year's team lost by."

"Which is?"

"This year, twenty-two points."

"You have a chance?" I repeated.

"Totally. I'm starting quarterback," he said, as if that explained it all.

"Good luck," I said. "About Gary: Tell me this—except for now, does he usually show up?"

"You mean, for practice?"

"Practice, games, class. Is he dependable?"

"Yeah, I guess. When I'm looking for somebody to hit

with a pass, he's always there," he added, defining *dependable* in the way that mattered most.

"Thanks, Morgan. One more thing. Who else is he friends with? Is he interested in any girls you know about?"

Another shrug.

"Didn't you tell me he'd asked Tory Wesley out?" Morgan's mother said.

"Oh, Mom!" Morgan flushed deeply, whether with anger or something else, I couldn't tell. "She's a geek. That was before he knew anybody."

"Knew any other girls?" I asked.

"Knew anybody," Morgan said, and what that meant was clear: before he knew the guys, knew who was cool and not cool, knew whom you could ask out, whom you'd better avoid.

I had Tory's name already, from my sister. I added *Wesley* to it, asked Morgan, "What about friends?"

"I don't know."

I gave Morgan a long look. He went back to his magazine. I checked the list I'd gotten from Helen. "His mother said Randy Macpherson."

"Yeah," Morgan said, uncaring. "Randy's a senior, he's a starter, but him and Gary hang out. Receivers, I guess they got stuff to say to each other."

"Randy's at camp this week?"

"Yeah."

I looked at the list again. "How about Paul Niebuhr?"

"Oh, shit!" Morgan shook his head and laughed.

His mother said, "Please watch your mouth."

"That kid is a total freak," Morgan said, not responding to his mother's words, as though she were not in the room. "Nobody hangs out with him. Just the other freaks."

"He's not a friend of Gary's? I heard they skateboarded together."

Morgan's look was pitying: How could anyone be so dumb? "Football players don't skateboard," he explained. "Coach Ryder says it's a dumb way to get hurt. You get

hurt, Coach says, it better be because some SOB was between you and the hole."

"Oh, Morgan," his mother objected, but Morgan was un-
touchable, because he was quoting his coach.

"Okay," I said. "Anything else about Gary you can think
of?"

Morgan shook his head.

"Thanks. You do think of anything else, here's my card."

He took it, read it, laughed again. "Private investigator.
Too fucking much."

"Morgan!" said his mother.

"Sorry," Morgan dismissed her. He stood. "Later," he
said, and that clearly dismissed me, too. He grabbed the
handrail, took the stairs two at a time. I heard a door open
upstairs, and slam.

I asked Mrs. Reed if she knew where Tory Wesley lived,
and she told me. "But I think they're away." I thanked her
and left her to her house and her son. From the car, I called
the Wesleys' number, got a machine, left a message. I called
the police again, but Detective Sullivan still wasn't available. I called Lydia and got her voice mail. I called my sister.
She answered on the first ring, as though she'd been sitting
by the phone.

"It's Bill," I said. "Have you heard anything?"

"No." Her voice when she answered had been quick and
anxious; now in that one word it grew dull again.

"Scott hasn't called?"

"Nobody. Have you found out anything?"

"Tory's last name," I said. "Wesley, does that sound
right?"

"I suppose so." She spoke as though I was sidetracking
and she was weary with it. "Is that all?"

"For now. I'm talking to Gary's friends; I'll call you
later."

We hung up, glad, I thought, to be rid of each other.

I called Paul Niebuhr's house. Maybe freaks answered
the phone for private investigators.

Paul didn't, but his mother did. I told her who I was and what I wanted.

"I'm sorry," she said, sounding genuinely so. "Paul's away."

"Can I reach him?"

"No, he's gone camping."

"Camping? Where?"

"Bear Mountain."

"Do you know what campground?"

"Paul doesn't go to a campground," she corrected me gently. "He has places deep in the woods where he goes. He's trying to get away from the stress of modern life."

Aren't we all, I thought. But this was a teenage kid: "Does he carry a cell phone?"

"Of course, but he probably won't answer it. He doesn't like to be dependent on modern technology."

I couldn't blame him. Though I'd bet he hadn't left the Polarfleece and ripstop nylon behind.

"Can I have the number?"

"Why did you want to talk to him?" his mother asked me.

"A friend of his seems to have run away from home. I'm working for the family. I thought Paul might be able to help me find him."

"Who would that be?"

"Gary Russell."

"Gary—oh, the new boy up the street. He's younger than Paul. He hasn't been over since school started."

"They're not friends?"

"Well, of course I try to give my children space. I don't quiz them on their friends. But I haven't seen Gary lately."

Of course. "His number?" I asked again.

"Well—yes, all right. I don't like to tell my children who they can and can't talk to. That's too much like censorship, isn't it?" She gave me the number; I wrote it down.

"Thanks," I said. "If you hear from him, will you ask him to give me a call? When do you expect him back?"

"He'll be back on Sunday. School starts Monday."

I called Paul Niebuhr's cell phone. He didn't answer. I left a voice mail, wondering if checking his messages was too twenty-first century for a kid trying to get away from the stress of modern life.

Well, there you are, Smith, I thought, sitting in the car on the peaceful suburban street. Zero for however many that was. I started the car, headed to the Wesleys', a few blocks over. If no one was home, I could leave my card; then I'd try the high school. The football coach, the assistant coaches, teachers, someone might be around who could give me some idea about Gary, who he really was, what was important to him.

The Wesleys' house was in the area where Warrenstown started to get fancy, where the yards began to spread and the houses were set far enough back from the street that driveways curved in front of them. The Wesleys' place had a Spanish feel, red clay tiles on the roof, heavy chocolate-colored window frames, wide front door. I parked in the drive behind a RAV4, walked up, and rang the bell. Nothing happened. Well, Morgan Reed's mother had said they were away. I rang again, took out a card, looked for a place to leave it. The mailbox was down by the street; the door had no mail slot. I went to wedge the card into a mullion in the sidelight by the door. My hand stopped halfway up as I got a look through the glass.

The place was a disaster. From the sidelight I was looking into a vestibule; if the inner door had been closed I couldn't have seen anything, but it stood wide, and I saw enough. Glass from smashed pictures sprinkled the stairs, glittering in the hallway lights still burning now, in full daylight. Broken furniture, maybe from the rooms upstairs, littered the landing. I looked left and right through the sidelight, then came back down off the porch and walked through the shrubs to the windows beside it.

They gave into the living room. The living room was wrecked. No furniture stood upright; a lot of it was ripped, stuffing hanging out, throw pillows thrown, side tables on their sides. One lone oil painting hung on a wall, its mates all fallen, their frames twisted, their canvases slashed. Beer cans, some crushed, some still round and upright, covered the carpet, the mantelpiece, any surface that could hold them, like an occupying army after a mighty battle.

I walked around the house, looked in other windows. The kitchen, dining room, den were no different. I took out my cell phone and called the police.

"It's Bill Smith," I told the young cop.

"Oh, hey, yeah, Sullivan's available," he said. "You want him now?"

"Yes. But not on the phone. Maybe he, or someone, better get out here." I gave the Wesleys' address.

"Why?" the cop asked. "What's up?"

"It looks to me like someone had a party."

four

I was sitting on the porch steps smoking a cigarette when the cops got there. They came up the curved drive in a blue-and-white with gold Warrenstown PD insignia sparkling on the doors. The cop behind the wheel pulled next to my Acura. A tall man ducked his head to get himself out of the passenger seat, reset his hat as I came down to meet them.

"Jim Sullivan," he said, offering his hand. "You Smith?"

"That's right."

"What's wrong here?"

"Take a look."

Our footsteps crunched over the expanse of marble chips that blanketed the drive. "You called before. You wanted to talk to me about Gary Russell," Sullivan said. He had a marine's weathered face, a marine's bristled haircut and straight back. He was an inch or so taller than I was, younger but not by much, and thinner, hard-looking, a man who still spent time in the gym. All the cops I knew who made detective grabbed the chance to go back into civilian clothes, but Sullivan wore a uniform, same navy pants and tie as the cop who'd driven him, flawless white shirt, short jacket with bars on the shoulders.

"I'm trying to find him," I said. "I came out here to see Tory Wesley. I heard she's a friend of his."

The bushes rustled as we pushed through them to reach

the living room windows. Sullivan said, "Oh, Jesus."

The other cop, the one who'd been driving, came to stand beside us. "Wow," he said.

Sullivan gave a short laugh. "Burke's new," he told me. "Your first, huh?" he said to Burke.

"Yes, sir."

"First what?" I asked.

Sullivan's look said it had just occurred to him I might be new, too. "Parents Are Away Party. P double-A P, they're called. Tradition in this town. Parents go away, leave the kid home alone. Kid invites a few friends over, have a little party Saturday night. Word spreads, next thing you know, every kid in Warrenstown's there. Usually ends up like this."

"Like this?" I said. "This place is destroyed."

"Like this. We get two or three a year, some not this bad, some worse. Two years ago they burned a house down."

"And this is what you call a tradition here?"

He shrugged, looked in the window, back at me. "You try to get in?"

"No."

Sullivan's eyebrows lifted. "PI, situation like this, you weren't curious?"

"Dying from it. But this isn't my problem. I'm looking for Gary Russell. I didn't want to have to talk my way out of it when you found me in the house."

He gave a small smile. "Smarter than you know. This town's real touchy about these things. Especially with outsiders."

"What does that mean?"

He shrugged again. "Something like twenty years ago, girl got beaten up, raped at one of these things. Boy who did it shot himself a few days later."

"I guess living down that kind of thing could make a town touchy."

Sullivan looked at me. "What made them touchy was, they'd already arrested the captain of the football team and it made the national news. Heads rolled over that." He turned to Burke. "Come on. We better see if we can get in. Gas may be on, something like that." He stepped back up on the porch, turned the door handle: nothing. He didn't tell me to get lost, so I stuck with them as they headed around the back.

"Can I ask you about Gary Russell?" I said.

"What's your interest?" Sullivan asked, as Burke rattled the handles on the french doors to the living room. One of them had a broken glass panel, but you couldn't reach the inside lock from it. We kept going. "Family hire you?"

"Not exactly. He's my nephew."

Burke was trying all the windows as we rounded the house. Sullivan said, "That right? You the mother's brother?"

"Yes."

"They didn't tell me she had a brother in the business. When'd they call you in?"

"They didn't."

"You're here."

"Gary was arrested last night in New York. That was the first I heard he'd run away."

"Arrested for what?"

"He picked a guy's pocket, but they dropped it. They released him to me. He ran again."

"Oh, shit."

"Right."

Sullivan's mouth twisted sympathetically. "Well, at least you can tell them he was okay last night. Bet you're in the doghouse, though."

I took out another cigarette, lit it in answer. I shook out the match, said, "How come you guys are involved? No offense, but most police departments don't put a lot of effort into teenage runaways."

"Your brother-in-law is from here. Played football with my chief. Called him the first day after the kid didn't come home."

"Old buddies, huh?"

Sullivan just looked at me.

"Hey, Sullivan," Burke called from behind some shrubs. "Back door's open."

"Go on in," Sullivan said.

"Detective," I said, and Sullivan looked at me, "if Tory Wesley was home alone and this was a party that got out of hand, where's she now?"

He eyed me. "Haven't seen her around town, it's true. You're thinking she ran away, too?"

"If it was my fault something like this happened to my folks' house, I'd run away."

"I might do the same," Sullivan agreed. "She tight with Gary Russell?"

We rounded the well-pruned plantings, followed Burke inside.

"I don't know. My sister thinks they saw each other for a while over the summer. I also talked to a kid named Morgan Reed."

Sullivan snorted. "Little bastard," he said. "Punk-in-training, Morgan Reed."

"Who does he train with?"

"Upperclassmen. Seniors and juniors. We got some doozies here, Smith. This is a quiet week, seniors are at Hamlin's."

"They're football players? All your doozies?"

"This town, you can do whatever the hell you want all week, long as you win on Friday night. Morgan says Tory Wesley and Gary Russell are an item?"

"Were. He says it's long over."

"Long over? Russell kid's only been in town a couple of months."

"Morgan said he only was interested in her before he knew kids who were cooler."

"Yeah," Sullivan said, stepping over the remains of a kitchen chair. "I guess that would be this crowd."

We all stood for a moment, looked around. "Shit," Burke said. "Stinks in here."

It did. The gas wasn't on, but beer, chips, and pizza had had days to meld with the ashes of cigarettes and joints and bake in the angled autumn sunlight. Flies buzzed and darted in the rancid air with the energy of an unexpected reprieve.

Sullivan took a pack of Camels from his shirt pocket. I gave him my cigarette to light off of. He offered his pack to Burke.

"I don't smoke," Burke said.

"Helps with the smell," said Sullivan; still Burke shook his head.

"Wonder where the parents are," Sullivan said.

I said, "Neighbors might know."

"Neighbors. Tell you something: less classy neighborhood than this, houses closer together, neighbors would have heard the party. Somebody'd have called us before things got this bad."

Things were pretty bad. Graceful dining room chairs lay crippled, broken, around a mahogany table with deep gouges in its shining polish. China shards sprinkled a corner of the dining room as though there'd been a dish-hurling contest. In one spot in the living room the pearl-gray carpet was still squishy underfoot; there must have been a lake of beer spilled there. Unexpectedly, a cat appeared at the top of the stairs and meowed. With clear distaste, it tiptoed down through the broken glass to join us, rubbed against Sullivan's leg. Sullivan bent down, scratched its head. "When's the last time anyone fed you, huh?"

"You want me to take a look around upstairs?" Burke asked.

"Might as well."

Burke's face said that was the wrong answer, but he went to do his duty. Sullivan headed back to the kitchen. He found the cat's plastic water dish under the radiator, filled it, pulled a can of food from a cabinet. When he ran the electric can opener the cat spun around like a whirlwind.

Sullivan put the can on the floor and the cat plunged its face into it. Sullivan started sifting through the papers that littered the terra cotta tiles, papers that had once been piled on the stone counter or held by magnets to the fridge. "Parents might have left the number of the place they were going," he said, cigarette dangling from his lip. He glanced at front and back, collected in his left hand papers that didn't help.

He was picking up papers and the cat was eating and I was smoking when Burke called from upstairs, "Sullivan! Oh, Jesus, Jim, you better come look at this."

Sullivan and I exchanged looks; he dropped the papers, rose, tossed his cigarette in the sink. I followed as he strode for the stairs, where Burke, white-faced, waited at the top. We worked our way over the debris. The second floor was pretty much in the same shape as the first: wrecked. It smelled worse, though, and the stench got stronger as Burke led us along the hall to a bedroom where we had to step over what was left of a desk to get in the door. When we did, we knew why Sullivan hadn't seen Tory Wesley around town, and why no one would ever wonder where she was again.

Sullivan and I stood on the lawn, watched the ambulance pull in, the medical examiner's man pull out. Huge trees with golden leaves blazed in the midday sun. The cop at the bottom of the drive was telling the neighbors, the joggers and dogwalkers, to go home because there was nothing to see. I'd given a statement, shown my license to Sullivan and various other people who wanted to see it, asked a few questions myself. Now we stood, watching.

"I've got to go see your sister," Sullivan said.

"I know. I want to be there."

"No. For all I know you knew all about this and came out here to cover it up."

I stared. "Then why did I call you?"

Sullivan considered. "Because you're an idiot?"

"That's true, but it's not what happened. If half the kids in Warrenstown were here, they're all as likely to know what happened to Tory Wesley as Gary is."

"He's the one who ran away."

"He said he didn't run away. He said he'd gone to New York to do something important."

"Yeah," Sullivan said. "Like run away."

"If that's it, why was he still in New York three days after he left home?"

Sullivan nodded thoughtfully, but he didn't answer the question.

"He may not have even been here," I said.

"We'll check that." A cop wearing surgical gloves carried a bag of trash, now evidence, from the house, dumped it in the back of a tech van. It would go to the lab, along with a dozen or so other bags, to be checked for prints. A lab director's nightmare.

"And we're tracking down the other kids," Sullivan said. "Starting with your buddy Morgan Reed. We'll find out who was here."

A fresh fall breeze shivered the leaves.

"I want to work together on this," I said. "You want to find out what happened to Tory Wesley. I'm looking for Gary."

"Could be we're looking for the same thing."

"I don't think so," I said, though a part of me was saying, hell, sure it could.

Sullivan was silent. Then, "No," he said.

"No, what?"

He turned to face me, spoke quietly. "What do you want me to say, Smith? That I don't think Tory Wesley died in her sleep, that I think someone who was at that party killed her and I think it may have been Gary?" He shook his head. "Until someone proves otherwise, Gary Russell's a suspect. You're his uncle. Drop it, go back to New York, keep out of my way."

"You don't really think I will?"

He looked over the lawn again. "You licensed in this state?"

"So far I'm not doing anything you need a license for. I'm just driving around asking questions."

"You carrying?"

"No." I opened my jacket to show him: nothing. I don't have a New Jersey carry permit, so the .38 I usually wear in a shoulder rig was back at my place. I had a .22 strapped up under the dash in the car, but he hadn't asked about that.

"Get out of town," he said.

"Sullivan—"

He shook his head. "You're Gary's uncle. You find him first, I'll never get my hands on him."

"You don't know that that's true."

He gave me a sideways look, didn't answer that. "You're looking for a runaway. I'm looking for a killer. Whether they're the same or not, my investigation takes precedence."

"I'm only interested in Gary."

"I'm sorry," he said, and it sounded like it might be true. "But you're in a bad position."

"Gary's in a worse one."

"I'll find him."

The wind gusted, stronger now. Leaves and shadows skidded around the unmoving trunks of trees. Sullivan slipped a cigarette out of his pocket. I offered him mine, for the light, but he took out a lighter, used that.

"I could refuse," I said. "To leave. As long as I'm not breaking the law—"

"I'll arrest you," Sullivan said calmly, breathing out smoke. "You'd beat it, but I could keep you out of circulation a couple of days. That might be all I'll need."

Or, I thought, I could drive to the next town, take out my cell phone, and call every kid in Warrenstown. Out of Sullivan's jurisdiction he'd have trouble making his threat stick. But there was no point in saying that. I'd do what I wanted and he'd do what he had to. I took a last drag on my cigarette, threw it onto the gravel. There was nothing left there. "Two things," I said to Sullivan. "If you find him, will you tell me?"

He nodded. "Once I have him."

"And I want to talk to my sister."

"I told you: No."

"Not with you. After you're done. She's my sister, Sullivan, her kid is missing and you're about to tell her he's a suspect in a homicide. I want to stay in town, see her after you're gone."

It sounded good. I didn't add that, before this morning, I hadn't seen her in years.

He fixed his eyes on me. "Then you'll leave?"

"I think you're wrong about this. But I'll leave."

"All right. I'll call you when I'm done with her. Where will you be?"

"I don't know," I said. "But I'll keep out of your way."

It took some work to get my Acura unpacked, to maneuver past the vans and cars, around the RAV4 that, according to a neighbor, had been Tory Wesley's sixteenth-birthday present from her folks. The crowd at the end of the drive parted, stared into my windows when I went past. I drove a little; where the streets were sunny and quiet, peaceful as though no one's child had died a few blocks away, I stopped, called my sister.

"Have you heard anything?" I asked. She'd picked up the phone on the first ring, the same as before. "From Scott, or anyone?"

"No. Have—?"

"Listen," I said. "Something bad's happened. Not to Gary. But the police are coming to talk to you."

"What do you mean?"

"That girl you told me about," I said. "Tory Wesley. She's dead."

Silence. Then, "Dead? I don't—"

"They think that's why Gary ran away, Helen."

"They think—what, that he knows something about it? But that's crazy. What do you mean, she's dead? What happened?"

"Detective Sullivan's on his way. He'll tell you the whole thing."

"Where are you?"

"He won't let me come. He thinks if Gary's involved I may be too."

"You—involved in what?"

In what. Jesus Christ. I stuck a cigarette in my mouth, lit it. "Answer Sullivan's questions when he gets there, that's all."

A small voice: "I don't understand any of this."

"I called because I didn't want you blindsided," I said. "I'm still in town. I'll call again."

I hung up, smoked, watched a gardener wrap burlap around some shrubs not hardy enough to withstand winter on their own. A car rolled by me, turned the corner. Eventually I took out the phone again and called Lydia.

"Hi," she said. "What's up? You don't sound good." Behind her words, a horn honked, a siren shrilled. She was on the street.

"I'm not." I told her what had happened, what we'd found.

"My God," Lydia said. "How did she die?"

"That'll take an autopsy. She was on the bed, naked," I added.

"Oh, Bill." Then the obvious, though I hadn't said it: "And they think it was Gary?"

"As Sullivan says, he's the one who ran away."

"Could it be? Could he have?"

I thought of Gary's exhausted eyes, the face that looked so much like mine. "I don't know."

"What do you want to do?"

"I told them about last night, gave them Hagstrom's name and number. They'll fax Gary's picture to New York."

"That'll make three," Lydia said. "Sets of pictures going around."

"My brother-in-law's there?"

"I haven't run into him, but one of the places I went, they already had a picture. A real one," she added. "Of Gary, not you. I took a copy. I've been passing it out with the other one."

"Well, now it's different. Now the police'll be looking for him as a suspect, not a runaway. They'll look harder."

We were silent for a few moments, me out here, stopped, in a peaceful town, where a house was destroyed and a girl was dead, Lydia in action in the never-still city.

And Gary, I thought, somewhere, alone, on the run, look-ing over his shoulder, trying to do something important.

"Bill?" I realized Lydia had spoken, was repeating her-self. "I said, do you want to hear about that camp?"

"Yes. Sorry." I didn't try to tell her it must have been the phone, because it wasn't the phone.

"Hamlin's Institute of American Sports, Plaindale, Long Island. Building Men by Building Character through Com-petitive Sports." Her voice told me what she thought of men built that way.

"Supposed to be any good?"

"If you like that kind of thing. It's been open about fif-teen years. Parents send kids over weekends and in the sum-mer. Sometimes schools send whole teams in the summer, too. And right now, they're running this thing called Sen-iors' Camp."

"I heard. Teams that make the play-offs, their seniors get to go to Hamlin's, to get their game ready for college."

"Right. I think there are about half a dozen schools with boys there. But Bill, it's only seniors. Gary's a sophomore, you said."

"I was hoping. Anybody out there seen him?"

"I talked to Tom Hamlin, the director. He hasn't, and he doesn't know why Gary would go there. Until Saturday," she added. "For the game. The Warrenstown underclassmen come here and play the seniors?"

"I heard about that, too. Listen, Gary has at least one friend who's there, a kid named Randy Macpherson, a re-ceiver. See if you can talk to him."

"So you want me to keep going?"

"Yes. Sullivan told me to lay off, but he didn't tell you to lay off."

"That wouldn't be because you failed to mention me, would it?"

"Well, yes," I said. "It probably would."

five

I closed the phone, thought how quiet it was here on this shady suburban street without Lydia's voice. The gardener was gone now; on the lawn where he'd been working a wood thrush flitted from branch to branch, tree to tree. It chirped a little on each perch, flew on to another one, seeming unable to find a place to settle. The fall weather had been warm so far, and maybe this thrush thought he wouldn't have to go south this year, could just stay and find shelter under golden-leaved trees until spring. Or maybe he already knew what he had to do, and was gathering his strength.

I sat for a while, just looking. Then I started up the car, headed into town: I was starving.

The Galaxy Diner occupied a prime spot in Warrenstown's downtown, a corner where from one part of the L-shaped room, the part that looked out on the streets, you could see who was coming and going, and from the part overlooking the parking lot you could see who'd decided to stay. I took a booth on the street side, ordered coffee and a turkey sandwich. The coffee came first. I drank it and watched the light change and tried to think of nothing.

The waiter was right on top of things, bringing back the coffeepot just before I finished my first cup. He filled it again and as he did a short girl, blond, maybe seventeen, slid onto the banquette across from me. She wore wide-legged jeans, a pink tee shirt with long white sleeves, a gray hooded sweatshirt she unzipped and pulled off as she sat. "I'll have some coffee," she told the waiter, smiling, and he smiled, too, and went to get her a cup.

"Hi." She leaned forward, turned the smile to me. "Stacie Phillips. Editor of the *Warrenstown News*—that's at the high school—and I cover high school affairs for the *Tri-Town Gazette*. That's published in Greenmeadow, but it also covers Warrenstown and a couple of other places around here."

"Sounds like a good job," I said. Her hair was chin-length and bouncy and she wore six gold earrings in one ear and eight in the other, from the lobe on up.

"Yeah." She grinned. "You're a private detective from New York. You're Gary Russell's uncle and you're looking for him. You were there when Detective Sullivan found—found Tory Wesley." The grin flagged. She looked around, luckily spotted the waiter bringing her coffee and my sandwich.

"That's true," I said.

She reached for the milk and sugar. Her hands were small and plump; her short nails were painted a pale pink. "Tell me about it." Into her coffee she dumped four sugars and as much milk as the cup could hold.

"I don't think so."

"Come on, it's news, it's not a secret." She raised her cup carefully, sipped coffee off the top.

"Ask Detective Sullivan." I salted the sandwich, took a bite.

"There's a press conference at three. Probably not Detective Sullivan, probably Chief Letourneau with his usual everything's-under-control-in-our-perfect-little-town stuff." A slight hesitation before *stuff* made me think that wasn't the word she'd have used if she weren't talking to a grown-up.

"If he's the police chief," I said, "then it's his job to say things like that, to make you all feel safe."

"He grew up here, I think he believes it. Anyway, I'll be there, at his press conference. But I wanted to talk to you first."

"How do you know who I am?"

"I asked Trevor." To my blank look she said, "The cop who was chasing everyone away at the driveway. He used to date my sister."

"And how'd you find me?"

"I followed you. Trevor'd already said about the press conference, and I knew there was no way he was going to let me up to the house. I mean, he knows I'm a reporter, but he's all, Hey, yo, this is my job, man." She said the last part in a deep, dumb-cop voice. "So when you left I followed you. You parked on Gillis and made a phone call. It's all one way around there, so I drove past you around the corner to Linden and waited. You had to come out that way."

I ate more turkey, thought back to the quiet street, the gardener. "Green Corolla?"

"Uh-huh."

"That's pretty good."

"So reward me. Tell me about it."

"How'd you hear what happened?"

"I have a police scanner in my car." By now she'd drained off maybe a quarter of her coffee. She poured more milk in, added another sugar. "And so does Stuart Early, who's the police reporter for the *Gazette*, and sooner or later he'll figure out about you, and I want to scoop him."

"This sounds more like his beat than yours."

"Tory went to Warrenstown High. It can be mine." She grinned again. "You share, I'll share. Maybe I can tell you something about Gary that can help."

"Did you know Tory Wesley?" I couldn't help asking.

Stacie Phillips's round-cheeked face clouded. She shook her head, maybe to chase the clouds away. "Not really. She's a sophomore. I mean, I saw her around."

"Tory Wesley's dead," I said. "This is the real thing."

"I'm a reporter," she said, looking me in the eye. "This is a real story."

I drank my coffee and looked at her, a kid whose life was about to start, asking me to tell her about a kid whose life was over.

"Tory," I said. "Was she close with Gary Russell?"

"Oh no, Mr. Detective," she said. "If I tell you, you have to tell me."

The waiter returned with the coffeepot, poured us both more coffee. "You want something to eat?" I asked her.

"No, thanks. But I think we need more milk." She poured what was left of the milk into her cup, gave the pitcher to the waiter with another smile.

"Sullivan said he'd arrest me if I didn't drop the case and leave town," I told her.

"No way."

"Yes."

"For real? Can he do that?"

"Uh-huh."

"Well," she said, looking around, "this isn't exactly out of town."

"I have a reprieve, maybe an hour. Then I have to go."

"I could put that in my story," she offered. "Abuse of police power. He might back down, if it's in the paper."

"No thanks. But he won't be happy to hear I'm talking to a reporter."

"Do you care?"

I thought about it. From Sullivan's point of view he was doing what he had to do, telling me to drop it, throwing me out of town; but he was also cutting me as much slack as he thought he could, promising to let me know if he found Gary, letting me stay to talk to Helen. If he got seriously pissed off he'd keep doing the job, stop doing me favors. On the other hand, Stacie Phillips might be able to lay out Gary's life for me in a way an adult couldn't do. And Sullivan might be out of favors already.

"No," I said.

"Me, either."

"You might get in trouble," I warned her.

"For what? He didn't tell *me* not to talk to *you*."

"I hear this town's sensitive about stories that might make them look bad."

"Because of what happened before? God, that was before I was *born*. When do people stop being sensitive about things?"

"Things like that, maybe never."

"Well," she said, "if they don't want to look bad they should stop doing things that make news."

I couldn't argue with that. "Sullivan might stop letting you into press conferences," I said.

"I don't think that's legal. Besides, he won't bother. He doesn't take me seriously anyway. None of them do." She grinned again. "I get some good stories because of that."

"Okay," I said. "I'll tell you about the Wesley house. But Gary's mother's my client and Gary's my nephew, so I'm not going to tell you much about that. And then you'll tell me what you know about Gary and his friends."

"Deal."

I described the scene at Tory Wesley's house, the garbage and the flies, the cat, the position and location of the body. I left out some things: what a body looks like, smells like, after a few days. It would take an autopsy to determine what killed Tory Wesley, but she'd been nude and bruised. Sullivan or the chief might cover some of that in the press conference, but I didn't see any reason to talk about it now, to another teenage girl in a sunny booth at the town diner.

Stacie Phillips took out a spiral pad, took notes in a round, open hand. She didn't interrupt, and except for a tiny pause, a stutter in her writing hand now and then, if anything I told her upset her, she didn't show it.

I finished, drank some coffee while she looked at her notes. She seemed to think about something, lifted her eyes to me. "Tell me the gross parts."

"What?"

"It's Wednesday. If Tory died Saturday night and was just lying there all this time . . ."

"You don't want to hear it."

"Yes, I do. Stuart Early can get all the facts, just like you gave me. I want a color piece. It's the only way I'll get a byline."

"This is someone you knew."

"And I'm just a kid?"

"Maybe something like that."

"Tell me."

Her eyes were brown, like mine, and steady, and I thought, who are you protecting, Smith, and why? If this kid's willing to go through this because she thinks it'll help her get something she really wants, who asked you to get in the way?

"Okay," I said, and I described the position of the body, the bloating that happens, and the flies. I told her about the snap as Sullivan pulled on latex gloves to run his hands between the body and the bedsheets, and the unexpected heaviness of a body, even a young girl's body, in a rubber body bag.

Stacie Phillips wrote and wrote, but she didn't look up.

After I was done we both drank coffee and for a while didn't speak. Then she took a breath, the reporter still, and asked, "Why did you go there? To the Wesleys'."

"My sister said Gary had dated Tory."

"He did?"

"I don't know. You tell me."

"Oh," she said. "This is the part where I tell you things?"

"I'm pretty much done. If you picked it up on a police scanner, you must've been there for the rest."

She nodded. "I guess I was." She put down her glitter-covered ballpoint, and I got the feeling she might have been relieved. "Okay. But if I think of questions later can I call you?"

"I might not answer them."

"If I don't call you, you definitely won't answer them."

"That's true." I gave her my card. She glanced at it, tucked it in the pocket of her jeans. She pulled out a card

of her own and handed it across the table. Well, why not?
I put it away.

"So: Was Gary Russell dating Tory Wesley?" I asked.

"I don't know, either. I'd be surprised."

"Why?"

"Well, Tory's not—wasn't, I mean, cool." Her fair skin
flushed, but she recovered.

"Gary is?"

"Well, yeah. He's a jock."

"That makes him cool?"

"Around here? Are you serious?"

"I don't know much about here."

"Jocks rule," Stacie Phillips said. "Totally. Warrenstown,
Home of the Warrenstown Warriors. You must have seen
that on the way into town. Whichever road you came on.
Even if you parachuted in. It's on the school roof, you
know."

"It is?"

"Of course. Trust me, it's true. Their world; the rest of
us just live in it."

"The rest of us, including you? You're not cool?"

"Me? No way. Come on, I write for the school paper."

"Why do you do that, if it's not cool?"

She gave me narrowed eyes, as if she thought I might be
making fun of her. She must have decided I wasn't, because
she drank more coffee and answered me. "I'm going to jour-
nalism school next year. Columbia, if I get in, or somewhere
else. You know some of the kids here have never been to
New York? All you have to do is get on a stupid bus." She
shook her head. "This place is sick. It really is. There's no
point in trying to be cool here if you're not a jock, it'll
never happen. The only thing is to get out."

Unless, I thought, you're new. Then maybe the thing is
to get in.

"So being a jock makes Gary Russell cool?" I said. "Even
though he's new here?"

"Sure. I mean, not when he first got here, in like June or
whenever, because no one knew him yet. If he dated Tory

Wesley, it must have been then. And maybe he did, because he kind of hung out with Paul Niebuhr then, too—Paul's a senior, he's in my class, that's how I know."

"Those aren't things you do if you're cool?"

"Puhleeze. Paul's so freaky I even have trouble talking to him. And I try really hard to talk to everyone. You get better stories that way," she told me seriously.

"And Tory Wesley? Also freaky?" I wasn't sure what defined *freaky*, but I didn't want to ask right then.

Stacie Phillips shook her head. "The reason Tory wasn't cool was she wanted to be so much."

"That's bad?"

"Of course that's bad. They can smell it the way a dog smells when you're afraid. It only gets you in worse trouble."

We sat looking at each other in momentary silence. I was thinking about Tory Wesley, and trouble. I don't know what was on Stacie Phillips's mind, but she turned to the window, drank her sweet, light coffee.

"About Gary," I said, after the traffic light had changed a few times, cars stopping, starting, rolling by. "When did he get to be cool?"

"Football tryouts," Stacie said. She turned back to me. "Early August. Gary blew everyone away. Every time a quarterback was looking for a receiver, Gary was open. Had more yards after catch than anyone else, even the seniors. By, like, double or better. Coach tried him out returning punts, he never dropped the ball. *I* even thought it was cool."

"You were there?"

"I covered it for the *Gazette*. Football tryouts in Warrenstown, now that's news."

"I think I'm hearing sarcasm here."

She shrugged. "It's a dumb story, but it gets me a byline. Colleges like to see that."

"So Gary's been cool since then?"

"Pretty much. Randy Macpherson, Mr. Big Deal, kind of adopted Gary." She dropped her voice, put on a superior, all-knowing frown. " 'The kid's not bad, but he's green.

Someone needs to show him the ropes.' " Back to her regular voice: "What that really means is, Randy's afraid Gary might actually be better than he is."

"Randy Macpherson's a wide receiver, a senior?"

"Yeah. How'd you know that?"

"I'm a detective. So what's Randy trying to do, bask in Gary's upcoming reflected glory?"

She cocked her head. "Wow. Can I quote you?"

"I don't know about this sarcasm thing, in a reporter."

"Sorry." She grinned. "Anyhow, I'm not sure that's really it. It's more like, he wants to be able to say Gary learned everything he knows from him."

"What makes Randy Macpherson Mr. Big Deal?"

"He's a senior. He's a jock. He's actually been scouted by a couple of colleges. And he's rich. And his father's Mr. Extra Big Deal, all the way back from when he went to school here, too. He was a famous Warrior, a linebacker. I mean, we have a mayor and everything, but Randy's dad is really who runs this town."

"I guess that's enough. Randy's at Hamlin's camp now?"

"Boy, you do know some stuff, don't you?" she marveled.

"I hate to be scooped."

"You're laughing at me."

"Never laugh at a reporter," I said. "Next thing you know, you're misquoted into oblivion."

"I can do that," she agreed.

"This Camp Week thing," I said. "I never heard of anything like this. When I was in school, if a team went to an away game, or anyone went on any field trip, they just made up the work they missed."

"Ah, but this is Warrenstown. Here we start school in the middle of August so we can close down during Camp Week so that the Warrior seniors don't have to make up any work."

"That's the whole reason?"

"Could there be a better one?" she asked, eyes innocently wide.

"And in the fall?" I said. "At the end of the season?"

"No one else does it. It impresses the college scouts with the players' dedication, their willingness to go the extra mile, their desire, the fire in their bellies."

"Is that from an article you wrote?"

"Are you serious?" She sounded insulted. "It's from the Hamlin's brochure."

"Sorry. How does—?" I began, but the cell phone in my jacket started to ring. "Sorry," I said to Stacie, took the phone out. "Smith."

"Sullivan. Just finished with your sister. You can go over any time."

"Any news?"

"About Gary? No. But I talked to your brother-in-law."

"He's back?"

"No, he's got a cell phone with him. She called him."

"He having any luck?"

"No. And he doesn't seem to like you much."

"He doesn't."

"Any particular reason?"

"Probably."

Sullivan waited, but I had nothing more to say, so he asked, "How come you didn't tell me he went to New York?"

"Does it matter?"

"It might."

"It won't. He's flying blind; he won't find him."

"He might know something we don't."

"I don't think so. And if he did, it would be something he hasn't told you for the past three days, so there's no reason to think he'd tell you now. But it would also be something he hasn't acted on for the past three days, and that's not likely."

"Well, he said he didn't," Sullivan conceded. "He said he went to New York because Gary'd been seen there. By you. He started to say some interesting things about you. But I told him why I was in his living room talking to his wife, so he said them about me instead."

"He doesn't like you either?"

"The only thing he liked about me was that I threw you out of town. Then he decided he didn't even like that, because it robbed him of the chance to whup your ass when he gets back, for coming here at all."

"Life is tough. Did he say when he was coming back?"

"After he finds Gary," Sullivan said dryly. "Where are you?"

"The Galaxy Diner, having lunch. Have you found out for sure Gary was at that party?"

"I'm going to talk to Morgan Reed now. You go see your sister, and get out of town."

"As soon as I finish my coffee."

"Hey, I'm doing you a favor. You don't want to be here when your brother-in-law gets back."

"Maybe he won't come back. Maybe he'll stay in New York, I'll run into him there, and he'll whup my ass. Think how lousy you'll feel then."

"I'll take my chances," said Sullivan.

I folded the phone, slipped it back in my pocket. "Sorry," I said again to Stacie Phillips. She had made no pretense of politely looking out the window, around the diner, down at her nails. Her shining eyes had been fastened on me the whole time.

"Detective Sullivan?" she said.

"You have a true reporter's nose."

She made a face, said, "Did he? Find out for sure Gary was there?"

"I told you, I'm not talking to you about Gary. You're talking to *me* about Gary."

"Oh? And who's whupping your ass?"

"No one, because they can't catch me. I have a few more questions, then I have to go."

"Or Jim Sullivan'll whup your ass?"

The waiter, who knew the drill by now, came by again, bringing the coffeepot and a full pitcher of milk.

"I'll take care of my ass," I said to Stacie.

She grinned. "You can't say that to me. I'm underage."

"I'm sure you know a lot worse words. I'm sure you know words I never heard of."

"You want me to teach them to you? It always helps to speak the language."

"Some other time," I said. I drank off some coffee. "Tell me about Warrenstown. Jocks are the only ones who're cool?"

Doing what she did with the milk and the sugar, Stacie nodded, said, "Totally."

"Who's not cool?"

"Everyone else. Some of us are less uncool than others, I guess. Freaks and stoners are the uncoolest. Then brainiacs and geeks, then the artsy crowd and tree-huggers—they're sort of the same—then cowboys, then jocks."

"Brainiacs are kids who get good grades?"

"And do Student Council and all that stuff. If they're like, Chess Club, they're geeks."

"Artsy, that would be you?"

She nodded. "And the drama kids, and the band, people like that."

"Cowboys?"

"They, like, drink and do dope and fight, and push everybody around. It's like being a jock, but without being on a team. So cowboys actually get detention or suspended or whatever, when they get caught."

"Jocks do all that, too?"

"Jocks do whatever they want."

"And don't get in trouble?"

She gave me the wide-eyed look. "Who would play on Friday night?"

"Uh-huh." I drank some coffee. "Are there girl jocks?"

"Not exactly. I mean, we have varsity teams and stuff—I play softball, I catch—but it doesn't make you cool. Nobody sort of notices." She shrugged.

"And freaks?" I asked. "Who are freaks?"

Stacie pursed her lips. "Kids who aren't anyone else. They hang out together but it doesn't mean they like each other. You just have to have someone to hang out with, I guess."

"Sullivan said half the kids in Warrenstown were probably at Tory Wesley's party," I said to Stacie. "Were you there?"

She shook her head, looked into her coffee.

"You knew about it, though, didn't you?"

She shrugged. "I knew her folks were going away."

"You mean, you didn't just hear about it afterwards, you knew before? That she was going to have a, what did Sullivan call it, a P double-A P?"

"I told you, she wanted to be cool. She didn't get invited to the jock parties. I'm sure she totally thought this would make her cool."

"If you knew it was going to happen, why didn't you tell someone?"

She looked at me. "Tell who? Tell them what? That some sophomore I don't even know is having a party Saturday night? So what?"

"According to Sullivan, those parties pretty much always end up like that. Shouldn't the police at least have been warned?"

"If they wanted to know," she said, "they'd know."

The waiter came to take away my plate and pour us more coffee. This time he brought a full sugar packet holder, which he traded for the decimated one on the table. I sat with Stacie Phillips for a while longer. She confirmed again what Sullivan had said: Chances were all the cool kids in Warrenstown had been at Tory Wesley's house Saturday night. She gave me some of their names, though I wasn't sure how I'd be able to make use of them, having been thrown out of town.

"If Gary Russell wasn't there," she said as the waiter put down the check, "it cut his chances of being cool way, way down. They'd have figured he was chicken. Especially," she added, "it was the night before the seniors went to Hamlin's. Randy would've been extra pumped, and it would've been a chance for him to show his protégé how it's done."

• • •

How it's done. I thought about that as I drove over to the
high school. How much of your life you spend, especially
when you're new, trying to figure out how it's done.

Stacie and I had walked to the parking lot together—
she'd insisted on paying for her own coffee, to keep her
journalistic integrity intact—and I'd watched her drive off
in her green Corolla. I wondered about the story she'd write,
how something like this looked when it happened in your
town and you were seventeen.

Then I'd made two phone calls. The first was to Morgan
Reed.

He answered the phone himself with a sullen, "Hello."

"Bill Smith," I said. "Cops leave yet?"

"Man, what the fuck are you calling for?" Rage boiled
through the phone. "Did you tell them to come here?"

"Don't be stupid. Detective Sullivan took one look at that
house, you were the first name that sprang to mind."

"Go fuck yourself."

"Don't hang up on me, Morgan, I'll just come over. I
want to know if Gary Russell was at Tory Wesley's party
Saturday night."

"Oh, fuck that party! I wish I never went to that fucking
party!"

"But you did go?" I said it as a question, but neither of
us thought it was.

"It's a fucking joke, too, because like I told Sullivan, I
was so fucking wasted, I came home early. People were still
coming when I left. Maybe Gary got there, maybe he didn't.
I didn't see him. Who cares?"

"I guess Jim Sullivan already asked you if you killed
her?"

"Fuck you!"

"Did you know she was dead?"

"No!" His voice tamped down. "I knew shit like that, I'd
tell somebody."

That's what you say, I thought, until you know shit like

that, and you know people you're tied up with are involved, will be in trouble if you tell somebody. I watched a car pull into the space Stacie Phillips had pulled out of. All right, I told myself, let it go. I asked Morgan Reed, "Do you know who killed her?"

"How could I, I didn't know she was dead?" The sneer was back. Another victory over a dumb adult.

"Did the reason Gary Russell went to New York have something to do with what happened at Tory Wesley's?"

"I don't know. I got no idea why he went and guess what? I don't give a shit."

"I don't buy it," I said. "You're a quarterback, he's your receiver. I didn't play, but I remember who was tight."

"The guy's new," Morgan snapped. "And him and me, we don't start." Meaning the thing that would tie them together, these boys, create a bond they would both remember as the best friendship they'd ever had: that thing hadn't happened yet.

"Okay," I said, and then because he was still a fifteen-year-old kid and some things were important to him, I said, "Have a good practice."

"I can't go to practice!" The real reason for his fury came out in a blast of outrage at the scale of the injustice. "My mom was so pissed when that asshole Sullivan came here and she found out about the party, I'm fucking grounded."

I called Lydia.

"That camp," I said. "Someone there has got to know something about this girl's death, what happened at that party. It might be one of them who killed her." I told Lydia about Stacie Phillips. "She said they were all bound to have been there, including Gary. And that Reed kid just about confirmed it. Whatever Gary's up to, it's got to have something to do with what happened there."

"I tried to call that kid at the camp, the one you wanted me to talk to, Randy Macpherson, but guess what—you can't talk to the kids."

"While they're at practice?"

"At all. No phone calls while they're at camp, except for certified emergencies."

"You're kidding."

"It sounded weird to me, too, but I decided it must be a guy thing. A football thing. You know, for building men."

"A lot of sarcasm going around today."

"Football brings that out in me. What do you want me to do?"

"About that, nothing, I think it's incurable. About the kids, go out there. This isn't just a social call, they'll have to let you talk to them. Sullivan'll be going there soon, but he'll have to hook up with the locals. Maybe you can find out something from the kids before he gets there."

With a note of caution in her voice, she said, "This is a homicide investigation now, Bill."

"That's in case I forgot?"

"It's in case you remembered and don't give a damn."

A Mustang racing out of the parking lot screeched its brakes when the traffic didn't stop to make way for it.

"I'm sorry," I said, rubbing my eyes. "You're right. If you don't want to go on with this—"

"Of course I'll go on," she said impatiently. "But I want you to pay attention. The way you would if this were any other case."

When we hung up, I watched the Mustang muscle into the street, then stand at a red light, engine stupidly racing.

six

I needed to see Helen once more, and I needed to get out of Warrenstown before Sullivan made me a short-term guest of the place. But there was one other thing I wanted to try, and if I was lucky I'd be able to get in and get out before Sullivan knew I'd been there.

Warrenstown High stood on the outskirts of town. Broad stairs led up to the doors and sunlight glinted off wide windows in the classroom wings on either side. Behind the classrooms rose the higher blocks of the irregular spaces: auditorium, library, gym. Everything was yellow brick and it all glowed triumphantly in the afternoon sun.

I climbed the steps past a group of kids sitting around killing time. Inside, a few more kids walked the deserted halls, opened lockers to exchange one set of books for another. These would be brainiacs, or geeks, or maybe the artsy crowd, doing what they did even over camp week. I asked directions, got pointed this way and that, and found my way to the gym, wondering how I'd feel if I were fifteen and new to this sprawling building on a crowded school morning, and everyone else was rushing around, and finding your way was confusing and difficult and really mattered.

The gym's polished floor gleamed in sunlight from high windows. The huge overhead lights, caged against damage, were off now, but they'd be on for evening practices, for

Friday night games. The place was empty; I stopped inside and my footsteps and the thump of the swinging doors echoed, faded. A wave of memory crashed over me as I stood looking: high school basketball in Brooklyn, the two years I lived there before I joined the navy; shipboard games under a net to keep the ball from the Pacific; college intramurals; pickup games in the park. Shouts, sweat, feet pounding, heart pumping, pulling out more than you thought you had from deep inside you again and again. I'd been a good shooter, but it wasn't the game-saver shots I was seeing now, not the cheers of the crowd I heard. What I remembered, what I'd forgotten, was a different thrill, and it was real, and better: making the no-look pass, setting the solid screen, nailing the timing on the alley-oop. Getting the pointed finger and the thumbs-up from the guy you'd made the pass to, set the screen for. Being depended on by a team full of other guys, and coming through; depending on them and not being let down. Long exhausting practices you looked forward to, coaches and trainers whose insults you let pass and whose orders you followed, pain you iced and ignored, because all that was the price of being here, on the hardwood, under the lights, in a place where you belonged.

I shook off the memory. There was no one here. I pushed out the swinging doors again, left them to echo by themselves.

Back along the corridor I came across the Warrenstown Wall of Fame: photos of boys, grouped by the sport they played, with plaques identifying them as school record holders, county champions, season MVPs. There were pictures of girls, too, in basketball and tennis uniforms, but fewer, and set farther from the propped-open double doors through which I could see the athletic field, spread wide in the glorious sunlight.

I stepped outside, where kids in maroon jerseys were lined up in rows along the field, doing stretches and jumping jacks. The stretches were led by a blond kid in a red jersey: the quarterback, who strained and shouted with the rest of them, grabbing this chance to show he could give orders, command respect.

Toward the end of any season, football practice was usually half-speed, to save the kids' battered bodies for the upcoming game; and here, especially, I'd have expected to see kids goofing off, messing with each other, feeling some kind of relaxed, exhibition-game mood. Warrenstown's season, after all, was over, and these kids—varsity juniors and sophomores, JV standouts—were here now only to get ready for a game they couldn't win.

But though they were in shorts or sweats, no pads but the bulging shoulder pads under their jerseys, these kids were anything but relaxed. This could have been August, a preseason practice to find the stars, weed out the failures.

It was like that, I supposed, as I watched them work with a concentrated fury that would have snapped a muscle in anyone over seventeen. They were preparing for the game where Warrenstown said good-bye to this year's heroes and got a look at next year's, and everyone wanted to be one.

On the screech of a whistle blown by a square-jawed, not-tall guy in maroon Warrenstown sweats, the warm-up session ended, and the kids lined up for wind sprints across the width of the field. Even allowing for the padding, these kids were huge: tall, wide-shouldered, their unpadded forearms and calves sharply muscled. The whistle blew and I watched them fly full-speed, bend to catch breath, turn at the whistle and charge again. I saw one kid slap another on the shoulder as he passed him, saw the second step it up, saw them end the sprint dead even. They were young and effort was rewarded and that extra burst was there when they needed it. I watched them run on the green field in the afternoon sun and I thought they were beautiful.

The guy in the sweats peered out over them all, eyes narrowed, mouth curved into a frown, looking for slackers, for losers, for fools.

I walked over, stood beside him. "Coach Ryder?"

He nodded without turning. "You found him."

Ryder had maybe fifteen years on me, a lined, ruddy face,

thinning sandy hair. "Bill Smith," I told him. "Investigator from New York. I'm looking for Gary Russell."

I waited. If news of Tory Wesley's, death had gotten this far, my name might have too, and Sullivan's order, and Ryder might tell me to go to hell. He didn't. What he said, nodding toward the field, was, "Russell. He's supposed to be here."

I looked over the field, too, the kids on their backs doing sit-ups now. "This is your juniors, your sophomores?"

"Except for Russell and Reed. Russell fucking takes off, Reed's mother grounds him. How the hell am I supposed to build a football team here if people do whatever they goddamn want?"

I had no answer to that question and I wasn't sure there was one. "I just need to find Gary Russell," I said. "Can you tell me anything about him, anything that might have been on his mind lately?"

"Anything's on their minds besides football, I don't want to hear about it," Ryder said. He blew his whistle once more and the sit-ups ended. He gave them thirty seconds, not quite enough to recover, and blew again. The kids strapped on their helmets. One group trotted down to run plays at the far end of the field under the eye of another guy dressed, like Ryder, in Warrenstown sweats. The rest stayed up here, lined up in groups of two and seven at the blocking sled. On an assistant coach's, "Down! Set!" followed by a whistle, the kids crashed the sled, pounding, thumping into it, imagining the enemy there. Ryder watched for a while, then stepped forward.

"Gelson!" he yelled in a voice that probably shook coffee cups down at the Galaxy Diner. "Goddammit, Gelson, your sister show you that? Go play with her, you want to play like a pussy! Take a lap, then get your fat ass back here and hit that fucking thing like you mean it!" A big kid close to us broke away from the others, headed around the dusty track; the others charged harder when the whistle blew for them.

"Gary Russell," I said.

Ryder turned to me for the first time. "I got practice going here."

"The kid is missing. He's fifteen."

"Missing, hell. He ran away from home. I hear he even left a note so his mommy wouldn't worry. Mommy's boys, how the hell am I supposed to work with that? What the hell you asking me for?"

"You're his coach. Coaches sometimes know what's going on with the kids on the team."

"Russell's new, I hardly know him. And like I said, if it's not football, I don't want to hear it. Ask me, I'll tell you during the season I don't want them thinking about anything but Friday's game. If they're JV, Saturday afternoon's, same thing. When Russell comes back, I'm not so sure I'll let him play."

Two boys crashed the sled together. The groups of seven were the offensive and defensive lines; the groups of two, backs and receivers. This wasn't really their job, and in most places coaches didn't expect as much from them on a drill like this; but Ryder, watching these two, scowled.

"Grades?" I asked Ryder. "Girls?"

"Grades—if they gave a shit they'd be bookworms, they wouldn't be playing football to start with. Girls you can't stop them from thinking about," Ryder snorted. "Especially here. Warrenstown High girls, cockteasing little bitches." The bitterness in Ryder's voice surprised me, and I wondered if he knew what had happened in Warrenstown, over the weekend.

"Coach," I said, "I don't know if you heard about this, but there was a wild party Saturday night, out at a girl named Tory Wesley's house. Detective Sullivan found her this morning; she's dead."

Ryder looked out over the field again, said, "I heard."

"Did you know her?"

Silence. Then a cold smile, and he said, "Tory Wesley. Warrenstown High girl."

Ryder started striding downfield, toward the red-shirted quarterback, who was firing passes at a receiver cutting fast.

"Davis!" Ryder shouted. The quarterback dropped his arm, waited. "Davis, if Reed doesn't play Saturday, you're all we have. You want that asshole Hamlin to let those seniors piss all over us?"

The kid shook his head. "No, coach."

"Then you have to be a lot better than that! We're playing fucking seniors, Davis! *Watch* your receiver! Throw where he is, not where you wish he was!"

I kept up with Ryder, stopped beside him. Davis threw another pass and Ryder cursed under his breath. He said nothing else to Davis, though, so I started again.

"Sullivan thinks most of these kids were probably at Tory Wesley's, Coach. Your seniors, too."

"Varsity had a ten o'clock curfew Saturday night, seniors going to camp Sunday morning. JV has curfew whenever varsity does."

"Kids in Warrenstown never break curfew?"

He turned to me with narrowed eyes. "These are good kids—Smith, you said your name was? These are good kids, Smith. They're boys; they're high-spirited. Look at them: They're working their asses off to play this game at a Warrenstown level. Sometimes they need to cut loose, blow off a little steam. Doesn't matter, as long as they can play on Friday night."

"Doesn't matter? Ryder, that house is wrecked and that girl is dead."

"These kids had nothing to do with that."

"You know that for a fact? You talked to them?"

"No, I didn't goddamn talk to them. Sullivan's going to come out here soon as practice is over, take their minds way the hell off their game. I got to get some work out of them before he fucks everything up."

Gary, I reminded myself, as I felt my jaw tighten. Don't go up against this guy; he's Sullivan's problem. Your problem is Gary.

"I think the reason Gary Russell left town is because of something that happened at that party," I said. Gelson finished his lap, ran back off the track, took his position. I could see his chest rising and falling as he waited for the whistle. When it blew he crashed the sled with a new viciousness, but his timing was still off, when to plant his foot, when to throw his shoulder. For his size, he didn't have the power he should have had. I said, "I think more than one of these kids probably knows what happened there."

"No idea," Ryder said.

"Who're Gary's friends on the team?"

"I don't know."

"I hear he's a buddy of Randy Macpherson's."

"I wouldn't know about that."

"Christ, Ryder, what's your problem? I need your help here. I'm looking for a kid."

Ryder turned his hard face to me. "I've been coaching here for thirty-three years, Smith. Kids come and go. You try your best to make men out of them. Sometimes you get pussies like Gelson over there and you can't, but mostly these are good kids. But guys like you, you just want to make trouble. Leave these kids alone."

"Thirty-three years? Then you were here when that other thing happened. The rape, and the suicide." Touchy, Sullivan had said. People around here were touchy. "That why you won't talk to me? I'm from outside, and this is too much like that?"

Ryder stepped forward, blew his whistle, two short blasts. Instantly everyone stopped what they were doing, began jogging in place. Ryder turned back to me.

"Get the fuck off my field."

He marched forward, shouting commands, and the boys scrambled to do as he said.

I didn't go back through the building, walked around it instead to get to my car. Way to go, Smith, I congratulated myself. Bring up something they don't want to hear about: a great persuasive technique for use on people reluctant to talk.

I was unlocking the car when my cell phone rang. I leaned against the door in the sunshine and answered it.

"Smith."

"You son of a bitch." It was Scott, the rage in his voice hemmed in by a hard, tight control. "What the hell do you think you're doing?"

"Looking for your son."

"Where are you?"

"Warrenstown," I said. "The high school. Where are you?"

"I'm in New York, you fucker! Goddammit, I told you to leave it alone!"

"You getting anywhere?"

"Fuck you! I can handle this."

"Christ, Scott, will you let it go?" I switched phone hands, pulled a cigarette from my pocket. "You can't stand me, fine. We find Gary, you don't ever have to see me again. Meanwhile, let me help."

"Oh, you're a big fucking help. The cops think Gary killed some girl, thanks to you."

"That's not how it happened."

"It's what they told me."

"Sullivan said that?"

"Fuck Sullivan, I called the chief. He said you were at that girl's house looking for Gary when she turned up dead. You weren't there, they'd never have connected him."

"Every kid at that party's a suspect right now."

"Other kids have private eyes calling the cops on them? Ratting out your family, nothing new there for you. But this is *my* family, Smith. Get the hell out of Warrenstown and keep away from my wife."

I felt hot blood flash into my face. I said, "My sister."

"She gave a damn she was your sister, she'd call you sometimes. She doesn't want to talk to you. We don't want you around, Smith, not my family."

"Gary gave the cops my name last night," I said. "Not yours."

"Oh, man!" Scott exploded. "Oh, you cocksucker!

You're fucked now, man. I'm telling you, you're fucked."

Three boys came around the building to the lot, pushing and shoving each other, laughing. I almost said something more to Scott, but I stopped myself, lowered the phone, thumbed it off. I forced my grip on it to loosen; I was surprised I hadn't broken it. I turned the ringer off, slipped the phone back in my pocket, left my brother-in-law in New York wanting me out of his town, his problem, his life.

I smoked another cigarette as I drove across town. I wanted another one after that, but I didn't light it. Screw Scott, screw his accusations, his threats and his anger. I parked in front of Helen's, slammed the car door, headed up the walk. Helen pulled the front door open before I go to it.

"Scott's mad," was the first thing she said.

I nodded. "He called me."

"I gave him your number. I—"

"Forget it. It doesn't matter. Sullivan was here?"

"Yes." She said that in the small voice, looked down, said nothing else. My shoulders, already locked after Scott's call, tightened some more.

"What the hell's going on, Helen?"

She flinched; I realized how loud that had been, lowered my voice. "Was Gary at that party?"

"I don't know." As I got louder she got softer. "He had curfew. I thought—we thought—he was upstairs in bed."

"He snuck out?"

"It's not like him."

"Stop saying that! You don't know what's like him, do you?"

"Don't yell at me!" Her face flushed and she thrust out her small jaw. "You can't tell me what my son is like! You don't know us!"

"Whose choice was that?" I said quietly.

In our silence, the dog came to the open door, stood behind Helen, stuck her face against Helen's hand. Helen scratched the dog's ears while the dog peered around her at me, wagged her tail once or twice, stopped.

"It doesn't matter," Helen said. "It doesn't matter anymore. Maybe you'd better go."

"What I did," I said, my voice suddenly as quiet as her own. "Back then. When I was Gary's age. You know why that was."

"It doesn't matter," she said again, and though it did, very much, I turned and left.

seven

I drove through town, headed east, toward the highway. It was all right with me, this business of leaving Warrenstown. If I were looking for Tory Wesley's killer, I'd feel differently; and maybe I was, but not from that direction. What I needed now was to move, to keep going, to stay a step ahead of Sullivan and stop him from shutting me down.

Or maybe I just wanted to think that my need to move had a connection to the pattern of the case. That it was what I'd feel if it hadn't been Gary standing in my living room last night, asking me for help. That it had nothing to do with my sister and what I saw in her eyes when she looked at me, or the slump in her shoulders when she thought I wasn't looking at her.

I tried the Bach in the CD player again; again, as it had that morning, it only irritated me and I turned it off.

I took out the cell phone, flipped it open, thumbed the first number on the speed-dial.

"Lydia Chin. Chin Ling Wan-ju." Lydia always answered in both her languages; you never knew who might be calling.

"It's me. Anything up?"

"No. I'm headed to that camp. How about you?"

"Me, too, but you'll get there first."

"Don't I always?"

"And when you don't, you still deserve to." I told her about the coach, about Scott's phone call.

"Nice guys," was her comment.

"A matched set. Who's your cousin who was kicked out of school and arrested for computer hacking?"

"Oh, right, throw my criminal relatives up in my face."

"I love your criminal relatives. Kwong, his name was."

"Linus Kwong. He's really the son of my mother's second cousin's brother-in-law."

She waited, but I couldn't dig out from under.

"And he wasn't kicked out of school, only suspended," she said.

"For, if I remember, the whole semester."

"And those charges were dismissed," she went on. "He was found innocent."

"That's 'not guilty.' No one's ever found innocent. And if the charges were dismissed, he wasn't found anything."

"Give the kid a break. He's just a bright high school student with an unquenchable curiosity. He didn't mean to do anything illegal."

"Uh-huh. He available?"

"For what?"

"Computer hacking."

"I'm sure he is."

Lydia gave me Linus Kwong's cell phone number and he was my next call. I identified myself, explained my connection to Lydia.

"Oh, hey, yeah, she's like my aunt or something," he told me. "She's awesome."

"Where are you?" Thumping music and blaring electronic sounds in the background made him hard to hear.

"Chinatown video arcade. Wait. Is this better?"

He must have walked outside, because the shrieks and beeps morphed into traffic noise and his voice came clearer. I told him what I wanted.

"This afternoon?"

"Right now."

"Dude, I'm winning here."

"You find something out there, you win even bigger."

We negotiated a fee. For just a bright high school student with an unquenchable curiosity, he had a pretty good sense of what his services were worth on the open market.

"How do I get there?"

"Rent a car. Send me the bill."

"Dude," he sighed at having to explain the obvious, "I'm fifteen. Hertz says you got to be twenty-five."

"Oh." I thought. "Call a car service."

"A stretch limo?"

"Don't push it."

"Okay, cool."

I gave him directions. "Listen, Linus," I said. "The mother'll let you in, but if you run into the father, blame me. Tell him I sent you and clear out."

"Dude won't be happy?"

"He'll explode."

"Cool," Linus Kwong said again.

I drove over the George Washington Bridge and straight across the Bronx, toward Long Island. I hit the beginning of rush hour, gritted my teeth as the traffic crawled. Most of the cars inching forward around me held no other passengers, just the drivers, men and women headed home, to their families, their houses, the places they lived. How was it, I wondered, where they lived, each of them? I saw in my mind the bright fall sun glowing on the fallen leaves and quiet streets of Warrenstown, the football coach making men out of boys, the party where a girl had died.

The drive took me along six-lane highways between ranks of apartment buildings, past wide, low shopping centers and two-family houses in rows with handkerchief-size lawns bordered by trimmed shrubs, chain-link fences, low brick walls—some way of saying, *mine*. Eventually the houses, though still close, began to be separated by driveways, and trees started to border the road. Where I pulled off the highway at Plaindale, the houses were bigger and the trees were older. I passed three- and four-story residential buildings and aging strip malls, bright new gas stations

and blank-walled tire warehouses, on my way to the address
Lydia had given me for Hamlin's Institute of American
Sports.

The place took up a lot of real estate, though it didn't
seem to be real estate many other people wanted. Flat,
cropped-grass acres, playing fields and training fields now,
probably potato farms once and meadow before that, spread
away to my left from a road lined on my right with discount
furniture emporiums and places that would fix your transmission, small grocery stores and even smaller bars where
you could drink away the news that your transmission
couldn't be fixed. The fields might have just kept going all
the way over the miles to Long Island Sound, but in the
distance they ran up against a scrubby woods, the kind of
trees that grow while people aren't paying attention. The
entrance to Hamlin's Institute was marked by a large sign,
which claimed, as Lydia had said, that HAMLIN'S BUILDS
MEN BY BUILDING CHARACTER THROUGH COMPETITIVE
SPORTS. It listed program dates through the fall and a number to call for the schedule for spring.

I turned left. The road into Hamlin's took me between a
parking lot and a baseball diamond wrapped with chain link,
its bleachers looking lonely, sagging a little, now that the
season was over and a cold winter would come and go before anyone would care about baseball again. Two long low
concrete block buildings, barrackslike, and a smaller square
one stood at the end of the road, fronted by another, smaller
parking lot. A tall building, maybe the gym, loomed behind.
A coat of thick yellow paint covered them all, the kind of
job you do once and don't have to worry about for twenty
years. Up close against one of the buildings, four hoops
hung on perforated steel backboards on asphalt courts. One
had no net and the painted lines on the asphalt were faded,
but basketball is an indoor game; these hoops weren't for
serious practice, just for fooling around.

And Hamlin's, it seemed to me as I parked, was a serious
place. I could hear the shouts, the thuds, the whistles; as I
walked around the buildings to the far side, I saw what the

institute cut off from the street and the town, surrounded and kept for itself: the football field.

Two squads of kids, most in blue jerseys or in Warrenstown's maroon, but some in the colors of other towns, other schools, were divided into groups on the field and on the track. They were in full uniform: helmeted, padded, in all ways looking prepared to play. Hanging over the fieldhouse doors was a large-lettered sign reminding one and all, YOU ARE NOTHING—YOUR TEAM IS EVERYTHING.

Some of the boys, in small formations, practiced the patterns of offensive plays over and over to the shouts and whistles of men in navy jackets with HAMLIN'S on the back. Down the far end, one lone kid in blue and one in maroon kicked the ball between goalposts. Each kid in turn waited for the ball, caught it if he could and raced it back to the coach, who set it up for the next kick while the other kid charged down to be ready for the catch. If a kid missed the catch, the whistle blew and he sprinted the width of the field. The kid in blue wasn't much of a receiver. I watched him do a sprint, found myself thinking kickers, in a game, never have to catch anything.

Across the field, quarterbacks-in-training threw passes to each other, high and long. I watched; the kids receiving stretched for the ball but didn't move their feet. If the passer didn't hit them with a bull's-eye where they stood, it was his bad, not theirs, and he did a cross-field sprint, too.

Everywhere, fierce concentration, full-out effort, grunts from the kids, whistles and shouts from the coaches. I walked up to stand on the edge of the track with a small knot of adults in civilian clothes. I looked for Lydia; in this entirely white, largely male group she'd have glaringly stood out, but she was nowhere in sight.

I stopped, stood with the others looking over the field. Near us, at full speed, a line of kids ran a zigzag course between close-set orange cones, cutting left, right, left, right. The man next to me turned to look at me, then turned back to the kids. He said, "Which one's yours?"

"None of them."

He gave me a sideways glance. "You're not from Warrenstown?"

"No. Where's the other team from?"

"Westbury. That's my boy there." Seeming to relax when he found I wasn't a parent of the competition, he pointed to a big kid in blue, part of a group throwing block after block against a line of kids in maroon. The long golden light of the late fall afternoon glinted off their helmets as they pounded each other again and again.

"He's big," I said, realizing that even allowing for the padding, most of these boys were huge. "He looks good."

"You're good, this place makes you better. You stink, they can make you good. Frank Edwards." He offered me his hand. "You thinking of sending your kid?"

"You'd recommend it?"

"My kids have been coming here for years. Gives them an edge. I don't think Frankie'd have made varsity otherwise. My younger son, he plays hockey. Best goalie in the county, twelve-and-under." He swelled with pride.

"Congratulations."

"What does your kid play?"

"My nephew. Football. Wide receiver."

I stood with Edwards, watched two lines of Warrenstown kids set up. An assistant coach behind one line shouted, "Down. Set!" and held the football the center snapped him. He dropped back the way a quarterback would, then stood waiting to see if the enemy would get through to him, or if his own men could protect him.

The defensive linemen mixed up their moves, and the offense tried to read and counter. The kids on offense were quick and strong, for the most part, stopping tackles and ends as they tried with spin moves and swim moves and sheer muscle and will to break through. But the defensive line was well-coached and well-led; the first time they ran the stunt the left guard didn't read it and the assistant coach was left face-to-face with a kid who'd have laid him out flat if he hadn't had a whistle around his neck. So the defense mixed it up and ran that play three more times, and the left guard missed it every time.

After the fourth missed stunt a whistle shrieked: not the assistant coach behind the line, but another man in a Hamlin's jacket, a man who'd been watching the drill with a deepening frown. The kids and the assistant coach all stopped, faced the man with the whistle.

"That's Hamlin," said Frank Edwards, beside me.

"The man himself?"

He nodded. "Hell of a motivator. The kids love him."

Hamlin walked slowly down the line of kids, looking them over. He turned, walked back, stopped in front of the left guard.

"Tindall!"

"Coach," the kid answered.

"Tindall, what position do you play?"

"Left guard, Coach."

"You throw the ball?"

"No, Coach."

"You carry the ball?"

"No, Coach."

"What the hell do you do, Tindall?"

"Protect the quarterback, Coach."

"Really?"

"Yeah."

"Oh. Thanks for telling me, because from what I just saw, I wouldn't know that! Take a lap, Tindall. No, two. Brown—" to the assistant coach—"get someone in here who knows how to play this position. Okay, back to work!"

He blew the whistle again. Tindall took off on the track around the field, another kid filled in his spot, the assistant coach shouted, "Down. Set!" and practice resumed.

"What do you think?" asked a quiet voice beside me. I turned; there was Lydia.

The late sun picked out the blue-black highlights in her hair and the silver snaps on her leather jacket. I looked at her and suddenly felt a strange sensation, as though I'd spent a long time in a foreign place, gotten used to it, had forgotten what it was like to be home.

Lydia stood on tiptoe, gave me a quick kiss on the cheek, and looked back over the field. "Does this look like fun to you?"

I looked with her at the boys, sweating and panting, charging, cutting, running in the golden autumn light. All that energy, speed and strength, all that reckless power. All that belief that effort mattered, that focus and concentration and trying mattered, that talent could be developed into skill and that skill brought good results.

"It's a practice," I said to Lydia. "Practices aren't supposed to be easy."

"I didn't say *easy*," she said. "I said *fun*."

One of the coaches down in the end zone was waving his arms and yelling at three kids, who stood silent, eyes ahead. To our left a group adjusted their helmets, prepared for the blocking sleds. Tindall finished his laps, rejoined his line, read the stunt the first time they ran it, but missed it the next time. The assistant coach ordered him on the ground for push-ups while the rest of the kids watched. On the next play he was hit hard. He started to stand, fell back, made it to his knees, then suddenly collapsed. He lay for a moment on the grass of the field, managed to rise halfway to his knees before he threw up.

"Ah, shit!" said Hamlin. His words rolled forward on a wave of contempt, but he smiled tightly, a man satisfied with today's accomplishments. He checked his watch, blew his whistle, three loud blasts. All over the field boys and coaches stopped, turned, jogged in. When they'd gathered, Hamlin stepped forward. He threw a disgusted glance at Tindall, who was dragging himself up from the grass to stand, shakily, with the others. "You men," Hamlin called, looking over the line. "Warrenstown and Westbury. Westbury, you won county, Warrenstown, you took your division. You other men, you're from winning schools, too. Because only winners come to Hamlin's Seniors' Camp. Am I right?" He paused. *"Am I right?"*

"Yes, Coach!" the boys yelled, their chests heaving, their voices raw.

"Then what the fuck happened?" He gave them a beat. "Too much partying? Beer and boobs? You fuck yourselves silly, drink yourselves stupid, because you thought the season was over?" Some of the boys snorted, jabbed each other. "All right!" Hamlin shouted. "The season is *not* over! Anyone wants to blow this game off, step out right now, you can go home!" No one moved. Hamlin swept his gaze down the line of boys, back again. "Warrenstown's juniors and sophomores, and some of their JV—their *JV*, for Chrissakes!—are coming here Saturday. They expect to lose. Even the way you men are playing right now, you might beat them. But winning's not the point, is it? *Is it?*"

"No, Coach!" the boys chorused, giving him the answer he obviously wanted, but looking confused.

"And what *is*?"

The boys were silent, their faces stricken. Giving your all and failing, any coach will respect that. But the player who doesn't get it, doesn't know what his job is, is the player the coaches despise.

Then a Warrenstown boy shouted, "Killing them, Coach!"

"What?"

"Killing them, coach!"

"I can't *hear* you!"

"Killing them, Coach! Killing them! Coach!" And then it was all the boys, in a rising, swelling shout: "Killing them! Coach! Killing them! Coach! Killing them! Killing them! Killing them!"

The shriek of Hamlin's whistle cut off the chant. "All *right*! And the way you're working now, you gonna kill them?"

The Warrenstown boy who'd started it knew his job and jumped to it: "No, Coach!"

"Damn right! So what am I gonna see tomorrow?"

"Work, Coach!" A Westbury kid, getting into the act, yelled, "We're gonna bust our asses, Coach!"

"You are?"

"Yeah, Coach!" the boys shouted as one.

Hamlin smiled, looked at them all. "Good," he said.

Hamlin blew the whistle again, three long loud blasts. The boys turned and jogged away, disappeared through the doors into the field house.

The men and women around us started to walk away. None made any attempt to talk to the kids.

"You can't," Lydia told me when I pointed that out. "I told you, it's a rule. You can only come watch after three in the afternoon, and you can't talk to them. 'While they're here, they're Hamlin's.' " She took a brochure from her pocket, handed it to me.

I glanced at the brochure, a glossy four-color job full of ringing endorsements, statistics, pictures of uniformed boys playing hard. "So you never got near the Macpherson kid?"

"Right."

"Even an investigator?"

"Mr. Hamlin wasn't impressed," she said dryly.

"You told him a girl had been killed and these kids might be suspects, at least witnesses?"

"He said suspects or witnesses, they're football players and they're not going anywhere, so whatever they have to say they can say at the end of the week. I told him the cops were coming out here so he might as well let me start, but he said sorry, this was practice." She added, "I guess he'll have to let that cop from Warrenstown—Sullivan?—he'll have to let Sullivan talk to them, but it won't make him happy."

"He doesn't seem like a very happy guy."

"He's sour and he's mean."

"One of the fathers told me the kids love him."

She gave me a long look. "If they do, it's because they're afraid not to."

We stood at the edge of the field as the lowering sun blazed in the windows of the gym. I was exhausted, I realized, as wiped out as if I'd done all that running, that cutting, all those push-ups that come from failure, myself. I rubbed my hand over my face, tried to clear my head. Gary's face came back to me, his tired, haunted eyes.

Maybe this was dumb, the idea that Gary would come here, that he really did have something important to do and it had to do with something, someplace, someone besides himself. Maybe he was just, as Sullivan had said, running away.

Lydia touched my hand. I hadn't realized what a chill had crept into the air until I felt her warmth.

"God, you look tired," she said. "What do you want to do? You want to see if we can find a way to talk to the kids anyway?"

I looked up and down the field, silent now, and empty. I reached into my jacket for a cigarette. "Well," I said, "maybe you could join them in the showers and distract the coaches, and I could get the kids to come out one by one and talk to me."

She looked at me, then turned away with a smile and a shake of her head. Sighing, she appeared to consider the suggestion. "No," she finally said. "I don't think so. If you want a distraction, you'd better come up with a different one."

"You mean, something more likely, like the Martians landing on the field house?"

"Exactly. Besides," she asked innocently, "if I joined them in the showers, why would the kids ever leave?"

"Good point." I smoked, said, "I don't know what to do. I'm not even sure what I want to do, what I want to have happen."

"I suppose," Lydia said, and now her voice changed, grew more gentle, "I suppose the best thing would be if we found Gary, and we found he had nothing to do with that girl's death."

I nodded. "For Gary, for my sister. But that town, that girl." On the empty field, the sinking sun picked out the sharp edges of each blade of grass, cast tiny shadows from each rough lump of chalk on the lines. "Helen said Scott brought them there because it was a great place to grow up."

"Maybe it is. Bad things happen everywhere. Even something like this doesn't have to change the place forever."

"I'm not sure," I said, "how much a place changes. Like a person."

"What do you mean?"

"If Warrenstown's such a great place, why did Scott leave as soon as he graduated and not go back for twenty years?"

"You left Louisville when you were nine," she said. "You never went back."

"I didn't want to leave; I was a kid. And I never went back because by the time I could've gone back there was nothing to go back to."

Cars started up around the other side of the buildings, parents driving away. I found myself thinking, but that's not true. If a place holds nothing, you might find yourself passing through there or not over the years, as currents take you. A place you avoid still holds something; and whatever that is still holds you.

Lydia said, "You never went back because you were happy there."

I stared at her. A breeze ruffled her short hair. I wanted to reach out, smooth it down for her, but I didn't.

"I'm sorry," she said. "It's none of my business."

"No." I shook my head, spoke slowly. "No, I think you're right. Those memories kept me going a long time, after we left. By the time I could have gone back everything was different there."

"So it did change."

"Not Louisville, I don't think. Just the little part of it I knew. I didn't want to see it."

"Don't," she said. "You don't want to see it."

"What?"

"Those memories still help keep you going."

The breeze came back, colder now. I turned again to the football field. The goalposts at one end were tipped with sunlight; at the other they were already in shadow.

After a minute Lydia said, "You're wondering what kept Scott away from Warrenstown for so long."

I wasn't; and it probably didn't matter. But I knew why she said it. I was grateful and I went along.

"Helen says Scott always talked about what a great place it was," I said. "But twenty-three years ago—while he was there—they had a rape and a suicide at the high school. It wasn't Eden then, and I don't think it is now, either." I watched the breeze fan the burning tip of my cigarette. "I think," I said, "I'll ask him."

"Ask Scott?"

"Ask him what his hometown was like, years ago."

Lydia tilted her head. "Are you sure you need to do that?"

"What?"

"Are you sure the answer matters? Or are you just mad and you want to hit something?"

I looked at her, small and still, outlined by the day's final sunlight. She looked back at me. She didn't say anything else.

"Shit." I crushed my cigarette against the bottom of my shoe, dropped it in the cellophane off the pack. Leaving a cigarette butt on Hamlin's track probably would be a deadly sin. "Don't you have something else to do? A shower to take or something?"

"Yeah," she said. After a moment she smiled again. "Come on."

We turned, walked off the field together, not holding hands, not touching, but together.

eight

Back around the buildings Lydia and I headed along the driveway and in through Hamlin's front doors, a steel-and-wire-glass pair that looked like the doors to any gym at any high school in the world. The lighting inside was fluorescent, a little grim, and the smells of disinfectant, sweat, and liniment punched me right back to Brooklyn.

A bored-looking guy, not much older than the kids on the field, sat at a cheap metal desk just inside. Behind him, above a second set of doors, hung a sign: THIS IS HAMLIN'S—NO ONE LEAVES THE SAME AS HE CAME IN. I guessed that was supposed to be a good thing.

The bored guy wore a security guard's uniform straining over huge, cut muscles. Like security guards the world over, he was leaning over the sports pages of the local tabloid. Also like security guards the world over, he glanced up at us with an annoyed, suspicious look, as though the one thing experience had taught him was that no one trying to get past his station was ever up to any good. The name tag above his pocket read BARBONI, and I got the feeling that that was more than he wanted you to know.

"Hi again." Lydia smiled.

Barboni smirked. "Hey, you still around? Like I said before, I'm off at seven. Anything you want to know about this place, I could tell you."

"Sorry," she said. She tilted her head, indicating me. "This is my partner, Bill Smith." Barboni leaned back elaborately in his chair.

"Can I help you?" he asked, addressing me, and I had to stop myself from saying, Probably, but if you do I'm sure you'll be as surprised as I will.

"We'd like to see Mr. Hamlin," I said. I gave him my card. He picked up Lydia's card, already lying on his desk, flicked their edges against each other. He lifted the receiver of the phone next to him, punched a button, threw a glance down the vinyl-tiled corridor toward a door that said OFFICE before bringing his eyes back to me, fixing me with a sharp look to make sure I didn't try anything.

"Yeah, hi, Coach?" he said into the phone. "There's a guy here wants to see you. Smith. A private investigator, his card says." Pause. "Yeah, she's here, too." Pause. "Okay, sure." He hung up the phone, looked at me. "Coach says go away." He turned to Lydia, brought the smirk back. "He says he already told *you* to go away."

Persuasion, reasoning, a convincing story—screw it, I wasn't in the mood. I reached across the desk, grabbed up the phone and punched the same button he had. He started to get up. Lydia leaned over, dropped her hands on his shoulders and shoved him back in his chair. She moved her jacket aside so her gun would show, smiled at him and put her finger to her lips. Barboni's eyes widened, snapped back and forth from Lydia to me. He made no move, confusion and anger throwing him into temporary gridlock.

"Yeah, what now?" snarled the voice of Coach Hamlin in my ear.

"It's Bill Smith, Coach," I said. "I'm not leaving and I want to talk to you, so you might as well come out."

"Who the hell—what, the detective?"

"Investigator. Yes."

"What the—where's Barboni?"

"He's here. I just thought this would be faster."

"Faster than what? What the hell is your problem?"

"Come on out and I'll tell you. Or just stay there, I'll come in."

I hung up the phone. Lydia snapped her jacket shut and we moved around the security desk.

Barboni jumped up, face crimson, traffic jam over. "Oh, no!" He grabbed my wrist. I threw my arm in a wide circle to break his hold, shoved him away. I turned, but when I felt his hand on my shoulder I spun in tight, socked him in the stomach, then on the jaw when he doubled over. I was reaching for him again when Lydia pulled my arm back.

"Stop it!" she commanded.

Barboni looked up at her, I looked down, and, glaring at me, she swept past him down the corridor.

"Fuck!" Barboni coughed, straightening up. By the time he started to come after us I had caught up with Lydia at the office door. She pushed it open. In the outer office the secretary's desk was empty, but the door to the inner office was open and the two men in there were on their feet. The one who wasn't Hamlin had about six inches on him, was dark-haired and broad-shouldered, was dressed in a suit and tie, and wore an equally angry glare.

They came out, we came in, and Barboni came from behind. Lydia smoothly stepped between him and me, weight balanced, prepared for whatever she had to do. Barboni was probably as pissed at her as he was at me, but he obviously wasn't sure whether it was okay to hit a woman, even one who'd manhandled him. My guess was he'd have come down on the side of pulverizing her to get at me after a few seconds' thought. I was tempted to let him try it, because it would have served him right, but I said, looking at the other two men, "If this guy touches either of us I'll kill him. I just want to talk, Coach, but I'm in a bad mood, so call him off."

It was the other man, not Hamlin, who said, "Who the hell are you?"

"Back off, Barboni," Hamlin ordered at the same time.

"Coach, they—"

"I said back off!"

Barboni, after a moment's hesitation, took an angry, grumbling step back but didn't leave.

"I'm Bill Smith," I said. "This is Lydia Chin. We're investigating a homicide and a runaway and we need to talk to some of these kids."

"Fuck you," Hamlin said with icy calm. "Get out. And you, too, Macpherson," he said to the other man. "Nobody talks to these kids while they're here."

Lydia's too good to give anything away, but I knew she felt the same small jolt I did, hearing the other man's name.

"The police are on their way," I said to Hamlin. "They'll be—"

"I already talked to Detective—what the fuck was his name—Sullivan," Hamlin cut me off. "I told him what I'm telling you. They come here with warrants, they can arrest any kid they want. Some kid's parents want to take him home, I don't give a shit who he talks to but he doesn't come back. You aren't cops, you're not parents, get the hell out of my camp."

The other man spoke. "Hamlin, I don't know who these people are and I don't give a damn what they want, but I'm going to talk to my son."

"Then you're taking him home, Macpherson. You know the rules."

"Christ, Hamlin," I said. "This petty tyrant bullshit may play to the parents, but you can't—"

"Shut the fuck up," Macpherson ordered me. My fists clenched and I felt the heat in my face; but as I started to move Lydia touched my hand. I stopped: she was right. I was bluffing. I had nothing to offer and nothing, really, to threaten with. But Macpherson was a parent. He was much more likely to be able to breach Hamlin's wall than we were; and once it was breached, maybe we could slip through the gap.

Macpherson kept his eyes on me just a second longer. His expensive suit, his silk tie, his Italian shoes would have told me, if his derisive half-smile hadn't, that he was used to people getting out of his way. Sure I was no more trouble because he'd told me not to be, he turned back to Hamlin. "Warrenstown raised fifty thousand dollars to send these boys here," he said in a voice like a ton of concrete. "A significant part of that money was mine. You're supposed to be improving my son's game, not holding him prisoner."

"He's not a prisoner, Macpherson. You can take him home any time. You signed a contract and you knew what was in it."

"We have a situation here that's different—"

"Different?" Hamlin shouted, startling us all. I looked at his eyes. They were as calm and cold as his voice was loud and raw. I thought, for effect; he did that for effect, planned and deliberate, not out of control at all. "I'm not coaching football here, Macpherson. I'm building men." He waved his hand around his office, showing us the citations, the awards, the photos of boys in uniform, alone and in teams, posed and in action. On his desk was a photo of two skinny kids with glasses, in tee shirts and shorts, laughing. I couldn't imagine they were his sons; no sons of Tom Hamlin would be scrawny, loose, like that. Whoever they were, they were probably there to remind him what his raw material was like, how hard he had to work to mold this unlikely clay.

Hamlin dropped his arm, looked at Macpherson. "You think this situation is different?" he said quietly. "Let me tell you something, Macpherson: every situation is always different. There are a million goddamn excuses. An excuse, Macpherson, that's like an asshole: everybody has one and it's full of shit. Either you do what you need to do, or you don't. At Hamlin's we teach boys to give everything they have. All the time. Every time. Not except when the situation is fucking *different*!"

He rested his eyes on each of us, one by one, and I thought again how cold they were, how unmatched to the heat of his words. A corner of his mouth turned up like a knife blade. "You can take him home," he said to Macpherson, "or you can let him stay. And you two"—he threw Lydia a glance, dismissed her, turned to me—"you can get the hell off my property before I call the cops myself." Hamlin reached for the phone. "You want him, Macpherson? You want to take him home?"

Macpherson, in his classy suit, was beet-red, the tendons in his neck bulging above his collar. He stared at Hamlin. "Fuck you." His voice was throaty, low. He turned and pushed past me to get out.

I looked at Hamlin, at Lydia. I lifted my hands, said to Barboni, "I'm leaving. No hard feelings. See you around." I walked past him, no sudden moves, followed Macpherson down the corridor. Barboni threw a glance at Hamlin. If he'd been given the signal he'd have charged, tackled me, probably with his nightstick already out. I half expected it, was ready for it. But I made it out the doors without hearing a sound behind me. After all, I was leaving, which is what they'd told me to do. What Hamlin and Barboni had to figure out was why Lydia was still there.

I wasn't sure, either, unless it was just to keep them off-balance, get me clear. I'd find out later; now, coming out into the chill twilight, I broke into a run, covered the yards to Macpherson's Mercedes SUV. I reached it as he was closing his door.

Yanking it back open, I said, "I need to talk to your son."

He hit the ignition. The big engine growled, as ready to leave as he was. His mouth was twisted around a cigarette. "Yeah, well, good fucking luck. Who the fuck are you anyway?"

"I told you. I'm an investigator."

"What the hell do you want with Randy? If this is about that girl, just forget about it, he doesn't know anything."

"I don't give a shit about that."

Which wasn't true, but it got his attention.

"What the fuck do you mean?"

"I'm looking for Gary Russell."

"Who the hell's that?"

"A new kid at Warrenstown. He's a friend of Randy's."

"Oh, fuck, yeah," said Macpherson, looking through his windshield to the lights of the roadway. "Scott Russell's boy. That's his name, Gary? I heard: he ran away."

"That's right. He's been gone since Monday."

"Scott's an asshole. His kid's probably an asshole. Maybe he killed that girl, that's why he ran away. But my boy doesn't know anything about it and if I catch you near him I'll break your neck."

"How do you know what Randy knows?"

Macpherson made a move, as though he was going to climb down out of the car and break my neck right there. Then he dropped back on the seat, threw the car into gear. I let go of the door and jumped back. His tires spat gravel as he took off. It was clear he wouldn't have minded dragging me along, or rolling right over me.

I watched his taillights speed down Hamlin's long driveway, pull sharply into traffic when he reached the road. I couldn't argue with Macpherson's assessment of Scott. But I wondered whether it came from the last few months, or was something he'd remembered over the decades, from the days when they were boys together, in Warrenstown.

I sat in the passenger seat of my car and smoked, waited for Lydia to come out. I checked for messages but I had none; I thought of calling Helen but I didn't. Twilight dropped into night, quickly the way it does as the year winds down. Lights in the windows of the buildings in front of me went off, came on, in a pattern that seemed random to me but had reasons, meanings, though anyone who knew them wouldn't be out here watching and anyone seeing it, like me, would be too much on the outside to understand.

Finally Hamlin's double doors opened, and Lydia walked down the drive, not looking back at the figure of Barboni looming in the doorway behind her. If we had to come back here, Lydia and I, we might have to find a way to do it on someone else's shift.

I didn't get out, hoping Barboni wasn't counting parked cars, would think I'd gone already. Lydia walked past her own rented Taurus and up to the driver's side of my car. She opened the door and got in.

"You think we're fooling him?" I asked while she pulled the door shut.

She shrugged, nodded toward the entrance. "He's gone."

I looked; he was. I'd have been willing to bet the doors were locked, too.

"You didn't have to hit him," Lydia said.

"I know."

"You're twice his size, he's not armed, and there were two of us."

I nodded, said nothing. For a while she said nothing more, either. After a few minutes she shifted to look at me. "Where's the music?" she asked.

"What?"

"You usually have music on while you're in the car." She pointed to the box of CDs between the seats.

I shook my head. "I've been wanting to listen to the Bach since morning, but every time I put it on it gets on my nerves."

She gave me a strange look, or maybe it was just the way the light fell from the high poles around Hamlin's entrance, casting odd, multiple shadows. She picked up the Bach CD, looked at it, sifted through the disks under it. She asked, "Did you try something else?"

"No." I wasn't even sure what else was in the box.

Carefully, she put the CDs back in the order she'd found them, saying nothing. Looking at me again, she asked, "Learn anything out here?"

"Macpherson thinks Scott's an asshole."

"This is not news."

"That Macpherson thinks so?"

"Macpherson strikes me as a man who probably thinks that about a lot of people. And from what I've heard, Scott is one."

I tamped my cigarette in the ashtray, smiling a little. "You can't say it, can you?"

"I could," she answered breezily. "But I don't intend to be dragged into the mud with all the other Neanderthals on this case."

"Me included?"

"Of course."

"Anything happen in there after I left?"

"Barboni asked me out again. It seems he gets excited by girls with guns who push him around."

"Here's a secret about men: We all do."

"Here's a secret about women: We all know you do."

"So why don't more of you carry guns?"

"So more of us can get asked out by guys like Barboni?"

"Or like the rest of us. I get your point."

"Anyway," she said, "I apologized for your thuggish behavior, and told Mr. Hamlin I understood how important it was for him to maintain discipline, and assured him I agreed he couldn't be expected to set a bad example for the boys by breaking his own rules."

"You'd better be going somewhere with this."

"No, I just didn't want to be associated with your approach. In case they ever need another security guard out here. It seems like kind of a good job. I like the ambience."

"And you could work the night shift with Barboni."

"Another plus. What I did was to ask Mr. Hamlin if the boys would be likely to have heard about Tory Wesley."

"And?"

"He carefully explained to me again that they're not allowed outside contact while they're here, so no, they wouldn't have. So I smiled and thanked him and asked him to keep his ears open, and to please let me know if he happens to hear any of the kids saying anything that might mean they know. Because if they do—"

"—it'll be because they knew already, before Sullivan and I found her body. You know, you really are a genius."

"You wouldn't just be saying that?"

"Sure I would. But you'd kill me if I didn't."

"That's true."

"You think he will? Let you know if he hears anything?"

"Fifty-fifty. He doesn't think very highly of me. But he'd love to prove to me how much more he knows than I do. He'd especially love to prove to me how much more he knows than *you* do. It's that male gorilla thing."

"Any gorilla knows more than I do, male or female."

"But that was strange, that thing."

"What was?"

"Well, usually, when a guy does that male gorilla thing and chases the other gorilla away—"

"Me?"

She gave me a silent look, went on, "—usually he follows it up with more chest thumping and a bad come-on line. To collect his prize."

"You?" When she didn't answer I asked, "Hamlin didn't?"

"As soon as you guys left and it was just the two of us it was like a switch turned off. He sat in his chair like nothing had happened and answered my questions patiently, as though he had all night."

"It looked to me like that was at least partly an act," I said. "All that yelling. And maybe more for Macpherson than for us."

"I had the same feeling. Well, I'm just as glad he didn't come on to me."

"Why? So you don't have to choose between him and Barboni?"

"A tough choice," she confirmed. "So, what do we do now?"

I thought. For a while in my car it was just silence and odd shadows, Lydia's leather jacket and the faint freesia scent of her hair. The wind came up, shifting the shadows around; Lydia zipped up the jacket.

"Cold?" I asked her.

"A little," she admitted.

"You know how to start a stick shift?"

"You'd let me start this car?"

"When you put it that way," I said, "no. Anyway, we'd better get out of here. Before Sullivan gets here."

"Can Mr. Hamlin really keep the police from questioning the kids?"

"Sure. Cops have no right to talk to anybody without a

warrant. It'll piss the cops off, but Hamlin doesn't seem like a guy who cares about that."

"He seems to me like a guy who likes it. Bill?"

I looked at her, waiting.

"Mr. Macpherson's a parent paying a lot of money to send his son here. You and I are just PIs who Mr. Hamlin doesn't know from Adam."

"Or Eve. And?"

"Well, wouldn't a parent be someone you'd want to at least try to keep on the good side of, even if you weren't going to let him have what he wanted? But Mr. Hamlin was going way out of his way to be unpleasant to Mr. Macpherson, much more than to us. He really seemed to be enjoying it."

"Because Macpherson's a lot more obnoxious?"

"You'll excuse me if I say I don't think, in terms of the events of this evening, that he was."

"You could be right."

"Then why?"

"I don't know."

"And another question: What was Mr. Macpherson doing here?"

"I assume he thinks his son knows something about Tory Wesley's death and he wanted to find out what."

"So why didn't he take him home, if that's the only way to talk to him?"

"Because the kid's a senior, he's been scouted by colleges, and this is football camp."

"If you had a son involved in a murder, wouldn't you think finding out just how involved would be more important than football?"

"I would. You would. But we're not from Warrenstown."

"He'll be back."

I looked at her, her dark eyes hidden in the shadows.

"He had to think about it," she said. "He had to decide what to do. But he'll decide he has to know, and he'll be back."

I nodded. "You might be right. I'll stay."

She stared out through my windshield, at the lights in Hamlin's buildings and the lights on the road. "And I'll go back to New York," she said, "and do what I was doing this morning." She opened the driver's door; then she turned back, leaned over, and kissed me, quickly, softly. She let her fingertips linger on my jawline. "I'll go back to New York," she repeated, "and find Gary." She got out, closed my door, walked quickly across the parking lot to her car. I watched her get in, start up. Her headlights, when she switched them on, changed the shadows entirely.

nine

I let Lydia go first, followed her down the long driveway.
She turned onto the streets of Plaindale, to work her way to
the highway, head back to the city. I U-turned down the
road from the entrance to Hamlin's, parked facing the drive.
I killed my lights and lit a cigarette, watched traffic drift
down the road. After about twenty minutes I reached into
the CD box, pulled out the first thing under the Bach. I
thumbed it open, slipped the disk in the player without looking at it. Brahms, it turned out to be, the F-sharp minor
Sonata. I wasn't sure how I felt about it, but I left it on.

The night grew darker; some stars came out. Cars rolled
by. The Brahms came to an end. A few blocks away, the
blue neon in the window of a diner seemed to glow brighter
and brighter. I wondered if I could slip down there, get
coffee and something to eat and still not take my eyes off
the road in case Macpherson's SUV came roaring back. I
was almost ready to try it when my cell phone rang.

"Smith," I said.

"Sullivan," it answered.

"I left town."

"I know. I've had guys on the lookout for your car, just
to make sure."

"Is that what you're calling to tell me? That you'll know

if I come back, so I shouldn't bother? Go to hell, Sullivan, I'm not in the mood."

"What's eating you?" he asked evenly.

I slipped out a cigarette, but I didn't want it. I shoved it back in the pack, threw the pack on the dash. "It's been a long day, Sullivan. You want something?"

"Yeah. I wanted to tell you that preliminary results on the beer cans and the inside of the Wesley house didn't turn up any prints that match anything at your sister's."

Sullivan's voice was fading in and out. He was on a cell phone, too, probably moving. Probably in a Warrenstown official car on his way to where I was right now.

I asked, "What are you saying?"

"I'm not saying anything. This is off the record. It doesn't mean he didn't kill her and it doesn't mean if he did I won't be able to prove it." He paused. "I still want him, Smith, and I'm still looking. I know you're still looking, too. I just thought, while you looked, this was something you'd want to know."

"You told me to stop looking," I pointed out.

"I'd have to be even stupider than I am to think you would. All I need is for you to stay out of my town and away from my witnesses. And if you do find him somewhere in New York there, I want you to remember what a good idea it would be for him to turn himself in. I thought this would help you remember that."

"This wouldn't be bullshit, would it, Sullivan?"

"No. It's too easy to check."

That was true. Any cop who owed me a favor, or wanted me to owe him one, could call any cop in Warrenstown and find out whose prints were on those beer cans.

"Whose were?" I asked.

"What?"

"Gary's prints weren't there. Whose were?"

"Not a chance, Smith."

"Thought I'd try."

"I'm not surprised, but no."

"Okay," I said. "Thanks. And if anything else comes up

that helps my side, let me know that, too, okay?"

"How do you know," he asked, "which side you're on?"

I didn't answer that. "You have autopsy results yet?"

"No. Tomorrow, maybe even another day."

"No preliminaries? Time of death?"

"Saturday night, early Sunday morning."

"Nothing else?"

"Nothing I'm going to tell you."

"The news about that party must be all over Warrenstown by now," I said.

"Pretty much."

"You talked to the other kids?"

"Except the ones at Hamlin's."

"You headed there now?"

"Who wants to know?"

"Let me save you some trouble. I've just come from there."

A pause. "Smith, if you—"

"I would have, but Hamlin wouldn't let me. He won't let you, either."

"What are you talking about?"

"You'll need warrants. You're hooking up with the Plaindale police?"

"Of course," he said warily. "What—?"

"Hamlin's position is, you can arrest them and take them out, or a parent can take them home. But if they leave they don't come back."

"Who the hell is he? Some of those kids may be material witnesses in a homicide."

Or killers, but he didn't say that.

"I mentioned that," I said. "He wouldn't let me near them. Randy Macpherson's father was there and he threw him out, too."

"Macpherson? He was there already?"

"Uh-huh. He and Hamlin don't seem to get along very well."

"Nobody gets along with Macpherson. What was he doing there?"

"He wanted to talk to his kid. Hamlin wouldn't let him. And tell me something else: Why haven't the parents of all the other kids who were at that party swarmed Hamlin's, too?"

"Maybe because we're being real tight-lipped about whose prints we found, so if someone's kid doesn't own up to it, they don't know for sure they were there."

"And the kids at Hamlin's can't talk to anybody, so they can't own up."

"And in Warrenstown," Sullivan said, "it takes a hell of a lot for people to want to mess with seniors' camp at Hamlin's."

"Business as usual, no matter who's dead?"

"This is Warrenstown," he said. "This is football."

We hung up. Sullivan didn't thank me for the heads-up about the warrants, but, though he gave me another lecture about keeping clear of his witnesses, he also didn't say he was giving my license plate number to the Plaindale police. That was a fair trade-off, I thought.

I stayed where I was. If the cops came, I'd leave. If Lydia was right and Macpherson came back, I'd see if that did me any good. Meanwhile, I sat in the car, surprised at how Sullivan's news made the night seem a little warmer, the road in front of Hamlin's a little less dreary. Whatever Gary was up to, if he hadn't been at Tory Wesley's party, then he hadn't killed her. Whatever he'd done and whatever trouble he was in, maybe it wasn't that.

I didn't even bother giving myself a hard time for thinking it might have been. I reached over, took the Brahms out of the CD player, put in the Bach. Single notes, flashing fast, wove themselves into crystal clear designs of sound, of rhythm. The French Suites: music for dances. Popular dances of their time, but dances we no longer understood, steps, turns, gestures we no longer knew. All we had now was the music, though you could feel, if you let yourself, the thrill of speed in one, the intricate, tight focus of another.

It sounded, I thought, pretty good.

I smoked, listened, thought about football, about basket-

ball and baseball and soccer: about individual players running formations and plays that have been run before,
running them differently, in different games, different circumstances. Organizing themselves into patterns, taking on
the obligation to create order from chaos.

I gave myself another cigarette, and I called my sister.

"It's Bill," I said. "You heard from anyone?"

"You mean Scott? No, he hasn't called."

"Or Gary."

"Gary? No. No, why? Do you—?"

"No. But I wanted to tell you this: So far the cops haven't
turned up anything that would prove Gary was at that party."

"What . . . what does that mean?"

"Oh, for Christ's sake, Helen! It may mean he wasn't
there. It may mean he didn't kill anybody."

I knew it was a mistake as soon as I said it. She was his
mother; what did I expect? "You thought he did? You've
been thinking that?" Her voice went up a pitch. "I can't
believe you could even say that."

"Don't start." I blew out a breath. "Family. They're all
saints, aren't they? They have to be. Or they're not family."

"That's not fair. That's really not fair. You—"

"Oh, shit. I can't, Helen. Not now. I'll call later."

And I hung up on her.

What did I expect?

What had I ever expected?

I got out of the car, stood breathing the cold night air. I
stopped myself from pounding my fist on the hood by heading down to the diner, for the coffee I'd wanted twenty
minutes ago, had needed for hours.

The diner coffee was strong and bitter and no cars turned
into Hamlin's driveway while I was buying it. I picked up
a cheese danish, too, bit into it while I headed back to my
car, so my hands were full and one of them was sticky when
my cell phone rang again.

I was tempted to let the damn thing just go on ringing.
It would take a message, and I'd call whoever the hell it
was back when I felt like it, which was unlikely to be soon.

But it could be Lydia. It could be Gary. It could be important.

I juggled the coffee and danish, flipped open the phone, told it who I was.

It told me, "Stacie Phillips, *Tri-Town Gazette*."

I sipped some coffee, started toward my car again. Bitter or not, the coffee was hot and full of caffeine, and Stacie Phillips was a seventeen-year-old kid who as far as I knew didn't owe me a thing.

"Hey," I said. "I'm having coffee. Can I buy you a cup?"

"Funny. Did you find Gary Russell yet?"

"You looking for a scoop?"

"Of course. If you promise me one, I'll trade."

"Trade what?"

"Information. I know something you might want to know. I'll tell you if you promise that when you find Gary I can talk to him first."

"First before the other reporters?"

"Of course, but mostly first before the police."

"I'm not sure I can do that."

"You could if you wanted to."

"I'm not sure I want to. What are you trading?"

"This: They haven't found Gary's fingerprints anywhere at Tory Wesley's house."

"This may ruin your day," I said, biting into the danish, "but I know that already."

A pause. "How?"

"Sullivan called me."

"No way. I thought he didn't like you."

"If everyone who didn't like me refused to call me I'd be a very lonely man. More interesting to me is, how do *you* know?"

"Sources."

"Come on. If this is all over Warrenstown, I want to know about it."

"It's not. It's confidential information."

"Sullivan called you, too?"

"Yeah, right. Hey, I have my own sources."

I thought back to Warrenstown, the bright sun, the yellow leaves blowing across the Wesleys' lawn. "That cop," I said. "Trevor."

I could hear the grin in her voice as she said, "I told him if he kept me filled in I'd try to talk my sister into dating him again when she comes home for Christmas."

"You think she will?"

"Ugh."

"And knowing that, you still promised? I'm getting seriously disillusioned about the press here."

"I only said I'd try. Hey, it gives the guy something to look forward to. How close are you to finding Gary?"

"I don't know."

"Where are you?"

"Hamlin's."

"Ohmigod," she said. "The promised land."

"Everyone seems to feel that way. What is it about this place?"

"They build men out there."

"So do the marines, and Dr. Frankenstein. What is it about Hamlin's that gets everybody all excited?"

She paused. "I think because Mr. Hamlin, he does it exactly like they do it here."

"What does that mean?"

"Well, you know Coach Ryder? Oh, actually, I guess you don't."

"No, we've met. I saw him at practice today."

"Then you know. I mean, I've never met Mr. Hamlin, but from everything I've heard he's just exactly the same as Coach Ryder. He thinks the same way about sports. And he even uses the same kinds of drills and things."

"And yells at the kids the same way. You know, you're right."

"Why do you sound surprised? Because I said something smart and I'm a kid?"

"No, because you said something true and you're a reporter."

"You better remember who can misquote who."

"*Whom,* I think. You won't get a job on the *Times* if you can't tell your *who* from your *whom.*"

"That's what rewrite people are for," she informed me. "You know, 'Get me rewrite!' They probably had that in movies when you were my age."

"They didn't have movies when I was your age. We lived in log cabins and walked five miles through the snow to get to school."

"Yeah, yeah, uphill both ways, I know," she said. "You must've gone to school with my dad. So you'll call me as soon as you find Gary?"

"Why would I do that?"

"Because I want the story!"

"Ah," I said. "But what do I get?"

She paused, giving me time for more danish.

"The power of the press to create public sympathy for him?" she offered.

"That's a reach. No, I want something more concrete."

"Like?"

"Whose fingerprints *were* in the house?"

"I don't know," she said. "That could get Trevor in trouble."

"I'll make sure no one knows I know. But it may help me work things out, to find Gary."

"Promise?"

She sounded like a kid trying to pin me down about a trip to the zoo. People lie, Stacie, I wanted to say. Even if they promise. A reporter better learn that. A cold breeze chased the steam from my coffee.

"Yes," I said.

"Okay. But Trevor only told me a couple. Mostly he wanted to tell me about Gary. He thought maybe I'd call my sister right away and tell her what a big help he was."

"Did you?"

"Are you my sister?"

"Well," I said, "I want them all. What you have now, and what you can get."

"And you promise? About the interview with Gary?"

"If I can."

"That sounds weaselly to me."

"I'm a weasel."

She accepted that assessment a little too fast, I thought, but I was the one who'd said it. I put the half-empty coffee and the half-eaten danish on the hood of my car, reached for my pen and notebook. Stacie gave me five or six names, fingerprints from the beer cans and broken furniture. Some I'd heard, some I hadn't. They were all boys. Morgan Reed was one. Randy Macpherson was another. I wrote them down.

"There might be some Trevor didn't tell me," Stacie said. "And there are a whole bunch they don't know whose they are. They have to go around town asking people if they can take prints from their kids' rooms. And the way people are here, Trevor thinks most of them won't let them."

"A little jargon for you," I said. "To help advance what I can see is going to be a distinguished career. You don't take prints, you lift them. But tell me something. About the ones you gave me—those people cooperated?"

"No way. They didn't need to. They have those kids' prints on file already."

"Why?"

"Give me a break. Those are jocks. They've all been arrested before."

"For what?"

"Speeding. Breaking people's windows. Driving their cars across people's lawns. Drinking in public. Peeing in public. Everything."

"Jails in Warrenstown must be full all the time."

"Oh, yeah, right. What happens, their parents just come to the police station apologizing all over the place. You know, he didn't mean it, boys will be boys. They pay a fine and they pay for the windows or whatever and the kid does community service, raking leaves in the park or something. We have a very clean park."

"What about the second or third time?"

"Hey, these guys are all in double digits already."

"Their parents never get sick of it? Decide to leave them in jail overnight, teach them a lesson?"

"If they're in jail, they can't play on Friday night."

I sipped my coffee, thought about that. I asked, "What if the arrest is for something serious?"

"Like what?"

"Drugs?"

"It never is."

"Kids in Warrenstown don't do drugs?"

"Well, of course," she said guardedly, "I don't actually know anything about that."

"Of course. But you have sources; what do you hear?"

"Well, I *hear* that if anything like that ever happens, Chief Letourneau has a long talk with the parents and the kid and explains the difference between a record with fifty hours of community service for breaking windows and one with four years in jail for possession."

"Most towns, these days, the police chief would do a clean-sweep, zero-tolerance thing."

"Chief Letourneau is very tolerant. Especially to jocks."

I leaned against the car for a while after Stacie Phillips and I hung up. I finished the danish and the coffee, which was cold now but still had some useful caffeine left. The neon at the diner still glowed blue, traffic was even thinner, and the night had grown chilly. I lit a cigarette, walked up and down to clear my head, stay awake. I thought about Warrenstown, and Westbury, and the other towns that sent their sons to Hamlin's. I thought about the grade school kids, the Warrenstown Junior Warriors, playing their pickup game on the school lawn before class. I wondered how well that left guard, Tindall, would sleep tonight. And how well Gary would sleep, and where.

I was back in the car with the Bach on again when Macpherson's Mercedes SUV swept by me. I watched him make the turn into Hamlin's drive, saw his taillights dwindle as he headed for the lot. When his lights went off, I followed with mine off, too. I went as far as Hamlin's entrance, parked across the drive. A bad spot to be in if Sullivan showed up, but I was betting on all the Plaindale judges to be home in bed and warrants for teenagers at Hamlin's Institute, requested by an out-of-state cop, to be a long sell.

I leaned on my car and waited for Macpherson to get back into his. It wasn't long before his lights flooded the lot and his engine purred to life, though I couldn't make out, that far down the drive, whether he was alone. His tires spit gravel as he drove too fast toward me, but he was the one in the late-model Mercedes. His headlights caught me and my roadblock; I squinted against the blinding light as he slammed on his brakes and hit the horn. I stayed leaning on my car until his had stopped completely, about four feet from me.

The driver's window powered down and Macpherson stuck his head out, his face knotted with rage. "What the fuck—oh, Christ, it's you? Move that fucking car!" He blasted the horn again, again, over and over.

I stepped fast to the passenger's side, yanked on the door. I'd figured Macpherson for a guy who wouldn't bother with wussy things like locking, unless he was driving through a place where he suspected the inhabitants of coveting what he possessed. And look, Smith, I thought, as the door pulled wide, you were right.

A broad-shouldered, dark-haired kid stared down at me from the shotgun seat, his already-angry eyes narrowed, the tendons in his neck knotted. "Who the fuck are you?" he snarled.

"Bill Smith. I'm a private investigator. I need to ask you a few questions, Randy."

Macpherson senior leaned across the seat, shouted, "Get out of my fucking way! Randy, don't talk to him!"

"He took you out of there, huh, Randy?" I said quietly. "So much for your week at Hamlin's."

The son threw a look of purest hatred at the father. "Yeah. Cocksucker."

Macpherson swung toward Randy. "Don't you talk to me that way!"

Ignoring me, Randy shouted back, "They have college scouts coming to the game! What the fuck am I supposed to do now?" Fury and desperation made his voice raw.

If you didn't have a game anyone had noticed already, I thought, I'm not sure two more days here would have given you one; but I didn't say that. "Who killed Tory Wesley, Randy?"

He jerked around to look at me. In the yellow glare from the high sodium lamps his face paled. "What?"

I looked at Macpherson. "You didn't tell him? You took him out of camp and you didn't tell him why?"

"What are you talking about?" Randy's voice was louder, insistent.

"Goddammit!" Mapherson growled, threw his door open.

I said fast, "She was killed at that party, Randy. Do you know who killed her? Was it you?"

Macpherson jumped down. I moved in front of his car, stood facing him. Off-balance, blinded by his own head-lights, he grabbed for me wildly. I sidestepped, pulled him toward me, the way he was coming already. He stumbled and I thought I had him, but his hand vise-gripped my arm. I dug into the gravel looking for footing; he used me for leverage and found his, too. He threw a punch, aiming for my face, clipping me on the ear. My head rang. My punch was as wild as his, but lower, and I was luckier: I found his gut. He groaned and I slammed another fast one. He doubled over. I grabbed him by the jacket and threw him to the ground.

Randy had exploded out of the car and was coming to-ward me, fists clenched.

"Don't!" I shouted, stepping back, putting distance be-tween us. "I don't want to fight you, Randy, but if I have to I will and I fight dirty. You want to play on Saturday?"

He stopped, looked from his father to me, eyes wild. His father rolled to his knees. Randy stayed where he was, but he was twitching: the wrong word, the wrong move, and he'd be all over me.

"Listen." I stayed still, kept my voice low. "All I want to know is this: where's Gary Russell?"

Randy Macpherson stared at me as though I'd asked him where the aliens were planning to land.

"Gary? What the fuck do you mean, where is he? How the hell do I know where he is?"

Of course, I thought. These kids were at Hamlin's; all the rest of the world could have come to an end and no one would have told them about it.

"Gary left home Monday," I said. "He hasn't been back. I saw him in New York last night and he said he had something important to do but he wouldn't tell me what. I want you to tell me what he's doing and where he is."

"How the fuck do I know? What are you talking about?"

"Tory Wesley's dead. What happened there, Randy?"

"I—it was just a party. What do you mean, she's dead?"

"Dead. Naked, all bruised up, stone dead. Who raped her? Who killed her?" I was reaching, but it worked.

"Raped her? Bullshit! We got a little wild, is all; that's how she wanted it."

"Rough?" I said. "She liked it that way?"

"Sure. Don't they all?" He gave me a man-to-man smirk, ghastly in the colorless sodium lights.

"It was you and her?"

"One time. But shit, man, she was up and partying when I left."

"Shut up, Randy!" came the hoarse command from his father. One arm wrapping his stomach, he pulled himself up on his car's bumper. Randy looked again uncertainly from him to me. He made no move to help his father up.

I asked, "Was Gary there?"

"Shut the fuck *up*, Randy!" Macpherson shouted. "How stupid are you? They're trying to do to you what they did to me. You!" His arm stretched out, fingers reaching for me, but he stayed back. His voice was ragged with rage. "You motherfucker. I'll tear your balls off. I'll shove you under a pile of shit. Do you know who I am?"

"No," I said. "But you don't have much of a right hook."

"You're dead. You're fucking dead, asshole. Your PI license, your car, every fucking thing you own, it's mine."

Headlights swept into the drive, brakes squealed on the other side of my car. Red and blue circling lights pulsed in the night.

"Well," I said, "if you want to start legal proceedings, now's a good time."

Four doors opened, two on each newly arrived car. Looking into the glare of their headlights I couldn't see anything, but the voice that shouted, "Goddammit, Smith, is that you?" was Jim Sullivan's.

"Yeah," I said, lifting my hands so everyone could see they were empty. "I have some fugitives for you."

"This your fucking car? What are you talking about?" Sullivan and two other men, one of them Burke, the young cop, and the other a cop in a uniform different from theirs, strode around my car to stand with Randy Macpherson, his father, and me. A fourth man stayed behind, standing at the driver's door of the lead car, ready to call it in if things got ugly.

"If you're here you must have gotten warrants," I said. "I assume one of them is for him."

Sullivan shifted his eyes to Randy. He looked to Macpherson senior for a few moments, then spoke to the guy next to him, the cop in a Plaindale uniform. "Randy Macpherson."

The Plaindale cop took out a pair of handcuffs, started to explain to Randy that he had a warrant for his arrest on charges of malicious mischief, destruction of property, leaving the scene of a crime.

"You sons of bitches, just hold on!" Macpherson shouted, stepping between them. "You can't—"

"Calm down," Sullivan said, "Maybe we don't have to."

"What?"

"The only way to get these boys out of Hamlin's is with

warrants," said Sullivan, shooting a glance at me. "But you took Randy out already." He turned back to the son. "I want to ask some questions and I want some serious answers. If you cooperate I might not have to arrest you."

"Fuck off, Sullivan. You touch my boy and I'll have your badge. Come on, Randy."

"I'm sorry, sir." That was the Plaindale cop, and he had his gun out.

Everyone stopped. The gun's barrel glinted in the head-lights of the cars on either side of mine.

"I have a warrant for this boy's arrest," the cop said, as if that would make a boy's father step aside, let him be handcuffed and led away.

"Let him talk to us, Macpherson," Sullivan said.

Macpherson fixed Sullivan with a look that would have chilled a colder night than this. "Randy," he said, "don't say a word. I'm calling Erickson. My lawyer," he said pointedly to Sullivan.

Macpherson turned from the rest of us, took out a cell phone. Sullivan nodded to the Plaindale cop, who put his gun away, handcuffed Randy, recited his rights as he led him to the patrol car.

"I don't have a warrant for you," Sullivan said to me, "but I don't need one. Obstruction of justice. Hamlin'll probably go for trespassing if I ask him to. What the hell is your problem, Smith? Am I hard to understand?"

"I was leaving," I said. "I saw Macpherson coming back. I wanted to talk to Randy and I knew you did, too."

In Sullivan's long silence the door on the Plaindale car slammed behind Randy. Burke shifted his weight from one foot to the other. Sullivan stared out over the high sodium lights lining the driveway to Hamlin's.

"Plaindale's pissed off already, the overtime they're go-ing to have to pay to process the six kids I'm pulling out of here," he said to me. "You have a good lawyer, would spring you if I took you in?"

"Yes."

He nodded. "I figured. Macpherson! Back your car up.

Now! Smith, get the hell out of here. And Smith: no more warnings."

"I get it," I said. "I'm gone. But can I ask you something?"

"Goddammit—" he started, then took a breath. "What?"

"Before you got here, Macpherson said to Randy, 'They're trying to do to you what they did to me.' Do you know what that means?"

At first he didn't answer, and I thought he might not, just tell me again to get the hell gone. But finally he said, "Twenty-three years ago, the hero linebacker they arrested for the rape? It was him."

He turned, headed for his car. Macpherson did the same, and I did, too. A little jockeying got me rolling down the driveway, toward the road. The police cars, red and blue lights circling, headed the other way, to collect five more boys from football camp and take them to jail.

ten

From the expressway, driving toward New York, I called Lydia.

"Anything?" I asked.

"No. You? Was I right? Did Mr. Macpherson come back?"

"Of course you were right. When were you ever not right?"

"What happened?"

"He threatened to kill me and sue me and Sullivan threatened to arrest me."

"He was there too?"

"He got his warrants."

"Why didn't they? Kill you and sue you and arrest you?"

"He didn't kill me because he's rusty and his timing's off. He probably will sue me. And Sullivan didn't arrest me because he's out of his jurisdiction and he's making enough trouble for the locals as it is."

I told Lydia about my roadblock, the abbreviated fight, the arrival of the police. "It's going to be a long night in Plaindale," I said.

"Will Detective Sullivan tell you if any of them knows anything?"

"Right now I don't think he'd tell me if they knew there was a bomb under my bed."

"I wonder what they do know," Lydia said. "I wonder if any of them know anything about Gary." Her voice was soft. I realized that the one piece of good news from this night was something she hadn't heard yet.

"I do," I said. "It looks like he wasn't there." I told her what Sullivan had said, and Stacie Phillips.

"Oh, Bill," she said. "Oh, that's great."

"Well, it's looking better," I admitted. "But he's still in trouble, and he's still missing. Listen, have you had dinner?"

"No."

"Want to meet me at Shorty's? I should be there in half an hour."

"Sounds good."

It did sound good. I folded the phone and put it away. Hands light on the wheel, I drove easily and fast, threading through the traffic, timing my moves to the speed of the cars around me, pulling away, cutting around. We wove a pattern, all working toward the same goal, though not known to one another. I listened to the Bach the whole way back to the city.

Almost there, I pulled a card from my pocket, made one more call.

"Stacie Phillips."

"Stacie, Bill Smith."

"You found him?"

"No. I want a favor."

"Ah," she said. "But what do I get?"

"Who taught you to think like that?"

"It's just something I heard."

"Okay," I said, "Point taken. And I don't know. But something interesting's come up. It might not mean anything. But I need it checked out."

"I thought detectives checked things out themselves."

"Actually, we call people. Sources."

"It may be a conflict of interest for a reporter to be a source."

"It'll broaden your base of experience to see how the other half lives."

"Yeah, right. So if I said yes, what would I be saying yes to?"

"You have access to the *Tri-Town Gazette* morgue?"

"Of course I do. What's in there you want?"

"Warrenstown's big scandal. The rape and suicide? I want to know who, what, where, when, why."

"That was before I was born," she pointed out.

"I know. And though nothing important could possibly have happened that long ago, still, humor me?"

"You better call me when you find Gary."

"You're on my speed-dial. Look, I'm heading into the tunnel. Fax me whatever you find."

I cruised into Manhattan, stashed the car in the lot I use and got to Shorty's before Lydia did.

I pushed through the etched glass doors, glad for the warmth, the quiet sounds, the welcoming smells of food and liquor. The bar was in the back and Shorty O'Donnell, as usual, was behind it; also as usual, he was watching the door, watching the whole place, everyone's moves, though you'd never see him do it. I made my way back there, exchanging nods, hellos, wisecracks with the other regulars. I'd lived two floors above this bar for sixteen years. Shorty had owned the building and the bar twice as long as that, and almost nothing had changed over those years: the green glass shades on the lamps, the faded prints of New York and of Ireland in equal numbers on the walls, the smell of burgers and beer. The conversations were the same, too, the quiet talk of men who knew each other, maybe not well, but long, who came here as much for the talk as the beer, to discuss the Yankees' chances this season, or the Giants' or the Knicks', and agree the mayor was a bum, every season, every year.

I looked around for Lydia, didn't see her, slipped onto a bar stool. Shorty pulled the Maker's Mark from the shelf, dropped ice in a glass, poured me a shot. He asked, "What's wrong?"

I sipped at the bourbon, looked up, was about to say something noncommittal, Just tired I guess, nothing's wrong, what's new with you? But I saw his face, creased now but smooth when I'd met him; his bristling eyebrows, gray where they used to be black; his dark eyes waiting. Shorty and his buddies: These men had known me since I was fifteen. Friends of my uncle Dave's, they'd been on my side, and had stayed there, though I hadn't been an easy kid to like. One or two of them, cops like Dave, had even arrested me in those years, but because Dave had never given up on me, they hadn't, either, cutting me every break they could, trying to help Dave, trying, in their ways, to help me. I'd never said thanks and I probably never would, but I couldn't look Shorty in the eye tonight and lie to him.

"Trouble," I said, lighting a cigarette. "I'm meeting Lydia, but I'll tell you about it later, if you have time."

He nodded. "Anything I can do?"

"I'm not sure."

He nodded again, went down the bar to pour someone else's drink. The etched-glass doors opened once more, and this time it was Lydia.

She got some looks as she walked through the bar, and some greetings from some of the regulars. She'd been meeting me here on and off over the last couple years, enough that she was part of the crowd now, someone the regulars would look out for, ask about if she hadn't been seen in a while. I got looks, too, every time she walked in, knowing ones from people who didn't know what they thought they did.

I stepped down from the bar stool, went to meet her, kissed her. Her skin was cold from the night air, but though our kiss was brief her lips warmed to it.

We separated; she waved to Shorty and slid into a booth. I put my drink on the scarred tabletop, sat down across from her.

"Still nothing?" I asked.

"I'm sorry."

I shook my head. "Not your fault."

"We'll find him."

I drank some bourbon, tried to believe what she'd said.

I wondered, suddenly, when she'd lose that, the optimism with which she approached everything, the cheerfulness, the hope. It would be a shame, when she did.

I put down my bourbon, said, "I learned something interesting." I was about to tell her what when we were interrupted by Caitlin, Shorty's new waitress. She brought Lydia a seltzer with three limes Shorty had sent over from the bar, setting it down carefully, on its Guinness coaster, along with two sets of cutlery wrapped in napkins, one by Lydia's left hand, one by mine. Young and still learning the job, Caitlin was, wanting to make a success of it. We ordered dinner—a bacon burger for me, a Caesar salad for Lydia—and when Caitlin left, I went on.

"I told you about the rape and suicide in Warrenstown, years ago?"

She nodded.

"Well, Randy Macpherson's father was the football hero they accused, arrested, then let go after the other kid shot himself."

"This would be the Macpherson who's going to kill you and sue you?"

"That Macpherson, yes."

"He sounds dangerous."

"Well, except it seems he didn't do it. It might be why he's been in such a lousy mood all these years, though. It could explain why he exploded at the idea of someone thinking his son had been involved in a crime."

"Does that need an explanation?"

I took out a cigarette, looked at her as I put a match to it. "No," I said. "No, I guess not." I drank more bourbon, felt it start to work, felt that distance begin, that slight separation between you and everything else that drink can give you.

"Anyway," I said, "I asked Stacie Phillips—that kid from the paper—to fax me whatever she could dig up on it."

"What are you looking for?"

"I don't know. Maybe nothing. Maybe I just don't like Macpherson and I'd like to have something on him."

"But if he didn't do it, then there's nothing to have."

"Maybe I just want to see what it was about. Or maybe," I said, "maybe I'm just mad and I want to hit something."

Her black eyes met mine, and held them. Sounds in the room faded. I had my drink in one hand and my cigarette in the other and I didn't want either of them.

Then Lydia smiled. Shorty put a Sinatra CD on, someone left the bar and someone came in, and everything was as it always was.

For a while we didn't speak, just sat together in this place I knew as well as the place where I lived, this place Lydia was coming to know, too. Caitlin brought our dinner, and either Shorty's food, always good, was better than usual, or the cheese Danish on the road in front of Hamlin's hadn't done much for me.

"You never ran into my brother-in-law," I said to Lydia, finally finished, rescuing a last fry as Caitlin came to take away our plates.

"We crossed paths. I told you. Some of the places I went, they already had pictures. I—" We were interrupted by the ringing of her cell phone.

She answered in both languages, listened, asked where and when, took out a pen and wrote on a napkin. She thanked the caller, flipped the phone shut.

"It's someone who thinks she saw Gary," she said.

Her phone's ring had silenced all other sounds in the room, for me. "When? Where?"

"Queens, this afternoon. A volunteer for One to One. One of those charities that have outreach vans for street kids? She was parked with her van near the Queens Plaza subway stop, but she didn't see Gary's picture until she got back to One to One's headquarters just now. He was okay," she said, heading off my question. "He was hungry, she gave him a couple of sandwiches, but he wouldn't stay around. He acted nervous, she said, kept looking around as though he was looking for someone. But he seemed okay."

"This afternoon? Goddammit—" I stopped myself, tried to take control as the heat flooded my face and my shoulders tightened. "I'm sorry," I said to Lydia. "I just—let's go."

She sat for a moment longer than I did, searched my face with her dark eyes. Then she nodded and stood. I waved to Shorty, pointed to our table so he'd know to put dinner on my tab. He sent a question in his look; I shrugged, shook my head. I dropped some bills for Caitlin, hurried through the room to the chill of the night.

The drive to Queens was short, not a lot of traffic at this hour. I took the bridge and Lydia didn't say anything until we were on it, rolling a little too fast out of Manhattan, across the river.

"Bill?"

I glanced over, saw her looking at me, the skyline and the dark water behind her.

"You have to get a better grip," she said. "I know it's important. I know there's more to it than I know about. But if you lose it, you're going to make it worse."

I looked at her again, then back at the road. I nodded, said nothing. Downshifting, I pulled out to pass, pulled back in right after I'd done it. I lit a cigarette. Lydia rolled her window down and didn't speak again.

The address we were headed for, the spot where the One to One van had been parked, was a few blocks from the place at Queens Plaza where six subway lines come together, four below ground, two above. Roosting pigeons swooped and dived as trains rumbled along steel trestles or over cracked concrete structures arched like Roman aqueducts. The streets and avenues below interrupted each other, crossed at odd angles, dead-ended and jogged and bent. Old office buildings and small storefronts, apartments above, lined them, the stores pretty much closed now, papers blowing along the sidewalks, roll-down gates locked tight. Some of the businesses were still open, the take-out Chinese place, the corner bodega, and we started with them, handing the countermen Xeroxes of Gary's picture with Lydia's cell phone number at the bottom. No one said they'd seen him; they all promised to call if they did, and we had to live with that, go on to the next place, show the picture again.

The night got colder, more storefronts closed, traffic thinned and we didn't find Gary. We made a wide circle of the neighborhood, stopped to post his picture on lampposts and hand it to people out walking their dogs. I bought a pack of cigarettes and Lydia got a cup of tea from the last corner deli still open. The lights on its sign went out as soon as we left.

"Are you going to call your sister?" Lydia asked. We walked a short way, stopped on the corner, for no reason except that we had nowhere to go.

I shook my head. "To tell her what? That someone thinks she saw Gary hours ago, but we can't find him now?"

We stood on the corner, me smoking, she warming her hands around her cup.

"We need to go back," Lydia said.

I didn't answer.

"We can't do anything here," she said. "He might have left a long time ago. It might not have been him at all," she added, something I was sure we'd both thought of but neither of us had said.

"I know," I said. "I know." I made no move to go anywhere. A gust of wind knocked some trash out of the can beside me.

"You didn't sleep last night," she said. "You won't be any good to anybody if you wipe yourself out."

A train clattered overhead, eastbound from Manhattan, people headed home. I stared up as its lights flashed by. Lydia was right. I was exhausted. Gary wasn't here. Going back, getting some sleep, now while there was nothing else we could do, would make sense. After a night's sleep tomorrow's choices would be clearer, the next step more obvious.

But I didn't want logic and I didn't want planning. I wanted to find Gary, give him the help he'd asked for. Someone needed to care about the kid; someone needed to stop him from screwing up.

Lydia touched my hand. She startled me; my hand jerked,

but she held me. "It isn't you," she said. I didn't know what she meant by that.

We were on the bridge headed in when a cell phone rang, mine this time. I had it out, open, barked "Smith!" into it before it rang a second time.

"Linus Kwong. How's it going?"

"Linus—oh, hey, yeah," I said, blanking, then registering. "Where are you? Did you find anything?"

Lydia turned, watched me as I spoke to her cousin.

"I'm in Chinatown. And I'm not sure, dude. I'm, ah, looking for, like, authorization."

"Authorization? To do what?"

"Well, see, it's like, that place you wanted me to go? That was a no-brainer, dude. The computer in your guy's room, there's nothing there but, like, school stuff."

For the second time that day I got the feeling *stuff* was the edited version, for adults.

"There's this other computer they have," Linus went on. "They just have like one online account with different passwords, and the lady, she gave them to me. So I go in there, and it's a snore. I mean, this is the heartland, right? These people, they're hitting like the NFL and Sears.com. Takes me maybe an hour, I've seen it all, dude. Your guy, he's not a game-player, he's not hooked up anywhere."

"I'm trying to follow you here, Linus. You're saying there's nothing there?"

"I'm saying, *he's* not hooked up. But I'm running through the back e-mails for each screen name, because, hey, you're paying me, you know?"

"I appreciate the professional thoroughness."

"Oh, hey, forget it, dude," said Linus, obviously pleased. "So your guy, he calls himself GRussell80, I don't know what that's about, but it's him. So like he has not so much e-mail, not his métier obviously, but there's this one dude, Premador."

He paused to give me a chance to catch up, but beyond a mental lift of the eyebrows at *métier*, it didn't help.

"Does that mean something?" I asked.

"Well, see, what I want authorization for, this Premador dude, I want to, uh, check him out."

"You're asking me to authorize you to hack into this guy's computer?"

"Oh, man, now don't say that."

"Listen, Linus," I said. "I can't authorize you to do anything illegal. I'm not a cop and I can't get a court order. And if I got you in trouble your cousin Lydia would kill me."

"I think she's my aunt."

"You'll have to straighten that out with her. But here's the point: The kid who's missing is fifteen, and I think he *is* in trouble."

"I get you, dude."

And Linus is fifteen, too, Smith. I pushed that thought away and asked, "What is it about this guy that interests you? Something in his e-mail to Gary?"

"No. One thing, it's all old, like a couple of months. And it's boring. But, like, his handle, dude."

"Premador, you mean?"

"Yeah. I don't guess you, like, follow Japanese books?"

"Japanese books?"

"Comic books, dude. They have them in English. The big ones, size of the newspaper?"

"No, I guess I haven't seen them."

"Well, there's this one series, *CyberSpawn*, you know, monsters and mutants and stuff."

"Okay."

"And this mutant Premador, he's real twisted. He was like a good mutant, but everyone messed with his head, and now he's bad. They're always trying to stop him, because he's like on a major mission."

"What's his mission?"

"To, like, blow up the world."

The conversation with Linus Kwong had taken us off the bridge and onto the FDR. While we headed south I told Lydia what her cousin had told me, or at least as much of it as I understood.

"So he thinks Gary's been exchanging e-mail with some-one who wants to blow up the world?"

"Gary's e-mail handle—"

"In English we call that a screen name."

I gave her a glance. "Thanks. Gary's screen name is GRussell80. Linus doesn't know what the eighty is for, but I think I do. One of football's most famous wide receivers, Jerry Rice? That's his number."

"So you're saying, your screen name is who you want to be?"

"I'd think so. You have e-mail. What's yours?"

She looked at me for a moment, then said, "Lydia Chin."

I dropped Lydia at home in Chinatown, promising to call her if anything developed. She promised the same.

"You'll go home and sleep?" she said. "You won't run around trying to do something when there's nothing you can do?"

"Yes," I said. "No."

She gave me a long, skeptical look. "And if you do," she said, "you'll call me so I can at least come?"

"Yes," I said again, and I couldn't help smiling. She got out of the car, waved from the sidewalk, entered the building she lived in.

I put the car in the lot for the second time that night, walked the half dozen blocks to my place. Guilt grabbed for me, tried to pull me into the bar to give Shorty the explanation I'd said I'd give. The promise of a drink double-teamed me, shoving me in the same direction, but I kept on going, un-locked the entrance to the steep stairs up to my place in-stead. Shorty had never known my sister, but he'd known me, met my mother and my father in the bad days after she'd left. He knew what had happened there, and he, like Dave, like all those men, had never been any less than stone certain that what I did was right. But they'd always been more sure than I was. And those weren't doors I wanted to open, right now.

Inside, upstairs, I took off my jacket, threw it on the couch, felt a hard chill in the air. The window, in the back room: It still gaped, jagged glass glinting again in the glow from the streetlight as it had last night. I rummaged through the desk, found enough cardboard to tape together a barrier between the night and me that should last until morning. I poured a drink, downed half of it, took a hot, pounding shower. Coming out of the bathroom for the rest of the drink I saw Gary's Warriors jacket over the back of the chair where I'd left it, after I'd searched and it had told me nothing. At least I knew now who the Warriors were.

I took my bourbon to the stereo, put on not Brahms, not Bach, but Copland, though I wasn't sure why: American music, maybe, something more raw, less reasonable. I crossed the room again, heading for the couch, planning to sit with my feet on the coffee table and drink and listen. Just before I got there I finally noticed the fax machine. It sat patiently holding a pile of papers, maybe a dozen sheets. Most of them were reduced Xeroxes of newspaper columns, their grainy high-contrast photos nothing but blurs of black and white, but their type tiny and sharp. The top sheet was a scribbled note in a round, clear hand.

"Ancient History 101," it read. "What are we looking for? And what do I get?" It was signed, "Stacie."

I don't know, I thought, and settled down to read.

eleven

This time the dream was about catching a train. Someone waited for me at a distant station as dusk grayed all color from a snow-dusted, hilly landscape. I was late, and the train we had agreed to take was the last of the day; there was no other that could get us to the event we were traveling for, expected at. But I couldn't find the things—the clothes, the papers—I was supposed to bring; I'd left them with the man who would be giving me a lift to the station, and he couldn't remember where he'd put them and didn't care much. I searched frantically, until seven minutes before train time; the station was ten minutes away. Then we left, empty handed, to see if we could make it, though it was probably too late.

I woke not because of the buzzer, which came a few minutes later, but because of the dream: some dreams you can't finish, and you can't leave. When the buzzer sawed through the night I was still lying on the couch, awake but not thinking, following the dream again, and the Copland Piano Sonata, which still played. My first coherent thought was that I couldn't have slept very long if the CD was still on. My second was that maybe I ought to get up and answer the door.

I stumbled to the intercom, pressed the button and asked

who was there. The sharp electronic answer from two floors below slammed me awake: "Scott Russell."

I thought about asking him what he wanted; I thought about telling him to go to hell. Instead I pressed the buzzer, threw off my robe, pulled on my jeans. I picked up my cigarettes from the desk, stood in the doorway and lit one, watched Scott climb the stairs. While he did, the music finally ended.

He gave me a look that said he felt the same way about being at my place as I felt about having him here. Well, hell, Scott, you're the one who came, I thought as I held the apartment door for him, shut it behind myself.

"What do you want?" I asked.

Scott looked around as Gary had, his eyes registering not surprise but disgust, though I didn't think it was the books, the pictures on the walls, not even the piano, as much as the fact that they were mine. He turned to me, a broad-shouldered, sandy-haired guy, stubble on his ruddy face. I had four inches on him, and Gary probably had two, might pick up two or three more before he was through.

"I want you to keep the hell away from my family," he said.

I looked at him for awhile, not moving; then I turned, walked past him to the kitchen, put water on. "You want coffee?"

"Fuck that! You were in Warrenstown all fucking day, Smith, you think I don't know that?"

"I wasn't trying to hide it."

"Are you hearing me? I only came here to say one thing: Stay away."

"Okay, you said it." I parked my cigarette in an ashtray, started the business with grinding the coffee, putting together the coffee press, because I thought it would be good to have something to do with my hands.

"You going to do it?" he said, raising his voice over the whine of the grinder, not yet moving from the spot he'd stopped at when he first came in.

I finished the grinding, dumped coffee into the press. "You find Gary yet?"

"Hey, you son of a—"

"Back off!" My voice was hard, and loud, and, I realized, as deliberately that way as Hamlin's had been, in his office, hours ago. "Who's Premador?"

He stared. "What the fuck are you talking about?"

"Premador's a comic book character who wants to blow the world up. Gary gets e-mail from someone calling himself that."

"So fucking what?"

"So maybe nothing. Or maybe Gary wants to blow the world up, too."

He stepped toward me. "What kind of bullshit—"

"No bullshit. No bullshit, Scott, not now." My hands gripped the edge of the wood counter between us. "You say stay away from your family. But they're my family, too, as much as you hate that. Helen doesn't like it, either. But you can't make it not true."

"Your family." He sneered. "You have no fucking idea what that means."

"You have no fucking idea," I said, my voice as slow, as flat and cold as ice on a deep winter river, "no fucking idea who I am. You don't know anything about me. I've kept away from your family for years because you wanted it that way. But Gary asked me for help."

"He must have been fucking desperate, to come to you!"

"I think he was."

That stopped him. Our eyes locked; in the color flaring in his face, the thrust of his shoulders, I could see how ready he was to explode. I clamped my jaw shut to keep from saying words to set him off, because part of me wanted that to happen, wanted him to rush me, wanted to fight Scott Russell right here, now, in my own place.

"You bastard," Scott said, his voice like gravel. "I'm telling you. I find you near them, you're dead."

I spoke as quietly as I could. "I'm not the bad guy here, Scott."

"What?"

"Whatever went wrong for Gary, it happened before he came to me. I'm sorry I couldn't hold on to him. But he needs help and I'm going to do whatever I have to, to find him. You can help or get out of the way. But you can't stop me."

Scott's eyes burned through me: blue eyes, like Gary's, though I couldn't see much else that was Gary, in him. Scott wanted what I wanted right then and I knew it. To hit, kick, beat someone down, exhaust yourself. To take the fear and helpless rage and turn them into something you can tell yourself you're proud of. To force someone to betray himself, to make him fail. To win. To prove you're really there.

Come on, Scott, I thought, come on, you son of a bitch, but Scott wasn't ready, not yet. With a violent turn, as though hefting a weight, he spun around, crossed the room, headed toward the door. He almost got there, and I almost let my breath out, but he had to kick aside the faxed pages I'd dropped when I fell asleep, and they caught his eye.

He stooped, picked up a few. "What the fuck is this?" He whipped through the papers in his hands, spun to look at me. "What the fuck is this? You're digging up this old shit again?"

I looked from the papers to him. "You know anything about it?"

"No! Goddammit, motherfucker! I didn't know anything about it then and I don't now. But I know Warrenstown doesn't need assholes like you digging through this old shit." He ripped the papers in half, threw them down. "My family," he said. "My town. Keep away, motherfucker."

I said nothing, didn't move. Just looked at my sister's husband as he stood in my room. Let him decide. I'd do it any way he wanted.

And then, the way things happen, the way so much of the time it's better if you don't get what you want, Scott turned, yanked open the door, and left.

Still not moving, I listened to the pounding of his feet on the stairs, heard the outside door open and slam shut. I walked slowly to the door up here, closed it, slowly again back to the kitchen. I lit a cigarette before I spotted the one I'd left in the ashtray, still smoldering. I ground it out, pulled on the new one. I poured the water in the press, stood while the coffee brewed, the full five minutes, not moving, looking at nothing. When it was ready I poured a cup. I took it to the couch, got the Scotch tape from the desk, put the papers back together, and began to read.

An hour later I'd been through it all twice, and the pot of coffee. I thought about calling Lydia, to tell her about it, talk it over; but it was late, and I'd gotten her up before six. And there was nothing in what I'd read that wouldn't keep. Some of it was interesting, showing me Warrenstown the way late sun breaking through heavy clouds can surprise you with something you thought you'd seen already. But I couldn't see how any of it mattered, to Gary, to the job I had.

I put on my jacket, left the apartment. I was going nowhere; I could do nothing. I'd run down my leads and hit dead ends. I'd been thrown out of Warrenstown, out of Plaindale, and I'd bet Bert Hagstrom wouldn't be happy if I turned up at Midtown South, either. I was a detective, looking for a kid; I'd had cases like this before and I'd failed before. Some people, some things, you never find.

But this one probably wouldn't end that way. Police in two states were also looking for Gary Russell, a clueless kid without a dime last seen on the streets of New York. He couldn't stay hidden; he wouldn't know how.

Is that a fact, Smith, I asked myself, turning my collar up as I walked into the cold wind near the river. When I was Gary's age and lived in Brooklyn with Dave, these blocks were sailor's bars, flophouses, warehouses and ship's chandleries. Now they'd all been converted for comfortable living; now there was a college here, a public one, where the sons and daughters of New York could come to prepare themselves for what was next.

I asked myself again, Is that a fact, that Gary won't know how to stay hidden? Because his mother did. For years. For as long as she wanted to, no matter what anyone tried.

Of course, though the police had searched for her, too, it was as a runaway, not a suspect. She wasn't the criminal. There was an arrest, and a trial, a conviction, a prison sentence; but though she knew about it all, she still didn't come home.

I crossed the highway, walked beside the river. They'd put a park here now, jogging paths, bike paths, trees. When it was warmer, hookers worked the park, bringing johns they'd picked up on the streets over the bridges to the shadows here: cheaper than a hotel, and easier to scramble away if a trick turned nasty. But on a cold night like this there was no one here but me. And though the waterfront was tame and pretty now and the windows of the new, prosperous buildings glowed behind me with their curtains drawn, the black water of the river still ran to the sea. You could smell the salt of the harbor, hear the water lapping against the wall you stood at. The river still carried things you didn't know were there, was still charged with currents that ran in unexpected ways. It was the same as it always had been.

I watched it for a while, watched barges and tugs whose workdays were not over, boats plowing through the cold river water late at night because they had to finish their jobs.

I lit a cigarette, smoked it through. I took out my cell phone, found the scrap of paper with the number Lydia had given me, dialed. When I got the voice mail I left a message. I was walking again, still headed north, away from home, when my phone rang.

"Smith."

"Hey, dude, Linus Kwong. You called?"

"Yeah, Linus. Sorry it's so late. I wanted to know if you found anything. This Premador guy."

"Is it late? Oh, shit, look at that. Man, no wonder I'm starving. This Premador dude, man. Been chasing his trail all day, found him once, but he's gone again. Captured some good shit, though."

Not 'good stuff,' anyway. "What does that mean?"

"I found, like, some sites where he goes, chat rooms, like

that. I wrote a program, so if he was on it would tell me. He came on once and I, uh, I—"

"Hacked in?" I was guessing, but it seemed right.

"Yeah, okay, whatever." Linus went quickly past that. "But I got his passwords."

"That sounds useful."

"Well, yeah, if he's online. Otherwise not so much. See, I think he's not using his own computer. Like he's in a cybercafé or something? 'Cause, see, if it was his, I could like get his address book or something. But it wasn't there."

"So what do we do now?"

"Well, I don't think he detected me, but he logged off and he hasn't been back. But I got his, like, history, too."

"History. That tells us something?"

"Oh, yeah, definitely. Dude hits some creepy sites. I don't think he likes anybody much."

"What do you mean?"

"You know. Skinheads, Vikings. The government wants to put a chip in your head. Get off the grid. Long live Waco. You know."

"I'm not sure I do, but it doesn't sound good."

"It's mightily bad, dude. Little guy's got no chance, government's gonna get you anyway, best you can do is take 'em with you when you go."

"Sounds like Oklahoma City."

"Sounds like all kinds of shit. I been holding my nose and posting to his boards, in case he comes back, but he's nowhere. But I'll find him. I do, you'll put him away?"

The question surprised me, coming from this confident voice, this kid with skills I would never match, couldn't even understand. But he was a kid, and kids look to adults to make it all right.

"Find him, Linus. I'll see what I can do."

With another, "Cool, dude," he was gone, and I was alone by the river again.

I turned, walked back south. A tug on the river, pulling a barge, was moving in the same direction I was, at the same speed. Old tires swayed from its sides and its cabin windows were lit. We shadowed each other until I came to the footbridge, and I turned away.

I was spent. My day was over. Scott and the coffee had jolted me awake, but that had worn off, and I was tired again, bone-tired and cold and played out. I'd done what I could. It wasn't enough, but I didn't have anything else. I headed back, to sleep.

The wind off the river pushed papers around as I walked. Sheets of newsprint, yesterday's stories, swirled toward me. I swatted at them and they fell away, a slow-motion receiver with empty hands eluding halfhearted tacklers.

I could talk to Lydia in the morning, I thought as I unlocked the street door, climbed the stairs. The idea warmed me. I took my jacket off, my shoes, headed for the bedroom shedding the rest of my clothes on the way.

Lydia, in the morning. That would be good. Lydia didn't look at things the same way I did. Sometimes, between us, we could see things neither of us had seen alone.

I went to bed and slept and if I dreamed I didn't know it. When I woke it was late, past eight, and I was sore, stiff, as though I'd had a hard workout the day before. I showered, shaved, made coffee, called Lydia.

"Hi," she said. "How do you feel?"

"Lousy. I need a vacation. Will you come with me to a South Sea island?"

"We went to one, and you felt worse when we were through."

"That wasn't the South Sea, that was the South *China* Sea. The islands are completely different."

"Oh. Then how about this: No."

"Just as I thought. Well, I can understand it. You're probably holding out for a football player."

"Oh, no, you found my secret. One of the really thick ones, too. Linebackers?"

"Linemen, they're even thicker. And it would serve you right. Will you come with me to breakfast?"

"In America?"

"You found me out, too. It was a trick question. I know this really great breakfast place on Tahiti."

In the end we settled on a diner on Varick Street, more or less halfway between us. I dressed, shrugged into my jacket, took the cigarettes and the cell phone, and headed that way.

The morning was gray, colder than the day before, one of those late fall mornings when you can smell winter in the metallic air, feel it in the weight of the clouds. Dead leaves and left-behind papers skidded along the sidewalk. The whispering sound they made was drowned out by the traffic, horns and brakes and the rush of tires, but I knew it was there.

Lydia was drinking tea in a booth by the window when I got to the diner. I unzipped my jacket in the sudden warmth. Lydia stood, touched my shoulder, kissed my cheek. I kissed her lips; they were warm and soft, but I kissed them lightly, as though this were just a greeting, nothing more.

"You smell good," I said as I slid into the booth across from her.

"I do?"

"Oh, wait, it's probably the waffles. Unless you use maple syrup perfume?"

A waitress, blond and bored, came to our table, said nothing, stood waiting. I ordered waffles, and coffee to go with Lydia's tea; she ordered poached eggs to go with my waffles.

"Scott came by last night," I said when the waitress had gone.

Lydia stopped, teacup in her hand. "To your place?"

I nodded.

"Why?"

"To tell me to keep away from his family."

She tilted her head, maybe to see me differently. "What is it between you and Scott?"

"He doesn't like me."

"As the kids say: Well, *duh*."

"I wouldn't know, I don't speak that language. But speaking of kids, I talked to your cousin again."

"Linus?"

"He's sort of obsessing on this Premador guy."

"Is it important?"

"I don't know. But it is to him."

I told Lydia what Linus had told me, from wherever he was, as I stood in the dark, by the river. "He wants me to put the guy away, if he finds him."

"For what?"

"Thinking bad thoughts."

"Did you tell him that's not a crime?"

"No," I said, as the waitress came back. "Let him learn that somewhere else." The waitress set my coffee down. Surprisingly, she'd brought Lydia not only more hot water, but another tea bag, too.

"So it'll be fresh," she said, not looking any less bored, taking the empty cup away.

Small kindnesses in unexpected places, I thought, sipping my coffee. Sometimes, the only ones there are; and sometimes, it's enough. Lydia unwrapped the new tea bag, dunked it into her new hot water.

"There's something else," I said.

"You're not going to tell me about Scott?"

I looked up sharply. "There's nothing to tell. We told each other to go to hell. What did you expect?"

"I expect," she said slowly, "that when even thinking about someone makes you tighten your shoulders and look like you want to punch something, maybe you'd want to talk about him."

I looked at my left hand, the one not holding the coffee cup, and uncurled the fist it had made. I breathed out. "You're wrong," I said. "I don't want to talk about him. Nothing happened. We growled at each other like a couple of leashed dogs. It was my territory so he pissed on something. Then he left."

"You can't mean literally."

"That he left?"

She rolled her eyes.

"No, of course not," I said. "He tore up some papers. Faxes. I'd tell you what was on them, but you don't seem interested."

"No, you're wrong. Since you insist on being your most guylike, refusing to discuss what's driving you craziest, feel free to change the subject to anything that will take my mind off the fact that guylike guys drive *me* crazy."

"Umm, yeah. So I got these faxes."

"From?"

"Stacie Phillips."

"Girl reporter."

"Right."

The waitress brought our waffles, eggs, syrup, toast. She poured me more coffee, slipped Lydia another tea bag, and this time she smiled. Lydia smiled back.

"Stacie Phillips," Lydia said when we were alone again.

"Uh-huh. I'd asked her to fax me whatever she could find from the local paper on that old story."

"And I guess she did."

"She did." I poured syrup on the waffles. It was real maple syrup, not flavored sugar; this diner was full of surprises. "Goes like this: After one of those wild parties like at the Wesleys'—"

"They had them twenty-three years ago?"

"Warrenstown's always had them, it seems."

"Well," she said, "I shouldn't be surprised. You're always telling me tales of your wild, misspent youth, and I guess that was about that long ago."

"I'm not going to get a break here, am I?"

"No."

"Okay, just so I know. So: A girl walking home from this one was dragged into a yard down the block, raped, beaten up. An early-morning dogwalker found her."

"She was there for hours?"

"Yes."

Lydia shuddered.

"She was hurt pretty badly. In the end she recovered," I added.

"You're telling me the end so I won't worry?"

"Isn't that a good idea? You like happy endings."

"Does this story have one?"

"Not really."

"Great. Okay, go on."

"It was a day or so before she was conscious," I said. "She admitted to being both drunk and high and she didn't remember anything after she left the party. But she remembered Al Macpherson had been hitting on her there. She'd told him to get lost, he'd told her dozens of girls would be happy just to have him look at them, given who he was."

"Who was he?"

"Football co-captain. Warrenstown Warriors linebacker."

"Oh. Of course. What do you suppose was wrong with her?"

I ignored that, went on. "She left, she said, because Macpherson was grabbing her, pushing her around. He left soon after she did, which surprised some of the other kids because he was a party animal and always closed every place up."

Lydia dipped toast into her poached eggs. "So they arrested him?"

I nodded. "New Jersey law, they can hold you seventy-two hours on suspicion. They did, and then they let him go."

"They had nothing to charge him on?"

"Everything was circumstantial. The paper said there were leads they were following up, but they must not have come to anything. But in the end it didn't matter." I sponged up a puddle of syrup with a forkful of waffle. "There'd been a rumor from the beginning that another kid, who hadn't been invited to the party, had a thing for this girl and had been following her around."

"Stalking, we call that."

"Now we do; they didn't then, but a lot of fingers started pointing at him. They arrested him and sweated him, got nothing, let him go. Another kid alibied him, a friend of his."

"Someone else who hadn't been invited? And I thought you didn't have to be invited to those parties, by the way. I thought you just charged in and tore the place up."

"You know," I said, pushing my plate away, leaning back in the booth, "I wasn't there. Really I wasn't."

She narrowed her eyes. "If you'd lived in Warrenstown then, you would have been."

"Maybe. Maybe not. I'm really a pretty nice guy when you get to know me."

"Which is not easy, incidentally," she said. "Okay, go on."

"Thank you. So this second kid, a few hours after the cops let him go, he shot himself."

She nodded. "The suicide."

I said, "He was seventeen."

"So Warrenstown did get a happy ending. A nut off their streets, the case cleared, everyone's girls safe."

"All of that, sure. But mostly, Macpherson was a brick-wall linebacker, he'd missed three days of practice already, and they needed him in the Homecoming game on Satur-day."

She raised her eyebrows. "I'm surprised at you. That sounds like something I'd say."

"It's not me. There was an editorial in the local paper."

"Saying that?"

"Saying the police had some nerve arresting a Warrens-town Warrior right before the big game, the grudge match against Greenmeadow everybody waited for all year. And if Macpherson didn't perform well on Saturday, the cops would be to blame."

"The cops would—what about the girl, the rape, the fact they had a crime to solve?"

I shrugged. "You'll love this. A reporter went to see the girl in the hospital. The football team had sent a big fruit basket. Her jaw was wired, but she managed to say, 'Go Warriors.' "

Lydia shook her head slowly. "Life can stink, you know that?"

"That sounds like something I'd say."

"No, you'd use worse words. Listen, this was a horrible story and I appreciate your telling it to me, but does it have anything to do with finding Gary?"

"Well, it tells us a couple of things. One, that the Al Macpherson we saw last night was the Al Macpherson that always was."

"Do we need to know that?"

"Probably not. Just some depressing confirmation that people don't change much."

"Only depressing if they were awful children. What's the next thing?"

"Warrenstown, from what I read, was thrilled when it turned out to be this other kid. Nobody'd liked him; today they'd call him a freak, I guess. Twenty years ago we just called those kids weird and everyone kept away from them."

"Someone seems to have liked him enough to give him a phony alibi."

"That's true. But here's my point: He was a loner. An outsider."

Lydia paused a beat before she answered. "Gary's a jock. A football hero already. Didn't you say that?"

"Yes. But everyone I've talked to so far has also started everything they've said about Gary with, 'He's new.' "

"I can see what you're thinking," she said. "But people don't get lynched in New Jersey anymore."

"When Al Macpherson was in jail," I said, "there was a candlelight rally at the police station in support of him."

"The football team, I'll bet."

"Their parents."

"You have to be kidding."

"Maybe people don't get lynched in New Jersey anymore. But they still get railroaded."

Lydia looked away, watched the blond waitress collect dirty plates from a table in the corner. She brought her eyes back to me, seemed about to say something; but she didn't, just tossed her head, maybe to rearrange her hair, maybe to push some thoughts away. "Okay," she said. "Then we'd better find Gary before anyone else does. We were planning on that anyway. What's our next move?"

"You haven't figured out that the reason I told you this story was to make it sound like I at least know something about something, when in fact I'm hiding the fact that I have no idea what to do?"

"You're not," she said, "hiding it very well."

"Okay, smarty, make a suggestion."

Lydia finished her tea in silence. "Well," she finally said, "I think all we can do is, you can call Detective Sullivan to ask if he's found anything—"

"Which he may or may not tell me."

"He will. He'll be thinking that the more you know the more likely you are to stay away from his case like he told you to."

I considered that. "You're probably right."

"And if he doesn't know anything, we can take our photos and spread them around some more. Just get out there and slog. I think that's it. All we can do."

Our eyes met. Hers were soft, and I thought maybe she didn't really believe I'd have been at that party, if I'd lived in Warrenstown then.

I took out the cell phone, called the Warrenstown PD. "Where are you?" was Sullivan's first question.

"New York. Eating waffles in a diner. Nowhere near your suspects or your crime scene."

"Keep it that way. What do you want?"

"I want to know if you've found anything."

"Like Gary Russell?"

"Anything," I said.

Sullivan's voice lightened up a little. "No. I got lawyers sprouting all over Warrenstown like mushrooms. No one admits to being at the party or knowing who was. 'My fingerprints were there? Gee, must've left them last week when I went over to do homework with Tory.'"

"On the beer cans?"

" 'Brought her a six-pack. Not my fault when she decided to crack it.' "

"This is why I never wanted to be a cop," I said.

"I'll get through to someone. Soon as I do, the whole thing'll fall apart. Just a matter of time. Pretty impressive, though."

"Yeah, great. Team defense. Are Tory Wesley's parents back yet? They have any ideas?"

"Due in soon on a redeye. I talked to them on the phone yesterday. They had nothing to offer, but hell, they were in shock."

I forced my mind from the image that sprang up: Tory Wesley's parents, white-faced, staring at each other in a distant hotel room, their world suddenly, with one phone call, changed in a ruinous way.

I said, "You get the autopsy report yet?"

"Not yet. You actually clean Al Macpherson's clock last night?"

"That what he says?"

"No, he says you never laid a hand on him, he slipped getting out of the car."

"He's got a tough punch, but he's too straightforward. I'm not that good, so I depend on sneakiness."

"Well, keep away from him. For a guy who slipped getting out of the car, he's got a real hard-on for you."

"Thanks for the warning."

"Now your turn. Didn't you say you talked to a couple of Gary's friends?"

"Only Morgan Reed."

"Not Paul Niebuhr? Max White? Marshall Nelligan?"

"Niebuhr, I left a message on his voice mail. He never called me back. The others I never heard of."

"Your sister didn't tell you about them?"

"Are they friends of Gary's?"

"According to some of the other kids around here."

"My sister," I said slowly, "doesn't know much about Gary's life, I think. Were those kids at the party?"

"I have their prints."

"Maybe they left them last week when—"

"Stick it. You never talked to them?"

"No."

"Oh. You find Gary yet?"

"If I had, would I be calling you?"

"If you do," he said, "you damn well better."

That was the end of that. I lowered the phone, looked out to the street, three lanes of traffic moving haltingly, with a lot of noise, in the same direction.

"Anything?" Lydia asked.

"He asked if I'd found Gary," I said. "He knows I haven't stopped looking."

"You said he wasn't stupid."

"He also didn't tell me to stop, or threaten me again."

"As long as you're out of his jurisdiction and not breaking the law, what could he say that he could back up?"

"That wouldn't stop a lot of other cops I know."

"It couldn't be," she asked, "that he actually expects you to keep your word and let him know if you do find Gary?"

I didn't answer that because I didn't want to think about it. I flipped the phone open again. "Let me make one more call," I said. "And then let's go."

"You know," Lydia said, "for a guy who claimed to hate that thing, who avoided getting one until—"

"Excuse me," I said, thumbing in a number. "I'm on the phone."

I listened through three rings, was rewarded with, "Stacie Phillips."

"Bill Smith. Just wanted to thank you for the history lesson."

"For a source, anytime. Especially one who can punch out Randy Macpherson's father."

"You heard about that?"

"I'm a reporter; I hear everything. You have anything for me?"

"Growing respect."

"Oh, great. Well, because thoroughness is important to a

reporter, I have something else for you," she said. "But part of it's bogus."

"Then why do I want it?"

"So you'll see how completely I hold up my end of a bargain. So when you find Gary—"

"Okay, okay. What is it?"

"Trevor called me this morning with more prints. This is from the furniture, not the beer cans. He really, really, wants to date my sister."

"I'm beginning to want to meet her myself."

"Let's not go there."

"She wouldn't date an old man?"

"Actually, she'd probably think you're cute. She's very weird."

"I'm sure you didn't mean that the way it sounded."

"Of course not," she said innocently. "Anyway: There's lots unidentified, and there are some of the same people I gave you yesterday, from the beer cans. Then there's Max White and Marshall Nelligan. They're sophomores. The bogus ones are the man next door, the cleaning lady, Tory's cousin Heather, and Paul Niebuhr."

"This is sad," I said, "but Jim Sullivan beat you to at least part of that, too."

"Sullivan's still speaking to you?"

"I have charms that aren't apparent."

"For sure. Actually," she admitted, "Trevor says he likes you."

"Trevor doesn't even know me."

A theatrical sigh. "You really did go to school with my father, didn't you? Wait, I know, the School of Hard Knocks. Are all sources like you?"

"Most are worse. It's our moment of glory. We like to milk it. But tell me why this information is bogus."

"Because those people weren't at the party."

"The guy next door and the cleaning lady I can see. But how do you know the cousin and Paul Niebuhr weren't there?"

"Heather Wesley lives in Cincinnati. Last time she visited

was over the summer. If her fingerprints were there, it just means the cleaning lady was goofing off. And Paul Niebuhr, no way."

"He wouldn't have been invited?"

"What part of 'no way' don't you understand?"

"What if he found out about it and just came?"

"To a jock party? No one would've let him in. They'd have poured beer in his pants and pushed him down the porch steps. You're talking about a guy Randy Macpherson locked in a locker once."

"So his prints must have been there from some other time?"

"Very *good*. And that means some of the others may be bogus, too, except if they're actually on the beer cans."

"Or the broken dishes. Well, that's certainly helpful."

"And now for me you have . . . ?"

"My phone number, for your sister."

"I have your phone number already. And you'd have to, like, fight a duel with Trevor."

I gave Stacie the same promise I'd given her before, hung up, paid for breakfast. Lydia and I walked out into the gray day, and I told her what Stacie had said.

"Are you going to tell Sullivan?"

"Tell him what? That Stacie Phillips has a crystal ball about who really was and wasn't at the party, based on the Warrenstown High pecking order? Besides," I said, "she's passing me information she's not supposed to have. Sullivan would be pissed at me, Stacie might get in trouble, and Trevor could lose his job."

"And all because Trevor wants to go out with Stacie's sister. Men are so amazing."

"You're saying you wouldn't jeopardize your career for a date?"

"I probably wouldn't even jeopardize my evening."

"It's that aloofness," I said, "that elegant disdain, that unapproachability, that makes men fall at your feet as numerous as leaves from the autumn trees."

She toed a clump of leaves tangled with newspaper and cigarette butts, wet with gutter water, as we stepped from the curb.

"Yes," she said, "and mostly, just as attractive."

twelve

The sun never showed that morning, so I had no real sense of the passing of time. In diffuse gray light that was always the same, Lydia and I covered the places where kids were. We walked past the flashing colors and disorienting, rushing perspectives of arcade video screens, bought coffee for thin, dispirited girls in greasy Alphabet City diners near the squats they lived in. We interrupted loud crowds of boys impressing each other in the skateboard corners of city parks or the plazas of office buildings where signs told you skate-boarding was among the many things not allowed. We talked to kids over the blasting bass beat of CDs in Tower Records and Virgin Megastore, on windy street corners near Cooper Union and NYU and Columbia. We didn't find Gary in any of those places; we weren't expecting to. What we hoped for was someone who'd seen him, or someone who would; someone who'd tell him his uncle was looking for him, that it was safe to come in.

We both had our phones with us and neither of them rang; we each handed out flyers and got no results. The light was the same and the guarded faces of the kids were the same and the answer was always the same. No, don't know him. He in trouble? Sure, if I see him. Hey, man, got a cigarette?

Once or twice, we got a variation on the answer: Yeah,

some cop was here already, asking about him. But from there, the answer always went back to, No, sorry, don't know him.

Finally, in Union Square, Lydia stood at the top of the curved steps looking out over Fourteenth Street and announced, "I'm tired. I'm cold. I'm hungry."

I climbed the steps to stand beside her, checked my watch. "It's a quarter to two."

"There," she said, as if my statement had proved hers.

"Okay," I said. I pointed at a restaurant called Hong Kong Bowl, a block away. "Noodles?"

"Sure."

"And then let's go back to Queens. It'll be about the same time your volunteer with the van saw Gary yesterday. Maybe some of the same people will be around."

We went and ate steaming big bowls of noodle soup, mine with beef, hers with shrimp and vegetables, and then we did go to Queens, though, as it turned out, for a different reason.

As we were chasing the last of the noodles around in our bowls, my cell phone rang. I put down my chopsticks, flipped the phone open, said, "Smith," and heard, "Linus. Got something, dude."

"What's that?"

"Chill, because it's not your boy and it's not Premador. But I got a place where he went."

"Who?"

"Like, *Premador*, dude. On one of his boards, he posted. He had an appointment. Dude calling himself Sting Ray. Yesterday."

"Who's Sting Ray?"

"I don't know who. But Premador, he was all excited, he was telling everyone on the board that Sting Ray, he has all good stuff, he's gonna hook him up. And I remembered I heard that name before. In your boy's e-mail."

"Gary's?"

"Premador said, meet me at this place, it's like beaucoup cool, and your boy said no thanks. But, see, he told him the address. The guy, the Sting Ray guy, he's in Queens someplace."

Electricity sizzled up my spine. Linus gave me the Queens someplace address.

It was two blocks from where the One to One volunteer had seen Gary, yesterday.

"Subway," I said to Lydia as we gathered ourselves up, dropped cash on the table. "It's right here."

Twenty minutes later we were back where we'd been last night, only this time we came pounding down the steel stairs from one of the train platforms that shadowed the streets. Pigeons circled and rerooted; a car horn blasted as I crossed the street on the cusp of a changing light. I walked like a man in a hurry, cutting corners, striding fast, and Lydia, wordless, did the same, although there was no reason for it. Premador, whoever he was, and Gary had both been and gone a day ago; speed can't make up for missed chances. Still, we rushed, and found the address, stopped at the building and met each other's eyes. The top buzzer said BRUCE RAY beside it on a press-on plastic label.

"Yeah?" a man's voice growled from the dented speaker box. The building was a three-story brick walk-up, a locksmith and a pizza place on the ground floor, apartments above. The street door was steel; peeling paint flaked from the wood window frames.

"Premador sent me," I said.

"Oh, fuck," said the voice. "He wants the rest? You got my money? I told that shit, no credit. Fucking Visa card, bite me. You got it?"

"I've got it."

No more words; the buzzer buzzed. Lydia and I walked up curling-linoleum stairs to the top floor, smelling garlic and pizza sauce, mold and old dampness, all the way. The door at the end of the one-bulb hallway wore the same number as the buzzer. When I knocked, there was action at the peephole. Then nothing. Then heavy iron clanks as multiple locks opened. The door moved as if by an invisible hand. Lydia stepped through first, me right behind her; the man behind the door pushed it shut, locked it, stood facing us with red-rimmed eyes.

He hadn't shaved today and he probably hadn't yesterday, a medium-height, thin man in a gray tee shirt that might have once been white. He wore jeans so greasy they shone, no shoes, stood smoking a cigarette in an apartment that reminded me of what Jim Sullivan had said about cigarettes when he lit one up at the Wesleys'. Chinese food containers, a grease-stained pizza box, crushed take-out coffee cups and aged magazines surrounded a sprung, worn couch where the pattern on the upholstery might have been flowers, or horses, or Jesus Christ and all the saints; there would never again be a way to tell. A doorless doorway on the right showed a galley kitchen with brown-spattered walls and tottering piles of dishes held together by congealed grease. An indeterminate number of socks, another tee shirt, and a jock-strap huddled exhausted on the floor, as though they'd been so overworked they couldn't make it to the laundry basket. The place was dim and it stank and I could hear water dripping from the kitchen faucet. Across the room a computer sat incongruously on a card table, its putty-colored case streaked with greasy fingerprints, coffee stains blotting its mouse pad, a layer of dust veiling its screen.

"Sting Ray?" I said. The man stood, waiting, hand still on the doorknob, making it clear that opening the door again and throwing us out was as attractive a proposition as any other.

"Yeah, sure," he said around his cigarette. He looked not at me, but at Lydia, a small, predatory smile on his cracked lips. "That'll work. Who the hell's this?"

"My driver," I said. "Security. Don't worry about her. She doesn't speak English."

"Why would I worry?" Ray said. "She know some hot shit Oriental moves or something?" With a sudden earsplitting yell he crouched into a kung fu stance he must have learned from a Steven Seagal movie, knees bent, hands chopping the air in front of him.

At the sound Lydia stepped back fast, took a defensive

position, body set sideways, arms up, leg ready to kick
Ray's head off. Then she assessed him. She relaxed. In a
gesture of complete contempt, she straightened up, looked
him in the eye, slipped her hands in her pockets.

"Ah, shit," Ray said, grinning, standing upright. "I don't
hit girls anyway, unless they want it. Wantee hitee?" he said
to Lydia. She gave him a stare that could have freeze-dried
a lava flow. He laughed, turned to me. "So what'd you come
for? All of them, just one, something else, what?"

I had no idea what we were talking about, so I countered
with, "I don't have enough cash for them all. I need to
choose."

"Oh, fuck that, man," Ray said without particular emo-
tion. "He and I went over this last fucking week." He took
the cigarette from his mouth, pointed it at me. "I told him
how much. He said he could get it."

"Didn't work out," I said.

"He's a fuckup. You shouldn't be letting him out, do
business on his own."

"He needed to get experience somehow." I wondered
how long I could keep this up.

"You his old man, what?" Ray asked, seeming to look
me over for the first time.

My heart pounded. I said, "Do I look like him?"

Ray gave me a leer. "Not even a little. Maybe his old
lady was doing nooners with the milkman."

"Well, the guy with him," I said. "The one who looks
like me. That's my nephew."

"What guy? That Premador asshole, he was alone, just
like last time, just like I told him to be."

"Oh," I said. "I guess maybe the kid waited downstairs.
Premador didn't say?"

Ray shook his head, mashed his cigarette into a pile of
butts that may have had an ashtray under it, maybe not. He
turned, walked into a bedroom even more disastrous than
the room we were in. He threw back a tangle of moth-eaten
blanket and yellowed sheet, grunted as he yanked a long
metal box from under the bed. He ran a combination, opened

the lid. Looking back over his shoulder, he said, "Well, don't expect me to fucking bring 'em out."

I moved aside so Lydia could go into the bedroom first, which she did with a muttered, "You owe me big," as she passed me. Ray crouched next to his box, smiling up at us, and Lydia and I stepped up and looked into it and my first thought was that there was more and varied ordnance in that box than I'd seen together in one place since my years in the navy.

Numerous handguns, mostly automatics but also a revolver or two, formed a disorganized metallic bed for five rifles—two with night sights—and a couple of shotguns, a sprinkling of supressors and long magazines, and three automatic weapons, one an Uzi and two I didn't recognize. None of them were particularly clean and many were scratched; whether from previous use or their stay at Sting Ray's was not clear.

"This is like the one he took," Ray said, shoving a shotgun aside, lifting the rifle that lay next to it. "And one of these." He showed me a 9 mm automatic pistol. "You want to see the others he wanted? Visa card, what an asshole."

I nodded and from the box Ray pulled another 9 mm automatic, a short-barrel Colt revolver a lot like the one I was wearing right then, and another rifle, with a night scope. "He also," said Ray, his sneer telling me that what he was about to say was about as ridiculous as anything he could think of, "wanted a couple of these." He rummaged through the box and hefted something I hadn't noticed before, a hand grenade. "He thought they're small, they must be cheap. Where'd you get an asshole like that?"

"Good help is hard to find," I said.

"Well, I hope he takes orders good," Ray said. "Because you're fucked if he ever starts giving 'em."

I crouched next to him, lifted the weapons he'd showed us. I looked at some others, felt the weight of the grenade. Ray lit another cigarette. "Did he tell you who we are?" I asked, as though if Ray knew that it would help him help me shop. "Did he tell you what we need these for?"

Ray took the cigarette from his mouth. "Deer hunting,"
he said in a deliberate way. "Funny thing about me. Any
time one of you guys starts telling me his shit, all I hear is
'deer hunting.' That's fine with me. Go hunt your fucking
deer. Though I got to say, you win some kind of prize here.
A fuckup like Premador and a slant-eye that doesn't talk.
Whatever you're into, good fucking luck." He eyed Lydia
again, said, "No speakee English at all, huh?"

"No," I said. "But she drives well. And she can kick
butt."

"Gotta tell you," Ray said, "I had a driver looked like
that, I'd spend a lot of time in the driver's seat myself.
Kicking butt," he finished, and laughed at his own joke.

When Lydia's working, she's working: She didn't blush,
didn't turn away, just kept the sullen, evil look of someone
who had no idea what was going on around her and didn't
care as long as she got her pay and got to stomp something
once in a while.

Sting Ray and I negotiated, smoked a cigarette or two
together, made some gun-guy small talk: reloads, black
powder, the five-day wait to buy at a gun show that could
be law by this time next year. I tried every way I could
think of to get Ray to give me anything Premador had said,
anything that would help me know who he was, how he
knew Gary, what the guns were for. In the end I decided,
not that he was holding out on me, but that he really did,
as he'd said, make it his business not to know anything
about his customers' intentions. Whatever Premador had
said, Sting Ray hadn't listened.

If I were in his business, I had to admit, I'd have done
the same.

Finally, I peeled two hundred dollars from the roll in my
pocket, took the 9 mm automatic and a high-capacity magazine. I told Ray I was interested, now that I'd seen the
merchandise, in the Uzi, maybe a few grenades, that I'd
have to come back for them.

"Listen," I said as we stood at the door, business concluded, Lydia and I about to leave. "If they come back, either one of them—"

"Who?" Ray asked.

"Premador, or my nephew," I said. "The one who looks like me."

"Oh. Yeah, him," Ray said without interest.

"If they come back, tell them to call me. I don't want them spending money on the wrong things."

"No problem," said Ray; though I had a feeling that if they did show up with money to spend, Ray would forget to mention I'd ever been there.

"My name's Smith," I said, just in case.

"Smith." Ray grinned. "Man, it's amazing. Every god-damn asshole who comes here, you know his name is Smith?"

"I have a lot of relations," I told him, and Lydia and I turned and left.

As soon as we pushed out the street door Lydia started striding fast and hard down the sidewalk, away from Ray's building. I followed beside her; only the fact that my legs are longer let me keep up.

"I'm sorry," I said. "I'm sorry I'm sorry I'm sorry. I'll buy you dinner. I'll buy you a vacation. I'll buy you a car. I'll buy your mother a car."

"You better never let my mother know you ever took me anywhere near a place like that."

"Never. Ever. Not in a million years."

"Why is it," she turned her head to me without stopping her downfield momentum, "that guys who sell guns from under their beds have to be so disgusting, too? Why couldn't he be doing that from some other part of Queens, someplace with nice houses on pretty streets?"

"I'm sure they're doing it there, too," I said.

"Gee, that's reassuring. What I need now is a bath. In Clorox. You have plans for that gun you bought?"

"Why, you want to go back there and blow his head off with it?"

"His head," she said, "would be second. And after I was

through with him, there would be you to think about."

I grabbed her as she was about to charge across the street into traffic. "Calm down," I said. "Forget about useless, revolting lowlifes like him and me. Think about not getting your own, um, self flattened here."

"I can take care of my own, um, self, thank you," she said. "And you better not have thought a single word he said was even faintly amusing. Driver's seat." She snorted.

"I didn't. Honestly, I didn't. You know, your mother makes that noise."

"Leave my mother out of this. And just remember, I can read your mind."

"I remember."

"And if you even smiled, even once, just a little bit—"

"Not me. Not once."

"Yes, you did."

"Only when I thought you were really going to demolish him."

"I wanted to."

"I could tell. It clearly took tremendous strength of character to hold yourself back."

"Well," she said, straightening her jacket, smoothing her hair, "well, there you go, then."

I wasn't sure where we went but at that point I'd have agreed it was July and we were in Tahiti, if Lydia had said so.

thirteen

We found a coffee shop and Lydia had a cup of tea and everything came back to normal again.

Except, as Lydia said, returning from the bathroom after washing her hands—I wondered briefly if she'd managed to find any Clorox—"This is not good news."

My coffee had already come, and I was already drinking it, sitting in the booth staring down the length of the restaurant, thinking the same thing.

"Can I say, 'Maybe it's coincidence,' so one of us said it and we can get past it?" she asked.

"I'm already past it."

"We have to tell Detective Sullivan," Lydia said, and her voice was soft. I shifted my gaze to her.

"I know." I made no move toward the phone in my pocket.

"You'll be doing him a favor. Gary. Whatever trouble he'll be in for buying guns, he'll be in a lot more trouble if he uses them."

"I know."

"The cops can make a deal with Ray. They can use him to find Premador. Then maybe we can find Gary."

She said *we*, not *they*, but that was just to make it easier for me and I knew it. It wasn't the way it was going to work.

But I didn't think it was going to work at all.

I shook my head, drank my coffee.

"What?" she said.

"He can't find Premador. I don't know much about computers, but I know anonymity is the whole point in a setup like this."

"They have experts—"

"They have anyone better than Linus?"

That stopped her. She picked up her teacup, sipped at it, said nothing.

"But," I said, "I have an idea. I—" My cell phone rang before I could tell Lydia what I was thinking. "Goddamn," I said. "Goddamn, goddamn, goddamn."

"Are you going to answer it?"

I took it out and flipped it open, though right then I'd rather have flipped it across the room. "Smith."

"Jim Sullivan."

Hell, I thought. The mountain comes to Muhammad. "Sullivan," I said, so Lydia would know who it was. "You need something?"

"I need you to tell me what you did to get my chief's balls in an uproar."

"Your chief? I never even met him. Letourneau, is that his name?"

"He just pulled me from the field into his office. Forthwith, now, immediately. He wanted to know who the hell you were, what I knew about you, what you knew about the Wesley case."

None of this was surprising; what was, was a new note in Sullivan's voice. Not yesterday's wary friendliness, not last night's irritated dressing-down. It was a tone I hear sometimes in the voices of repeat clients, calling to offer a new job, a lousy one they know I'll take because I don't want to lose them. Or from sources, calling with information they're hoping will net them a few bucks. It's not something I hear often from cops.

I looked a question at Lydia, though she had no idea what I was asking.

"What'd you tell him?" I asked.

"What should I have told him?"

"Oh, Christ," I said. "Do we have to do it this way?" Sullivan said nothing, so we did it that way. "You know who I am. I'll fax you my goddamn resume if it'll help. I'm a PI, I'm Gary Russell's uncle, and I don't give a shit who killed Tory Wesley if it wasn't Gary." That wasn't quite true, but it was good enough for government work. "You know everything I know about that case, including the fact that you threw me off it, and you know everything I know about where to find Gary, which is zilch." After where Lydia and I had just been, that wasn't a hundred percent true, either. But I wanted to see where this was going, whether I was right about the tone behind Sullivan's words, and if I was, what the offer was.

"He knew all that already," Sullivan said. "Before he called me in."

"And?"

"The chief," he said conversationally, "grew up around here. I think I told you," he added, "that I didn't?"

"You didn't mention your early years."

"Oh. Well, I'm from Asbury Park. But the chief's from Warrenstown. In fact, he played varsity with Al Macpherson."

"Well, then maybe that's all it is. He's pissed off at me because his old buddy Macpherson slipped getting out of the car last night."

"I asked. Macpherson did call him, see if there was any way to back me off and simultaneously throw your ass in jail. Chief told me on the q.t. that he's inclined to like anyone who can knock some wind out of Macpherson's sails. But that doesn't seem to include you. He still wanted to know what the hell you were up to."

"I'm not up to a damn thing," I said. "I spent the morning in New York passing out pictures of my nephew to kids on the street."

"Any luck?"

"No, but the word's out."

"Word's also out the NYPD wants him, for us."

"Any luck?"

"So you have no idea what my chief's problem is?"

"No," I said, "I don't. Maybe he's just in a bad mood."

"Everyone is, around here," Sullivan said. I heard the ripping sound of a match being struck, the brief pause of a smoker drawing on a cigarette before speaking again. "About the warrants, and me pulling all those boys, especially Randy Macpherson, out of Hamlin's."

"You know," I said, wishing I were somewhere I could be smoking too, "I hadn't thought about it until just now, but I'll bet you're about the least popular guy in Warrenstown today."

"Department's getting screaming phone calls, not just from Macpherson," he agreed. "Got four at home last night before I unplugged the phone. Found two 'For Sale' signs on my lawn this morning. Last time that happened was Coach Ryder's lawn, five years ago, when the Warriors didn't make the play-offs."

"Sounds bad." And it did, to me; but I could swear I'd heard the small, distant smile in his voice.

"Yeah, well, market's soft, so I think I'll stay. But the chief told me to back off the boys, until I get something definite. I asked if he meant until after the Hamlin's game."

"You must have a good union contract."

"That I do. I hear Coach Ryder's trying to negotiate with Hamlin, get him to take back the boys I pulled out."

"Will he?"

"Don't know. Hamlin seems to be getting a kick out of this."

"Hamlin gets his kicks in strange ways. But this means the boys you arrested, you let them go?"

"I can't hold anyone without evidence."

"You could have scared up something."

"I can't hold anyone without evidence," he said again.

"On this case, according to your chief, you mean."

He didn't contradict me. "Chief also said, you come back to Warrenstown, I have to pick you up."

"You told me you were going to do that yesterday, on your own hook, before the chief ever heard of me."

"Now every cop in town's heard of you. Got your picture in the briefing room."

"I'm flattered."

"Wrong answer. And Smith, whatever you're doing that's pissing my chief off?"

"Yes?" I said.

"When you figure it out," Sullivan said, "let me know."

He hung up. I lowered the phone, wondered if by some miracle of the city council you actually could smoke at coffee shops in Queens. I looked around: No one else was, so I settled for finishing my coffee. It was cold.

"You didn't tell him," Lydia said.

"No."

"Why?"

"Withhold judgment," I said. "Until you hear."

"Working with you is often a matter of withholding judgment. I'm listening."

"His chief just chewed him out over who I am and what I know."

"And?"

"Usually, a guy's boss is teed off, it makes the guy teed off."

"I appreciate your delicate use of language. Sullivan isn't teed off?"

"He told me, when I figure out what I'm doing that got to the chief, let him know. Not stop doing it, just let him know."

"Hmm," she said. "This is a guy who threw you out of town yesterday."

"Just what I was thinking. He's also a guy who's been told to ease up, by that same boss."

"Really?"

I told her the whole thing.

" 'For Sale' signs?" she asked, when she'd heard it. "They're crazy out there. That whole town is nuts. But."

"But what?"

"But, I think you're saying that Sullivan's been told to back off, which he understands, but he's also been told that you're a menace, which he doesn't. And he's asking you to find out why. Am I right?"

I nodded.

"So you're not telling him about Sting Ray and the guns because of that?"

"I just wanted a minute to think about it."

"Have you thought?"

"What are you trying to say?"

"I'm *saying*, there are two boys out there who bought guns yesterday and said they were coming back for more."

"One boy. Premador was alone."

"Bill." Her voice was sharp, her black eyes hard as coal. "It doesn't have to be Sullivan. But we have to tell somebody."

We sat like that in the diner, looking into each other's eyes, for a long few moments. I slid out of the booth, dropped a five on the table, pushed out the door into the cold afternoon. I knew Lydia was right behind me; I didn't look at her as I shook a cigarette from the pack, cupped my hands to light it, or as, drawing deep on it, I pulled the phone from my pocket, thumbed the number at the Warrenstown PD.

A young cop on desk duty, a long wait, and then, "Sullivan."

"Smith."

"You're telling me you figured it out already?"

"No. I've got something big and I'm giving it to you for free."

"Nothing's free."

"That's true. Maybe I just don't know what I want, yet."

"Well," Sullivan said, "if it's big enough I'll make a note that I owe you. Unless it's something you should've already given me. Then I'll make a note to bust you."

"Just happened." I told him: Ray, Premador, the gun locker. I told him the meaning of Premador's name and I gave him Ray's description, his address. Then, at the end, when I couldn't cover for it anymore, I gave him the link. "I got to this Premador guy through Gary's e-mail. And there's someone who thinks she saw Gary a couple of blocks from there yesterday."

"Oh, shit," Sullivan said softly. "You're telling me we have a couple of kids think they're cartoon mutants or something, buying guns off some asshole in Queens?"

"I don't know. Ray only saw Premador. He asked if I was Premador's father, so he must be a kid. But he never saw Gary."

"But someone did."

"Thinks she did."

"Yeah. Shit. All right." Sullivan blew out a breath. "This is the kind of thing, has to go through channels. Christ, Smith, you shouldn't have bought that gun."

"What the hell was I supposed to do, tell him, 'Just browsing, thanks?' I'll turn it over."

A brief silence. "All right," Sullivan said again. "I'll call the NYPD, tell them I got a tip. Anonymous. I'll keep you out of it if I can. That'll be what you get, for giving this up."

"It may not be what I want."

"I know," he said. "But it's all I have."

"Gary?" I asked.

"I have to tell them. About Gary, and that other kid. You know that."

"Yeah," I said. "I guess I do. Sullivan, one more thing."

"What?"

"School's out in Warrenstown, until Monday. If no one's got their hands on this Premador kid by then—"

"Yeah," Sullivan said. "I'm ahead of you. But shit: Gary's new here. If he's talking to this Premador kid by e-mail, he doesn't have to be from here. He could be anywhere."

We hung up again, Sullivan and I, and I slipped the phone back in my pocket, looked out across the street, watched people go about their business, cars roll by, a dog sniff at a trash can.

"I'm sorry," a soft voice said, and of course it was Lydia, beside me.

I shook my head. "You were right."

"I'm still sorry." She took my hand, gave it a quick squeeze, let it go again. I nodded, looked away.

"I was thinking," she said.

I turned back to her, waited.

"There must be reporters in Warrenstown by now, covering the Wesley investigation."

"There probably are."

"You didn't tell Sullivan I was with you at Ray's. He has no idea I exist."

"You want to go to Warrenstown?"

"I'm young, I'm small, I'm a girl, I do 'Gee whiz' really well."

In spite of myself, that made me smile, and when I smiled she did, too. "You also," I said, "do evil kick-ass psychotic sidekick well. If Ray had a brain, he'd have been scared of you."

"I endeavor," she said, "to give satisfaction."

So we made a plan. I'd stay here, around the neighborhood, talk to the woman in the One to One van when it came, try to turn up someone else who'd seen Gary. I'd keep an eye on Ray's place, see if anyone came or went before the NYPD showed up. Lydia would rent a car and head out to Warrenstown.

"It'll be supper time by the time I get there," she said. "Maybe I can find kids hanging around the McDonald's or someplace."

"I can call Stacie Phillips, find out where the kids hang out," I said. "If I get her I'll call you. But I'm not going to tell her who you are. If you come across her, you can talk, girl reporter to girl reporter."

"I can't wait."

She took my hand again, and I leaned down, kissed her, and then, in the chill of the gray afternoon, let her go. I watched as she crossed the street, as she trotted up the subway steps. I stood there and smoked another cigarette until the train came and I knew she was gone. Then I took a picture of Gary from the envelope Lydia had left with me, and started to slog.

I worked the pictures for forty minutes or so, getting nowhere. The One to One van didn't come, and though I checked Ray's block half a dozen times, I saw no action. It's hard to get a warrant on an anonymous tip, though it can be done; whoever Sullivan had called in the NYPD was probably taking a little time to figure out how to do it in a way that would stick. That was okay with me, and I told myself it was okay because I wanted to be sure it would stick, too. Though if that were the whole truth, my heart wouldn't have pounded the way it did when I saw a tall, broad-shouldered kid walking down Ray's block, and the current wouldn't have flashed up my spine later when a different, dark-haired kid in a letter jacket turned the corner. Neither of them was Gary, and neither went into Ray's building. No one else that age came close, and I accomplished nothing. I kept at it, though, because sometimes going on, even when you're exhausted and winning is hopeless, is easier than quitting.

I walked up and down the blocks and I handed out the flyers and I thought about being fifteen. I called Stacie Phillips and got her voice mail. I talked to people and had another cup of coffee and smoked more cigarettes and was almost relieved when my cell phone rang.

"Smith."

"Please hold for Mr. Macpherson," a woman's voice told me. I stepped out of the flow of sidewalk traffic and held. After that extra half-minute so I'd be sure to know that, though he'd been the one to call, he had more important things to do with his time than talk to me, Al Macpherson came on the line.

"This Smith? I want to see you."

His voice was as it had been yesterday: loud, fast, a voice used to saying things once and being obeyed.

"Last night you wanted to drive over me," I pointed out.

"And you better believe I still do. Come up here. My office."

"You make it sound so inviting."

"Fuck you. I could have you arrested for last night. But first I want to talk."

First. "Do I have a choice?"

"You can do any damn thing you want. But it'll work out better for you if you come up here."

"Work out better how?"

"Two-forty-one Park. Macpherson Peters Ennis and Arkin, sixteenth floor. I'm here until six."

I checked my watch. Four-thirty; plenty of time if I wanted to do this.

"Yeah," I said. "All right. Half an hour, forty minutes."

"That the best you can do?"

"Well, yeah, but an important guy like you could probably do it faster. You want to come here? I'm in Queens."

"You don't know when to stop, do you? Half an hour, Smith? I don't like to wait."

He hung up without saying anything more.

I detoured along Sting Ray's block on the way to the subway, but nothing was happening: no young kids armed to the teeth, no NYPD cars racing up, no plainclothes detectives scoping the place out. I had the gun I'd bought from Ray stuck in the back of my jeans and the .38 I usually wear in a rig under my left arm. I had a sudden urge to take Ray's gun to the range and see if it actually worked, but I knew I wouldn't. At Sullivan's nod I'd turn the thing over to the NYPD, never fire it. I wondered about the gun Premador had bought, whether it would be fired, and where, and by whom.

I used the wait on the subway platform to call a lawyer friend and ask about Macpherson Peters Ennis and Arkin.

"Trusts and estates," he told me. "Divorces, if there's serious money involved. You about to shuffle off and leave someone a bundle?"

"No, I'm breaking up with my girlfriend. She's filthy rich and I'm looking for palimony."

"If that were true," he said dryly, "Macpherson would be your boy. He does the divorce work, a husband's man. Defends beleagured millionaires and their offshore assets against bloodsucking women and children."

"Good to know someone's willing to step up and do what has to be done."

"By all accounts, the man loves his job."

The subway rumbled through Queens and under the river, brought me back to Manhattan seven blocks up and two over from Macpherson's building. I took those blocks in long strides, moving in a rhythm, not slowing as I cut around other pedestrians, stepped off the curb, made lights or beat them. I stopped only once to wait for one to change, and cut in front of a slow-moving cab the second it finally did.

241 Park turned out to be a gray glass box on a corner, and Macpherson Peters Ennis and Arkin turned out to be a law firm big enough to take up three floors of it. The directory downstairs told me the senior partners, the ones with their names in the title, were on the sixteenth floor; I wondered, as I was shown to Al Macpherson's corner office, if they limited themselves to four senior partners because the building was square.

Macpherson's office was large, the leather furniture and hefty gold-lettered volumes lining the bookshelves meant to reassure clients that here was a man of weight and substance. You'd congratulate yourself, they said, for being smart enough to place your legal needs in his hands. This satisfying thought was echoed by the complicated maroon-and-blue Persian carpet sitting superiorly on the beige wall-to-wall; by the oil painting of a sailboat regatta, glowing under its own brass frame light; and by the breakfront bearing a dozen golf trophies, evidence that Macpherson played the game and played it well.

The paralegal leading the way had opened Macpherson's office door for me; the door was heavy, dark wood, silent on its hinges. Now he shut it again behind me, never saying a word. Macpherson stood as I came in, not out of polite-ness, but as a linebacker takes a stance waiting for the ball to snap, the play to start.

"Smith," he said. He looked pointedly at his watch; the trip had taken me nearly an hour.

"How's Randy?" I asked, stepping up to stand in front of his weighty desk, taking position. "He make it home last night, or did he spend the night in a cell?"

"You're an asshole," was Macpherson's response. He was shaved and groomed and his muscled, athletic frame was dressed in another expensive suit: navy this time, pale blue white-collared shirt, blue-and-yellow rep tie. He didn't look like a man who'd been in a fight last night and he especially didn't look like a man who'd lost. "You're a god-damn asshole and you don't know what trouble you're in."

"But you're about to tell me, right? If that's all this is about, write it down and fax it, Macpherson. I don't have time."

"Sit down. I want to ask you some questions. If you're smart, you'll stop fucking around and give me answers."

"We've already established I'm an asshole." I stayed standing. Macpherson did, too, looking me over, my jeans, my jacket, my boots. World-class players, his eyes said, didn't walk around in raggedy-ass uniforms.

"Why the hell didn't you tell me you're Scott Russell's brother-in-law?" he demanded.

"When did you ask?"

"Where's Scott's son?"

"If I knew that I'd be out of your life."

"You'll be out of my life soon anyway, Smith. What's he up to, the Russell kid?"

"Why do you care?"

He gave me another look and a slow, cold smile. He dropped himself abruptly into his big leather chair. It was maroon, I noticed, Warrenstown's color, though in leather they call that oxblood.

"That asshole Sullivan," he said to me. "Fifty thousand dollars to send those kids to Hamlin's. Randy didn't kill that girl and neither did anyone else on the football team."

"They were at that party."

"Says who?"

"Some kid'll break down. Some kid'll start saying who was there, and then it'll all come out."

"Bullshit. All that'll happen is Sullivan'll fuck with their heads and there goes the Hamlin's game, maybe even next season. Warrenstown's a great place, but Warrenstown cops have always been assholes."

"Yeah," I said. "I heard about that. Been true for over twenty years, I guess?"

Macpherson appeared motionless, gazed steadily at me; but I sensed all his muscles tightening under his skin, the way you know, sometimes, which way the guy with the ball is going to move, just by looking in his eyes.

"That," Macpherson pointed a finger at me, "is your biggest fucking mistake. Big. Warrenstown doesn't need that shit dug up again. And I—" He stood, planted his fists on his desk. "—I sure as hell don't need it dug up, either. You know that arrest ruined my college career?"

I looked at the laminated diploma hanging by the bookcase. "You went to Harvard."

"Harvard fucking Law. Rutgers undergrad, where I worked my fucking ass off to get into fucking Harvard. Because I was going to goddamn be somebody, Smith. Because I couldn't play football."

"Why not?"

He blew out a breath. "It's a big fucking deal in Warrenstown to get recruited, you know that? Suburban schools, Eastern schools, colleges write you off. They like big colored boys from Texas, or dumb-ass bohunks from steel towns. I was recruited, Smith. By a Division One school. Notre Dame. But they were the only ones. And tight-assed Catholic pricks, after I was arrested they kissed me off."

"I don't get it. You were released, never even charged. Another kid killed himself, for Christ's sake. Or am I wrong?"

"Jared Beltran. Stinking little shit. But the party, it was

all over the newspapers. Sex, drugs, rock and roll. Remember those days?"

"I remember."

"I was a middle linebacker. I never fooled myself, I knew where I stood: I would've started second string at Notre Dame. But that would've been enough for me, just to get the chance, just to show them what I could do."

A brief pause, and I almost thought I saw, behind this looming, arrogant bully of a man, the faint outline of a boy who wanted nothing so much as a chance to play.

"Not good enough, in other words, for them to keep the offer up after the bad publicity." The man's sneering words swept the boy's ghost away. "They had other candidates, they didn't need me. They thought I'd be a liability for the fucking alumni. These days, trust me, they wouldn't give a shit. They'd call it 'youthful indiscretion,' say I was a better human being and a better football player for it because I'd no doubt learned from my mistakes. No doubt. No fucking doubt. But that was then, and they didn't say that then."

"Couldn't you have played somewhere else?"

"Division Two? You're kidding me, right? I'm going to take that kind of punishment for a bunch of second-raters, no one comes to the games, team never makes the papers?"

"My mistake."

He leaned forward. "Randy plays his position as well as I played mine. Better. He's All-State, two years. I am not, *not*, going to let his career get fucked up the way mine did. And especially not over some Warrenstown High bitch."

"Did you know her?"

He took a breath, straightened up. "Tory Wesley? No, of course I didn't know her. She was a sophomore. Randy's a senior. His older brother graduated two years ago."

"Sons," I said. "No daughters."

"What I want to know is how you knew her."

"I didn't."

"I have to listen to this shit? That asshole Scott Russell shows up in Warrenstown after twenty years, his son disappears and his fucking brother-in-law who *happens* to be a private eye *happens* to find a girl's body a couple of days later and you tell me you didn't know the girl?"

There seemed to be a lot of assholes in Macpherson's life. "I didn't know the girl," I said.

"What were she and the Russell kid up to?"

"Were they up to something?"

"Smith," he said, "what exactly are you trying to do?"

"Find Gary Russell."

"I don't think so. Scott says if he catches you near his family he'll kick your teeth in."

"That's his problem."

"What's your interest in Tory Wesley?"

"None at all, if people would stop saying Gary killed her."

"Someone did."

"Someone at the party. Looks like Gary wasn't even there."

"Sure he was."

"Randy tell you that?"

"Scott says he didn't hire you. He says for all he cares you can rot in hell. Who hired you?"

"Gary."

That stopped him dead. For a moment, nothing. Then he walked around the desk and stood, feet planted, weight balanced, facing me. "What the hell does that mean?"

"Gary asked me to help him. I'm trying."

"Help him do what?"

"I don't know."

"You stupid son of a bitch." Macpherson's face filled slowly with color. Oxblood, I thought, but it would have been a bad time to laugh, so I didn't. Macpherson drilled me with a piercing stare, probably very effective in the courtroom. "This wise-ass shit is a bad idea, Smith." His voice took on a deadly quiet tone. "You're a stupid son of a bitch, and talking to me this way is a bad idea. It may work with the kind of people you usually run into, but I'm losing patience. I want to know what the hell you're up to."

I shrugged. "So do I."

A very long silence filled Macpherson's office. Through the window behind where Macpherson stood I couldn't see the avenue; we were up too high for that. All I saw were the two ranks of buildings facing each other across it, tall, sharp-edged, and, to the eye, completely still. There was no sign, on their hard and solid exteriors, of the unceasing movement inside them.

Macpherson finally spoke, still in the quiet, cold voice. I could imagine Randy dreading that voice, when he was small.

"Sullivan told you to stay out of Warrenstown," Macpherson said. "I'm telling you to stay out of Warrenstown's business. I filed assault charges against you in Plaindale last night. If you go back to Hamlin's, you'll get picked up. If you go back to Warrenstown, you'll get picked up."

"I heard about that."

"Cops in New York, on Long Island, in two fucking states are looking for fucking Gary Russell. They'll consider any involvement on your part to be interference and—"

"—I'll get picked up. If the questions are over and you're moving on to telling me what trouble I'm in, I think we're done."

"The question," he said, "is whether you're smart enough to quit before your ass gets caught in a meat grinder."

"If that's it," I said, "the answer is no, I don't think I am." I turned, crossed his office to the silent door, let myself out.

fourteen

Back on Park Avenue I stood on the corner, breathing in the cold air, watching the pedestrians weave freely around me, the traffic flow along its straitened path. The day had ended; the night was beginning. Lights in the Midtown buildings had been on all day, but now they were visible in the purple twilight. People hurried past me to the subways, the buses, to go home. I wondered if the cops had gotten to Queens; I wondered if Lydia had gotten to Warrenstown.

I stopped into a deli closing up for the day and bought a cup of coffee, headed downtown at a slow walk. No one was calling me and I had no reason to call anyone: I didn't know anything now I hadn't known before my visit to the wood-paneled offices of Macpherson Peters Ennis and Arkin. But I had some things to think about. A few questions, probably meaningless, probably just something to persuade myself I was doing something, hadn't been stopped after all today's work with no ground gained, a little lost.

Forty minutes later twilight was gone, night was complete, and I was almost home, when my phone rang. I took it out, answered it, and heard, "This is Stacie."

"Hey," I said. "How are you?"

"Terrible. Can you come here?"

Her voice was weak, her words unclear. "What's wrong?" I said. "Where are you?"

"Greenmeadow. It's the next town over from Warrenstown."

"What's going on?"

"I'm in the hospital."

Cars and people around me disappeared; there was nothing but the phone, and Stacie Phillips's voice. "What happened?"

"I'll tell you when you get here. Can you please come?"

She sounded like a little girl, and she sounded close to tears. "As fast as I can. But it'll be almost an hour."

"That's okay," she said, and though her voice was shaky she sounded like the Stacie Phillips I'd gotten used to hearing when she told me, "I think I'll be here."

I made the lot where I keep my car inside of five minutes. I sliced through the streets until I was back uptown, at the approach to the George Washington Bridge. By the time I reached the bridge, rush hour was almost over, but I hit the tail end of it and had to slow down. I didn't lose any time, not really, but I still had to work to keep myself from sitting on the horn, from cursing out the other drivers, from driving in a way that would either have gotten me where I wanted to go or gotten me killed. When I was finally off the bridge and moving I pulled out the phone and called Lydia. I got the voice mail, left a message, and heard from her about five minutes after that.

"Smith."

"It's me. What's wrong?"

"Stacie Phillips. She's in the hospital."

"What happened?"

"I don't know. I'm on the way. Can you meet me there?" I told her where.

"Yes."

After that I just drove, concentrating on the road, the other cars, their lights and their maneuvers. The miles of commercial strip, ugly in the bright sun of yesterday morning, seemed even uglier now, lit by their own sodium and neon and fluorescent glows. I turned off the strip road again as the hills came closer, black bulks tonight, the fall colors hidden in the darkness. Then I made a left onto a road I hadn't been on yesterday morning, the road to Greenmeadow, where the hospital was.

I thought I might be too late for visiting hours, and was ready to swear I was a doctor, a priest, or Stacie Phillips's long-lost uncle, but when I shoved through the revolving door I found visiting hours lasted until nine o'clock and Lydia was already there with a pass to room 577, Stacie's room.

"She called me," I said as Lydia and I rode the elevator, which was large and, it seemed to me, slow. "She asked me to come. I don't know what happened."

The doors opened on the fifth floor, we turned down the hall, and though when we found Stacie's room I still didn't know what had happened, I saw the result.

She was in the bed near the door; the other bed in the room was empty. As we entered she turned to us, her face so purple, so raw and swollen I almost didn't recognize her. Her eyes were black-ringed; one was shut completely. Her lip was split, a bandage on her head probably covered stitches on her scalp, and her right ear was taped and padded. All those earrings, I remembered.

"Hey," she said.

"Hey. Did I ever tell you how beautiful you are?"

"You know," she said, "my dad just left. You should go find him and talk about your old school days." Her voice was stronger than on the phone, and I felt my shoulders loosen.

"What happened?" I asked.

Stacie looked at Lydia, back at me.

"This is my partner," I said. "Lydia Chin."

"For real?" Stacie lifted her left hand to the hand Lydia extended. On her right a steel splint bound two fingers together.

"For real," Lydia said.

"You're a private eye, too?"

"Yes."

"Is it fun?"

"Right now I get the feeling it's better than being a reporter."

Stacie grinned weakly, the grin I felt I knew well, though I'd only seen it for the first time yesterday. A tooth was missing from it, but the grin was the same. "Being a reporter can suck," she said.

"Is that what this is about?" I asked. "Being a reporter?"

"I don't know," Stacie said.

"What happened?"

"I was mugged."

"Lots of people get mugged," I said. "Some of them aren't reporters."

From her one open eye Stacie shot me a look. "This was a guy in a goalie mask, like he was Jason or something."

"Jason?"

"Jason," Lydia filled me in. "From *Friday the Thirteenth*."

Stacie moved her one-eyed gaze to Lydia. "Maybe I should talk to you."

"No, go ahead and talk to Bill," Lydia said. "I'll do the simultaneous translation."

Lydia sat in the chair that, according to Stacie, Stacie's father had just vacated. I pulled one over for myself.

"Comfy?" Stacie asked when we were seated.

"Better than you, I bet," I said.

"They just gave me a shot of Demerol. It's really nice."

"You'll be asleep in a minute."

"So be quiet and listen to what happened, then."

I raised my eyebrows, said nothing.

Stacie went on, "So this guy jumped me in the school lot. The lot's almost deserted Camp Week anyway, there's almost never anyone around."

"Except geeks like you?"

"I thought you were going to be quiet." She turned to Lydia, told her, "And I'm not a geek. I'm an artsy type. He can't get it right."

"He has that problem sometimes," Lydia agreed. "What were you doing at school?"

"At the paper we can keep going through the break if we want. Researching stories or the graphics people can do layouts or whatever. It's extra credit."

"So lots of people would have known you were there?" I asked.

"Oh, a detective question. I guess so. We can work after two-thirty, any days we want. I'm the editor, so I come in every day. I guess people know that."

I said to Lydia, "She's the editor, you know."

"I can't believe," Stacie said, "that I'm in the hospital and you're picking on me."

"I got shot once working with him," Lydia said. "I was in the hospital for four days and he visited every day and picked on me."

Stacie's one open eye opened wider. "You got shot, for real?"

"He's a dangerous guy to know. I'll show you my scar later if you want."

"Cool."

"Can we get back to why you're here?" I asked.

"I'm here because this guy jumped me. He kept hitting me and kicking me." Stacie's voice started strong, but suddenly wobbled, at the end. I reached out, squeezed her hand. Surprisingly, she didn't let go. She said, "Don't you want to know why *you're* here?"

No wise guy retorts: I just nodded.

"He kept asking me, 'What do you have?' I didn't know what he meant. Then he switched to, 'What did Tory Wesley have?' "

"That's it?" I asked. " 'What did Tory Wesley have?' "

"I kept saying, 'I don't know, I don't know.' Then he cursed me out, and then he told me I'd better not tell anyone what he said, and I'd better drop it or he'd be back." She looked at me. "What did he mean? What do I have? What did Tory have?"

"I don't know," I said. "That was all he said?"

She nodded. "Over and over."

Lydia got up, took the plastic cup from Stacie's bedside,

filled it with water for her. Stacie released my hand so she could hold the cup.

"Could you identify him?" I asked. "Anything about him?"

She gave Lydia back the cup. "I don't think so." She seemed to sink into the pillows a little. "He kind of growled, like a really hard whisper, not talked, so I don't think I'd know his voice if I heard it again. He wasn't real big, but he wasn't real skinny or anything else you'd notice. Just sort of average."

"Just your average mugger."

"In a Jason mask," Lydia added.

"Did you tell the police? Sullivan?"

"I told them about the mask and stuff but not what he said. It wasn't Detective Sullivan. I would've told him, I think." She sounded not quite sure of that. "But it was Bobby Sánchez. He's not a detective, just a cop."

"Why didn't Sullivan come? Is he off duty?"

"No, he's someplace else."

Oh, right, I thought. In New York, with the NYPD, picking up a gun dealer in Queens.

"Besides," Stacie said, "from what it looked like, it was just, like, a mugging. They didn't think they needed a detective, I guess."

"But you think they're wrong."

"Of course I think they're wrong." She turned her battered face to me. "What does he want me to drop? What *do* I have? What did Tory have?"

"I don't know," I said. "But I'll find out. And if anyone ever comes near you again, I'll kill them."

She gave me the grin, weaker and more weary this time, but real. "Could you put that a different way? So I can keep, like, dating?"

"I can't believe," I said, "that you're in the hospital and you're picking on me."

I left first, waited in the hallway while Lydia showed Stacie her bullet scar. Lydia and I rode the elevator down and walked out in silence, stood in the hospital parking lot by my car.

"I can see why you like her so much," Lydia said. "She's great."

"I meant it," I said. "I'll kill him."

Lydia gave me a long look under the sodium lights. "It would be better," she said, "to figure out who he was and what he wanted."

"Shit," I said, and then, when I'd gotten a cigarette going, smoked half of it in silence, said, "I know that."

"When you called," Lydia said, after a moment, "I was talking to a girl I wanted you to talk to anyway."

"Someone in Warrenstown?"

"Yes. One of a crowd I found hanging out in the park. I guess you'd call them freaks. Dyed hair, pierced noses, those things. None of them had anything to say, but I gave them my card and about half an hour later this girl called me. Do you want to talk to her?"

"You think it'll help?"

"I don't know what will help," she said. "But I know this is what we do."

Lydia made a call from her cell phone. We got into our separate cars and navigated down the hill from Greenmeadow Hospital into the town.

We were meeting Lydia's contact on the playground at Greenmeadow Elementary School. I'd offered coffee, or dinner, but the girl told Lydia she wanted to make it somewhere less public. I would have been reluctant in any case to go back to Warrenstown until I had to; but it was she, not I, who had suggested meeting outside of Warrenstown.

I stopped to buy coffee, and tea for Lydia, and caught up with Lydia on the street in front of the school. I parked behind her and we walked to the playground that filled the lot between the school and a baseball field. A fence surrounded it but the gate was open. I dropped myself onto a picnic table bench, leaned back against the table. I stretched my legs, stared across the street at the neat little houses with their windows glowing an inviting yellow. Lydia sat on the table itself, arms around her knees, sipping her tea.

"Her name's Kate Minor," Lydia said. "She's a senior at Warrenstown High. She thinks I'm an investigative reporter for New York One."

"She's seen your business card," I said.

"I used the reporter ones," she said, lifting her eyebrows as though I should have known that.

"You had them with you?"

"I always do. You never know."

Never, I thought. You never know.

It was ten minutes before Lydia's contact showed up and we spent it in silence, sipping from cardboard cups, watching the evening. I wanted to tell Lydia where I'd been that afternoon after she left for Warrenstown, what I'd been thinking about on my slow walk downtown. But I couldn't, right now. Right now all I could do was drink coffee and smoke a cigarette and try to push away the images of Stacie's face, and Gary's, the echoes of their voices asking for help, the echoes of Macpherson's voice and Scott's and Hamlin's and Coach Ryder's telling me to go to hell, and my sister's small bewildered voice saying she didn't understand.

At one point Lydia reached a hand out, kneaded my shoulder. Even through the thickness of my leather jacket I thought I could feel her warmth. I don't know why she did that, but when she did the faces and the voices faded, and the fence and the streetlights and the night became, again, what was real.

Finally an Audi a few years old pulled around the corner, parked behind my car. The driver got out and headed through the playground fence. Lydia slipped down off the table, stood and waved. The figure walked slowly toward us, and now I could see it was a girl, large and heavy; as she neared us I saw the spiky black hair, the moon-pale face, the ring in her nostril and the one in her eyebrow. She came to stand before us, hands in the pockets of her army-surplus jacket. She scowled, and she shifted from foot to foot, looking as though at any second she might turn and leave.

"This is Bill Smith," Lydia said. "My partner. We're working this story together. Bill, this is Kate Minor."

I put out my hand and Kate Minor's scowl deepened. I didn't move and finally she offered her hand, withdrew it after a perfunctory shake.

"Sit down," I suggested, as though this were my office and I was trying to be hospitable. After a moment she did, straddling the bench, hands thrust deeply into her pockets. I sat on the end, where I had been, and Lydia perched on the table again, between us.

Lydia took out her small notebook. "I asked Kate and her friends," she said, "whether they could tell me anything about Tory Wesley, or the party, or the boy who disappeared. Gary Russell?" She said that as if to refresh my memory. "Or anything they think viewers would be interested in. Things people should know."

Kate Minor looked down at her feet, at the tufts of grass drained of color by the streetlights at the playground's edge. Looking back up, her eyes belligerent slits, she said, "I don't want anyone to know I'm doing this."

"Of course not," Lydia said. "Our sources are confidential, always."

"Because I could get in trouble."

"I understand."

Kate looked at me and I nodded.

"It's only—I mean, it's always been really shitty, but now they finally killed someone. I mean, they *killed* someone."

Her eyes wore heavy rings of coal-black makeup and her lips were painted a dark-outlined brown. She looked at me, and then at Lydia, and behind the toughness I thought I saw, in her eyes, a little girl asking us to say this all hadn't happened, no, everything's all right, you don't have to do this, go home. But we couldn't say that. Lydia asked instead, "Who did, Kate?"

"The jocks did," Kate said, her tone suspicious, as though if Lydia and I didn't know something that obvious, maybe there was no point in talking to us. "Those fucking jocks.

They own Warrenstown and we all live with that, but they can't just *kill* people."

"Tell us why you say they did."

"Killed Tory? Who else do you think was at that party?"

"Were you there?"

Kate Minor stared at Lydia. "I'm fat, I'm a freak. I get straight A's in honors calculus and computer science. Do I seem like someone who'd go to a jock party?"

A cold wind swept the playground, ruffling Lydia's hair, though it made no impact on the spikes Kate wore. Lydia's hand touched my shoulder again, and it was a good thing, because a hot wave of impatience had swept through me as though embers I'd been trying to ignore had been fanned into flame by the wind. This girl could tell us nothing: She thought it was news that the jocks in Warrenstown were capable of murder. She was here to persuade us with her hate, but it was all she had. I wanted to go. I wanted to move. This was useless.

Lydia, her hand still resting on my shoulder, said to Kate, "There must have been seventy-five kids at that party. If one of them killed Tory Wesley, do you know who?"

Kate Minor shook her head. "No," she said bitterly. "But I know why."

fifteen

Kate Minor kicked the dirt beneath her feet at the play-ground picnic table and told us what she thought.

"When they don't get what they want," she said, "it's totally fucked."

"The jocks?" Lydia asked.

Kate nodded. "It's, like, this famous tradition in Warrenstown. It goes back years."

"And it's still true?"

Kate didn't look at us. "Like, last year, this one senior, Cody Macklowe? He wanted me to do his algebra homework for him."

"When he was a senior and you were a junior?"

"Yeah, but I'm in honors and he was in, like, last math."

"Not his subject?" Lydia tried a smile, and I knew it was to tell Kate, relax, it's okay. But Kate didn't smile back.

"Whatever," she said. "He might have done okay in it, except half the time he never went to class or took notes or anything. He was a big football star."

"He didn't get in trouble for cutting classes?"

"He started both ways," Kate said, offering this as an obvious reason a kid wouldn't get in trouble for delinquent behavior. "We only had one other player that did that."

Lydia nodded, asked, "What happened? About the homework?" as if she had any idea what it meant to start both ways.

"I told him to shove it. He kept telling me to and I kept saying no." Kicking the dirt again: "So he beat up my dog."

"He beat up your dog?"

"Lucky, my dog. We got him when I was eight. He came home all bloody one day, he couldn't walk right. We thought he was hit by a car. The vet said he almost died. In the morning I found a note on my locker that said, 'Next time, I'll beat his fucking brains out.' It was stapled to Cody's homework assignment."

"What did you do?"

From inside her army jacket Kate took out a pack of American Spirits. I lit a match, held it for her. She seemed slightly surprised, like when I'd offered to shake hands. Exhaling, looking away, she said, "I did his homework for the rest of the semester."

"You didn't tell anybody?"

"If I told somebody," she said, "and Cody got in trouble and couldn't play, the whole fucking town would be pissed at me. And Lucky," she said, took another long drag on her cigarette, "Lucky would be dead."

The wind gusted, lifting thin veils of dirt from the baseball diamond, herding them across the outfield grass along with a few stray gum wrappers, a sheet of newspaper, a Styrofoam cup. Over in Warrenstown, the park was kept clean by jocks in trouble: You'd never find this kind of trash there.

Lydia spoke. "Kate? What did you mean, about Tory Wesley? The jocks wanted something from her and she said no?"

I had a pretty good idea what Kate meant and I guessed Lydia did, too: What a teenage boy wants from a teenage girl. But as it turned out, I was wrong.

Kate Minor shifted on the bench. "The jocks. They can't—couldn't—stand Tory. She's too smart, and she dresses wrong, and she has zits." Kate switched back and forth between the present tense and the past when she talked about Tory Wesley. I'd seen that before, when a death is too fresh, too new, not yet worked into the pattern of your life. "She was like, young. I mean, not really, but she acted like it. Kind of clueless. She didn't *get* it, you know?"

"Get what?"

"How things are. How they work. She doesn't—she wasn't *cool* at all. You know?"

"And that was a problem for the jocks?"

"Well, sure. They say what's cool and then if you're not that way, you're just, like, totally nobody. But Tory, she wanted them to like her so much she'd do anything. It was pathetic. Especially last year. They used to tell her to do stuff just so they could laugh at her, like carry their books to class, or get their lunches from the cafeteria line and stuff."

"And she'd do it?"

"Last year she did. At least they were paying attention. But this year she thought she found something better, that really would make them like her."

"What was that?"

Kate took a hand from her pocket, rubbed her mouth. Looking away from us, she said, "Dealing."

I hadn't said anything yet and I didn't now. After a moment Lydia asked, "Dealing drugs? Tory Wesley was dealing drugs?"

"I wouldn't tell you," Kate said insistently, as though we needed, all three of us, to understand that, "except . . ."

"I know," said Lydia. "It's okay."

Kate lifted her black-outlined eyes to the playground again. "It's not that hard to get drugs in Warrenstown. Everyone does grass and hash, I mean, it's no big deal. But trippy drugs, acid and things, it's a little harder. Jocks are into those because you can drop them after the Friday night game, party your ass off, and by Monday practice you're cool again." She glanced at Lydia. "What?"

"I guess I'm just a little surprised. That jocks would do drugs during the season."

"Are you serious? They party harder than anyone else.

They're used to it, they've all been juiced on andro and shit for years."

"Andro?"

"Steroids," Kate said impatiently. "To make them big."

"Where do they get them?"

"Andro, that one's legal. You get it at the health food store."

"Androstenedione," I said. "Mark McGwire was taking it."

Kate nodded. "And prescription ones, they get them from dealers. Jocks'll drop anything that'll get them high or make them big. You didn't notice them, how huge they are? They think it makes them hot." Her lip curled.

Lydia asked, "And Tory was dealing those drugs?"

"Not the steroids. The trippy ones."

"I'm sorry, but I have to ask this," Lydia said. "Is this something you know firsthand, or something you heard?"

Either Kate missed the implication, or she didn't care. "A guy I know. A friend of hers," she said. "He tried to make her stop. He said it was dangerous, the people you get mixed up with. But she was into it."

"And you think she got mixed up with people who were dangerous?"

Kate shook her head, snapped, "I'm not finished."

"I'm sorry."

Kate tossed her cigarette on the ground, mashed it with her toe. "She'd been dealing since school started. I don't even think she was making any real money, either, but anyway she had the jocks coming to her all the time."

"Do you know which jocks? Their names?"

"Not really."

I doubted if that was true, but we were talking about a place where it was dangerous to refuse to do someone else's homework.

"Anyway," Kate went on, hands back in her pockets, coat pulled around her hunched shoulders, "anyway, for that party? She went around telling everyone she'd have ecstasy." Kate darted an unsure glance at Lydia and one at me. "That's a club drug. You know, a designer drug? You know about it?"

"Yes," Lydia said. "I've heard of it."

Kate seemed relieved, maybe that she wasn't going to have to explain what happened when you took ecstasy. "It's hard to get around here," she said.

"Harder than acid?"

"You can only get it in New York. I mean, maybe Newark, but nobody goes to Newark."

"But people do go to New York."

"Not a lot. Tory never went. I don't know where she was getting it from. But she promised. Everyone was psyched."

"And did she?"

Kate kicked at a clump of grass, over and over. She finally uprooted it. "No," she said.

"How do you know?"

"Paul told me. He told her she'd better leave town and forget about the party. He said she'd be fucked if all the jocks came looking for ecstasy and she didn't have it. But she was so into that party. She so thought it would make her cool. She had acid and crystal meth and coke and she thought they wouldn't care."

"But you think they did?"

For the first time, Kate Minor looked directly at Lydia as she spoke. "Totally. It was what they wanted. They went over to Tory Wesley's and didn't get what they wanted. When the jocks don't get what they want, it's totally fucked."

Kate held Lydia's eyes for a few silent moments. The wind had stopped and no one moved. From a distance, the three of us could have been any group of friends, lingering at a picnic table on a playground, reluctant to end the evening, not ready to go our separate ways to the pleasant houses with their glowing yellow windows.

Or we could have been the last people left in a vast, hostile wasteland, each one afraid to go out into the night alone.

Kate suddenly stood. "I hope you can use this," she said.

"I hope you can fry them." She started to walk away, turned back. "But remember, anything you heard about anything in Warrenstown, you didn't hear it from me."

She turned, strode toward the fence. I stood. "Wait," I said.

She pivoted around, her black-rimmed eyes wide. "What? What do you want?"

"Who's Paul?"

"What?"

"Tory's friend, the guy who told her she should leave town. You said Paul. Paul Niebuhr?"

"I didn't say Paul. I didn't say anybody's name." Kate's words were rushed, as though speed would convince me they were true.

I stood silent.

"Me talking to you," Kate said, "that's, like, me. Because the jocks . . . it's too fucked. But anybody else, if I talk about them, I could get them in trouble. I didn't say anybody's name."

I nodded. "Okay. I guess it doesn't matter. Reporter's instinct, trying to nail everything down. Just a few more questions?"

Kate darted her eyes toward her car. "What?" she said. "What?"

"Gary Russell. Is he a part of any of this? Does he buy drugs, deal them, anything?"

"I don't know anything about him. He's a jock. He's new."

"Okay. Who's Premador?"

She blinked. "From CyberSpawn? That mutant?"

"Gary Russell gets e-mail from someone with that screen name. Do you know who that is?"

She looked down again, shook her head. A brainy, heavy girl at a school where the jocks ran wild, she'd probably spent a lot of her teenage years looking at the ground.

"Just one more thing, Kate. You said Warrenstown has a 'famous tradition' of jocks making trouble. Were you talking about what happened twenty-three years ago?"

"Yeah, and before that, and every day since."

"Can you tell me about that?"

"About what? What happened then?" She shrugged. "I don't know, some kid raped some girl and then killed himself."

"A jock?"

"No, some geeky kid."

"What did you mean then, about the jocks, if it wasn't a jock who did that?"

"Well, because the biggest deal about the whole thing was they arrested a Warriors player. Randy Macpherson's dad. He was co-captain. The whole town went crazy. When they came to arrest the other kid, the geeky one, they had to stop a couple of jocks from beating the shit out of him. And then they beat him up again after the cops let him go."

"I didn't know that."

"That kid," she said, "he's . . ."

"He's what?"

"Well, it's stupid. I mean, he raped a girl, and that's really bad. But, see, she was in the jock crowd."

"And?"

"And, well, some of the guys. . . . It's like he's Robin Hood or something. He raped one of the jocks' girls and then he got away."

"Got away? He killed himself."

A distant, sharp light shone in Kate Minor's eyes. "Got away *from them*. The cops let him go, but there was only one way to get away from the jocks and he knew it. And he had the guts to take it."

"There are other ways," I said, and though she didn't move, didn't speak, I was aware of a gate closing, iron bars slamming shut between Kate Minor and me.

"Okay," I said. "Thanks. You've been a help. Kate?" I said, as she turned away from me. She turned back, waited. "I hope the dog's okay."

She shrugged, nodded. As she spun around and ran to her car I thought I saw tears in her coal-circled eyes.

. . .

After Kate left nothing moved and nothing changed on the playground or anywhere I could see. The wind was gone; everywhere was tired silence, quiet and cold. I dropped back onto the picnic table bench, arms resting on my knees, stared at the ground as Kate Minor had. The clump of grass she'd uprooted lay in the dirt. By tomorrow it would wither and the wind would carry it away.

Lydia slipped off her perch on the table, came to stand in front of me. "Bill?"

After a moment I straightened, looked at her. Her eyes were soft. I stood. "Let's get out of here."

"Where are we going?" Lydia asked as we walked across the playground, out through the fence.

"I don't know." That struck me as funny. A famous Smith family tradition. In the years after we left Louisville, none of us had ever known how long we'd stay at any post or where we'd go next. When my sister left home, no one knew where she'd gone. I didn't know where Gary was, now. And finally here I was, not knowing where I was going, either.

But I had Lydia, walking beside me. "We're going to eat," she said.

I looked at her. "We are?"

"You bet we are. Fill the stomach, feed the brain."

"That's an ancient Chinese saying?"

She shook her head. "My mother. Making sure we were well-fueled before we did our homework."

We got into our separate cars and headed out of Greenmeadow, to the strip highway that would lead us, when we were ready, back to New York. About half a mile down that highway I spotted a steakhouse among the brightly lit, interchangeable concrete buildings. I pulled into the lot, Lydia following.

Inside, low lights, heavy wood trusses, rough board paneling, and a wagon wheel or two tried their damnedest to drive the neon, the six lanes of traffic, and the last hundred years from diners' minds. It didn't work, at least not on me; but the sizzling sound of meat on the grill and the aroma that floated from someone's sirloin going by on a waiter's tray were, on the other hand, pretty persuasive.

We were seated, we ordered drinks and nachos, we left the table to wash our hands. I was back first; just after I sat the drinks and nachos came. Lydia's drink was, as usual, club soda; mine was bourbon, though the ersatz nature of the decor extended to the bar and my only choice was Jack Daniel's.

Lydia came back, sat, sipped at her drink and said nothing, except to order dinner when the waiter asked. She waited until I was halfway through the Jack, until I'd downed a few nachos, until I'd shifted in my chair, lifted my glass again, and looked around the restaurant. A young couple in a booth beside us gazed into each other's eyes. At a round corner table, three little blond kids tried to behave as their parents cut their steaks for them.

"Better?" Lydia asked.

"You were right, again."

"I'm always right. You know that."

"I forget sometimes."

"Think how much easier your life would be if you remembered."

"My life would be much easier if I could think."

I took another sip, felt the liquor cut a warm track inside me. Lydia asked, "Speaking of thinking, do you think that's it?"

"Do I think what's what?"

"What Kate Minor said."

I looked at my drink, swirled it around in the glass. Jack Daniel's might not be a favorite of mine, but I had to admit it worked. "No," I said.

"You think she's wrong?"

"I don't know if she's wrong. She could be right. A bunch of kids who think they own the world go to a party expecting the high of their lives. Probably they're already high when they find out they're not getting it. One of them gets pissed off, goes a little crazy. It could happen."

"Then what was the *no* for?"

"It could happen, and maybe it did, but that's not all that's going on here."

"What else?"

"It doesn't explain Gary. Unless," I said quickly, before she could, "it was him. But it doesn't explain what happened to Stacie Phillips."

"And you think it's connected."

" 'What do you have?' " I quoted Stacie. " 'What did Tory Wesley have?' "

The waiter came with my steak and Lydia's chef's salad. The steak was on a pewter platter the size of Texas, maybe to make it feel at home; Lydia's salad came in a bowl you could toboggan home in if you were caught in a sudden snowstorm.

"So," Lydia said, "what *does* Stacie Phillips have? Tory Wesley's drugs, do you think?"

"That thought crossed my mind." I cut into the steak; it was tender and rare. "But why beat her up? Why not just buy from her, if she's dealing now?"

"Maybe she wouldn't sell. Maybe she's not telling us the whole story."

"Maybe. But then why call me?"

Lydia nodded as she folded a lettuce leaf onto her fork. "If it's not the drugs, what does she have?"

"Me."

She looked up from her bumper crop of romaine. "You?"

"She talked to me at the diner. It wasn't a secret. We've been on the phone half a dozen times since. She faxed me that stuff from the *Gazette*."

"Fascinating as you are to those of us who know you," Lydia asked, reaching onto my plate for an onion ring, "in this case, what would it be about you?"

"I don't know. If you ask me, all I'm doing is looking for Gary."

"So maybe someone wants to find him as much as you do."

"Maybe. But I'm also getting the feeling someone thinks I know something about something else. And they're afraid Stacie knows it. And that Tory Wesley knew it, too."

"If that's true, why hasn't anyone asked you?"

"Someone has."

I ate steak, told Lydia about my visit to Macpherson Peters Ennis and Arkin. "He was doing more than telling me I was in trouble," I said. "For one thing, he's not the type who'd have bothered to get me up to his office for that. He was fishing."

"For what?"

"I'm not sure. He wanted to know where Gary was, what he was up to. I thought, well, he's looking for someone to blame Tory Wesley's death on, take the pressure off his son and the other kids. But then he started asking what Gary and Tory were up to. He wanted to know how I knew Tory and he didn't believe me when I said I didn't."

"Why does he think you did?"

"He said he didn't buy the whole coincidence, me being Scott's brother-in-law, Gary running away, me being there when her body was found. The more interesting question is, Why does he care if I did?"

"Because he knows his son killed her, and he's trying to find out what you know?" She frowned. "No, that wouldn't explain anything, would it?"

"No, because if I knew her, and she and Gary were up to something, it would be before that happened."

"Which goes back to what he thinks you know."

"Try this on." I finished the last of the Jack. "According to Macpherson, as much of a loser as I am, my biggest sin was digging up the old rape, his arrest, that whole story."

"I can see why that wouldn't make him happy."

"Uh-huh. But how did he know I was doing it?"

"Hmm." She came back for another onion ring. "Someone at the *Gazette* told him Stacie had faxed that stuff to you?"

"Possible. Or Scott told him he'd seen the faxes at my place."

"Oh," she said. "You think so?"

I looked at her, took out my cell phone. "Keep your paws off my onion rings." I dialed the number at Greenmeadow Hospital.

Lydia said, "You won't finish them."

"Especially if you eat them all first. Hi, Stacie? It's Bill. Did I wake you up?"

"No. I don't think so," Stacie said. "This Demerol, you just sort of lie there. It's very cool." Her voice was a relaxed drawl.

"I'm going to ask you something. Don't be insulted."

"If you insult me, I will be." To someone else she said, "It's okay, it's a friend of mine. Yes, okay, Daddy." Back to me: "My dad says I can't talk long. You want to talk to him when we're done, about the old days at Corny U.?"

"Some other time, thanks. Now listen: Tory Wesley was dealing drugs. Did you know that?"

"No! Are—? How—?" She stopped.

"You can't ask questions because your dad's there, right?"

"Right! So just tell me!"

"No. Later," I said, when she started to protest. "Tomorrow. Now here's the insulting part. Do you have her drugs and are you dealing them now?"

"*What?* No, Daddy, it's okay."

"Don't get excited," I said, "it's bad for you."

"What made you *ask* that? Are you crazy?"

"Yes. One more question, before your dad cuts us off. Did anyone at the *Gazette* know you'd faxed me that stuff from the morgue?"

"You ask the weirdest questions. I think you're nuts."

"Did they?"

"I don't think so. The morgue's in the basement. I Xeroxed the file and faxed it myself."

"What happened to the Xeroxes?"

"I put them in my background notebook for the story."

"Anyone see that?"

"No, I always keep those very private so I don't get scooped. What's going on?"

"Okay, hang up before your dad gets mad."

"You're not going to tell me why?"

"Tomorrow."

"Oh, sure."

"Sorry."

"I hate you."

"You can't hate your sources, or if you do, you can't let them know."

"I'll work on the not letting you know part."

"I'll talk to you tomorrow. Get some sleep."

"How can I sleep—?" she started, but I hung up.

I put the phone away. Lydia had left me half a dozen onion rings. I ate them and finished my steak while I told her what Stacie had told me.

"That leaves Scott," she said.

"Uh-huh," I said. "Scott. Who Macpherson says is an asshole."

"One among thousands."

"Still."

I signaled the waiter, asked for coffee, tea, and the check. "Well," I said, "if what I'm supposed to know has to do with what happened back then, I think it's time we found out what happened back then." I took out my phone again, pressed in a number.

"I want you to remember who gave you your first cell phone," Lydia said.

"I remember everything you've ever done. Every move you ever made. Every time you winked at me or wiggled your hips."

"I don't wiggle my hips."

"But go ahead if you want to, I'll remember."

In my ear I heard, "Sullivan."

"Smith. I want to talk."

"Every time we talk, things get worse," he pointed out.

"Not my fault."

"So you say. Where are you?"

"At a restaurant," I fudged. "I'm finishing up. Where are you?"

"As it happens, I'm in Queens."

"You picked up Sting Ray?"

"Not me, the NYPD."

"He have anything to say?"

"Why don't I tell you," he suggested, "when we talk?"

sixteen

Sullivan assumed I was in the city and I didn't correct him.
I chose as a meeting place a bar I knew on the Upper West
Side, and as a time forty-five minutes from now. I told him
that was to make sure he had time to get there, traffic over
the bridge from Queens being what it was.

"I hope traffic over the bridge from New Jersey isn't
what it is," Lydia said as we walked through the steakhouse
lot. "It would be embarassing if you were late."

"I'll just tell him I had a hard time ditching this cute little
Chinese girl I was out with."

After some discussion, we'd decided Lydia wasn't coming along. She agreed, with a sigh, that it would be prudent
to keep Sullivan ignorant for the time being on the subject
of her, and she admitted it was curiosity, not a sense of the
requirements of professional practice, that made her impa-
tient with the demands of prudence.

"I'll call you as soon as I get home," I promised her. "I'll
tell all."

So we got in our cars and headed to New York, Lydia
to Chinatown and home, me to JL's, a sidestreet tavern in
the west Nineties.

Traffic on my bridge was light. On Sullivan's it must
have been heavy, because I got to JL's in time to order a

beer and work on it for about five minutes before Sullivan walked through the door.

JL's was the kind of place there used to be a lot of in New York, a bar with captain's chairs, heavy square tables, a pool table in the back. You could get a burger, fries, a BLT, and that was about it in the food department; you could watch the game, or talk about the game, or listen to other guys talk about the game. The guys you listened to would be your blue-collar neighbors, a dwindling species in this rising neighborhood. JL's was too shabby, too scruffy to attract the young, hip crowd, and JL and Mrs. JL, both of whom had spent every day in this bar for the last thirty-six years, worked hard to keep it that way. They sold no microbrewed beer, single-malt Scotch, or any vodka you'd ever heard of; they hadn't painted or, some said, changed a lightbulb in the place in decades, and neither of them had a pleasant word for anyone under the age of the bar, including their own grown sons.

The game tonight was college football, two Division Two teams playing under the lights someplace far away. The home team was setting up for a second and seven deep in enemy territory when Sullivan came in. He stopped right inside the door, let his eyes sweep the room methodically, the same way I do in a new place. He spotted me, threaded his way across the floor, and pulled out a chair. I had a cigarette going; Sullivan lit one, too. He was in uniform, navy jacket, starched white shirt, pressed navy pants, tie held in place with a Warrenstown PD tie clip. He wore no gun. Cop or not, he wouldn't be licensed in New York any more than I was in New Jersey. I wondered if he kept a weapon taped up under his dashboard, too, for times like this, but I decided not to ask.

Mrs. JL wove through the tables to take Sullivan's order. She was a big, wide-faced woman, her hair the same white-blond I'd seen on the three little kids at the New Jersey steakhouse, a color that in real life doesn't last past third grade. She smiled at Sullivan. Sullivan was my age, but even if he'd been a rookie, he'd have qualified for a smile.

The one exception to the age-of-the-bar rule was for cops: The JLs liked cops. If any of their sons had become cops, they might have gotten themselves a pleasant word every now and then. "What'll you have?" Mrs. JL inquired of Sullivan.

"Beer."

"Bud?"

"Draft?"

"Bottle."

"What else you have?"

"Rolling Rock, for gourmets."

"Bud."

"You want a glass?"

"No."

Mrs. JL smiled again; that was a trick question and he'd had the right answer. She went to get the beer, and I asked Sullivan, "This mean you're off duty?"

"Hours ago."

"Just hanging around New York because you like it here?"

"Change of pace. You seem to like New Jersey, same reason."

"I hate the place."

"Even Greenmeadow?"

I drank from my Bud, said, "Rotten town. You having me tailed?"

"Just lucky. Deputy whose wife had twins saw your car in the lot, visiting hours. He was out of his jurisdiction, though, and he had better things to do than look for you to run you off. He just reported it and went in to see his wife."

"Twins'll be a handful."

"Yeah," Sullivan said as Mrs. JL brought his bottle, put it down on a Michelob coaster left behind by some hard-working distributor's rep who'd for sure gone away empty-handed. "Mind telling me why you were there?"

"Not at all. It's why I called. But first I want to hear if Sting Ray had anything to say about Premador."

The small smile. "If I had anything to trade, Smith, you

better believe I wouldn't give it up first. But," he pulled on
his beer, "I've got nothing. Ray was up to his ass in hot
water and he would've given us his grandmother. But we
had no use for her, and he couldn't tell us anything about
Premador—or Gary Russell—that we didn't already know."

"Which is?"

"One of them bought guns from him for cash. The other
was seen in the vicinity, but not by Ray."

"You find the woman who saw him?"

"The charity lady." He nodded. "Positive ID on the picture."

"Anybody else?"

"Hot-dog vendor, one dog-walker. Both tentative. Willing to do a lineup when we take him up."

"Christ," I said, blocking out Sullivan's *when* in favor of
if. "I handed out pictures all day, got nothing."

"You should have been with an NYPD uniform. Works
wonders."

I ground my cigarette out. "Any description from Ray on
Premador?"

"Medium height, brown hair, teenage kid."

"Nothing else?"

"Well, a lot of assumptions on Ray's part, some about
the kid's mother."

"You show him pictures?"

"Of Gary, yeah. Otherwise, of who?"

I shrugged. "The Warrenstown yearbook?"

"You know," he said, setting his beer on the table, "that's
not a bad idea."

"Go ahead. It's yours for free."

"I'll take it as a down payment."

"On?"

"Why you were at Greenmeadow Hospital."

I told him, "A friend of mine is there."

"That would be?"

"A high school girl named Stacie Phillips."

He said, "The reporter? She okay?"

"Not right now, but it looks like she will be." I made a

mental note to be sure to tell Stacie how Sullivan had identified her. "Some guy jumped her and beat her up."

He drank, looked at me. "Why?" he asked.

I told him what I knew. When I was done, he said, "When'd she get to be a friend of yours?"

"Yesterday. She hunted me down, Sullivan, not the other way."

He nodded, and I had the feeling he was putting that aside, to come back to if he needed it.

"Let me tell you what else I think," I said.

"Can't wait."

He had to, though, because Mrs. JL, picking up empties from the next table, asked, "You boys want another?"

We did, and she brought them, and then I said, "I think this all has to do with what happened in Warrenstown twenty-three years ago."

Sullivan frowned. "The rape and suicide?"

"Al Macpherson called me this afternoon, ordered me up to his office."

"Must not've known you don't take orders well."

"I went. He wanted to know how I knew Tory Wesley, told me I was lying when I said I didn't. He told me to stop digging into the old case or he'd have my head."

"I know Macpherson, that's not the part he wants. You digging into the old case?"

"Just curious, at first. But it's the connection between me and Stacie: She faxed me old articles from the *Gazette*. My brother-in-law saw them at my place, blew up at me, and the next thing I know, Macpherson knows I have them and someone beats the crap out of Stacie. I think someone, and I think it's Macpherson, thinks that's what I was hired for."

"Hired by who?"

"The kids. Stacie, Gary, Tory Wesley."

"Why?"

"Because there's something hidden there, and they wanted what Stacie calls a scoop?"

"Is that what happened?"

"What?"

"Is that what you were hired for?"

The smoky room erupted with shouts as on the TV screen the visitors picked off a pass, ran the ball back nineteen yards. I stared at Sullivan. "You're kidding."

He tamped his cigarette methodically in the ashtray, didn't speak.

"Okay, you asked," I said. "The answer's no. All I'm doing is looking for Gary Russell."

He drank some beer, stared thoughtfully at the TV. "You're telling me your brother-in-law tipped off Al Macpherson to your interest, and Macpherson hired someone to lean on Stacie Phillips, find out what she knows?"

"And what the dead girl knew. And," I said, "I'm telling you my interest is what your chief is pissed off about."

He looked at me without speaking for a while. On the TV, because the ball had changed hands, the action was stopped while the teams sent in new squads. "Serious accusation, Smith."

"Well, I could be wrong."

He didn't answer.

"Listen," I said. "You know the details of the old case?"

He waited, finally said, "Just what I remember from being a kid on the other end of the state."

"Is there any chance," I asked, "the suicide was something else?"

"You mean," he said, "is there any chance Macpherson did what they said he did, then framed the other kid and killed him?"

"That's what I mean."

Again Sullivan was silent for a time, letting his gaze wander the bar, watching JL rack glasses, watching the game.

I said, "There's something else."

He brought his eyes back to me.

"I hear Tory Wesley was dealing drugs."

"You do? From who?"

"I hear."

"I never heard that, in Warrenstown."

"Just since school started, this year. Psychedelics. To the football team."

"You're not going to tell me where you got that?"

"No. But you may be able to use it for leverage when you talk to the kids."

"Yeah. After the Hamlin's game."

"That's two days away. Your chief can't really keep you off the case until then?"

"I'm not off the case. My orders are, I can do any damn thing I want as long as it doesn't involve subpoenas, warrants, or arrests. Unless I'm so sure I've fingered the killer I'm willing to bet my career on it. But no fishing."

"That means you can only talk to people willing to talk to you."

He nodded. "As my chief points out, we don't have the coroner's report yet. Tory Wesley could have died from natural causes. No killer, think of all the trouble I'm making for nothing."

"Think of it," I said. "Two days before the Hamlin's game."

Sullivan didn't answer.

"Well, this drug thing could mean something," I said. "I still think it goes back to the old case, but this could mean something."

Through cigarette haze, Sullivan peered at me. "A lot of things going on here, Smith."

"Meaning?"

"If my nephew'd disappeared the same time a girl was killed," Sullivan said, "then turned up with a gun dealer in Queens, I might try blowing smoke everywhere I could."

"If my boss backed me off a homicide when all I was doing was interviewing witnesses, I'd want to know what was going on."

He nodded, finished his beer. "What do you want?"

"The old police reports, to start with."

"Can't give you those."

I'd expected that. "Summaries?"

"Maybe."

Nothing was free. "What do you want?" I asked him.

"Whoever killed Tory Wesley."

I knew what that meant. Whoever; not, whoever unless it's Gary Russell.

"Smith?" Sullivan said. "You play high school football?"

"No."

"I did, for Asbury Park."

"Offense?"

"D."

"You don't look like you have the meat for it."

"I worked my ass off. And I could read the plays. I could see them coming."

Sullivan drove north from JL's, to the bridge and home to New Jersey. I drove south, through the night streets of New York. I thought of calling Lydia but she was probably home already, where her mother exasperated her, where her four older brothers dropped in unannounced and drove her crazy, but all from caring, from worry, from wanting to protect her. I saw her, sometimes, as a flowering plant—maybe the elegant, spare freesia whose scent I'd learned to recognize because Lydia wore it—reaching for the vast wild sky, angry at the soil for keeping her anchored. Rootless myself, I could only wonder what that must be like.

And wonder what she would say if I ever, ever let it slip that I thought of her that way.

I put my car in the lot, zipped my jacket as I headed up the street toward my place. I passed the door to Shorty's, but I didn't go in. JL's beer had taken the edge off my night, and Shorty wouldn't have forgotten I'd promised him an explanation I still wasn't ready to give.

As I put my key in the lock I heard a shout, my name. I spun around, ready, saw a car door open on the other side of the street, saw Scott Russell climb out.

I waited on the sidewalk; he said nothing until he was across the street, standing in front of me.

"Jesus fucking Christ, Smith!" he spat. His eyes burned

into mine, like the eyes of a wolf in a circling pack, waiting for the leader's command to rip the throat from the prey. The sense of that was so strong I found myself checking the street for the rest of them. No one; Scott was alone. He snarled, "What the hell is your problem?"

"A lot of people asking me that today," I said. "Your friend Al Macpherson, for one."

"I ought to fuck you up right here and now, then you'll have a problem."

"Macpherson tell you he talked to me?"

"He said you were a pain in the ass."

"He doesn't seem to think very much of you, either."

"Who the hell asked you?"

"I just wonder why you're going out of your way to protect him."

"Him? You think this is about Al?"

"What is it about?"

"Helen!"

"Helen?"

"Al said, if I don't want my wife's brother rotting in jail, I better get you off his ass. Me, I don't give a shit what happens to you, but I'm trying once more, Smith. Back the fuck off."

"I think it's true," I said, "that you don't give a shit. So why are you here?"

"For Helen. She doesn't like you any better than I do, but you're family and she doesn't like to think of her family in jail." He hit each of those words, *her family in jail,* like a hammer.

I wanted to step back because I didn't trust myself near him, but I didn't want him to see me move away. I forced myself still, said, "You ask her?" No answer. "I didn't think so. What's this really about, Scott?"

"I told you, leave it alone. I told you, I'll handle it."

"Who beat up Stacie Phillips?"

"Who the hell is that?"

I looked at him, broad shoulders, balanced stance, hot blue eyes. I said, "You know a friend of Gary's bought some guns illegally yesterday, and Gary was there?"

He missed a beat. "Fuck you," he said. "Fuck you, I do know. How the hell do *you* know?"

"What happened in Warrenstown when you were Gary's age, Scott?"

He took a step toward me. I didn't move. "You're the fucker who dropped the dime on them, aren't you? Like with that girl who died." I watched his arms tense, his fingers flex, ready.

I said, "Does Gary know how to shoot?"

"Of course, asshole. My father took me hunting, I take Gary. Fathers and sons, that's what they do." He stood very close to me now. Briefly, he smiled, sunlight glinting on ice. "But you don't know about that, do you?"

"Your guns—do you know where they are?"

"In a cabinet in the den. All locked up nice and safe."

"What are the ones they bought in Queens for?"

"Gary didn't buy any fucking guns in Queens. He wouldn't. He's a stand-up kid, Smith. Probably he wasn't even there, only now you've got the cops thinking he was. It was you, right?"

"What happened in Warrenstown, back then?"

"What happened is over. What's happening now is, my kid is wanted in two states and if some asshole cop sees him, he'll shoot him."

"Not unless Gary shoots first."

"Bullshit!"

Scott lunged, grabbed my jacket, slammed me against the wall.

Pain jarred my arm from elbow to fingers, I lost my breath, and I thought, Good, good, it's now. Blazing, I swung my arms to break his grip, kicked out and connected. He staggered back cursing, feinted left, threw a right I just barely blocked. He grabbed for me again. Only one hand caught and I could have come up under it, lost him that way, but instead I sliced down from above, on the wrist, heard him howl. He let go, clutched his hurt wrist to his chest. I stepped up, plowed my fist into his face, spun him around. I hooked my leg around his; he fell. I leaned over him, punched, punched again, pulled my fist back to go for his face another time but something stopped me, someone held me. Scott wasn't alone. I twisted, reached, pulled the new guy down. He was small, rolled with my pull, hit the ground and bounced to his feet again in one smooth motion. "Stop it!" he shouted, and my world spun, righted itself again, but looked all different now, because this was Lydia.

"Stop it!" Lydia said again. Everything did stop, sound and motion, breath and heart. Then things began again, and I climbed to my feet as Scott scrambled to his, both of us staring at her.

"What the fuck—" Scott began.

"Shut up." I closed on him, breathing hard. "Get the hell out of here. Don't come back. I don't care what you think of me or what your buddy Macpherson wants. I didn't ask you to come back into my life and the only one I give a shit about is Gary. The rest of you better just stay the hell out of my way."

Without waiting to see what he did I walked away, unlocked my door, took my stairs two at a time.

I could tell from the sound behind me that Lydia was taking them that way, too.

seventeen

We reached the top; without looking at Lydia I stood aside, let her in. Silence, and neither of us would break it. Finally, from me: "What the hell were you doing here?"

"Watching your back."

Now I turned to her. Our eyes locked. I forced my shoulders to uncoil, my breathing to even out. "What?" I said. "What does that mean?"

She breathed, too, spoke in a quiet voice. "I did some shopping on the way home. By the time I got downtown I thought you might be back, so I drove down the block to see if your lights were on. I was going to go home when I saw you weren't here, but I spotted that guy sitting in his car across the street. Just sitting. I drove around a little and came back. He was still sitting. So I stayed. That was Scott?"

"Yeah," I said. "That was Scott."

"Tell me about it," she said.

"Tell you what? You were there."

"No," she said. "Tell me what it is between you, why you hate each other so much."

"I never thought I hated him. I never had much to do with him. He's a short-tempered, self-righteous SOB."

"And if I asked him, what would he say about you? What is it he thinks you are?"

I didn't say anything at all, and the silence sank in again, spread itself between us. A truck rumbled by on the street below, but that was far away. I didn't know if Scott had left or not. "I don't want to talk about it," I said.

"In all the years I've known you, you've never talked about it," she said. "Now I need to know."

"Why? What the hell do you mean, you need to know?"

She walked through the room, ran water into the kettle, put it on the stove. I realized with a shock that I didn't want her to do that. I wanted her out, didn't want her staying, in my room, in my place; and this was the first time for that.

"In Chinatown, when I was a kid," she said, "a boiler blew up in the basement of a building. Three people were killed and the building was so damaged they had to tear it down. The super blamed himself for the rest of his life." She turned to look at me. "It had been acting strangely, steam leaks here and there, and he'd been repairing it now and then. But it turned out those were just small problems. He never saw the real one, and the pressure just kept building until it exploded."

I stared at her, then shrugged out of my jacket, dropped it on the couch. "That analogy lacks your usual subtlety." I drew a cigarette from the pack, threw the pack on the desk.

Lydia risked a smile. "Truth is a poor substitute for fiction."

"And what are you, the super?"

The smile faded away. "I just don't want to wonder for the rest of my life if there was something I could have done."

"You think I'm in danger of blowing up?"

She considered me. "I think you punched out that guy Barboni at Hamlin's yesterday when you didn't have to. I wasn't there when you fought with Al Macpherson, so I can't really say about that. But I'm watching you smoke more and drink more over the last two days than I've seen, and drive too fast, and I think you would have beaten your brother-in-law into pulp if I hadn't been here."

"You don't think he deserved it?"

"He probably did. That's not the point. The point is, it isn't like you."

"Isn't like me," I said. "Maybe it is. Maybe you don't know."

"I want to know."

The kettle started to whistle. Lydia opened my cabinet, took out a tin of her tea. She reached for a mug, rooted around in a drawer and found the strainer.

I guessed that meant she was staying.

I moved around the counter into the kitchen myself. Lydia stepped aside so I could reach into one of the cabinets for a glass. I dropped in some ice, poured Maker's Mark, went and sat on the couch. That lasted five seconds. I stood, crossed the room, stared out the big front window. Scott was gone, but that wasn't why I was there.

In the glass of the window I saw Lydia's reflection as she sat. Generally, she liked the big chair, but if she chose that now her back would be to me. Because mine was already to her, she sat where I usually did, on the couch, her face turned toward me. Steam rose from her tea. She held the mug in both hands, as though she were cold. I was cold. I sipped from my bourbon; it did nothing to warm me.

"Until I was nine, we lived in Louisville," I said. "With my father's folks. In the house where he was born." I drew on my cigarette; Lydia didn't speak, and her reflection didn't move. "I remember my grandfather as a big, strong man who taught me to fish, had just started taking me hunting when we left. My grandmother taught me to play the piano. Louisville was a great place for a kid and Helen and I were both pretty happy." I spoke quickly, trying to get past the images of the white house, the broad, shady porch, the black walnut tree waving its branches in the front yard.

"My grandfather had a temper," I said, "mostly directed at my father. We didn't feel it too much, the kids. He was careful about that. My father had one, too, but we didn't really feel that either, because my grandfather kept my father on a short leash. His house, he said, his rules. Too short: Something had to give, and eventually my father got fed up and took us away. He was an army quartermaster, working out of Cincinnati. He was some sort of efficiency expert and the army wanted to send him around the world to teach whatever it was he did to quartermasters on other bases."

I stopped, watched the traffic on the street below.

"What was it he did?" Lydia asked quietly.

"I don't know. It bored me and I never paid attention." A station wagon, looking lost in place and time, drifted unsurely down the block. "My mother hadn't wanted the foreign postings because she thought it would be hard on Helen and me, but he finally just said the hell with it, we're going." I had more to drink. "When we left, things started to get bad."

I waited for Lydia to ask what that meant, but she didn't. The wait got long. It occurred to me it wasn't Lydia I was waiting for. "It seemed he'd always hit my mother," I said. "Knocked her around. We didn't know that, Helen and I, but now we saw it. And now he started to hit us."

Lydia said, "Your grandfather had been stopping him?"

"I don't think it was from altruism. I think we were the prizes in a contest: Who will the kids like better? Kindly sweet grandpa or grumpy old dad? I think he beat my father when he was a kid."

"And now? . . ."

"And now dad was free to pound on us any time he wanted." I drank more bourbon, felt nothing. "I was big even as a kid and in the years we were away I grew fast; by the time I was twelve I was bigger than my mother. Helen was seven when we left and anyway she's small, like my mother was. It wasn't all the time; it wasn't even all that often. But when he came home all pissed off about something he'd start in on the first person he saw. It was better if it was me."

"You mean, he liked it better?"

"I mean, it was better for everyone."

My cigarette had burned down to the filter. I looked at it, crushed it in the ashtray.

"We finally came back to the U.S. when I was fifteen

because my mother couldn't take it anymore."

"Couldn't take the beatings?"

I shook my head. "Me. I kept getting in trouble wherever we went, worse and worse. I was arrested in the Philippines, in jail overnight even though I was an army brat, and in Amsterdam after that. I was a punk. I was uncontrollable."

"Because of your father?"

I shrugged. "My mother thought it would be better here. She told my father she was taking Helen and me and moving to New York, to Brooklyn, where she was from and where her brother lived."

"Your uncle Dave."

I nodded. "She said he could come or not but she was going. It was the only time, the only thing she ever did to stand up to him."

"She never tried to get him to stop hitting you?"

"She said if we behaved better, Helen and I, it wouldn't happen. She said he never hit anybody, including her, who hadn't set him off. She was always so helpless, so goddamn helpless."

Lydia waited; when I didn't go on she said, "You came to New York? . . ."

"We were here two months before he managed to resign his commission, but he stayed with the army as a civilian employee, a sort of consultant. He got himself posted out of Amsterdam to Fort Dix, close enough to Brooklyn to commute." I looked at Lydia in the window glass, insubstantial, a pale outline in the dark. "It was good, those months. I liked my new school and I got to know Dave. He'd been down to visit us in Louisville a few times but my father never liked him so he didn't come often, and of course I hadn't seen him since we left. You know I'm named after him?"

"I thought you must be; I mean, I knew that was your real first name. But you don't use it."

"That was the deal. My mother could name me after him, but they wouldn't use it. William was my grandfather's name. The one in Louisville, my father's father."

I looked into the dark again. Lydia prompted, "And after your father came?"

"Then it was just like before." I sipped at my bourbon. "The difference was, I had had a few months without him. And I was almost as big as he was by then. I started fighting back. I could never beat him, but I knew someday I would. I could feel it, coming closer."

I looked into the glass at Lydia, caught her eyes. They seemed liquid, as bottomless as the night, and I looked away.

"One night Helen stayed out way past curfew. She was as wild as I was by then; we'd both realized it was pointless to try to be good. My father wanted to know where she was and didn't believe I didn't know. He beat the shit out of me.

"It wasn't any different from any other time. But in the middle of the night I woke up and found Helen sitting by my bed. She asked what had happened and I said, nothing in particular. She asked, Was it about her? More and more those days it was, but I told her no. She said it wouldn't be, anymore. She said she promised. I didn't know what that meant, but I was tired and hurting and all I wanted to do was sleep."

I finished the bourbon. I crossed the room, got more ice and the bottle, all the time not looking at Lydia. She sipped her tea and didn't speak. It must be cold by now, her tea, I thought. I walked back to the window, talked to the night.

"I don't have very clear memories of the next few days. My father pulling me out of bed, pounding the hell out of me, screaming, 'Where is she? Where is she?' My mother in the doorway, crying. An ambulance, I remember the siren. Dave leaning over me. I woke up in the hospital. Helen had run away, left a note saying she couldn't take living there anymore. My father thought I knew about it, the way he always thought. He cracked my skull. He almost killed me."

I drank, went on. "I was there for weeks. He'd racked me up pretty bad, not just the fractured skull. Dave came every day. He told the hospital not to let my father up unless I wanted to see him. I didn't want to see him and I didn't want to see my mother, either. Dave tried to talk me out of that but I meant it, so she didn't come. They tried to find Helen, but she was gone."

My head hurt now, maybe from the fight with Scott, though I couldn't remember him connecting.

"One day, sometime in that first week, I overheard a doctor who'd just examined me saying to a nurse that if I'd been some bum on the street and not the guy's son my father would be in jail by now. I thought about that all day, and when Dave came I asked him if it was true. He said, if the bum swore out a complaint there'd have been an investigation, and if they could prove who did it, the guy who was guilty would go to jail, yes. He was very careful, talking about it. I asked if I could swear out a complaint.

"In the end that's what happened. It was a little more complicated, because I was underage, and in those days this kind of thing was swept under the rug as much as possible. But I wouldn't give it up and eventually they arrested my father and charged him with assault.

"See, I was thinking that if my father went to jail, maybe Helen would come home.

"And maybe then it could be like it was those first few months in Brooklyn, when he wasn't there."

I finished the bourbon, wondering when this stuff had stopped working for me. I stood at the window, silent so long that Lydia must have wondered if I was going to go on. But she said nothing, legs folded under her, empty mug on the table now.

"It backfired," I said. "They held off the trial until I could testify. Dave had spent a lot of time talking it out with me, making sure I wanted to do this, and when he was sure, he and his cop buddies rounded up witnesses, my teachers and coaches and other kids at school, the paramedics who'd been on the ambulance, the doctors. Helen's teachers, too, from times I hadn't been home or hadn't been what my father wanted.

"It could have gone either way, especially if my father had seemed sorry, had said he was crazy with worry over Helen, something like that. He didn't. He wouldn't let his lawyer do any of that; he just told the court I was an arrogant son of a bitch, a delinquent and I'd always been one. He asked just what the hell he was supposed to do, a father with a son like me?

"The prosecutor put his witnesses on the stand, one by one, and last he called me. I didn't look at my father. Or at my mother. She sat behind him and held his hand. I told my story, answered the DA's questions and my father's lawyer's questions. I didn't remember afterwards anything anyone had asked me. Dave told me I'd done well."

I put the glass and the bottle down, shoved my hands into my pockets. "He got three years."

I don't know how long the silence was then, but finally Lydia spoke. "What do you mean then," she asked softly, "that it backfired?"

"Helen," I said. "Helen never came home. She knew what was happening. She was keeping in touch with some of her friends and they told her. One night, near the end of the trial, she called me. I was living at Dave's by then; I moved in with him right out of the hospital. Helen said I had to stop, I couldn't send my own father to jail. I told her he'd almost killed me and if he'd found her that night he might have killed her. She said still, it wasn't right. I said I had to do it and I wanted her to come home. She hung up. She was crying."

I stopped, watched the darkness outside. Cars drove down the street, someone walked up the block. They meant nothing to me. That was it. That was as far as I could go. I thought, good, now Lydia knows, now she knows it all. Now she'll leave, get the hell out of here, leave me the hell alone. I stood where I was and waited for that.

That wasn't what happened. What happened was she got up off the couch and came and stood beside me, just stood there, two ghost people looking into the night. A couple of guys full of beer and laughter came out of the door below,

Shorty's door, and headed for the subway. A steel gate rumbled closed over a storefront somewhere around the block, somewhere we couldn't see.

We stood there for a long time. It wasn't that I felt rooted, it wasn't that I couldn't move, it was that there was no place I wanted to go and nothing I could think of to do. People and cars appeared and disappeared in the limits of my window as though we were seeing the backstage comings and goings in a theater while the play, the action that made sense, went on somewhere else.

"It wasn't fair," Lydia said softly, after a while. Her voice was like music from far away.

"What wasn't?"

"For you to have to make that choice at that age. It wasn't fair."

I turned from the window, walked through the room, dropped heavily onto the couch. I reached for my cigarettes. If she'd said, you did what you had to do, if she'd said, I'd have done the same, what you did was right, then she'd have been just like everyone else. Then I could have told her, yeah, well, thanks, I appreciate it, now I'd like to be alone for a while, I'll call you in the morning. If she'd offered a reassuring hug, a supportive squeeze of the hand, I'd have known I'd been right all these years, not to tell her.

She said nothing else and she didn't come near me. She went into the kitchen, put on more water. I looked up, surprised, when I heard the coffee grinder. She found the press, did the whole thing, brought me a mug of coffee and more tea for herself. I was on the couch now, so she sat in the chair she liked.

"Gary's fifteen," she said. "He's in a tough spot and he needs help."

Steam rose from her tea, from my coffee as we held them. I had the sudden insane idea that our images, thin and inconstant as the steam, still stood in the window, in the night, looking in.

"He's fucking up," I said. "He needs someone to find him and stop him."

Lydia nodded. "All right," she said. "Then we will."

eighteen

Not much more was said in my apartment that night. Lydia left soon after. I wandered around for a while, cleaned up, went through the mail. The place was still cold; I'd have to get that window fixed soon. I thought about music, but I couldn't come up with anything I really wanted to hear, and practicing, after all I'd had to drink, was out of the question. For all the effects I could feel of the bourbon and the beer I might as well have been pouring it down a hole, but I knew it would be in my fingers just the same, making them even more slow and stupid than usual, and I wasn't ready to face that. Finally I went to bed. The bourbon kept me from dreaming, and that was good; the coffee didn't keep me awake, but it also didn't do anything to stop the hangover that rocked me when I got up in the morning.

Head pounding, I downed three aspirin, showered, made strong coffee in the press Lydia had used the night before. Partway through my second cup the phone on the desk began to ring, making me wonder what the hell the point of coffee was if a damn little bell ten feet away could still feel like jagged glass between my eyes.

"Smith," I said, half hoping it was a telemarketer so I could curse a blue streak and slam the thing down the way it deserved.

"Sullivan. You okay? You sound lousy."

I grunted. "Hung over. You?"

"Bright-eyed and bushy-tailed out here in the clean country air. City living's unhealthy, Smith."

"Living in general. What can I do for you?"

"Me, for you."

"Even better."

"The old case. I pulled the files. Some interesting things. But about the suicide being anything else? Forget it. Kid shot himself in front of witnesses. In the park."

"In the center of town?"

"Right. Four people saw him, more heard the shot. He yelled so they'd turn and look, then pulled the trigger."

"Jesus."

"Left a note."

"Contents?"

"Classified."

"Damn."

I heard the small smile as he said, "Paraphrase: I know you're coming to get me. You'll be sorry. You bastards can all go to hell."

"Hmmm. It doesn't say, 'I raped that girl'?"

"He shot himself."

"Okay. Assuming you didn't mean the note, what did you mean, interesting things?"

"Two things. Macpherson had a half-assed alibi, a kid who tried to say he'd seen him at the party late, hours after the girl left. He dropped that after a dozen other kids confirmed Macpherson'd left right after she did. Said he was just trying to help out his buddy. Shit, Smith, that was my chief."

"Letourneau?"

"I told you they played varsity together."

"Yeah," I said, "okay, don't bite me. You also told me Letourneau isn't particularly fond of Macpherson."

"Now."

"All right."

"Explains why he wouldn't want it dug up, though. Whether Macpherson did it or not, the chief was lying for him. Not something you'd want everyone in town to know."

"It would tend to undermine his credibility," I agreed.

"Also," Sullivan said, "I can see why he wants me to take it easy on the boys. Probably wishes someone'd taken it easy on him."

"Yeah, well, be careful what you wish for. What's the other interesting thing?"

"They also thought they had a witness. Another kid. Said at first he thought he'd seen the girl and Macpherson arguing on the street right after she left the party. He was never sure. In the end he said it probably wasn't them."

"What about it?"

"Scott Russell. Your brother-in-law."

I took the phone to the stove, poured more coffee. "Oh," I said.

"Oh," he echoed.

I drank, walked to the desk for my cigarettes. "The alibi," I said. "Jared Beltran—that was the suicide, right?—he had an alibi. A friend who was supposedly with him. Who was that?"

"Kid named Nick Dalton. Nicky the Nerd, they used to call him."

"He around?"

"I don't know where he is now. I can look."

I thought of Luigi Vélez, thought, So can I.

"The girl." I shouldered the phone, lit a cigarette. "Who was the girl?"

"She was underage. Rape victim."

"Twenty-three years ago."

"Yeah," he said. "I can't give you her name."

"Sullivan—"

"Can't. What's the difference? If the suicide was suicide, there goes your theory."

"I don't know where it goes. I just know Macpherson's pissed off, Letourneau is pissed off, my brother-in-law's pissed off. And someone beat up Stacie Phillips over what she and Tory Wesley both knew, only Stacie doesn't know anything and Tory Wesley's dead."

"Macpherson and Letourneau might just not want the

past brought up, bad memories and bad press for both of them. And from what I hear about your brother-in-law, he spends a lot of time pissed off." In a more conciliatory tone he said, "I'll go over and see Stacie Phillips later this morning."

"All right," I said, reminding myself that even the small amount he'd given me was crossing a line Sullivan didn't like to cross. "Thanks."

"Stay out of trouble," he said. "And," he added, "stay out of Warrenstown."

I drank coffee, smoked and thought. I called Stacie Phillips at the hospital.

"Hello?" Her voice sounded stronger.

"It's Bill Smith. How are you?"

"Now I'm starting to see how much this hurts. I'm really mad."

"That's good. It'll help you heal faster."

"I thought you didn't like sarcasm."

"I'm completely serious."

"Did you figure out what's going on yet?"

"No, but I'm working on it."

"Great. Well, take your time."

"Maybe I just don't like sarcasm in *you*. Listen, did your folks grow up in Warrenstown?"

"Not my mom," she said, sounding a little surprised at the question. "My dad did. Before he went to Corny U. with you."

"I'd like to talk to him."

"Well, he happens to be right here. They think they're going to let me go home today. They just kept me overnight to see if I had a concussion."

"Reporters never get concussions, their skulls are too thick. Can I talk to him for a minute?"

"My dad? You have to tell me why."

"About the old days at Corny U."

"No way."

"It's complicated."

"I'm the one holding the phone."

"That's extortion."

"And your point? . . ."

"When you get your Pulitzer," I said, "I want you to mention me."

"In what context?"

"As the guy you practiced on. Okay, look: I think what happened to you, and some of the other things that are going on, has to do with that stuff you faxed me about what happened in Warrenstown in prehistoric times. I want to ask your dad about it, see what he remembers."

"You do? Like what?"

"Uh-uh. Pass the phone."

"I—"

"Uh-uh."

"We'll talk," she said. Then, "Dad?" in muffled tones, "this is Bill Smith. The private investigator? He wants to talk to you."

A different voice, a man's: "Hello?"

"Mr. Phillips, Bill Smith. I'm a friend of Stacie's."

"She told me about you." He sounded suspicious. Well, I thought, why wouldn't he be?

"I know you're worried about Stacie," I said. "I'm trying to get to the bottom of what happened to her."

"The police are working on it."

"I know. Detective Sullivan will be there a little later, to talk to her."

"You're working with Jim Sullivan?"

He seemed to let up a fraction when he asked that, so I said, "We're sharing information. We have different theories."

"Well," he said, "what did you want me for?"

"You grew up in Warrenstown?"

"That's right."

"Did you play football?"

"Football? Yes."

"What position?"

"Defensive end. Why?"

"Just wondering. This is my real question: Were you

there when the rape and suicide happened, twenty-three years ago?"

He paused, then answered. "I was a sophomore in college by then."

"But you knew about it?"

"Everyone knew about it."

"Do you remember the name of the girl?"

"The girl? Bethany Victor. Beth."

How easy it was, I thought, to get information from people who didn't know they were supposed to classify their memories.

"You knew her?"

"By sight only. She was a freshman when I was a senior."

"Do you know where she is now?"

"Now? I don't have the faintest idea."

"She doesn't still live in Warrenstown?"

"No. What does this have to do with Stacie?"

"I don't know, Mr. Phillips. But my theory is that it does."

"Does Jim Sullivan think so?"

"He's not as sure as I am."

I waited while he was silent. Finally he said, "All right. Is there anything else you wanted to know?"

"How about a kid called Nick Dalton?"

"Nicky the Nerd? Jesus, where'd you dig him up from?"

"He tried to alibi the kid who killed himself."

"Jared. That's right, I remember. Boy, they were a pair."

"A pair of what?"

"Creeps, I thought then. Now I'm a father, I look at kids differently."

"What would you say now?"

He took a minute. "Jared and Nicky, they weren't jocks. That's what it took to be somebody in Warrenstown then."

"Now, too, from what I hear. Tell me about them."

"They were, I guess you'd call them late bloomers. Skinny, small, couldn't dance. Still thought girls were icky. You know the type."

"I hear Warrenstown jocks are hard on that type, these days."

"I suppose we were, too, I'm sorry to say. Aren't all kids hard on kids who're different? What did you want to know about Nicky?"

"Do you know where I could find him now?"

"Nicky? Not a chance. I heard he joined the army instead of going to college, but that was so ridiculous I figured it must be a joke."

"Ridiculous why?"

"We didn't call him Nicky the Nerd for nothing."

I asked Stacie's father not to tell anyone aside from Sullivan, if he asked, what I'd wanted to know, and then I spoke to Stacie again, told her the same thing.

"You find Gary yet?" she asked.

"If I had, you think I'd still be on this case?"

"You mean you wouldn't be trying to figure out what happened to me?"

"You? You're a reporter. Lower than the dust."

"Just wait until I'm on the *Times* and you call up wanting something."

"Stacie," I said, "you know I'll never rest until I have the guy who attacked you on his face in the mud, trussed up like a hog."

"When you do," she said, "call me before you do anything else. So I can send a photographer from the *Gazette*."

I called Vélez. "Oh, shit," he groaned when he heard it was me.

"Come on, Luigi, you know you don't mean that."

"Why not? Don't you got something else you need done yesterday?"

"Yes."

"Like I said: Oh, shit."

"Two kids who were teenagers in Warrenstown twenty-three years ago. I need to know where they are now."

"*Ay, Dios mio.* I'm working here, man."

"Put it aside. This is more important."

"You wouldn't say that if you was my other client."

"I sure as hell wouldn't. Bethany Victor and Nick Dalton."

"You know anything about these people besides their names?"

"Not much."

He sighed. "Give me what you got."

I did: their names again, the crime, the year it happened. "A guy I talked to said he'd heard Nick Dalton joined the army out of high school," I said. "But he thought it probably wasn't true."

"Why not?"

"Because," I said, "Dalton was skinny like you."

It took Vélez an hour and forty-five minutes to get back to me. I spent that time at the piano. Sometimes, when I'm working a case, stuck on something, practicing helps. The work on a piece keeps everything else away, keeps me from running all my questions around and around on worn tracks, digging ruts so deep I can't see over them. When I'm done and I step back into the solid world, out of a world where nothing lasts long, where everything starts to vanish the second it's born and memory is never complete, I sometimes find even hard facts that haven't changed look startlingly, jarringly different.

There was no way I could play anything right now, not a piece of real music, not something that required focus, concentration, understanding. But I could do technical work, practice scales, finger positioning, go for speed or fluid movement or variations in tone. I did that waiting for Vélez and when he called I jumped, annoyed at first the way I always am when something interrupts my practicing. For a second I was angry with myself for leaving the phone turned on, and then I remembered why I had.

"Smith."

"Yeah, yeah. I'm gonna give you what I got now, because you're in a hurry. You want more, I can keep going," Vélez said.

"Thanks, Luigi. Shoot."

"The girl, she was easy. Married and divorced three

times, lives up in Mountain Glen now, name of Beth Adams."

"Adams is her third husband's name?"

"Second. I guess she liked him best."

"Where's Mountain Glen?"

"Small town in the mountains. Near the border."

To Vélez, the only border that counted was New York's; every place else might as well be labeled, HERE THERE BE TYGERS.

"In New Jersey?"

"I didn't say that?"

"No, but I guessed. Address? Phone?"

He gave them to me.

"And the guy?" I asked. "Nick Dalton?"

"Different thing, *chico*. This guy, he's gone."

"What do you mean? He's dead?"

"Dead, you got a death certificate, maybe insurance, something."

"Not if someone stuffs him in the landfill."

"Yeah, but you get whacked, you got loose ends. You don't make your car payments, they repo your car. Evict you from your place if you don't pay your rent, shit like that. That shit, I can find it."

"And I guess you didn't?"

"This Dalton guy, he got no loose ends. No car, no rent. Check it out: Guy has three bank accounts, closes them all, cancels his credit cards, same day. Day after he got out of the army."

"He did join up?"

"Like you said. Served three years, honorable discharge. Then he disappears. Discharge papers got no address on them. Passport and social security number never used again."

"Could he be in prison?"

"They send you away, you keep your social security number."

"What the hell does this mean, Luigi?"

"It means, *chico*," he said patiently, "this Nick Dalton guy, he wanted to be somebody else."

I told him to keep looking, get back to me with whatever he found.

Then I called Lydia.

"Hey," I said.

"Hey."

"I have a hangover."

"I didn't ask."

"You were about to."

"I wasn't, but thanks for filling me in."

"Got a minute?"

"Sure."

"I talked to Sullivan this morning. About the old case." I told Lydia what Sullivan had said, and what he hadn't. I told her about Stacie Phillips's father, and my conversation with Vélez.

"Wow," she said. "All I've done so far today is the laundry."

"That may prove more productive, in the end."

"What are you going to do?"

"I think I'm going to drive out to Mountain Glen."

"You want me to come?"

I stopped to light a cigarette. "You think there's any more you can learn in Warrenstown?"

"Like what?"

"Tory Wesley was dealing drugs," I said, "and Gary used to date her."

"You want to know if he was dealing drugs, too?"

"Or the other way: Maybe he stopped seeing her because she was dealing. He started out being friends with that kid Paul Niebuhr, too, and dropped him after school started. Be interesting to know why."

"Well, I probably could dig up some more if I went back to Warrenstown."

"Then I'd rather you did. And something else: Do you think you could go see the Wesleys?"

"Tory's parents? They're back?"

"Yesterday morning, on the redeye, according to Sullivan."

"God," she said. "I hate those interviews."

"I know. You want me to do it?"

"No, because I also hate the kind of interviews where you're on one side of the bars and I'm on the other."

"Come on, now. That hardly ever happens."

"Well, I get the feeling if you go back to Warrenstown right now, it's a real possibility. No, I'll go."

"Thanks. But I want to bounce a question off you first."

"Go on."

"What was my brother-in-law up to?"

"Scott?"

Her voice had taken on a strange tone and I added quickly, "Not last night. Back then."

"Oh," she said, shifting gears. "You mean, saying he thought he'd seen Al Macpherson arguing with the girl, then changing his story?"

"Was he trying to set Macpherson up? And then he chickened out?"

"And if so, why?"

"Why try, or why chicken out?"

"Both. And I have a question, too," she said.

"Okay."

"Stacie Phillips's father, according to you, said Jared and his friend Nicky were late bloomers. I think the phrase you used was, 'thought girls were icky.' "

"What about it?"

"Teenage boys who think girls are icky don't usually stalk them. Or rape them," Lydia said.

We talked awhile longer, set up our plans for the day. Neither of us said anything about what I'd told her last night and I hung up feeling as though I'd been holding my breath without knowing it.

I walked down to the lot, picked up the car. It was another bright day, yesterday's heavy clouds forced away by the wind. I went out the tunnel again, drove without music, without much focused thought on anything beyond the cars around me and the turns I needed to take.

Mountain Glen was about an hour and a half into New Jersey. It lay on the southern fringe of the Catskills, north of the rolling suburban prettiness of Warrenstown and Greenmeadow and the ugly strip roads that connected them. As I got near, the hills grew steeper, less tame. Scarlet, rust, and orange splashed their sides. Here and there yellow birch leaves still glowed against white bark, set off by moss green stands of pine that seemed permanently in shadow. Yesterday's heavy clouds had delivered rain, up here, and the hollows on the shoulder of the road held puddles that reflected the colors in the hills. Whole stretches of road went by without buildings, without people. The village of Mountain Glen itself was almost not there, a post office fiction to gather together a collection of houses, cabins, shacks, and trailers strung loosely along wandering roads and give them something to belong to.

The address Vélez had given me for Beth Adams turned out to be a wooden structure somewhere between a cabin and a shack, set in a spongy field half a mile past anything that could be called town. I turned in, parked behind a rust-pocked Olds Cutlass that was probably as surprised as anyone every time it found itself running. Mud clutched at my shoes as I walked to the porch, and the steps creaked as I climbed them, to remind me they could collapse whenever they wanted to so I should consider myself warned. There was a doorbell and I pressed it, but I heard no sound and nothing happened. I pressed it one more time, then knocked hard on the door. Immediately from inside I heard a dog scrabbling and barking, but nothing else. I lifted my hand to knock again harder. Before I could, the door opened and a woman's bleary face appeared. She blinked against the daylight and flinched from my upraised arm.

"Beth Adams?" I pulled my arm down. The dog, a small scruffy one, yapped and jumped, but stayed behind her.

She blinked again. "Who're you?" Her voice was deep

and scratchy. She told the dog to shush, and he did, stood behind her growling.

"My name is Bill Smith. Can I ask you a few questions?"

She stared at me as though she wasn't sure she understood the request. Her graying blond hair was curly and disheveled, caught roughly with a red plastic clip where it would otherwise have fallen in her eyes. She wore khakis and a white cotton sweater and she didn't wear them well. The sweater was coffee-stained, loose threads hanging at the sleeves and hem; the worn pants were a size too small, pulling across her dense legs and belly as though the thickness of her body was something she hadn't noticed.

"What do you want?"

"Just a few questions. It won't take long."

She started to close the door on me. "Don't like questions."

I held the door. "Please."

She didn't try to push back. "What do you want?" she asked again.

I said quietly, "I want to talk to you about what happened in Warrenstown, years ago."

"No!" She shouted loudly, shoved the door toward me. The dog started yapping again. She caught me off guard; I barely managed to wedge my foot in. "No," she said again, still pushing at the door, but not with any strength, as though she knew it was useless. "I told him I don't remember. I told him to leave me alone."

"Told who?"

"Al. I told him to leave me alone."

"In Warrenstown, when you were a kid?"

Her face changed; she gave me a triumphant sneer that reminded me of Morgan Reed's. "In Warrenstown. No, dummy. Here, last night."

"Al Macpherson was here last night?"

"Go away."

"What did he want?"

The sneer again. "He wanted to help me. Al's going to help me, hoorah, hoorah."

"Help you with what?"

She turned from the door, left it open as she walked back into the house. "Fuck it," she said. "Want a beer?"

I wiped my feet on a worn mat, followed Beth Adams and the dog through a dank hall to a sticky-floored kitchen. I took the can of Bud she handed me, and then followed again into a living room sloppy with old magazines and *TV Guides*. The dog sniffed at me, wagged his tail tentatively, skittered away when I bent to pet him. The cloud of dust I raised when I sat on the broken-down couch danced in the sunlight.

Beth Adams sat on an equally decrepit chair which was set up, I saw, directly facing a large-screen TV. Half a dozen empties stood on the table beside her. As soon as she sat, the dog jumped into her lap. The room smelled of stale beer, damp dog, and neglect. "Who the hell are you?" she asked again, without hostility, looking at the beer she was popping open, not at me.

"Bill Smith."

"You from Warrenstown? Do I know you?"

"No. Did Al Macpherson come here last night?"

"And you're here now. My, my."

"What did he want to help you with?"

"Al wants to make sure," she slurped foam off the top of the can, "Al wants to make sure everything's all right with me. Al's a big lawyer now."

She stopped, waited, so I said, "I know. Macpherson Peters Ennis and Arkin."

That seemed to prove my credentials. "Al says maybe I could get money from Jared . . . from Jared's parents . . ." She trailed off.

"That's why he came?"

She narrowed her eyes at me. I popped the top on my beer, too, took a swig. I hadn't eaten, just had a lot of coffee, but this was clearly a requirement of conversation here. Beth Adams smirked, drank again, went on. "He said, if I could remember what happened, maybe we could sue. He sues people now, Al. That's what he does."

"What did you say?"

"I told him, I don't remember. I never remembered. People kept asking me and I never remembered. But I remembered something."

"What's that?"

Big smile. "I remembered I don't like Al. He was a big football hero and I didn't like him anyway. All the girls liked him but I didn't."

"Is this the first time you've seen him since you left Warrenstown?"

"He looks just the same, too. Big and pushy. If he sent you to ask what I remember you can go to hell, too."

"He didn't send me. I don't like him either," I ventured. "But that's what I came to ask."

"I know what this is about." She winked at me, took a quick gulp of her beer.

"What?"

"Money."

"What do you mean?"

"That's how lawyers like Al get rich." She told me this in a tone of voice that said I was lucky to be talking to someone who knew the ways of the world. "He sues people and keeps a third. I know all about it. I," she said, downing a long swallow of beer, "*I* have been married three times. Bums every one of them, but I cleaned them out." She waved the Bud at the living room, showed me her loot: mismatched lamps, a stained and threadbare carpet, the big TV. "Three tries at the brass ring," she said, not really to me. "Fuck it." She gulped some more beer. "Al wants me to sue Jared's folks so he can make money."

"What did you tell him?"

"I told him to go away."

"Did he go?"

"I told him," she said, as though she hadn't heard, "I told him I don't remember." She was looking at the sunlight slanting in the windows. The grime on the glass was bright; you couldn't see past it. "I don't remember and I don't like to think about it." Her voice had changed and her lip trembled. The arm she had wrapped around the dog tightened as she pulled him closer to her. The dog squirmed and rearranged himself but didn't try to leave. "We wouldn't get anything from Jared's parents and I don't care if we would, just so I don't have to think about it. I told him to go away."

"Did he go?"

"He said if I ever changed my mind I should let him know. He left me his business card."

"Can I see it?"

She turned her gaze to me, stared for the first time directly into my eyes. "I threw it away. I ripped it into little pieces," she said, "and threw it the hell away."

nineteen

I drove away from Beth Adams's house, back down the empty roads, thinking how bleak autumn sunlight can look sometimes, shining off the vivid colors of leaves about to fall.

I steered carefully, searching for someplace I could get a cup of coffee to cancel out Beth Adams's beer. I found a gas station with a mini-mart, fueled the car and myself, and took off again. The coffee held me until I was out of the hills and back on a strip road headed south. Then I pulled off· at a diner whose blue neon sign read EAT HERE—GET FAT. Direct and to the point, I thought, unlike so much in life.

I ordered scrambled eggs and sausage, and more coffee. After the first cup I told the waitress I'd be right back, took my phone out into the sunshine and called Lydia.

Traffic whizzed by in both directions, exhaust filling the morning air. I dialed, waited until she'd answered in both languages, then said, "It's just me."

"Oh. How'd you do?" she asked.

"I talked to her. She doesn't remember what happened that night. She says she never has. But that's not the real news."

"What is?"

"Al Macpherson was there last night asking her the same thing."

Sunlight glinted off chrome as a big rig pulled into the diner lot. Lydia said, "Our Al Macpherson? You're kidding."

"Never. I'm all business, you know that."

"Uh-huh. What did he want?"

"He said he wanted to help her make big bucks suing the parents of the kid who killed himself. If only she could remember what happened."

"That's unbelievably ghoulish. Not to mention," she said, "plain unbelievable."

"I know," I said. "Twenty-three years later? All of a sudden, last night?"

The driver of the big rig climbed out, a long-limbed beanpole of a guy who ambled across the parking lot like a walking challenge to the diner's mission.

"How did he find her?" Lydia asked.

"She wasn't hiding; Vélez found her for me in under two hours. Macpherson could have had somebody do the same. Or he could have been keeping track of her all these years."

"So what did he really want?"

"Must be to see what she remembered. He must've thought dangling money in front of her would make her think harder."

"What did she remember?"

"Nothing. Except that she didn't like him. She threw him out."

"Good for her," said Lydia. "It does sort of give you the feeling, though, that there's something to remember."

Through the diner window I saw my eggs arrive. "Listen," I said, "I love you but my breakfast's here. You have anything to say?"

"About your breakfast?"

"About your place in my heart."

"Just behind eggs?"

"Before eggs. But behind coffee."

"Not a word, except that if you're eating it now, it's

lunch. But in case you're dying to know what I've been up to, I've been talking to these kids some more."

I checked my watch. She was right about lunch. "Nothing fascinates me more than your movements. Except my coffee. Find anything?"

"I seem to be confirming what Kate Minor said. Consensus is Tory Wesley was supplying Warrenstown High with hallucinogens and designer drugs."

"The kids are telling you this?"

"It's more like, I'm saying 'what if' and they're not denying much. It comes out the same. But no one seems to think Gary's involved. Though from the kids I'm talking to, you always get, 'Of course, he's a jock.' "

"Meaning there's a whole jock life mortal kids know nothing about?"

"Seems to be."

"Kate said jocks do hallucinogens and steroids. Did they get the steroids from Tory, too?"

"I haven't heard that."

"How about where Tory was planning to get the ecstasy that never came through?"

"I asked that; no one knows."

I looked back in the window of the diner. "I'm going to have my breakfast, or whatever it is," I said. "Those eggs are calling me. After that I'm going to come meet you. I know someone who'll know."

Lydia tried to talk me out of going to Warrenstown but it was no good. This was something that had to be done in person, not over the phone, and by me, not by her.

"Competent as you are," I said, "indeed, even skilled, talented beyond my own humble abilities—"

"I'm going to be sick."

"It always comes down to that, doesn't it?"

We compromised on a meet in the Greenmeadow Hospital parking lot, mostly because we both knew where it was. I plowed through the eggs and sausage, decided that food like this was breakfast no matter when you ate it.

It took me another forty minutes to get to Greenmeadow;

when I did I found Lydia already there, leaning on her car in sunglasses and black leather. We left my car behind and took hers, so at least it would have to be my face and not my license plate that alerted the Warrenstown PD that I was around.

"I spoke to the Wesleys," she said, turning left out of the lot, me beside her trying not to press my brake foot to the floor every time we neared another car.

"Learn anything?"

"Not about the party, who might have been there. They had no idea about the drugs, according to them. They did say Tory had trouble 'fitting in.' She didn't seem to have many friends." Lydia fell silent; I turned to look at her.

"And?"

After more silence she said, "They told me her social life started to look up this summer when she began seeing a boy who was new here."

"Gary."

Lydia nodded. "But after football tryouts, he started hanging out with the jock crowd, and he stopped calling her."

"That's what Morgan said: He dated her before he knew who was cool."

"Her mother said Tory was really upset. A couple of times she found her crying in her room. She told her mother she'd do anything to be cool, to be one of the crowd. Her parents thought it was just teenage melodrama. They told her it didn't matter who liked you, as long as you liked yourself."

I turned back to the windshield. In a front yard, a guy was raking leaves. A gust of wind charged into his leaf pile, tossed the leaves around his lawn. It shook the branches of the oak tree above him, raining down more leaves, and blew the maple leaves from his neighbor's yard over to him. The man straightened up, stood holding his rake, staring around him, as the leaves swirled.

"You want to hear the really awful part?" Lydia said.

"Oh, sure."

"The town's cutting them dead."

"Meaning?"

" 'What was your daughter thinking, throwing a party the night before the boys went to Hamlin's?' 'Why did you leave her home alone, what's the matter with you?' 'Dealing drugs? What kind of a girl was she?' 'Look what she's done to this town. Look what trouble she's gotten the boys in.' That sort of thing. Bill, they're burying their daughter, and the town's blaming her. And them."

I had no answer to that. I rolled down the window, lit a cigarette. We sat in silence until we neared Warrenstown, when Lydia took out her phone, made a call to a number I gave her.

"Morgan Reed, please . . . Oh . . . Can you tell me when he'll be in? . . . I'm calling from the school library, about some books he reserved. . . . Oh, has he? . . . Oh, fine, I'll call him then. Thank you very much."

She flipped the phone shut as I said, "He's ungrounded?"

"Only to go to football practice. He has to come right back home when it's over."

"Sounds like Warrenstown," I said. "But football practice starts at three. It's barely two."

"He's not allowed to drive."

"The Reeds live more than three miles from the high school."

"That's why he left early. He's walking."

I directed Lydia to the Morgans' well-kept wooden house, and from there we cruised along the most likely route to Warrenstown High. The yellow school bus passed us carrying children home from the elementary school. Suburban cars rolled down the street on suburban errands. At a Tastee-Freez Lydia pointed out to me two of the kids she'd talked to.

"None of the jocks will talk to me at all, and of the kids who will I can't get anyone to admit they were at that party."

"Neither can Sullivan. I guess they know it could get them in big trouble."

"Having been there could get them in trouble with Sullivan," Lydia said. "Admitting it, the kids tell me, could get them in trouble with the jocks."

We spotted Morgan Reed's tall, lean form about a mile and a half from the school. He was ambling down one of Warrenstown's newer residential streets. He wore his letter jacket, maroon and white like the one Gary had left behind, and his uniform pants, white, skin-tight, ending just below the knee. His maroon jersey swung from his hand. It was knotted and it bulged with his shoulder pads and the rest of his gear.

The street, in the way of suburban streets in the middle of the day, was deserted. Lydia pulled over just ahead of Morgan, kept the engine running while I stepped out of the car. "Hi, Morgan," I said.

Morgan stopped short, scowled. "Oh, shit. What the hell do you want?" He tried to keep walking. I blocked the sidewalk. "Get the fuck out of my way."

"Last time we talked, you were grounded," I said.

He smiled, squinting in the sun. "Coach Ryder called my mother. So did a couple of neighbors. The assistant principal, too. Everyone said it was real important for me to be at practice."

"Well, then," I said, "I'll give you a lift."

"Fuck you."

"Or," I said, "I'll knock the hell out of you right here on the sidewalk and you'll never make it to practice."

"What the—?"

"I only want to talk. But you're a hard man to talk to."

"You're fucking crazy."

"Get in the car," I said. "I'll get you to practice on time. Or you can try to get past me. But I wouldn't advise it."

He glanced at the car, at me. "Come on, man. I don't make practice today, I don't play at Hamlin's tomorrow."

I nodded. "That would be a shame, Morgan. I saw Davis at practice Wednesday. Not much of an arm. You guys wouldn't have any chance at all with him at quarterback, would you?"

He licked his lips. "What do you want?"

"Just a few questions," I said, holding the door for him. He shook his head. "Out here, man. And make it fast."

I gave Morgan a long look, then waved Lydia out of the car. She smiled at Morgan from behind her Ray-Bans as she came around from the driver's door to stand on the sidewalk behind him.

"My partner," I told Morgan. "Lydia Chin. Morgan," I said for Lydia's benefit, "is a quarterback. Young, but they say he's pretty good. They say he's smart, can react to the situation."

Lydia nodded her approval.

"Well," I said to Morgan, "here's the situation. Tory Wesley—you remember her, Morgan, she died Saturday night—Tory Wesley was dealing drugs to you and your friends."

Morgan turned from Lydia to me. "I—"

"Don't bother, I don't really care," I said. "I'm mostly interested in a few other things. First, I want to know who beat up Stacie Phillips last night in the school parking lot."

Morgan stared. "Stacie? Hey, she's cool. She, like, covers us for the *Gazette*. What do you mean, beat her up?"

"Split her lip, blacked her eyes, knocked out a tooth. Tore up her ear. Broke a finger, bruised a couple of ribs. She's at Greenmeadow Hospital."

"Shit, man. That's, like, fucked. Who did that?"

"I'm asking you."

"Me? How would I know?"

"It was someone in a goalie mask, Stacie told me. Like Jason." Lydia's brows lifted above her Ray-Bans when I said that.

"I don't know," Morgan said. "I never even heard about it until just now."

"Well, think. And while you're thinking, answer this: Gary Russell. Does Gary do drugs? Does Gary deal drugs?"

The change of subject seemed to throw him. "Gary Russell?"

I nodded.

Morgan laughed. "You're supposed to be a detective?

Man, don't quit your day job. Gary Russell is a very straight dude. Very, very straight. His old man would scalp him, he caught him doing drugs."

"Any drugs? Grass? Speed? Even steroids?"

"You shitting me? You met his old man?"

"If Gary did want steroids," I said, "where would he get them?"

"What are you asking me for?"

"Because from what I hear the whole varsity and half the JV uses them."

"That's crap."

"I don't think so. Unless there's something in the water in Warrenstown that grows huge mutant teenage boys."

Morgan shrugged.

"You want to get to practice?"

The familiar arrogance that had begun to fill Morgan drained away like water. "Man, I don't know what you're talking about. I don't touch that shit."

"Dammit, Morgan!" He pulled back, startled by my shout. "I didn't ask if you used them. I asked where a kid in Warrenstown could get them. Answer me!"

"Man," he said, looking automatically to Lydia, his voice back to pleading. When dad's on your case, you can try mom, if you happen to live in one of those families where that works. He found no help, shook his head. "I don't fucking know."

"You're lying."

"Bullshit."

"Goddammit! I—"

"Bill," said Lydia calmly, "cool down. Morgan?" The car keys jingled in her hand as she slipped her hands in her pockets. She smiled, her sunglasses hiding her eyes. "Morgan, I'm not sure you understand how serious this is. Tory Wesley's dead and Gary Russell's disappeared and Detective Sullivan is quite concerned." At Sullivan's name Morgan's eyes narrowed, as though he saw more trouble coming his way. "I know you want to get to practice and we'd like to help you out. Maybe it's true you don't know where the steroids are coming from, but I still think you can help us. Will you try?"

Warily, Morgan said, "I don't know anything."

"Well, let's see. We heard that Tory Wesley was dealing acid and other drugs. She's dead, so you don't have to worry about whatever you say about her. We'd just like you to confirm what we've heard."

The street was totally still, not even a breeze to disturb the perfect composition of blue sky, green lawns, red and orange and wine-colored leaves. Morgan swallowed, glanced at me. I must not have looked as though I'd cooled down, because he answered Lydia's question.

"I guess so. I mean, I heard that."

"You heard that. Fine. Now, what did you hear about Tory Wesley's party on Saturday?"

"I don't know. Just that there was gonna be one."

"That's all?"

"Yeah."

"*We* heard," Lydia said, "that she was going to have ecstasy there."

Morgan didn't answer. Lydia said nothing more, just drew her hand from her pocket with the car keys in it. She glanced at her watch, letting the car keys jingle, and gave Morgan her little smile.

"Fuck!" Morgan burst out. "Yeah, fuck it, she was supposed to have ecstasy. Some of the guys said. They were, like, into it."

"Where was she getting it?"

"I don't *know*. I don't fucking *know*! Come on, you guys." His voice took on a whining note as he looked from one of us to the other. I wondered if that worked at home.

"The same place she got her other drugs?" Lydia asked.

"No."

"How do you know?"

"Well, if she could have, she would have before, wouldn't she?" Morgan said. "I mean, the guys, some of them, they were saying a long time they wanted it."

"Maybe she could have," I said, "but she was afraid of what would happen if she did."

"What do you mean?"

"We heard that some of her friends were worried about Tory. They were afraid it was dangerous to deal drugs to guys like you."

"I *told* you, I don't—"

"Of course not, Morgan. It's the other jocks I mean. Some of them are dangerous, aren't they?"

"Don't be stupid. The guys just wanted to, like, party."

"Some of Tory's friends—"

"Bullshit, some of her friends. You mean that freak Paul Niebuhr, right? He's the only one. He says all kinds of bullshit."

"It's bullshit?"

"From that little prick? He was all over her to quit dealing acid. Said she'd get mixed up with the wrong people and get in trouble. Like the people he hangs out with are so cool." Scorn filled Morgan's voice, and I thought of Kate Minor, who considered Paul a friend. "Randy had to talk to him," Paul added.

Lydia said, "That talk, that was when he locked Paul in a locker?"

"Shit, no, that was last year. Paul's just so annoying, you know? With that fucking skateboard, all his shit. Jesus, what a twerp—"

"I see," I said. "So to prove Paul's wrong about the jocks being dangerous, Randy locks Paul in a locker?"

"I told you, that was *last* year."

"And this year? The jocks have new ways to deal with annoying kids this year? Like beating them up in parking lots?"

"Shit, no, man. Nobody'd do that."

"Someone did. Was it Randy?"

"Shit, no," he repeated. "And he didn't touch The Prickless Wonder, either. You know, Paul. Randy's not that way." I thought about the Randy I'd seen at Hamlin's, reserved my judgment on what way he was. But Morgan, next year's star, was intent now on clearing the senior star's name. "He just kind of said to leave Tory alone. Just to, like, let her do whatever she wanted."

"Sell whatever drugs, you mean?"

"Just to leave her alone."

"And what happened?" Lydia asked.

Morgan shrugged.

"Paul left her alone?"

For the first time that afternoon I saw Morgan's sneer. "He stopped telling her what to do. But he didn't leave her alone."

"What does that mean?" said Lydia.

"That night she had that party? He was there the whole time."

"Paul Niebuhr was at the party?"

"*At* the party? No fucking way. He was outside."

"Outside?"

"In his car. Just sat there, all fucking night."

"Paul went camping, at Bear Mountain," I said. "He left Friday, right after school."

"Bullshit. Who said that?" Morgan asked.

"His mother."

"His mother?" Morgan rolled his eyes. "His mother doesn't know shit. She's, like, some hippie or something." His face took on an unfocused look, and in a slow, soft voice he breathed, "I like to give my children space." Back to normal: "Did she tell you that?"

"Yes, she did."

"Yeah, well, what that means, she gives them a few bucks, tells them to go down to the Tastee-Freez for supper, because she's, like, meditating or some shit. The woman is way lame. She's clueless."

"Paul told you this?"

"Paul? I don't, like, hang out with Paul. But you can see it, man. I mean, the guy is, like, a total loser. After the locker thing, I heard his mom told him he must have been, like, putting out negative energy, or otherwise no one would've gotten so pissed at him. His own mom? I mean, what kind of shit is that?"

"Good point," I said. "On the other hand, I'll bet he never gets grounded."

Morgan turned down Lydia's offer of a ride to school with, "You're shitting me, right?" She and I stood and watched him jog along the sidewalk, disappear around the corner with a quick glance back as though he was worried we were going to drive over the grass and scoop him up again.

"Next time," Lydia said, "I want to be the bad cop."

"And I'd be the good cop? Who'd believe that?"

"You always say that."

"It's always true."

She sighed. "Did you notice the change in him when he started telling us about Paul Niebuhr?" Lydia asked. "He became positively talkative."

"Steering us away from his friends. Did you believe him?"

"Fifty-fifty."

"Which fifty?"

"I think he knows where the steroids are coming from. But if Gary isn't taking them or dealing them, we probably don't care."

"And the other fifty?"

She turned to me. "I think Paul Niebuhr was in town Saturday night."

"Watching Tory Wesley's house," I said.

"Until all the other kids left."

"Your thought is . . . ?"

"Well, Kate said they were friends, and that he was worried about what would happen when the jocks found out she couldn't get the ecstasy."

"So he was watching over her to make sure she was all right?"

"Could be."

"But she wasn't all right," I said, "If he found her, why didn't he tell anyone?"

We looked at each other, the afternoon silent around us.

I said, "If he was here Saturday night, then his mother was either lying to me, or she's as clueless as Morgan says."

"And you're thinking we ought to go find out."

I was thinking exactly that. Lydia started up the car and we drove the well-kept streets of Warrenstown once more.

twenty

Paul Niebuhr's family lived near my sister, beyond the other end of the development of mirror-image houses in their gently rolling landscape. At the far edge of the subdivision, on the side where Helen lived, maples, oaks, and birches in their autumn colors showed you what the woods had been like that had stood there until the houses came. On this side, beyond the new ring road we drove along, the softer contours of the treeless land and the muted golds and browns of the wild grasses said that this place had once been farms. The farmers had retreated now, leaving the squash and corn fields unturned, unplanted, waiting for bulldozers, concrete, and sod.

In the sameness of these houses and the careful distances between them the Niebuhr's house was a surprise. We found it on the wrong side of the ring road, across from the development, the only house there. Set back on a little rise, with two ancient apple trees in front, it was brick, small-windowed, old: one of the original farmhouses, its porch shadowed and wide, though from it the only view now, repeated, was the lawns and driveways and tasteful gray houses of the neighbors.

A rainbow-striped windsock billowed in the breeze as Lydia pulled in and parked behind a Volvo with a few years on it. We climbed the scuffed porch steps. The front door,

like the wood trim at the windows, needed a coat of paint.
I pressed a rusted doorbell sandwiched between a SAVE THE
WHALES sticker and one with the universal cross-out symbol
over the cinch-waisted tower of a nuclear power plant.

Grasses rustled and the breeze brought the smell of damp
earth as Lydia and I stood waiting on the porch. The door
was answered by a woman of medium height, barefooted
and heavy in the hips under her ankle-length cotton skirt.
Her hair was doeskin-brown on its way to gray and hung
long down her back. She looked from Lydia to me with a
serene smile. "Yes?"

"Mrs. Niebuhr?" I asked.

"Cooper-Niebuhr," she corrected me gently. "Niebuhr is
my husband's name. Marriage should be a synergy, my husband and I believe, not a case of one person losing her
identity." Her voice, as on the phone on Wednesday, was
unhurried, Mrs. Cooper-Niebuhr willing to give each ele-
ment of her thinking the time required for its expression.
She waited a moment; then, almost as an afterthought, she
added, "Did you want something?"

"I'm Bill Smith. This is Lydia Chin, my partner. I called
two days ago asking to speak to Paul. About Gary Russell?"

At first her look was pleasant but blank. Then she said,
"Oh, yes, the missing boy. Paul's not back yet. He comes
back Sunday. He's camping. I think I told you?"

"You did. Right now it's really Paul I'd like to talk to
you about. Can we come in?"

"About Paul? Is everything all right?"

"Just a few questions. It won't take long."

She hesitated, then opened the door and stood aside.
"Would you please take off your shoes?" Lydia slipped off
her shoes, I untied my boots, and we entered the Cooper-
Niebuhrs' house in our socks.

Paul Niebuhr's mother showed us to a living room of
mismatched wooden furniture scattered with Kente cloth pillows, draped with Navajo blankets, presided over by a Bed-
ouin camel saddlebag on one wall and a Mexican striped
serape nailed to another. The floor was bare except for scat-

tered crayons and childish drawings, some completed, some just begun. In a few places crayon lines continued past the edges of the paper onto the floorboards, joining up with older crayon lines in more faded colors.

"Janis, if you're finished with a project, it's appropriate to leave the area as you found it," Mrs. Cooper-Niebuhr called into the general atmosphere. She seemed to expect no answer and when none came she smiled at us. "My youngest daughter," she said. "She's very creative." She stepped over the crayons and sat on a leather ottoman. From the drawings it looked like little Janis was about four. Some parents would have taken a moment to check and see where she was and what she was up to, but Mrs. Cooper-Niebuhr clasped her hands around her knees and looked peacefully at Lydia and me. "What's this about?"

"When did Paul leave?" I asked, sitting with Lydia on a futon-frame sofa covered loosely with an India-print bedspread. The sofa was already occupied by an enormous orange cat, who opened one baleful eye, shifted grudgingly a quarter of an inch, and went back to sleep. "For Bear Mountain."

"Friday, right after school. Didn't I tell you that before? I'm sorry."

"Yes, you did. But one of the other boys said he saw Paul in Warrenstown Saturday night."

"I don't see how that can be. He left on Friday."

"Could he have come back, just for a while?"

"Why?" she asked, as though the question could not really have an answer. "He went camping. To meditate, in the woods. It would interfere with the process of his meditation to come back to town."

"You know," I said, "that a girl in Warrenstown died at a party on Saturday night?"

Paul's mother smoothed her skirt. "Yes, I heard. It's difficult sometimes."

"Difficult?"

"The wheel of fate. To understand how it turns. Nothing

happens without a reason, of course. But I do feel the pain of her parents."

I opened my mouth to ask another question, but before I could, Lydia, nodding gravely, said, "Difficult to understand. But important to accept, whatever your karma brings you."

"Yes, well," Mrs. Cooper-Niebuhr replied, "that's the challenge of life, isn't it?"

The two of them sat there smiling gently at each other like junior members of some holy sect willing to help each other to enlightenment in any way they could. I wondered how badly my karma would be affected if I lit up a cigarette.

Lydia's face grew solemn. "Mrs. Cooper-Niebuhr—"

"Phoenix. Please call me Phoenix. It's the name I've chosen. Titles put such distance between us."

"Phoenix." Lydia smiled. "We think that the boy we're looking for, Gary Russell, may know something about this girl's death. And we think we were led here because your son may know something about Gary."

That wasn't true; the reason we'd come here had nothing to do with Gary. But it was Lydia's game and I let her play it out.

"Paul?" Phoenix Cooper-Niebuhr asked. "What could he know?"

"They're friends, aren't they, he and Gary?"

Phoenix stared into the infinite, thinking. "When the Russells first moved here, in the summer, I think Paul and Gary spent time together," she said. "But I haven't seen Gary lately."

Not since Gary learned which friends let you belong in Warrenstown, I thought, and which ones kept you from that.

"Well," Lydia said, "some of the other boys seem to think they're still friends." What we'd heard, actually, was the opposite. I wondered where she was going. "Has Paul said anything to you about Gary recently?" she asked.

"No, I'm afraid not."

"You don't know whether they see each other at school?"

"Paul doesn't speak very much about school. He finds

the rules confining and the sense of community forced and artificial. In Warrenstown there's a lot of emphasis placed on football," she added by way of explanation.

"Paul doesn't like football?"

"Not at all. Football gives off extremely negative energy. All that hitting and pounding." She shook her head sadly, perhaps over the damage football players were doing to their own karma. "Paul prefers to be alone," she told us. "He has a solitary nature."

Lucky for him, I thought, since none of the other kids will speak to him.

"But Gary Russell," Phoenix Cooper-Niebuhr added, "he's a kind boy."

"Even though he plays football?"

"He has a strong sense of right and wrong. He brought back Paul's skateboard. Paul was very grateful."

"Paul had loaned it to him?"

"Oh, no. The football coach won't let the boys on the team play with skateboards. That's why it was clear they were working out a deeper issue, when they took it."

"I'm not sure I follow you," Lydia said.

Phoenix's large eyes rested on Lydia. "Oh, because they didn't want it for itself. It was just after school started. I told Paul the most productive way to deal with the situation would be to focus on the real issue, and engage them in a dialogue over that."

"Engage—" I started, but Lydia flashed me a look.

"Did he do that?" Lydia asked.

"I don't know. I don't interfere with his relationships with the other children. A child can never learn anything if you do that."

I clamped my mouth shut as Lydia said, "But this boy Gary Russell, he brought it back?"

"Yes. He came over two days later with it, and said he was sorry."

"He was the one who'd taken it?"

"No. But he felt bad that the boys on his team had done something as negative as that. I felt a strong sense of tribal identification from him toward the other boys."

"That's what they say a team is," Lydia said. "An outlet for our tribal feelings."

"I suppose that's true." Phoenix looked thoughtful, as though this hadn't occurred to her before. "He gave the skateboard back to Paul, and then he left."

Lydia smiled at Phoenix. "That's a kind act," she said. "The act of a friend. Now, Phoenix, I'm going to ask you a rather big favor," she said. "In case it could help us. I'd like to ask if we could see Paul's room."

Phoenix Cooper-Niebuhr's brow furrowed. "In this house we don't enter another person's room without permission."

"I understand. If Paul were here we'd certainly expect to ask him. But this situation is different. It's so important . . ." Lydia let that trail off, let her sweet smile linger. I thought of what Tom Hamlin had had to say last night about situations that were different.

"Well, I don't . . . " Phoenix began, but a crash and a small cry from another room stopped her. Lydia and I jumped to our feet, and Phoenix rose, too, but without haste. Serenely, she headed to the back of the house. We followed, and there, in the kitchen in front of the open refrigerator, we found a smudge-faced little girl looking helplessly at the shattered remains of a pitcher dotting a puddle of milk. The milk had splashed out in all directions when the pitcher hit the floor, and the puddle had the form of a daisy with a pottery-shard center. Uh-oh, Smith, I thought, block those flower metaphors.

Phoenix crouched down and said mildly to the little girl, "Now, Janis, I know you like to do things independently. But sometimes it's better for a small person to ask a big person for help."

And sometimes, I thought, it's better if a big person forgets about the hand-thrown ceramics and leaves the milk in the cardboard quart it came in, which a small person who likes to do things independently can probably handle. I bent down and began picking up pottery. Lydia went to the sink for a sponge and started soaking up milk.

"I want some milk," Janis said.

"That was all the milk," her mother told her.

"I want some!"

Phoenix shook her head sadly. "Well, you shouldn't have spilled it all. Now no one will have any until tomorrow."

Janis looked stricken. Her face scrunched up. Phoenix, standing, said to me, "It's very important that they understand the consequences of their actions."

I thought, when they're four? Janis started to wail. I asked, "How about some juice? Maybe there's juice in the fridge."

In midhowl, Janis paused, suspicious, but giving me a chance to come through. I checked the fridge, and there wasn't any; but the freezer compartment held frozen organic grape juice. I mixed it up in another pottery pitcher, because that was what Phoenix, with raised eyebrows, handed me. I poured a glass for Janis as Lydia finished with the floor. The little girl took her juice and ran off.

"Thank you." Phoenix Cooper-Niebuhr smiled at Lydia and me, looking around at her newly clean floor and her newly mixed grape juice. "It feels good to be with caring individuals."

Lydia smiled back. I did too, wondering again how many extra lifetimes I'd have to spend in the insect world for indulging in tobacco products in this house, and whether karma granted you extenuating circumstances.

"Janis is a lovely child," Lydia said. "Obviously creative, as you said. We were talking about taking a quick look at Paul's room? . . ."

Phoenix looked from one caring individual to the other. "Yes," she said. "Yes, I suppose that would be all right. I don't have the sense that Paul would object."

Lydia and I followed Phoenix up an uncarpeted wooden stair to a short hallway with one door off to the left and three to the right, all closed. Only the bathroom door stood wide.

"This is Janis's room, and this is Grace's," Phoenix said. "This is Paul's." At each of those doors a pile of clean and folded laundry waited to be taken inside and put away.

Phoenix stood where she was, at the top of the stairs; it seemed the responsibility for actually opening Paul's door and invading his space was to be ours, not hers. Lydia, smiling yet again, reached and turned the knob, and the life of Paul Niebuhr was revealed to us.

The place was a mess. Dirty underwear, used towels, open magazines, pens, videotapes, a pack of cards, and a flock of gum wrappers carpeted the floor. Pulled window shades cut the sunlight to whatever managed to leak in around the edges, but even in the dimness we could see an unmade bed, cluttered bookcases, a TV where a flung sock hung over the screen like an unruly lock of hair. Paul had a computer on his desk and at some point he'd painted his walls a dull black. The room smelled of sweatsocks, stale marijuana smoke, and unwashed sheets. Paul's mother's face fell as she stared through the open door and I wondered how long it had been since she'd been in the room where her son spent his time.

Lydia entered and I went after her. Paul's mother hesitated in the hall, the house prohibition against trespassing obviously strong. She overcame it, though, and stepped over Paul's threshhold to stand behind us. But by then Lydia had found the light switch and she and I, looking around, had been stopped dead by what was clearly intended to shock like a blast of cold water. It had that effect, though not for the usual reason.

On the wall opposite the door hung a huge poster. Its violent, slashing graphics, the thick red blood and bare jagged bones among the grinning, contorted faces, were meant to bring ice to your spine. What did it for us, though, was the grafitti-tag lettering triumphantly rising above the five figures who howled in the center of the whirlwind of death and gore. These were the Avenging Mutants. These were the CyberSpawn.

And in a corner of the poster, out of reach of the others, a sixth figure mocked them as he disappeared into a blast of light. They swore they would stop him. They screamed his name.

He was Premador.

"Oh, my God." Lydia looked at me, I back at her.

"Oh," said Paul Niebuhr's mother softly. "Children are sometimes so difficult to understand, don't you think?"

Lydia glanced at Paul's computer, then at me. She turned to Phoenix, seemed about to speak. Then: "Oh, excuse me." She took her phone from her pocket, opened it as if to read a message. "It vibrates instead of ringing," she explained to Phoenix, her smile back in place. "I'd rather not answer it when I'm doing something else. I like to keep my attention in the moment. But sometimes . . ." She checked the read-out. From where I was I could see nothing was on it; Lydia had gotten no call.

I caught on. I moved to the desk, began going through papers, slowly lifting and reading only what was out, careful not to violate Paul Niebuhr's privacy by opening drawers or cabinets. I flipped through an algebra workbook, looking for notes scribbled in the margins; I glanced at a battered Spanish text, sketchy chem lab reports, Cliffs Notes to *Of Mice and Men.* Lifting a small silver frame, I inspected the photo: the thin face of an adolescent boy, smiling at the camera with that I-can't-wait smile of youth. The photo was grainy, as if cut from a newspaper, and I wondered how long it had been since Paul Niebuhr had smiled that smile.

Lydia meanwhile was placing a call.

"These things," I said to Phoenix, by way of distraction. "They're all Paul's?"

"These things?" Phoenix looked at me blankly.

"I just wondered if you saw anything that wasn't his. That may belong to the boy we're looking for. Gary Russell."

"Well, I . . ."

"Take your time. Look around. We don't want to interfere with Paul's things."

Lydia was speaking into the phone in rapid Chinese. Phoenix glanced at her. Lydia smiled, then turned back to

her call. Phoenix looked around the room. It was obvious
to me she had no way of knowing what in this room was
her son's and what belonged to the man in the moon.

Lydia flipped the phone shut. "I'm sorry," she said again.
"My cousin. A family problem. Well, not really a problem."
She moved to the desk, switched Paul's computer on. I
crossed away from her to the other side of the room, began
picking up things from the floor, looking them over. Paul's
mother glanced from one of us to the other. "I'm from such
a big family," Lydia explained, "that half the time someone's not speaking to someone else, and of course there's a
banquet coming up—" A box appeared on the computer
screen and she typed in *Premador*. "—you know, the Autumn Festival, and I'm expected to make peace, get them
all to sit down happily together—"

"I'm not sure Paul would want you to be doing that,"
Phoenix said as Lydia typed something else. This appeared
on the screen only as asterisks, but it caused the screen to
change. Another box appeared and Lydia typed again, saying, "Oh, anything Paul wants to keep private he'll have
hidden behind passwords and things. The kids all do this so
much better than we can." She smiled ruefully. "I'm just
hoping I can find his address book and maybe find Gary
Russell's screen name." The screen had changed again;
Lydia did a few more things, then shook her head. Just as
it seemed Phoenix was about to object once more, Lydia
turned the computer off.

"Oh, well, I'm not very good at that. Bill, did you come
up with anything?"

The answer Lydia wanted was obvious in her eyes, so I
said, "No. I don't think there's anything here."

"I guess we'd better go." Lydia smiled, headed toward
the stairs, no longer interested in Paul's room or anything
in it. Phoenix and I followed. I closed the door.

When we'd reached the bottom of the stairs I said, "Can
I ask you one more question?"

Phoenix looked expectantly at me.

"Gary Russell can shoot. A gun," I added, in case the

concept was alien in this house. "Can Paul?"

Surprisingly, she nodded. "Teenage boys have an instinct for aggression," she told us. "It's natural, a gift of evolution. Of course, for social creatures that aggressiveness can be a problem, but Paul's father and I feel it's healthier if you help children redirect their antisocial impulses than to try to repress them. Children have to learn to work through their needs and turn them to positive ends."

I let most of that go. "Does he have a gun?"

"Paul asked for a rifle last year for Christmas. If we'd forbidden it, it would just have become more desirable. Of course, he only shoots targets and skeet. That's an absolute rule. He understands how wrong it would be to kill living beings. He doesn't hunt."

As I laced up my boots in the front hall, I thought, that's what you think.

"Is it here?" I asked.

"Is what here?"

"His rifle."

Phoenix Cooper-Niebuhr cocked her head thoughtfully. "I don't know," she said. "I'm not sure where he keeps it."

Paul's mother closed the door behind us as we went down the porch steps. Lydia and I walked back to her car through the long golden light. Perfect for meditating in, I thought. Especially if you sat facing the unplowed fields, your back to the world you lived in.

Lydia and I met each other's eyes as she started the car.

"That was Linus you called?" I said.

She nodded. "Premador has two passwords, a two-layer system. He gave me both of them."

"And?"

She stared ahead of her, easing the car down the gravel drive, onto the smooth asphalt road. "They worked."

The fields curved by on one side, the houses on the other, both glowing peacefully in the sunlight. On the right a rabbit, startled by our passage, dashed into tall grass. On the left a woman and a small boy carried groceries through their front door. I pulled a cigarette from the pack, lit it up, dropped the match in the ashtray.

I filled my lungs with smoke, said, "Gary hunts."

"I know," said Lydia, and as we drove into town she said nothing else.

I finished the cigarette, then took out my phone, thumbed in a number.

"Sullivan."

"Smith. Where are you?"

"Where am I? Where a cop belongs: behind my desk. Why?"

"I'm coming to see you. Ten minutes."

A brief hesitation. "I hope you're coming by helicopter. I hope this doesn't mean you're in Warrenstown now."

"Arrest me when I get there, Sullivan. This is important."

Silence; then, "I'll be waiting."

Lydia dropped me a few blocks from the police station. We saw no point in her talking to Sullivan. There was nothing she knew about Premador that I didn't, but there were things she might be able to get from the kids that I couldn't. She drove off to see.

A young cop I hadn't met before was behind the desk this time. I told him who I was; he nodded toward the door under the Warrenstown Warriors banner. I went through, found Sullivan alone in a three-desk room, papers tacked to boards on the walls, a window behind him that gave onto the parking lot. He stood when I entered, regarded me. "You were in my platoon, you'd be in the brig," he said.

"I spent some time there. Sullivan, I found Premador."

Tiny muscles moved under Sullivan's skin, a wolf catching a scent. "Tell me."

"Not found him," I corrected myself. "Found out who he is."

"Tell me."

I met his eyes. "Not yet. I want to talk to your chief."

He stared. "What the fuck does that mean? You have a problem with me?"

"God, no. It means I need your help."

Sullivan walked slowly around his desk, came to stand in front of me. He was as tall as I, muscled and thin. "What game are we playing?"

"No game. I'm asking, Sullivan. You say no, I'll give you what I have anyway. But I have questions for your chief and I don't think he'll answer them unless there's something he wants, too."

"What questions?"

"About what happened twenty-three years ago, and why it still matters."

"What makes you think it does?"

"For one thing, Al Macpherson went out to talk to Bethany Victor last night, to see what she remembered."

A pause. "How the hell did you get her name?"

"Dammit, Sullivan, this is what I do. I found a source. What's the difference?"

"Jesus, Smith, you're a piece of work." He turned to his desk for a pack of cigarettes, pulled one out, lit it up. I recognized that move: It's partly for the smoke, partly for the time, both to help you think. "Macpherson," he finally said. "No shit?"

"No."

Sullivan's steady, pale eyes didn't waver. "The chief's a good cop. You could wreck his career over a dumb mistake he made when he was a kid."

"That's not what I want. But I need to know."

He nodded slowly. "And you'll withhold evidence that could aid in the apprehension of a felon—an armed homicidal teenage boy—until your curiosity's satisfied?"

"If you want to look at it that way."

"You have another way?"

"No."

A corner of his mouth tugged up. "Goddamn," he said. Eyes still on me, he reached for his desk phone, punched a button. "Chief? Jim. Got a minute?"

Letourneau's office was at the end of the hall, and from him I got no smile. "You know who this kid is, you don't tell me *now*, I'll lock you up, and not just for withholding evidence." He stood at his desk, square jaw and square shoulders set. The chief of the Warrenstown PD was a big man, his sandy hair short and thick; his skin was pale and his hands were huge. "It'll be weapons possession for the gun buy, and accessory before the fact if anything else goes down." His knuckles jabbed his paperwork. His voice was louder and harder than it needed to be, matching the excess in the threat: jail's jail, no matter how many charges you pile up on each other. I wondered how many times in his high school career he'd been called for unnecessary roughness.

"You can do that," I said from across his desk. Sullivan stood beside me, waiting to see how things fell. "But I have a good lawyer. You might win, but the whole thing will take a lot of time. I don't think you have that kind of time. School starts Monday."

Letourneau looked at Sullivan. Sullivan shrugged. Letourneau asked me tightly, "What the hell do you want?"

"I want you to answer some questions for me."

"Questions about what?"

"Al Macpherson and Beth Adams. Victor, excuse me— Bethany Victor."

Skin as pale as Letourneau's flushes deep, and quickly. "Fuck that. That's ancient history."

"I'm not so sure. The last person who told me that got the shit beat out of her."

Letourneau's eyes narrowed. "Stacie Phillips?"

"Friend of mine."

"What's it got to do with her?"

"Guy who beat her up kept asking what she had, Chief," Sullivan said in his easy drawl. "And what Tory Wesley had. Stacie has no idea what that meant. Only thing she'd done out of the ordinary lately was fax Smith here background on the Victor rape from the *Gazette* morgue."

Letourneau said to me, "That's how you got that?"

I nodded. "And you knew I had it because Scott Russell told you. Why?"

"Why'd he tell me? Goddamn embarrassing for me, all that old shit comes out, don't you think?"

"And Scott was just doing you a favor, as an old friend?"

"Friend? Russell? Guy's a jackass, always was." Letourneau shook his huge head. "But yeah, I suppose that's what he thought. In case he needed a favor himself someday, maybe."

"Like if you found his son?"

His eyes flared. "That what you think?"

I looked from him to Sullivan. "I think that may be what Scott was thinking. But no, I don't think it would have worked."

"Damn right it wouldn't." He snorted, backed down a little. "Anyway, what's this got to do with anything?"

"With what happened to Stacie? I think it does," I said. "And so did the person who beat her up."

"Bullshit. They were asking about Tory Wesley, it's about drugs."

"You knew Tory Wesley was dealing drugs?"

"I heard rumors."

Sullivan's eyebrows went up, and Letourneau caught the motion. "Rumors," he said to Sullivan. "I was going to tell you, check it out. When the kids got back from break."

"And when she died," I said, "you didn't think that was about drugs?"

"Might be," Letourneau answered. "We'll find out."

"After the Hamlin's game."

Letourneau shrugged.

"Okay," I said. "I never saw a town with its head so far up its ass, but I don't care. You answer my questions, I'll tell you who Premador is. You agree, I'll even tell you first, so you can get the hunt started. You don't, you can throw me in jail and we can all wait and see what happens." Letourneau held me with a hard stare. Sullivan was relaxed and still beside me. He knew what I did; that I was blowing smoke. There was no way I was going to keep Premador's identity to myself. School started Monday.

But Letourneau didn't know that, and Letourneau, his

voice tight, finally spoke. "What if I say I'll answer your fucking questions, and then after you give it up, I don't?"

"Then the *Tri-Town Gazette* might wonder why."

"This is bullshit," Letourneau said. "It's extortion."

"It's a trade. If it has nothing to do with anything, that'll be the end of it."

Letourneau shifted his glance to Sullivan, who looked at him steadily. Sullivan had told me Letourneau was a good cop. Letourneau turned to me. "Just what the hell," he said, "do you want to know?"

twenty-one

I kept my part of the bargain and Letourneau kept his. To start, settled in a chair across the desk from Letourneau, I gave him and Sullivan a condensed version of the visit to the old brick farmhouse. My first instinct was to leave Lydia out of it, to keep a weapon in reserve. But as soon as Sullivan spoke to Phoenix Cooper-Niebuhr—and that was sure to be his next move, when he'd heard me out—he'd find out about her, and there was no point in pissing Sullivan off even more than I already had.

"I went out to Paul Niebuhr's house," I said. "With my partner."

Letourneau said, "Your partner?"

"Lydia Chin. Small Chinese woman, you might have seen her around town."

"I thought she was a reporter," he said. "One of the New York cable channels."

I shrugged. Sullivan gave me a level gaze, said nothing.

"Paul wasn't there. We talked to his mother," I said. "We saw his room." I told them: the poster, the passwords.

When I ended the story, silence. Then, "Goddamn," Sullivan breathed. "Paul Niebuhr. God*damn*."

Letourneau's brow furrowed. "Skinny little nobody, right? I have the right kid?"

"Skateboarder." Sullivan's voice was noncommittal on

the question of whether Paul Niebuhr was a nobody. "Permission, Chief?" Letourneau nodded, and Sullivan reached across the desk and pressed the speakerphone button. "Denise, that Warrenstown yearbook," he said. "That go to Crossley at the NYPD yet?"

"The messenger's on his way here for it," a woman's voice crackled into the air.

"Cancel him. I'm in the chief's office; bring it here."

A few moments later a tall woman, a civilian clerk, came in and handed Sullivan a manila envelope. Sullivan tore it open. He slipped out a maroon leather volume, last year's Warrenstown High yearbook. He flipped the pages; Letourneau and I leaned forward to see. "Bingo," Sullivan said, finger on a photo in a row of photos. I craned past him to have my first look at Premador, who was on a mission to blow up the world.

I expected a slightly older version of the grinning boy I'd seen in the silver frame on Paul Niebuhr's desk, but this was a different kid: thin, pale, a young-looking high school junior when the photo was taken, which would have been this time last year. He wore aviator glasses; his thick brown hair was combed into submission, but barely. Most of the other boys had dressed in jacket and tie for their yearbook photos. Paul Niebuhr wore a black tee shirt, and he did not smile.

"Denise, have this enlarged," Sullivan said. "I'll call Crossley right now. Fax him this. This is the guy he's looking for."

I looked into Paul Niebuhr's expressionless eyes. A chill went through me. "Do you have a photo of Jared Beltran?" I asked Sullivan.

"In the files. What the hell for?"

"Did you know he's a hero to some of these kids?"

"Beltran? Some of what kids?" Letourneau said in disbelief.

"The freaks, the misfits. Because he one-upped the jocks. Raped one of their girls and then gave them the finger, killed himself so they couldn't get at him. I hear when the police came to arrest him a couple of jocks had to be pulled off him."

Letourneau didn't meet my eyes. "We'd heard. About him following Beth around. A few of the guys . . . Anyway, it was lucky the cops got there when they did."

"Yeah," I said. "Real lucky. I think his photo was on Paul Niebuhr's desk."

Letourneau said, "His photo?"

"From the paper."

"Shit. Denise, the file on the Victor case—"

"It's on my desk," Sullivan said.

His chief stared at him. "What—?"

Sullivan didn't answer. Denise left, to get the file.

What followed were two conversations in which Letourneau and I had no part. In the first, Sullivan explained to a detective at the 108th Precinct in Queens that he'd identified Premador as a Warrenstown High School senior named Paul Niebuhr, that they should run the photo he was about to receive by Sting Ray, that Paul Niebuhr should be considered armed and dangerous. "The kid with him, too," Sullivan said. "Gary Russell . . . Yeah, our runaway, you have that photo already. . . . I don't know. . . . They could be, or maybe they've split up. . . . Monday . . . Yeah, I know. Okay, thanks, I'll keep in touch."

Next Sullivan called the state police in Newark, explained the situation, asked for a computer expert. "No, off-site. We'll bring it here, soon as I get a subpoena. . . . Right . . . Far as I know, maybe one other kid . . . Yeah, and his'll be here, too, right . . . They might, I don't know. . . . And the car, at Bear Mountain? Yeah, good. Thanks."

He replaced the receiver, looked from his chief to me.

"You keep saying *they*," I said. "Gary may have nothing to do with this."

"Yeah, and pigs may fly. Until I see it, I'm operating on the assumption. What were you doing in Warrenstown, Smith? You, and your partner?"

I shook my head. "Later. We had a deal."

Sullivan held my eyes; then he nodded and stood. "I'm

going to do the paperwork, get it over to Judge Wright. Back in fifteen minutes."

"You're that fast with paperwork?" I said. "I'm impressed."

"Small town, emergency situation. Judge'll cut me some slack. And," he added, "chambers are right next door."

He left, shutting the door behind him. It was true he needed to fill out the forms, swear out the statements, do what cops did to get warrants from judges. The Warrenstown PD would want to search the Cooper-Niebuhrs' house, and, at this point, my sister's, take the kids' computers to the station, see if they could find a way to track Paul and Gary down. But I had the feeling he was glad to leave the room before Letourneau answered my questions, in case anything came out that it would bother Letourneau for years to know that Sullivan knew.

Nothing did that I could see. After Sullivan left I turned to Letourneau, waited; Letourneau scowled, but we had a deal. Letourneau's story was short, not much I hadn't read, heard from Sullivan, or filled in myself.

"All that," Letourneau said. "Back then. It was no big deal. I didn't commit a crime. I was trying to help out."

"You tried to give Al Macpherson a bullshit alibi," I said.

"Because it was a bullshit rap! That asshole Scott Russell—your brother-in-law," he added with weight, "—what the hell did he have to open his fat mouth for? He saw Al arguing with Beth. Or maybe not. Or maybe it was someone else. Or maybe it was later. Or earlier. Or in his dreams."

"Did he see them?" I said.

"How the hell do I know what he saw? He didn't know either, he should have kept his mouth shut."

"In the end he did."

Letourneau gave me the smile he probably gave, in his football days, to the player lined up against him.

"You told him to, didn't you?" I said slowly. "You told him he'd better take it back, say he didn't know what he saw. You threaten him? You beat him up?"

Letourneau shook his head. "Didn't have to."

"Meaning?"

"Russell was a benchwarmer. He was a senior."

"So?"

"He'd never started. Two years on JV, two years varsity, some games he never got in at all. Homecoming game was coming up."

It took me a minute. "And if he took back his story, he'd get to start? The Homecoming game?"

"Wouldn't have been much of a game," Letourneau said, "without Al."

Letourneau took out a pack of cigarettes, so I did, too. Like most places these days, the Warrenstown PD was officially smoke-free; like most cop houses I've ever been in, that extended no farther than the front desk, and the desk sergeants usually complained about having to wait until their break for theirs.

I said, "Al Macpherson left the party in time. He could have raped Beth Victor."

"He left in time," Letourneau said, cigarette between thick lips. "Eight other kids said that back then. But Al didn't do it, Jared Beltran did."

"Eight other kids," I said. "A lot of pressure on you and your phony alibi."

"Wrong. There was no pressure. Everyone in Warrenstown *wanted* to believe me. They did, until there was just too much on the other side."

"Then what?"

"Then I said gee, I must have been so drunk I couldn't tell time, sorry about that."

"And that was that?"

"Sure. Even people who knew I was lying thought I was the good guy, out to save Al's ass. And as it turned out, Al wasn't the only one with a bullshit alibi. Jared Beltran had one, too."

"From Nicky the Nerd."

Letourneau's eyebrows went up. "You have been working this, haven't you? What the hell for? It was twenty-three years ago."

"I'm looking for Gary Russell," I said. "That's all I wanted, when I started. All the rest of this keeps getting in front of me. I couldn't go around it so I'm looking for a way through." Letourneau, without an answer, pushed a paper coffee cup across the desk for me to use as an ashtray. I tapped my cigarette against it, said, "Jared Beltran had been stalking Beth Victor?"

"Yeah. When we found that out—"

"Found it out? I thought it was well known."

"Maybe. I didn't know it. Anyway, they picked him up and he denied raping her and Nicky alibied him. But then he killed himself so there you go."

There you go. "How did they find out he'd been stalking her?"

"One of the teachers tipped off the police. Said they'd heard the kids talking about it, and they'd seen Jared in the halls, sort of sneaking around after her. Said one of the kids said he'd left creepy things outside her locker. Dead flowers, shit like that."

"Which teacher?"

"They kept that a secret. Teacher wanted the kids to feel like it was safe to talk to her, or him. None of those people's names ever came out, the teacher or the kids who reported that stuff, either."

"What if they'd arrested Jared Beltran and it had gone to trial?"

"Then I guess the teacher would have had to testify, and probably the kids. But it didn't get that far."

"Do you know who any of them were, the kids?"

"The ones who said they'd noticed stuff? A couple of guys told me afterwards they'd seen him in class, kind of drooling in her direction."

"Afterwards. But you'd never heard anything like this before the rape?"

Letourneau shrugged, said nothing. He tapped his cigarette against a heavy glass ashtray.

"What happened to Nick Dalton?" I asked.

"Nicky? He was a pain in the ass. He kept saying Jared

really had been with him, that the alibi was good. I mean, the kid was dead, what the hell difference did it make?" He flushed. "I think some of the guys gave him a hard time for a while."

"Some of the guys. The jocks, you mean?"

He nodded, didn't look at me. "Anyway, he left town as soon as school got out. Didn't even go to graduation."

"Any idea where he is now?"

"No. Haven't heard anything about him since."

I asked about a few more things, including why Letourneau thought Macpherson might have gone to see Bethany Victor last night. He had no answer.

Just before Sullivan came back, Letourneau told me this: "I want you to understand something, Smith. Warrenstown football, it's like a family. What I did, I was trying to help out a friend. A brother. Yeah, it was a lie, yeah, it was wrong. And it probably sounds stupid to you, but I became a cop to sort of make up for it. Do the right thing, you know? But I knew that rap on Al was bullshit. We were co-captains, I knew the guy. I knew he wouldn't do shit like that."

"Did you really know that?" I asked. "Or did you just know you couldn't win the Homecoming game without him?"

Letourneau said nothing, just looked at me.

Two quick raps on the door, and Sullivan put his head in, paused to see if he should enter. I shrugged. Letourneau nodded.

Sullivan shut the door behind himself. "It's done," he said. "Warrants'll be issued in ten minutes. I'll pick them up and roll. I already sent Chávez and Huber down to talk to any kids they could find, see if anyone knows where Paul Niebuhr might be. The state'll bring Paul's car back from Bear Mountain, take it to the lab in Newark. I have rangers looking at likely campsites there, in case he's hiding up there until whatever it is he's planning." He handed me picture out of a file folder he held. "Jared Beltran."

I fingered it, a newspaper photo of a skinny, grinning

kid. I put it down on Letourneau's desk, nodded.

"That was Beltran's junior yearbook picture," Sullivan said. Letourneau, silent, stared at the photo.

Sullivan looked from his boss to me. "Your curiosity all satisfied, Smith?"

"No," I said. "But it'll do for now."

Sullivan perched on the arm of the next chair. "Okay, then, satisfy mine. What the hell were you doing in Warrenstown today?"

I dropped my cigarette into the coffee cup, listened to the sizzle. "I needed to talk to Morgan Reed."

"After I told you to keep away from my witnesses?"

"You weren't using them."

A long look; then he said, "What did you want from Morgan?"

"I wanted to know where the steroids were coming from."

Sullivan nodded slowly. "All those thick-necked football players."

"You know?"

"Know they're on them? Just look at 'em. They're not twice as big as we were because they drink more milk. But they all deny it."

"What about urine tests?"

He glanced at Letourneau, gave me the small smile. "Warrenstown won't allow them. Interferes with the boys' right to privacy."

"Or with Warrenstown's right to grow huge football players."

"Uh-huh. Why did you want to know and what made you think Morgan would tell you? And did he?"

"He said he didn't know but he's lying. I wanted to know because one of the other kids said Tory Wesley was killed because she didn't come through with ecstasy for her party. That kid didn't know where that was coming from either and I thought the source might be the same."

"Ecstasy?" Sullivan looked to his chief again, then back to me. "You didn't tell me that yesterday."

"Sullivan," I said, "I'm dealing with kids who're afraid of you, and more afraid of the other kids. I'm trying to use what they're giving me and protect them at the same time. The only reason they're talking is that, with all due respect, they feel like the situation has gotten out of hand and they can't take it anymore."

"What the hell do you mean, situation?" Letourneau demanded.

"The jocks," I said. "The jocks who run Warrenstown High. The other kids live in the shadows. They go where the jocks let them and do what they tell them. When you're that age high school is your world and here, the jocks run that world."

"This is bullshit," Letourneau growled. "This is a football town. Same as half the towns in America. So people look up to athletes. So what?"

"Yeah," I said. "Like they looked up to Al Macpherson when you were in school."

"Okay," Sullivan said, in an even, quiet way. "That's why you came to town. But it doesn't explain what made you go out to Paul Niebuhr's. His mother told you on Wednesday he was at Bear Mountain until day after tomorrow."

I looked at him. "Morgan told me he'd seen Paul in town Saturday night. Parked outside Tory Wesley's house."

"He was at that party?" Letourneau leaned toward me.

"The kids say no. Outside."

"A freak like that—"

"Uh-huh," I said. "Here it comes."

"What?"

"You'll do anything in this town to avoid making trouble for your jocks. You'd love to pin Tory Wesley's death on Paul Niebuhr. A freak like that."

"For Christ's sake, the kid went to Queens to buy guns!"

"I'm not denying he's dangerous, Letourneau, maybe even crazy. But there was a lack of enthusiasm around here for investigating any of the jocks before Paul Niebuhr's name ever came up. Warrenstown has a history of that."

"Oh, for shit's sake! That history crap, that's bullshit! That freak Jared Beltran raped Beth Victor and that's all there was to it! It has nothing to do with this!"

"Yeah," I said. I stood. "You guys have work to do. So do I. See you around."

"Smith—" said Sullivan.

"Yeah," I said, and I left.

twenty-two

I walked a block from the police station, took out the phone and called Lydia. "Law's a-coming," I said. "To talk to the kids. You want to buy me a cup of coffee?"

"Your case, your expense account," she said. "Are you telling me to make myself scarce?"

"I'd suggest it. Meet me at the Galaxy Diner."

"You want me to pick you up?"

"No, I'll walk. Sullivan seems to have given up on the idea of arresting me, for now."

The police station wasn't far from the Galaxy; nothing in Warrenstown was all that far from anything else. The air held a fresh fall chill; I zipped my jacket and started over. Star-shaped maple leaves lay here and there on the slate sidewalk, their wine color bringing out the blue of the stone. The scent of cinnamon drifted through the air as I passed the bakery where I had sat with Helen; I glanced at the shop window and saw, through my own reflection, one of the grandmotherly ladies behind the counter taking a tray of cookies out of the oven, for afternoon snacks. Cars drove slowly down Main Street, people stopped on corners to talk to their neighbors, and everywhere golden sunlight draped Warrenstown like a protective blanket.

I stopped on the sidewalk, took out my cell phone, called my sister.

"Hello?" Again, the tentative voice, the one that asked, *Am I taking up too much room in the world?* Again, the tightening in my shoulders.

"It's Bill. Is Scott there, or can we talk?"

"He's not here, but Bill, he doesn't want me talking to you anymore. He says—"

"I don't give a damn what he says. Listen to me. Things are bad. The police think Gary's with this other boy, Paul Niebuhr, and they think Paul's dangerous."

A little intake of breath. "Paul? Oh, God. Will he hurt Gary?"

"I don't think so. I'm not even sure they're together. But the police have a warrant and they're coming to search Gary's room. I think they're going to take his computer, and the one in the family room, as evidence."

"Evidence?" It was almost a wail. "Evidence of what? Scott said the police have the whole wrong idea about Gary, because you—"

"I'm calling," I cut her off, "same as before, just so you have some warning. I want you to cooperate with them, Helen. Tell them anything you know, anything they ask. No matter what Scott says. He thinks he can protect Gary his way, but he's wrong. Do you understand me?"

"I . . . but Gary . . ."

"Helen! *Do you understand me?*"

"Yes," she whispered, a sound like the leaves skidding across the sidewalk.

"I'll talk to you later." I snapped the phone shut, stuck it in my pocket. I turned up my collar; the wind had come up, and I was cold.

At the Galaxy I took a window booth, ordered coffee. I watched the Warrenstown traffic start and stop. When I was halfway through the cup I saw Lydia's Taurus pull into the lot, saw her get out, lock the car, head to the diner. She moved, as always, quickly, with an athlete's grace and sureness. Or maybe, I thought, sipping coffee, the grace was something she'd been born with, and the sureness had nothing to do with strength, with agility or endurance; maybe it was purely the certainty of youth, the confidence that comes from not yet knowing it's just not true that you can have whatever you want badly enough, whatever you work hard enough for.

I lost sight of her as she rounded the building to reach the door; then there she was inside, scanning the room for me, smiling when she found me. "What's up?" she asked as she kissed my cheek. She slid into the booth across from me. "You look worried."

"I'm older than you are."

"You just figured that out?"

"No, but I always saw it as a flaw in *you* before."

"Clearly a mistake, since for one thing I have no flaws."

"Right, now I remember," I said, and then the waiter came by, refilled my cup and took Lydia's order: tea and one of the flaky crescents with almonds on top that she'd seen in the dessert case on her way in.

"You find out anything new?" I asked her.

"Nothing at all. No one I found had anything to add, about where Paul might be, or anything else."

"That's strange."

"Why?"

"All these kids," I said. "These school shooters, Littleton, whatever. They all talked about it beforehand. It's one of the things they all have in common."

"Then maybe it means Paul's not one. That that's not what's on his mind."

"Maybe."

She brushed hair from her forehead, said, "How was your visit to Sullivan and his chief?"

"I'm not sure I learned anything. They did, though, and they're moving on it. That's why they're talking to the kids. And they've got warrants for the Niebuhrs' house, and for Helen's."

"Helen's? Oh, Bill. Did you speak to her?"

"I called." I sipped my coffee.

"Was Scott there?"

"No. But he told her not to talk to me anymore."

Lydia's eyes met mine, held them for a moment. "You know," she said, "I don't get any of this."

"Any of what?"

"The stuff between you and Helen. Why she can't get past what you did and see why you did it. Why you didn't try harder to keep in touch with them, and to prove you were different from what they thought."

"I don't have to prove anything to them."

"No, you don't have to," she said. "But they're all the family you've got."

I had nothing to say to that, nothing to say at all, and I looked out the window, watched the light change over and over. I was barely aware when the waiter came back with Lydia's tea and pastry, went away again.

"If you break that cup," Lydia's voice came softly, "they probably won't give you any more coffee."

I looked down, saw white knuckles gripping my coffee cup. I forced them open, forced myself to breathe, forced myself to look at her. The same dark eyes, the same still mouth, short hair so black its highlights glinted blue. Waiters and customers moved around us in the diner and a sappy love ballad threaded through the air, sometimes heard, sometimes lost in the sounds of people getting on with it.

"Yeah," I said. "And God knows that would be a disaster, me without caffeine." I drank down some of that caffeine as she gave me a soft smile. I asked, "Can I tell you about the chief?"

She nodded. I told her Letourneau's story, partly because as my partner she needed to know, and partly just to be talking to her.

"Let me get this straight," she said, nibbling on an almond she peeled off her pastry. "Scott changed his story for a chance to play in the Homecoming game? And don't tell me 'This is Warrenstown, this is football.'"

"Okay," I said, "but it is. And if he wasn't sure what he saw in the first place—"

"Yeah," she said, "but what if he was?"

"This is Warrenstown," I said. "This is football."

She didn't answer that, just looked at me. She shook her head, sipped her tea. "What are they going to do if they don't find Paul by Monday?"

"They'll secure the school." I told her what Sullivan had told me. "They'll call out the state police and the National Guard if they have to."

"They can't do that forever."

"No."

"You know," she said, "they may be wrong about him. *We* may be wrong about him. He may show up on Sunday just like he told his mom, say, gee, it was a little cold for camping, but I had a great time."

"He may."

"He might have bought that gun just to see if he could. He might actually *be* at Bear Mountain now. Meditating."

"Possible."

"We might just all be spooked, by Littleton and things like that."

"We might."

"But," she said, "it would be insane to wait and see, wouldn't it?"

That didn't need an answer. Lydia ate another forkful of almond crescent—I have never in my life eaten a diner pastry with a knife and fork—as the Muzak shifted into Randy Newman's "Short People." I smiled at Lydia. "I'll bet you hate this song."

"On the contrary. It's stereotypes like this that enable people like me to sneak unseen right up into the faces of people like you, and clobber you."

"You think so?"

A forkload of pastry stopped halfway to her mouth. "Who says who plays?"

"Who plays the music? I don't know, probably there's a tape player—"

"No! Who plays *football*."

"What?"

"Letourneau and Macpherson were co-captains, okay, but

it's not the captains who make the decision about who goes in, is it?"

I stared at her for a moment. "No," I said. I reached for my wallet, dropped bills on the table. We both stood. I said, "It's the coach."

My car was still in the hospital lot in Greenmeadow, so Lydia drove us out to the high school through the fading autumn afternoon. We found the doors unlocked, the halls nearly empty. Linoleum gleamed and the lockers lining the corridor stood to attention as we passed by. We headed toward the gym, found the coach's office. The furniture was new and the office spacious; I wondered briefly if the English department had facilities like this. Two desks, along with file cabinets, took up the outer room and a desk sat facing us from the inner, with a crowded trophy case in each room. Ranks of framed photos, championship teams, covered the walls, here and there basketball or softball, but mostly football, through the years. The outer room was empty, the inner one dark. A faint blue glow filled the darkness as, seated in an easy chair in front of a large TV, Coach Ryder reviewed Warrenstown Warrior game tapes.

We reached the inner doorway. The coach's eyes remained glued to the screen.

"JV practice over, Coach?" I asked.

Ryder glanced up, looked back to the TV. "Busy," he grunted. "Go away."

"I need to talk to you, Coach."

"You speak English? Go away."

"It's about Bethany Victor."

"I don't coach the girls. Your kid got a problem, talk to Tina Meyerhoff Monday morning. She's girls' head coach." Not looking at me, he clicked the remote, rewound, and watched a second time as an opposing back, his timing perfect, soared into the air and intercepted a pass meant for a Warrenstown receiver. "Asshole," he muttered, scrawled something on the clipboard on his lap. "Fucking candy-ass.

You see that?" He raised his voice, asking the question of
me. "That kid, Chambers. Best hands I've seen in years.
Can catch anything he can touch. But fuck if I know how
to teach the asshole to come back to the ball."

"He needs to stop thinking about the guy who's covering
him," Lydia said from beside me. "And about the guy who
threw the pass. It needs to be just him and the ball, on the
field alone."

Ryder turned now, to stare at her. "Well, is that a fact?"

"Yes," Lydia said.

"And just who exactly the hell are you?"

I took it. "I'm Bill Smith. I was here Wednesday, at JV
practice. This is my partner, Lydia Chin."

"Your partner?" He flicked his eyes over Lydia, asked
me, "Is that some politically correct way of saying you're
shacking up?"

"No, it's a way of saying we're in business together.
We're investigators."

On the screen, a new play started. Ryder clicked the remote to pause, stared at me from his chair. "Oh, you. You
wanted to know where Russell was. You're a pain in the
ass. You a pain in the ass, too?" He gestured the remote at
Lydia.

"Yes," Lydia said.

Ryder gave that a razor-edged smile. "You find that asshole?" he asked me. "Because if you did or not, I'm not
letting him play at Hamlin's tomorrow. That why you're
here?"

"No, I just told you, I'm here about Beth Victor."

Ryder's face darkened, as though hearing me for the first
time; but all he said was, "Who the fuck is Beth Victor?"

"Warrenstown High girl," I said, and even in the blue-lit
dimness I could see Ryder's eyes narrow, considering me.
"Ryder, she was raped in Warrentown twenty-three years
ago, and you know who she is."

Ryder lumbered out of his chair. "Don't take that fucking
tone with me."

"I'm not a kid you can browbeat or a parent you can

intimidate, Ryder. I'm an investigator trying to do my job. Bethany Victor was raped, Al Macpherson was arrested, and the only real witness was Scott Russell, who changed his story so he could play in the Homecoming game. Was that your idea, or Letourneau's? Or Macpherson's?"

He planted his feet, faced me square-on. "In case you didn't hear, some other pervert shot himself over that. A little asshole who'd been stalking her."

"I did hear, and I don't know why he did that, but I don't think he ever stalked her and I don't think he raped her. He had an alibi."

"Yeah, his buddy tried to say they were together."

"And kept saying it, even after the suicide."

Ryder shrugged. "Candy-ass like Nicky the Nerd, who'd've figured him for a stand-up guy? Tell me this, big shot: What the hell do you care? About this old shit?"

"I care because people keep telling me I don't."

"Like who?"

"Al Macpherson, for one. I thought I was looking for Gary Russell; next thing I know, Macpherson's offering to shove my license down my throat."

"Why are you looking for Russell? His father says he told you to back off."

"Scott told you that? He talked to Macpherson about it, too. Cozy little town you have here."

"Answer the question!"

I held myself back from telling him not to take that fucking tone with me. "I'm looking for Gary because he asked me for help. Not your business, Coach. Except there's this: Someone beat the crap out of a Warrenstown High girl yesterday, and I think it's all connected, all goes back twenty-three years, all has to do with me. See, I think people are getting the idea I was hired by the kids to look into this *old shit*. The kids, you know: Stacie Phillips, Tory Wesley, Gary Russell, Paul Niebuhr. And it's interesting: One of them's dead, one hospitalized, two are missing."

"Two?" Ryder frowned. "Russell and who else? Niebuhr?"

"I know he doesn't register on you because he's not a jock, but he's been gone for days."

All I needed now was a fishing pole, I thought, and one of those vests with a million pockets to hold things that, in the end, you never find a use for. But I kept silent, feeding out the line.

"What the fuck is going on?" Ryder asked. "Little snot-nosed shits, what do they want to know?"

"Not them," I said. "Me. None of those kids has anything to do with it. And what I want to know is: What happened back then, Ryder? What's Al Macpherson hiding, and what are you hiding?"

Ryder gave me a long, calculating look. A good coach is flexible: He can alter his strategy, play to other strengths if he sees trouble with the game plan he originally set out.

So Ryder shrugged his shoulders, rubbed his neck, projected the air of a man giving in. "Macpherson was in trouble," he said. "I didn't know if he did it or not and I really didn't give a shit."

"I'm not sure I believe that. You were his coach. If you'd asked him, Macpherson would've told you. You'd have been the one person he'd have told."

"Believe what you want." He shrugged. "Warrenstown High girl," he said. "Flashing her tits at a party. What's the difference who it was? She probably enjoyed it."

Beside me, Lydia stood still, as unmoving as the kids on the TV screen. I knew that was because if she let herself, she'd break Ryder's neck.

"So you had a talk with Scott Russell?" I said.

"Just to make sure he was absolutely positive, what he saw. Because if he wasn't, we had a really big game coming up."

"And the team needed both what Al Macpherson could contribute, and what Scott could. Is that what you told him, Ryder? Is that how you put it?"

The razor-edge smile again. "He'd improved a lot, Russell had. He was ready to start."

"Jesus." I looked into Ryder's eyes, and he into mine.

Behind him, a play was frozen on the TV screen, home team and visitors straining after the ball.

"That's all," Ryder said. "That's all there was, a talk with one of my players. Nothing illegal, maybe a little bad judgment, I'd rather it didn't get out, that's all. Now excuse me. I have work to do."

"So do I," I said. I stayed where I was.

"What does that mean?"

"The kid who killed himself. The story is, it was a teacher who came forward with the stalking thing. I just talked to John Letourneau, and he said he didn't know anything about it until the story started going around, just before the kid was arrested."

Ryder shrugged. "Tunnel vision, Letourneau. All his life, something didn't happen right under his nose, he didn't know about it."

Lydia spoke. "Even now, as police chief?" she said. "Like the fact that all your boys are on steroids? That's right under his nose. You think he knows about that?"

Ryder stared at her as though he'd forgotten she could talk. "Oh, Jesus God. What the fuck is this? The guys buy this shit, Andro, whatever the hell, at the health food store. It bulks them up, I'm all for it."

"What I heard is, they get prescription drugs illegally, from a dealer," Lydia answered.

"What you heard, toots, is crap. And if it was true, you think anyone in Warrenstown would give a shit? It makes them big. It makes them win."

"What happened to Nicky Dalton?" I said.

"Dalton? Mommy's boy. Who the hell cares what happened to Dalton?"

"He joined the army right after graduation, and disappeared the day he came out. Nobody's heard anything about him since."

"So?"

"Maybe he disappeared because he was afraid."

"Of what?"

"I don't know yet. Maybe, whatever it was that made Jared Beltran kill himself."

"That little perv killed himself because they were going to put him away for a long, long time. In a place where I promise you he'd have been a receiver, not a quarterback." He smiled a nasty smile. It faded, and he said, "And about Dalton, when you find him, don't call me, because I don't give a flying fuck."

He turned back to his TV screen, clicked the remote. The frozen play took up motion again: The guy the pass had been intended for caught it, hugged the ball to his chest, was immediately smashed and smothered by half a dozen opposing players, even more teammates. "Now," said Ryder, settling into his armchair, absorbed in the action once more, "get the hell out."

Lydia looked at me; I nodded. We turned, walked back down the silent hall. A janitor pushed a mop bucket along the corridor; the fumes of lemon-scented detergent filled the air.

"Alone with the ball, huh?" I said.

"I hope you're filled with admiration for my restraint."

"I'm filled with admiration for everything about you, as always."

"Did we accomplish anything, besides raising my blood pressure?"

"For one thing, I wanted to get across the point that if what I'm doing is what's getting everybody's back up, the kids aren't involved in it. I'm not sure Ryder's the guy to say that to, but I'm hoping it'll get around."

"Are you sure it's true?"

I lit a cigarette, considered her question. "No."

"Okay," she said. "But anyway, we told him. Did he tell us anything?"

"I'm not sure. What did you get?"

"Well," she said, "he admitted to something that could be construed as tampering with a witness. That could be bad for him, for his reputation, even if it wasn't actually illegal."

"You mean, it could be true that that's all he's hiding?"

"Could be."

"But you don't buy it."

"No."

"For a reason, or just because you hate him?"

"That's a reason. Can I ask you something?"

"What?"

"Did he remind you of Mr. Hamlin?"

"Stacie said that, too. That that's what Warrenstown loves about Hamlin: He's just like Coach Ryder."

"Where do you suppose he learned that?"

"That coaching style? I hate to add to your disillusionment with organized athletics, but it's a fairly common one."

"Bill, they use the same *words. Candy-asses. Pervs. Mommy's boys.* Everyone else in the world says *momma's boys,* except these two guys."

I glanced at her as we left the school, walked together down the stone steps. "Well, I suppose Hamlin could have coached under Ryder," I said. "Or played under him, when he was a kid."

"Ryder's been at Warrenstown for thirty-five years, and Hamlin's not much older than that. That would mean Hamlin's either from here, or he worked here for a while."

"That could be."

"Why didn't anyone tell us that?"

We reached her Taurus, shadowed now that the sun was low. The wide lot was almost empty, just half a dozen cars spotted around the asphalt, none close to any of the others. I thought of Stacie Phillips, unlocking her car, her mind on the work she'd just done, or her plans for the evening, or anything but a man in a hockey mask grabbing her, kicking her, shouting over and over a question she didn't understand.

"And?" Lydia said, standing by her car, keys in hand. "Now what?"

The wind turned sharply, cut back across us, pulling Lydia's hair across her forehead, snaking under my open jacket. I zipped up, leaned against the car, stuck my hands in my pockets. I watched leaves skim the surface of the lot, watched the wind move through the branches they'd fallen from.

"Where to now?" Lydia asked.

"Shit," I said. "I don't know." I didn't want to get into the car, didn't want to head somewhere else, down another nowhere road to ask more futile questions, didn't want to keep going, playing a game where I didn't know the rules, didn't know where I stood, didn't even know what outcome I wanted.

Cops in two states were looking for Gary now, as they looked for Paul, and when they found them they'd find how all this tied together. Or not. But I had nothing they didn't have, except suspicions they didn't want to hear. And maybe they were right. If I'd been a cop, I'd be putting everything I had into finding Paul Niebuhr. Even the death of Tory Wesley would have to wait, never mind a case twenty-three years old, until the threat to a school full of kids was stopped.

"Come on." Lydia's voice, though soft, was clear over the wind. "I'll buy you a drink."

I turned my head to look at her. "I thought you said my case, my expense account."

"It's a one-time offer. Because you look so pitiful."

"That works? Looking pitiful?"

"In your case, it may be the only thing that works."

I pulled the door open, got in the car. I was prepared to take her up on it, even if it meant admitting to pitifulness. She started the car, but we weren't out of the lot when my cell phone rang.

"Goddammit," I said under my breath. I took the phone out, opened it. "Smith."

"You fucking son of a bitch!" Scott's voice practically scorched my ear. "You sent the cops here! Bastard, I'm coming for you—"

"Don't bother," I said. "We'll come to you."

I thumbed the phone off, put it away. "The drink will

have to wait," I told Lydia. "But I'll need it more later. Make a left up here."

"Where are we going?"

"To drop in on my relations."

twenty-three

Lydia and I drove over to the development on the edge of town. The pale gray house sat peaceably in the twilight, brass lantern shining softly over the front door, windows glowing gold. Scott's Lumina sat behind Helen's Blazer in the driveway, as though guarding it from harm. Lydia parked the Taurus on the street.

"This won't be fun," I said to her.

"For *you*." She got out of the car, stood waiting on the sidewalk. I looked at her but didn't answer as we headed up the chrysanthemum-lined path.

At a nod from me Lydia pressed the doorbell, and the soft chimes I'd heard for the first time two days before, the bell at my sister's house, echoed from inside. For a moment, the twilit scene was peaceful, calm, just the graying sky and the carefully spaced houses, me standing next to Lydia in the glow of the lantern. Then the door flew back as though afraid, a brighter light sliced out onto the step, and Scott stood before us, his face red and twisted with rage.

"You cocksucker!" The still air exploded with his voice. "You son of a bitch! That's some fucking pair—!" The Doberman raced into the vestibule, drowned out his shouts with barking. She lowered her shoulders, planted her feet. She looked ready to rip the throat out of whatever was threatening her home.

So did Scott.

"We need to talk, Scott," I said, my voice raised over his, over the barking.

The dog yelped more furiously, picking up on Scott's tone, his stance. Behind her, Jennifer and Paula appeared, coming to see what the noise was about. The dog growled and snapped. Scott looked at the girls, his face dark with the heat of his anger. He put a restraining hand on the dog's collar. "No," he said. "Stay." He stepped outside, closing the door on the dog, and on his daughters. We stood together in the twilight, Lydia and Scott and I, the dog's barking muffled now. No other sound came into the silence between us and nothing moved except the tops of the bare trees behind the house as the wind blew through.

I said nothing, waited. Scott finally spoke. "You motherfucker." He locked his eyes on mine, spoke very deliberately, very slowly. "I ought to let that dog tear your heart out."

"Scott, can we—?"

"*No, we fucking can't, asshole!* You tore one family apart for Helen, now you can't wait to do it again, can you? Jesus Christ, why couldn't you leave us alone? Who fucking asked you?"

Gary did, I thought, but my blood was pounding in my ears and my fists were tight and that wasn't what I wanted to say to him. There were a dozen other answers surging through my mind, ways to show my brother-in-law that my anger burned as hot as his, my contempt ran as icy cold. I opened my mouth to speak, took a step forward. I waited to feel Lydia's hand on my arm, her cool reasonableness; I was ready to shake it off, to step to where Scott was, to let the heat of my anger ignite his. No one would get hurt in the firestorm that would come of that except Scott and me, and that would be all right.

But Lydia didn't touch me. Lydia didn't move. And I looked at Scott, saw he was ready too, and I thought, this is over. Scott and I will always be like this, never change.

No one will ever win. This will never end, and so it's ended. It's over.

I stepped back, opened my hands. "This isn't why I came." I wasn't sure that was true, but I had had another reason, too. I stood without moving, looked into Scott's eyes. Suddenly, for a second, the door and the stoop and the trees vanished. I was on an asphalt half-court in a Brooklyn playground, facing my opponent, both of us waiting. The explosive rage of my youth, that anger that never left me, was compressed into a small, tight, fiery place deep inside, where I could draw on it for the extra step, the burst of speed, the stretch in a jump; and as long as I could keep it there, not flowing through, around, over me, I could see clearly, keep a cold eye on my opponent, understand completely my situation. Only in a game or at the piano could I do this, when I was young. Now, there were other times, too. I breathed deeply, spoke to Scott.

"I know the police were here and I'm sorry," I said, "but I had nothing to do with it."

Suspicion came into his eyes, not, I thought, at my words—he had long established in his mind my guilt, my cravenness—but at the tone I used, the stance I took, my surprising unwillingness to settle what we'd started the night before, what we'd started years ago.

"That asshole Sullivan." He ground the words out. "He came to my house with a fucking search warrant because you—"

"No, because your friend Letourneau sent him. They're looking for a boy who could be planning to shoot up the school. Paul Niebuhr. Gary's a friend of his."

"And they're looking for Gary because you fucking said—"

"No, they're looking for Gary because he's a friend of Paul Niebuhr's."

"You—"

"Scott, goddammit, *listen.* Whatever reason Gary had for leaving home, it came before he called me. It's connected to things going on in Warrenstown, and things that went on here. I didn't cause that, Scott, and I'm not looking to screw anybody over. Not even you. Not even you. I want to find your son."

He stared at me, and I don't know what answer he was planning to make. If our positions had been reversed, if I'd been standing where he was as the twilight passed into night, the best I'd have been able to manage would have been, "Go to hell." At my most controlled, I would have been able to turn, walk back into my warm, bright house, leave him alone and shut out in the dark.

Maybe he'd have done that, or maybe he'd have tried again to spark the explosion we both wanted. But the door behind him opened. Yellow light spilled onto the stoop once more, and my sister stood in it, one step outside her home. "What are you doing?" She looked from her husband to her brother, her high voice quavering. "What are you doing?"

Scott, eyes still on me, stepped back, pulled shut the door behind her. Now there were four of us under the glow of the porch lamp, darkness everywhere beyond except where a streetlight pooled to light the way, or where windows shone in other people's homes.

The silence was long, no one moving. Then Scott looked at Lydia. "Who's this?" he said, his voice so low the wind almost masked it.

"My partner," I said. "Lydia Chin."

"You were there last night," Scott said to her. She nodded. Scott considered her another moment, turned his gaze to me again. Helen and Lydia waited, spectators; Scott, jaw tight, waited, too, for my move.

"When I saw Gary in New York," I said, "he wouldn't tell me what he was doing, but Scott, he said you'd approve. 'My dad would be cool with this, if he knew.' You tell me you're close with him. You take him hunting, you go to his games. What can that mean? What is he doing that he thinks you'd approve of?"

The wind was gathering strength now, and the night was complete. In the trees, the moon had come up, but the wind

had brought clouds; all I could see was a ragged bright patch
in the dark.

"I used to beat that kid's ass," Scott said, "I used to make
sure he felt it, when he lied. He fucked up, he came clean,
he got off a lot easier than if he lied about it. I thought I
could make a man out of him, a stand-up guy. But if he
said that, he's lying now, because there's not a fucking thing
I can think of that would make it okay, what he's putting
his mother through."

Helen bit her lip. Her eyes started to fill, tears glistening
in the porch light. From deep within, the fire swept through
me, and the words burst into my mind: *I'll kill him.* My face
burned and my heart pounded when I saw her tears, and I
thought, *Someday I'll kill him.* I stepped toward Scott, felt
my fists clench, my blood race. Then Lydia did touch my
hand. She just brushed it with her fingers, but her skin was
cool and smooth, and when I felt her touch, the hot mist in
my own eyes cleared. I saw who it was I was looking at,
and I saw, in my mind, who it was I wanted, and they were
not the same. I forced myself to stop, stand, forced the fire
to retreat again.

"A couple more questions," I said, my words gravelly
but under control. "Then we're gone."

"Why?" Scott's voice was as cold as the wind in the
trees. "Why the hell should I answer any questions from
you?"

"Because you were here," I said. "Because I think this
thing comes out of what happened here years ago."

"Bullshit."

"Maybe. But the cops are already working on the present.
What can you lose, answering me?"

He didn't speak, but he stayed. That was enough.

"Beth Victor, Jared Beltran," I said.

"It's bullshit," he said again.

"What I need to know," I said, speaking quietly, meeting
Scott's eyes, "and I'm asking you because you were here,
Scott, because I don't know anyone else who was a kid here
in those days and I don't have time to find someone—about

Jared Beltran stalking Beth Victor. Had you ever heard that before the rape?"

I expected something from Helen, a flick of her eyes toward Scott, a frown of confusion, a flush of embarrassment at the topic. She stood, instead, calm and still beside her husband, and I realized he must have told her. I wondered how much he'd said, whether she understood his role, but I wasn't here for that.

Scott's look, and the silence, were very long. Finally, he said, "No."

"It wasn't true, was it?"

A long pause; then, "I don't know."

"Who was the teacher the tip came from?"

"I don't know."

I nodded. "What happened to Nick Dalton?"

"Nicky? Fuck Nicky, who the hell cares what happened to him?"

"Do you know where he is now?"

"Now?" A smile burned across Scott's face. "Fuck that asshole, maybe he's here now. Maybe it's him."

"What does that mean?"

"Nicky. Nicky the fucking Nerd. He always said he'd come back, he'd make us all sorry. Fuck that asshole, maybe this is all about him. That what you think, Smith? You think Nicky's behind all this, Nicky kidnapped my son, Nicky killed that girl, Nicky came back to get us all? Well, good luck. Keep looking. You just keep on looking for Nicky and stay out of my fucking life!"

Scott reached back, pushed open the door to his house. He held out a hand to my sister. She took it, turned away from me, and went inside with him.

I was headed down the walk before the door closed. I wanted to keep going into the wind, away, anywhere, any distance, not look back again, not ever. But Lydia's car was at the curb and Lydia's footsteps, light and sure, sounded behind me. I stopped at the car; after a second, I brought my fist down hard onto the hood. I heard my voice throwing a curse into the wind, felt pain jar my arm to the shoulder.

Then I thought, No! Goddammit, no. I stood, head down, hands on the cold steel of the car, trying again to force the fire back down into that small, controlled place.

Lydia said nothing. After a moment she went around and unlocked the car. I got in. She started it up and we drove away along the well-laid-out, gently curving streets. The people who'd planned this place had tried to eliminate sharp turns, hidden ways, any chance of anything unexpected. There was supposed to be nothing here to make you suddenly have to change where you were headed, take another path. But up ahead a dog sniffed his way onto the street from behind a parked car. Lydia stamped on the brake, pressed the horn. The dog, startled, snarled and sped across. It could have been a kid on a bike, on a skateboard. It could have been a police car racing up the street, or fire trucks at a burning house. I thought of the planners, and an icy contempt filled me, both for the intention, and for the fact that it had failed.

I rolled down the window and lit a cigarette. Lydia hadn't been to this development before but she seemed to know well how to get out, how to leave these houses, and Warrenstown, behind. She put us on the road to Greenmeadow, back to where we'd left my car.

We drove in silence. Not until we were pulling into the hospital parking lot did Lydia speak. She said, "That's why he hates you."

I looked over at her as she stopped her car beside mine. I tried my voice carefully, not sure I trusted it. "Why?"

She turned the key in the ignition, faced me. "His testimony could have sent a friend to prison, and he took his story back."

"And I didn't?"

"That's right."

Her eyes were steady and clear; it was I who looked away.

"And I'm even worse," I said. "Because in my case it was family. And in his, he wasn't sure of what he saw."

"No," Lydia said. "He was sure."

I watched her face, soft in the shadows. "You think so?"

"He was. Al Macpherson raped Beth Victor; Scott saw them, just before. The stalking stories, the coach started that. The teacher who wanted to stay anonymous. He picked that boy, Jared, because he was weird anyway, so people might believe it. And because he was expendable."

"Then why did Jared shoot himself?" I asked her, though I thought I knew.

"Because he was a nerd at Warrenstown High, and now they said he was a pervert. His life was already hell, and all he had now was a choice between going to prison, or worse hell."

"No other way out?"

"In a town where the parents held a candlelight rally in support of Al Macpherson?"

I slipped another cigarette from my jacket, rolled it around in my fingers.

"Scott's always known that," Lydia said. "That the coach's lies and his own silence killed that boy. He's spent his life telling himself that what he did was the stand-up thing to do, for his friend. Not the kind of thing a coward would do who was afraid of the other jocks, and the coach, and this town, and who wanted to play in the game."

I said, "He's spent his life trying to make a man—a stand-up guy, he said—out of Gary."

An ambulance pulled into the parking lot, no siren howling, no lights flashing. It rolled slowly around the building to the emergency entrance. It was headed there, I supposed, because that was the entrance ambulances used; but it was in no hurry, carrying no one who could be helped.

"And he hates you," Lydia says, "and calls you a coward, because you had the guts to do what he should have done."

The car was hot and close; I couldn't sit there anymore. I got out, stood in the wind. Lydia got out also, and came around the car to stand beside me, and this time she took my hand. I thought of Scott, and fire, and boys forced to make choices men are forced to live with; I thought of Gary, without a jacket, without help on the cold streets; I thought of a lot of things, a lot of places, and through it I felt the solid warmth of Lydia's hand.

"Why did he come back?" I said.

"Scott? To Warrenstown?"

I nodded.

"My guess?"

"Yes."

"Gary was getting to be the age Scott was when Warrenstown made a man out of him."

"So Scott brought him here?"

"To prove he'd been right, what he'd done. To prove he had nothing to be ashamed of."

"Prove to whom?"

She didn't answer that, because she didn't need to.

"Do you think Gary knows?" I said.

"What Scott did? Probably what he knows is that Scott stood up for his friend."

"And that's what Gary's doing now, that Scott would be proud of? Standing up for Paul? By helping him get ready to shoot the school up?"

"We don't know that's what he's doing."

"We don't know anything."

She shook her head, looked at the ground. A gust of wind lifted her hair; she pushed it back off her cheek, said, "You know who I feel bad for?"

"Besides me, because I'm so pitiful?"

That caught her by surprise; she smiled, and our eyes met. I thought again of fire, but a different kind. I don't know what she thought of, but her smile grew; then she looked away, and it faded again. "That other boy," she said. "Nick Dalton. Watching that happen to his friend, and there's nothing he can do."

"He said he'd be back, and get them all."

"Umm-hmm," she said. "Does he seem to have?"

The wind turned and blasted across the parking lot, pounding into us like a weight. I shook my head, saw Jared Beltran's face, the grinning kid in the newspaper photo, the kid who was excited at the idea of what lay ahead.

"Jesus Christ." I was suddenly cold and it had nothing to do with the wind. "Oh, shit. Oh, sweet Jesus on the cross!"

Lydia lifted her eyebrows. "Am I to understand from this that an idea has hit you?"

"That picture! I've seen that kid before."

"Which picture? Which kid?"

"Get in the car, I'll tell you as we go."

"Which car?"

"Oh," I said. "Oh. Both cars."

"Where are we going?"

"Hamlin's." I dropped her hand, fished for my keys. "He has a picture on his desk."

"Two skinny kids on the beach? Bad haircuts, glasses?" She'd seen that one, too, but she hadn't seen the photo from the Warrenstown PD case file.

I nodded. "Nerds. The one on the left is Jared Beltran."

twenty-four

We talked on the phone for a while, as we drove away from Greenmeadow, past Warrenstown, to the bridge, but the questions we had were not really for each other. Both of us knew the way to Hamlin's, so we didn't worry about traveling together, just set up a meeting place at the head of the driveway there.

After we hung up I pressed another number into my phone. I braced myself for Vélez's, *"Ay, dios mio,"* when he heard it was me, and after it came, I said, "Hey, it's not four in the morning, what's your problem, Luigi?"

"I ain't about to tell you, *chico,* because you ain't about to care. What you got now, you want done in ten minutes?"

"Tom Hamlin," I said. "Runs a place called Hamlin's Institute of American Sports, in Plaindale. Long Island," I added, in case Vélez's definition of the borders of New York didn't extend to Long Island. "Whatever you can get me. And Luigi? Forty minutes," I said generously.

I drove the bridge, the Cross Bronx, the Long Island Expressway. Commuters heading home crowded the roads, and traffic was thick, slow, but it kept moving. Lydia was with me, just ahead or just behind; in the darkness I couldn't tell which, but I knew she was close. Somewhere in there, at just under half an hour, Vélez called back.

"This guy," he said. "I got his address, his phone number,

his driver's license, his credit rating—and his credit's good, *chico*—and all this shit about this institute thing."

"Like?"

"Used to be a army reserve base, decommissioned and sat around for a while growin' weeds until this guy Hamlin bought it fifteen years ago."

"Does it make money?"

"Makes enough. Pays him, assistant coaches, trainers, nurse, maintenance people, all shit like that."

"No extra money? Nothing being laundered, maybe?"

"That what you're looking for, you shoulda told me that up front, *chico,* make my life easier," he grumbled. "Uh-uh. Hamlin and his other coaches, they're making a living, but no one's getting rich out there."

"Sorry, Luigi," I said. "It was a stab in the dark. I don't know what I'm looking for."

"You ever do? But I do got something interesting for you, amigo, no extra charge."

"And what's that?"

"All of this shit I got, it's right up front, you know? Anybody could dig it up, not just a genius like me. Like the guy's not trying to hide nothing. But I'm telling you, he's hiding *something*."

"Why?"

"The man's life's an open book, but the book don't go back no more than twenty years."

"What do you mean?"

He sighed. "Twenty years, *chico*. Like this guy was made in a lab, put out on the street then."

"Nothing earlier? Birth certificate, grade school, high school graduation?"

"Old driver's license, old address, medical records, credit, college, military. No nothing, *chico*. Like that other guy, from yesterday, that one who disappeared? This guy could be the negative of him."

"Yeah, Luigi," I said. "I think he is."

I called Lydia, told her what Vélez had said. As I pulled off the highway onto the streets of Plaindale I found her, in my mirror, following. We met up, left her car up the street from the diner on the road outside Hamlin's, and drove down Hamlin's long drive in mine.

Barboni was behind the desk again, and his surprised scowl when he saw us held a shadow of dark pleasure: the unexpected chance for a rematch.

"No," I said, holding my hands up, palms out, as he started to rise. "Your boss wants to see us."

"I don't think so."

"You're wrong." I took out a business card, wrote *Nick Dalton* on the back. "Give him this."

Barboni read the card, hesitated, and might have been about to rip it up and haul off and sock me, but Lydia winked at him. He flushed scarlet. She smiled, ran her hand through her hair, and as she lifted her arm her jacket moved and revealed a flash of the gun clipped to her waistband.

He scowled again, then said gruffly, "Wait here, and don't touch nothing!" and slipped through the double doors behind him.

"That's the same as wiggling your hips," I muttered to Lydia as we stood waiting, touching nothing.

"How little you know," she answered.

Barboni came back, wordlessly held the door for us. He followed Lydia with hungry eyes as we walked through.

Tom Hamlin was standing behind his desk in the inner office; the outer one was again empty. He held my card out in front of him, looked from it to me as though comparing a picture. I was ready for the full fury, the withering scorn, of the Coach I'd seen on the field and in this office. But after a moment Hamlin just smiled, asked not unpleasantly, "Who exactly are you?"

"I was going to ask you that," I said, a little thrown, then remembering Lydia's words: *It was like a switch turned off.*

"Tom Hamlin." The smile spread on his weathered face. He opened his arms, showed us his photo-lined, trophy-packed world. "Builder of men."

I picked the framed picture up off his desk, looked at the grinning kids. Jared Beltran, on the left. On the right, another kid, taller, bigger but still skinny, looking into the camera with a sunnier version of the same smile Tom Hamlin was wearing right now.

I handed the picture to Lydia. "Formerly Nick Dalton," I said. "Of Warrenstown, New Jersey."

Hamlin dropped my card on his desk, reached over and took the picture from Lydia's hand. He set it gently back in its place, facing him. "Warrenstown, New Jersey," he said, "is a shithole."

"I'm not sure you'd get an argument from me on that," I said. "But they just spent a big pile of money sending their seniors to you for a week, so you could make men out of them."

"A week in the fall for the seniors," Hamlin agreed, "summer camps, weekend clinics. Sometimes we have a three-hour program on a weekday evening, and do you know some of those assholes will drive an hour and a half to bring their kids to those?"

"Do they know who you are?"

He raised his eyebrows. "Tom Hamlin."

I shook my head. "Nick Dalton was in the army. They'll have his fingerprints." I asked again, "Does anyone in Warrenstown know?"

He shrugged, dropped into the desk chair. "Goddamn unlikely, don't you think? Although I'm not so sure they'd give a damn. Sit down." He leaned back comfortably. Lydia sat on a chair facing him, and I pulled over another one.

"Why wouldn't they give a damn?" I said.

"Me and Warrenstown, that's ancient history. Warrenstown's always been a forward-looking place. No one there ever gave a shit about what happened. Just what's going to happen. Focused on the future. Results-oriented. 'It doesn't matter how you play, as long as you win the game.' The town motto of Warrenstown, New Jersey. And," he added, "words we live by here at Hamlin's Institute."

"We know what happened," I said.

"Good for you. You think anyone else gives a flying

fuck? What Warrenstown cares about is *men*. And just look
how many men I've built for them."

"Fifteen years' worth?"

"Absolutely. We guarantee it." He nodded his head
gravely. "You remember that senator, Shane Fowler, youngest state senator ever in New Jersey? Had a hell of a career
going for a while, until they caught him with a sixteen-year-
old girl? He was one of mine, from Warrenstown." He
looked into space, smiled as though at a pleasant memory.
"I had a Warrenstown kid, Brandon Doyle, playing football
for Harvard three years ago."

"Doyle? He was a linebacker," I said. "Got thrown out
in a cheating scandal, I remember that. He was from Warrenstown?"

"You bet," Hamlin said. "Oh, and just last spring, one of
my Warrenstown boys, a freshman halfback at New Hampshire, got so shit-faced at a frat party he showed the highest
level of blood alcohol ever recorded in someone who wasn't
dead. Almost dead, after they peeled his car off a light pole,
but not quite dead."

"You sound proud of him."

"Proud of them all, Smith, proud of them all. They're
men."

"I don't get it."

"Oh, come on. These boys own the world. Warrenstown
tells them that, I tell them that. Work hard enough, tear your
muscles, fracture your bones, shit your pants and puke on
the field, you can get to play football like a motherfucker.
Play football like a motherfucker, you own the fucking
world. You can have it all, do whatever you want, no one
will stop you. I'd apologize for my language," he said, turning to Lydia, "but I really don't give a damn."

"That's what it's like in Warrenstown," I said.

"Goddamn right. And that's what it's like at Hamlin's."

"Revenge," Lydia said, her voice low and clear. "Nick
Dalton said he'd be back for revenge."

"I'm giving them," Hamlin said, "what they want."

"You're making their boys into monsters," I said.

"In Warrenstown, they know what they want." He smiled again.

"Coach Ryder's drills, his attitude, his words. Everyone in Warrenstown loves Hamlin's because you do it just the way they do it there."

"Makes them feel like they're looking in a mirror. And you know what? They are. They made me, Smith. And I make men out of their boys. See," he said, "see, Jared asked me to. He said, 'Nicky, will you help me? Will you get them for me?' And I said, 'Sure,' even though I didn't really know what he meant. I said, 'Sure.'"

"Jared Beltran asked you? When?"

Hamlin looked at the photo on his desk. "The guys from the football team got him the next day, after the police let him go. Like they had before he was arrested. They beat him up some more. Broke his glasses. Made him say, 'I'm a fucking pervert' over and over. They found some dog shit and made him eat it."

"Jesus," I said.

"He asked me to help him, and I said I would, and then he killed himself. It bothered me for a while, that I didn't help him. Then it hit me, you know, even if I couldn't help him, I could still get them. That's what he asked me to do, and I could do that."

He raised his eyes calmly, met mine. Hamlin's office was brightly lit, heated well enough, but I was looking into his eyes. I felt a chill that nothing could warm anymore, saw a darkness nothing could ever light.

"You alibied him," I said.

"He was with me." Hamlin shrugged. "We were at my house. They had *Night of the Living Dead* on TV. He didn't go home until way after that girl left the party."

"It was Macpherson, then."

"Oh, yeah, sure it was," he said without particular interest, a man telling a story he'd learned long ago that no one wanted to hear. "One kid even saw them together, but he changed his story. That's why they let Macpherson go, and they needed someone else. Me and Jared, we were both losers, but my dad had money."

"You must have had trouble with them, too," I said. "The kids on the football team. Because of the alibi."

He rubbed his mouth. "Yeah," he said.

"Do you know who it was who spread the stalking stories?"

"Never did. Doesn't matter. The thing about that was, it was so completely stupid, only a place like Warrenstown could have bought it."

Doesn't matter, I thought. But maybe that was true. I wondered how much would change, if he did know.

"What about the other towns?" I asked quietly. "Westbury, places like that?"

"No one makes them send their boys here."

"Hamlin," Lydia said. "The Pied Piper. He led the children away."

Tom Hamlin said, "Only the ones who wanted to go."

"In the story," said Lydia, "that was all of them. Except the crippled one. He wanted to, but he couldn't."

"Led them away," I said, "because the parents wouldn't pay."

Hamlin said, "They're paying now."

I watched his eyes. His right hand held his coach's whistle, turned it over, around. He met my gaze, smiled again. "And you're the first asshole—" He turned to Lydia. "—excuse me, ass*holes*, who ever figured it out. You know, I've had that picture on my desk since I opened this place, no one's ever looked at it?"

I picked it up, looked at it now. "The mouth's the same," I said. "Not the nose, the ears. Plastic surgery?"

"Of course. Not much, just enough so those jerkoffs could keep from seeing what they didn't want to see. Mostly, I spent three years in the army, five years after, bulking up. Borrowed money, hired famous coaches and pro athletes because I knew those names would impress those motherfuckers. Kept my rates low in the beginning. Now, of course, I can charge whatever I want. They'd give me their firstborn. Oh, hey, they do, don't they?" He beamed.

"And no one's caught on?"

"You don't get it about those guys, that town." He corrected me mildly, as though just to help me understand, not because what we were discussing mattered to him. "They don't want to see. I went out to Warrenstown to pitch the camp to them the year I bought it. Just eight years after I graduated. Nobody—Coach Ryder, nobody—even said, 'Hey, don't I know you?' Well, you saw: That pervert Macpherson was in here the other night, probably the tenth time we've met. Up until then, I was his best buddy. He fell all over himself to give me money for the Warrenstown boys. And even pissed off like he was that night, it never crossed his mind I had a reason to be breaking his balls."

I thought about what he was saying, what he'd done, and how reasonable and even clever it seemed to him. I thought about some of the things I'd done in my own life, about what Paul Niebuhr and Gary Russell might be doing now.

"Tell me about bulking up," I said, leaving the rest of it for later. "Lifting, conditioning, training?"

"Worked five years after the army in a place like this, upstate New York. Hey, I had a lot of sports to learn."

I gestured at the picture, its back to me now. "And you were a skinny little guy."

Something dark flicked across his face, but it passed. "Ancient history," he said.

"So maybe you needed some help bulking up."

"Everyone needs help. The army was great for that. Helpful guys, no worries about pain or long-term damage, sissy shit. Just 'Get up, Dalton, unless you're dead!' Helped a lot."

"Chemical help, too?" I asked.

"Like?"

"Steroids?"

"Well, now, you have to be really careful with steroids," Hamlin said, his face taking on a mock earnestness, a fake concern that chilled my spine. "You have to really know

what you're doing. Especially if you're a kid." He smiled
again. "Could fuck up your life."

"But you know what you're doing."

"I know all kinds of shit."

"And you tell the kids."

"They're here for their education."

"You tell them, for example, where they can get steroids."

"I don't have to. They know."

"What do they know? That they can get them here?"

"Here? Back off, Jack. No fucking way. Nothing illegal
goes on at Hamlin's. Kid comes here with a can of beer,
he's out on his ass. My goal is to stay out of trouble and
stay in business. I'm building men here, and I love my
work."

I was aching for a cigarette, but I didn't do anything
about it. I couldn't tell what kind of an edge Hamlin was
on, and I didn't want to push him. "So if the camp were
searched right now, we wouldn't find any drugs?"

"Give me a break. We don't strip-search them. Some kid
has a few pills in his wallet, vitamins, this and that, I guess
I wouldn't know about it. But they don't get them here.
Besides, what's the big deal? They want to be big. They
work like sons of bitches, two-a-day practices, weights,
homework until three in morning because they were in the
gym until midnight, and their parents tell them how proud
they are. Why shouldn't they get a little help from modern
science?"

"Where do they get them?"

"What?"

"The steroids, Hamlin. Where do they get them?"

"Oh, here, there, who knows?"

I said, "I need to know."

"Well, I'm sure sorry I can't help you."

"There's a big problem." Lydia spoke up in a cool and
steady voice, fixing Hamlin's attention. "A girl is dead, and
other people may die, unless we unravel what's going on.

Where the boys in Warrenstown get their steroids is one of the questions we've got to have answers to."

"These people who're going to die," Hamlin said, his voice easy, his smile wide and suddenly venomous, "are they in Warrenstown?"

Coach Hamlin, furious and vindictive on the field; Nick Dalton, aka Tom Hamlin, mild-mannered and reasonable in his office.

Well, I thought, whatever works.

I was around the desk before Hamlin could stand up. I yanked him out of his chair, slammed him against a file cabinet. The trophies crowding the top rattled and one fell to the floor as Hamlin's head hit the steel.

His eyes flew wide. "What the fuck is your problem?" He tried to grab for me, but though he'd built his muscles and changed his life what he'd become was a bully, and bullies are bad fighters. I danced back; he grasped air. I shouldered in again, this time smashing him against the cabinet's hard edge. He yelped. I took him by the shoulders and shoved him face down on his desk. Twisting his arm behind him, I shouted, "Where?" My shout and the sounds of rattling, crashing, pounding, brought Barboni to the door.

"Hey!" He charged in, but Lydia was up with a yell to distract him and a sweep of her leg to pull his feet out from under him. She sent him sprawling.

"Fuck!" Hamlin growled. "Jesus fuck, what's the big deal?" I let up some on his arm but kept him pressed to the desk. "Any Warrenstown boy could tell you where they get them, what the fuck are you beating on me for?"

"They could," I said, "but they won't. You will."

"Yeah, all right. Jesus." I let him up. He stood rubbing his shoulder. "Well, why not? Can't hurt me, and probably won't hurt my business, either. Of course, if you say you heard it here, I'll say you're a liar."

"Where?"

Hamlin smiled, that smile that was wide and warm in the photograph on his desk, dead and cold in here. "It's almost funny, now I think about it. It's the only difference between him and me anymore, really. Besides him thinking that what we both do, the way we build men, is a *good* thing. The only other difference between us, now, is that Coach Ryder deals steroids to the kids, and I don't."

twenty-five

I called Sullivan from my cell phone while Lydia and I stood in the wind in Hamlin's parking lot, Barboni watching us through the wire glass of the locked double doors.

"It's Smith," I said.

"I'm busy."

"You'll be busier. Did you know Coach Ryder is the guy dealing steroids to your football team?"

Silence; then, "If I knew that, you think I'd be sitting around with my thumb up my ass?"

"It's Warrenstown."

"You can't—"

"No," I said, "I'm sorry. Anyway, you know now."

"Yeah, well, now, Smith, right *now*, I'm kind of occupied. I'm looking for a couple of kids with guns."

"Take a break, go arrest the coach."

"On what evidence?"

"Nick Dalton's."

"What?"

"He's been under your noses for fifteen years." I told Sullivan about Hamlin, about his camp and his reasons.

"I don't believe this," he said when I was through.

"Worry about it later. Arrest the coach."

"On the word of a suspect's uncle about the word of a nut? Listen, this guy may not be Dalton, Smith. He may be some loony who heard the story, met Dalton in the army maybe—"

"And decided to devote his life to being Dalton's avenging angel?"

"Or his evening to pulling some PI's chain."

"That's crap. But even if it were true, he could still be right about Ryder. Pick him up."

"I can't do that."

"Why, because he's fucking St. Coach in Warrenstown and they'd hand you your ass on a platter? Christ, Sullivan, then pick up a kid. Any kid. One of those guys with the thick necks—Randy Macpherson, maybe. Or try my pal Morgan Reed. You have the answer, they'll break down and confirm it for you."

"Look," he said. "I'll look into this. If it's true, I'll build a case and when it's ready I'll arrest him. But right now—"

"No, Sullivan, now. Because if the steroids and the ecstasy were coming from the same place, Ryder may know something about Tory Wesley's death, and if he does, he may know something about where those boys are."

"The steroids and the ecstasy—that's *your* theory, Smith. I didn't buy it then, and if it's the coach, no way. Ryder handing out steroids, yeah, okay. Make them big, give them an edge. But party drugs, I don't think so. This is a coach who benches them, he finds them smoking, drinking coffee."

"Maybe it's wrong, maybe it's bullshit," I said. "But you say you're looking for those boys: What else do you have?"

A very long pause. The wind blew harder, colder; the stars and the moon had disappeared above a heavy weight of clouds. "Tomorrow," Sullivan said, "is the game at Hamlin's. Last time the seniors will ever play, most of them. Whole town goes out there to say good-bye to this year's heroes, see if *St. Coach* can beat them with what he's got for next year. You want me to pick him up for questioning, on the hearsay evidence of a nut. Smith, only way I could pick up Ryder before this game would be if he had some kid's blood dripping from his teeth."

"I think he does."

"*You* think." Another silence; then, "I'll call you." The phone went dead.

I folded it, put it in my pocket. From another pocket I slipped a cigarette. "Where to?" I asked Lydia.

"Excuse me? Your case, your car, your bright ideas. This, by the way, was a prizewinner."

"Yeah," I said, striking a match. "I want a trophy."

Lydia looked at me long and hard. The wind was messing with her hair; she ran her hand through it, and said, "Home."

"What?"

"You're exhausted. And I am, too," she added, overriding my objection. "Let's get away from this place, go have dinner, maybe get some sleep. The police are working on this, in high gear. Give them a chance. Unless you come up with another bright idea—"

"—or you do; it may be my case but I'm not proprietary about it. You're welcome to have bright ideas, too."

"Thank you, this *is* mine. Let's go home."

The wind pushed her hair across her forehead again, and this time I smoothed it for her. "You know," I said, "if this were your case and your nephew and I said let's go home, you'd break my kneecap."

"Undoubtedly."

I looked into her eyes as the wind turned again, whipped across us from the other direction. I wanted to be with Lydia someplace else, on a broad empty field like this but someplace where the wind was still and the air was warm and sweet and the sky was covered with stars. I brushed her hair back one more time although it didn't need it, felt its silkiness under my fingertips. I thought I smelled the freesia scent she so often wears, though in the wind, in the cold, that wasn't likely.

"Okay," I said. "Home."

We had brought both cars so we each drove alone, along a highway much less crowded, going into the city at night, than it had been leaving it at rush hour. I didn't know what

Lydia was doing in her car: maybe she had the radio on and she was catching up on the news, or she'd found some local college station where they played freshly burned CDs by garage bands from around the neighborhood; or maybe she was on the phone, talking to her mother, or a brother or a cousin, checking in with her family, sharing her day. I usually drive with music, but now my speakers were silent, the CDs stacked in the holder between the seats. I had the window open, and I felt the cold push of the wind, the damp heaviness in the air. I tried not to think, just to drive, beating the traffic around me but not by much, pulling into the right lane occasionally for drivers—usually young men—whose need for speed was greater than mine.

I was almost to the tunnel when my cell phone rang. I slipped it out, thinking it might be Lydia, and flipped it open. "Smith."

"Linus Kwong, dude. He's back."

"Back?" The wind roared into the car; I pressed the button, sent the window up, so I could hear. "What do you mean?"

"Premador, dude! I've been, like, scanning his chat rooms and message boards. You know, in case. And just now, I found a post. From, like, today."

"When today?"

"No way to tell."

"What does it say?"

"Basically: Yo, and remember, you knew me first."

"First?"

"He says he's about to be famous. His name's gonna be everywhere, he says."

"When? When is that going to happen?"

"Doesn't say. That's all of it, dude. You dudes knew me first, remember that when I'm famous."

"He doesn't say what he's going to do that's going to make him famous?"

"No. You got a clue what it's about?"

"Maybe. Linus, can you get in touch with him?"

"I already posted to that board, but he didn't answer yet.

It could have been hours ago, he may not even be online on anymore."

"You can't tell? You can't talk to him?"

"It's a board, dude, not a chat room."

"What does that mean?"

"It's not real time," he said, sounding a little suspicious, as though this must be a trick question because the answer was so obvious. "You post your message, it comes up later. You could be signed off or somewhere else, by then."

"But there are places you can talk in real time?"

"Yeah, sure. He has rooms he goes to. I've been scanning, but he's not around."

"Is there a way to find out where he, uh, posted from?"

"You mean, physically?"

"Yes. I mean, where he is."

"Sometimes. But you gotta go through the service, though. I mean, it's not something I can do." He sounded embarrassed at this admission.

"Who can?"

Even more uncomfortable: "Cops can," and I remembered why Linus was so available, this semester, for this kind of work.

"What information do they need?"

"They need his screen name and the URL of the board. They got to find the administrator, somebody at the service provider and maybe if they're using a remailer—"

"Linus, you could be speaking to me in Chinese. I'm going to give your number to a cop I know."

"Oh, hey, dude—"

"It's okay, Linus. Just tell him whatever it is you were just telling me. Tell him everything you know about Premador, the Web sites he goes to, everything. You won't get in any trouble."

"I—"

"You wanted me to stop this guy," I said. "If he's about to be famous, I don't think it's for anything good."

Pause. "Yeah, okay. But if I get in trouble again, you got to talk to my mom."

"I promise. And don't worry about it. You can always move in with your cousin Lydia."

"Oh, dude, that is *so* not happening! Her mom's a crazy lady!"

"Yeah," I said, "tell me about it. Listen, Linus? Good work."

"Hey, thanks, dude."

"And keep looking. He might turn up somewhere else."

"Yeah, I know. I'm all over it."

I called Sullivan again.

"Goddammit, Smith—"

"Christ, Sullivan, you're a hard guy to help. Picked up the coach yet?"

"Smith—"

"Okay, okay, don't hang up. Your computer expert from Newark show up?"

"Just got here."

"Tell him—"

"Her."

"Even better. Tell her Premador's back online."

"What the hell—"

"I was just talking to a kid who found a post from him on a message board," I said, hoping I had the words right. "From today. He says he's going to be famous soon."

"Shit," said Sullivan.

"Right. Here's the kid's number." I gave it to him. "He can tell her how to find the bulletin board, and he thinks she may be able to trace where the post came from. The physical location."

"She might, but that kind of thing takes time. He may be long gone from wherever that was."

"Yeah," I said. "Or he may not."

Sullivan said he'd get on it. By then I was at the tunnel. I closed the phone, waited until I was threading through the streets of Manhattan to call Lydia. I told her about her cousin and what Premador had said.

"Oh, no," she said quietly.

"It's not like we weren't expecting it."

"No. But I was hoping."

"I know," I said.

We met, as planned, at a Shanghai-style restaurant we both liked in Chinatown, where we ate cold smoked fish and four-flavor bean curd and fried pork dumplings. The food was as good as always, and I was hungrier than usual, but even after a beer I still felt that edge, that tight-drawn sharpness I couldn't shake. A busboy behind us dropped a glass and I spun round in my chair, ready.

"Christ," I said to Lydia, turning back.

She smiled. "I know. We have that in common."

"We have something in common? God Almighty, what?"

"We both hate being on the bench. Oh, no, did I just use a sports metaphor?"

"Don't let your mother know. She'll send you back to China for reeducation." I waved to the waiter, pointed to my empty beer bottle. "I just feel so goddamn useless. Gary asked me for *help*," I said.

Lydia said, "Jared Beltran asked Nick Dalton for help."

I stared at her. "What are you saying?"

"I'm not sure. Just that it isn't straightforward. You do your best, but that doesn't mean the result will be something you wanted."

The waiter brought my new beer and I took a long drink. "Is this a way of telling me to lay off?"

"I think what I'm saying is, we've come to a point where there's nothing we can do for a while, and we think that's a bad thing, but it might not be."

"Sit down, let the first-stringers play."

"It's the reality of the job, Bill. The police have the people, the access, the resources. Sometimes it's our job just to get them to take a case seriously. Then we step back and they go to work. If we insist on staying in, we really can screw things up."

"Where did you pick up crap like that?"

She smiled again. "You taught me."

"You know," I said, "there are times when a talented rookie would be better off ignoring a know-it-all veteran."

"I was young and impressionable then. I ignore you all the time, now."

"So I've noticed." I signaled for the check. "All right. I'll be a good boy, go home and go to bed. But if Sullivan doesn't call by morning I'm going to go out there and pick up Ryder myself."

She nodded. "I'll go with you."

I walked Lydia home, kissed her at her door, watched her disappear inside the building where she's always lived. Then I turned and kept walking, not going anywhere, not paying much attention to where I went. The wind kept up, blowing grit and papers through the air, making street signs shiver. On a sidewalk in SoHo two young women left a trendy bar, laughed as the wind sneaked up from behind and wrapped their coats around them; in the East Village, theater patrons trying to steal a smoke between acts cursed as the wind waited for them to light matches and then blew them out. As I crossed into the Seaport the wind brought sprinkles of rain. When people opened umbrellas it gusted harder, turned them inside out to make them useless. At Battery Park the rain started to come down hard; by the time I reached Laight Street I was soaked.

I stopped in front of Shorty's, then walked past, to my door. With my key in the lock I changed my mind, turned and headed back. Inside, the bar was warm, smoke-filled, smelling of burgers and of wet cloth and leather; I wasn't the only one who'd been caught in the rain. Quiet talk shared the air with the TV's low-volume commentary on a college football game. I watched the TV screen above the bar for a few moments as I stood in the doorway: It was an unimportant game in an unimportant conference, but it had been chosen by ESPN for this Friday's broadcast, putting these kids on national TV for what would be for most of them the first and last time. The home team was clobbering the visitors as the third quarter wound down.

I made my way to the bar, found a stool near the end. Shorty, behind the bar as always, looked my way; I nodded and he brought me a Maker's Mark over ice.

"You're all wet," he said as he set it down.

"I usually am." I picked up the drink. "Can I ask you something?"

"About what's going on?"

"How do you know something's going on?"

"You looked like hell last time you were in here. You said you'd tell me about it next time I saw you and then I didn't see you." Shorty's voice was raspy, the way it had been as long as I'd known him. I listened for accusation, searched his face for anger, found neither, just fact.

"When I was fifteen," I said. "What I did."

"What about it?"

"You and Dave, the other guys, you always said it was right."

"So?"

"Was it?"

"Yes."

"I sent my father to prison."

"Your father was a lunatic. He almost killed you."

"He was my father."

"That wasn't your fault."

"It didn't work out. My sister didn't come home."

"It was still right."

"Whether or not it worked?"

"Since when is that the judge?"

His eyes caught mine. I nodded. I finished my drink in silence after that, and then I left.

twenty-six

Upstairs, I poured another bourbon, turned on ESPN, watched the end of the game. The visiting team couldn't dig out from under; they lost by over twenty points. I left the set on, caught the commentary, which was short because there wasn't much to say. As I finished the drink I drifted with the station into a late-night rewind of some set of Extreme Games held earlier that day somewhere in New Hampshire. I watched as young men, and a few women, flew through the air on mountain bikes, leaped on Rollerblades over parked cars. They were going for both speed and danger, and I remembered that, remembered thinking at that age that the risk was worth the thrill, because you don't understand what you're risking. Manic announcers called the events, their shouted half-sentences tumbling over each other as though broadcasting were another Extreme sport.

After a beer commercial came the main event: skateboards racing down and then up a pair of huge concrete ramps. The competitors tried for flips, twists, airborne jumps as they sped between the two. The third kid to start, reigning champ according to the broadcaster, pulled off the double somersault he was going for but wiped out on the landing, his board flying one way, he another. He hit hard and didn't get up. Medics swarmed around him, and other kids did, too. One brought back his board. He held it out as though the sight of it would be enough, could make the kid rise, could roll the clock back just far enough to make this a mistake, a ref's bad call that could be rethought and revised. "You hate to see this," the commentator said in a hushed voice, the same guy who'd whooped and shouted, "Yes! He's going to try it!" when the move began. And I thought, do we? Do we hate it, or is it seeing this—the football player rushed off the field in a cervical brace, the race car bursting into flames as it smashes the wall—is it this that gives us the limit, reminds us of what we forget as we go through our days: that something is actually at stake here? Sometimes the only way to know where the line is, is to cross it. Is this young kid, motionless at the bottom of the ramp, the threat and the promise we keep coming back for?

The kid moved his arm, blinked his eyes, tried to sit. The camera was right there to record it all. Two medics helped him up, walked him off the ramp, his eyes empty, his legs stumbling. "Looks like he's going to be all right," the commentator said. "Thank God. They're clearing the ramp, and Lachappelle's up next." I turned the TV off and went to bed.

I slept badly, the room too hot and then too cold, the sirens too loud in the street, the lighted dial on my clock too bright. Dark images from the depths of my dreams kept forcing me to the surface, but vanished before I could catch them, hold them, look at them straight on. I was half-awake, drifting, waiting to sink again, when the cell phone rang.

I'd left it beside the bed. I groped for it, flipped it open. "Smith," I rasped, coughed, reached for a cigarette. The clock said 7:30; I registered that as I heard Linus Kwong's voice.

"I got him, dude! He's right here!" The echo told me Linus was on a speakerphone.

"What?" I said.

"Premador! I'm in a chat room with him! What do you want me to say?"

"You're talking to him now?"

"Bingo, dude! Eric+Dylan.com! What should I *say*?"

An electric jolt swept the dream images away. I swung my legs off the bed; my head pounded from last night's bourbon. "Eric and Dylan? Those were—"

"Columbine, dude! It's one of his sites I've been scanning. Come on, help me out here!"

"Shit," I said. "Okay, Linus. What's he saying?"

"He can't sleep. He's too excited."

"Ask him why."

"Some other dude already did. It's too close, he says."

"What is?"

"Like yesterday: He won't say."

"Okay." I rubbed my eyes, tried to think. "Okay, say this to him: Tell him you've been looking for him online. Tell him you admire him, you think he's cool, great, whatever."

"Yeah. Okay." I heard the click of a keyboard.

"Did he answer?"

A pause. I stood, headed into the living room. Linus said, "He says, wait. It'll get even better."

"Tell him you don't want to wait. Tell him you want to be part of it."

"What?"

"Tell him!"

"Okay."

I pulled on the cigarette.

"No answer yet," Linus said. "Other guys are posting, too."

"Tell him you're in—in Philadelphia. Tell him you want to be part of it, ask if he's somewhere you could get to in time. Tell him—Linus, tell him you have an AK-47."

"A what?"

"AK-47. Modified, semiautomatic, but still fast as hell. Powerful. And you have the clips for it, a lot of them. Tell him that."

"Shit, dude." More keyboard clicks. I listened while I reached for the desk phone, dialed Sullivan's number.

"Sullivan," I heard in my right ear, the alert voice of

someone who'd been awake for hours. He'd probably already run five miles before the sun was up.

"Premador's online right now," I said.

"What?" said Linus.

"Both of you," I said, "I'm on two phones. Linus, keep doing what you're doing, let me know if he answers. Sullivan, he's on a Web site called Eric and Dylan dot com—"

"With one of those plus things, not the word *and*," Linus interrupted, catching on. "No spaces."

"Thanks. All run together, with a plus sign, Sullivan. He's in a chat room. Linus, do I have that right?"

"Totally."

"Live, right now," I said to Sullivan.

"I'll call Newark," Sullivan said.

"I'm hanging up. Not you, Linus. Sullivan, I'll call." I put that phone back, said to Linus, "What did he say? About the gun?"

"It's coming now. He says . . . he says thanks, but he's got all the weapons he needs."

"Make a case, Linus. Tell him you want to be there with him, with Premador, when it goes down. You want your name to be linked with his. You want to be someone, like him."

"Yeah. He says, no, that's cool, but no. He says this is something he has to do alone."

"Alone? Linus, I think there's someone with him. I don't think he's alone."

"Yeah . . . yeah, no, he is. I asked him, can't I be one of the other guys with him. He says no, this is just him, just Premador, on his mission."

"I—"

"But he says we should all check it out. He says it'll be different. Bigger, and better."

"Tell him—"

"Shit. He's signing off. Oh, shit, dude!"

"What?"

"He signed off. But the last thing he said, he said, good luck to all of us, keep the flame burning, make Eric and

Dylan proud, make *him* proud. He said, when we see it,
we'll know it's him. And dude, he says it's today."

Though it was early morning, the sky was a low leaden gray,
the light dull and featureless. Because it was Saturday, the
traffic heading east out of the city was about the same thin,
smoothly flowing stream as the lanes heading in, but still I
pounded the horn, slammed the brake when I had to,
swerved around cars whose drivers had no sense of urgency,
didn't seem to care. Beside me, Lydia held her tea out in
front of her so it wouldn't slop over. "The police are probably already there," she said, but I knew that, and I didn't
slow down.

As soon as I'd hung up with Linus I'd called Sullivan's
number again. I'd gotten voice mail, which probably meant
Sullivan was on the phone with the computer expert in Newark. I'd left a message, then called Lydia, got her voice mail,
too. I'd just hung up from my message to her when Sullivan
called back.

"He was gone by the time she got on," he said.

"We were wrong, Sullivan," I said. "It's not the school.
It's Hamlin's."

"What?"

"Today. He says it's today. Different, he says, bigger and
better. The Warrenstown game at Hamlin's, Sullivan, next
year's team against the seniors. It's got to be."

"Jesus Christ."

"Call it off."

Silence. Then, "I'll call my chief."

I took a fast, cold shower to quiet the pounding in my
head. I was dressed, reaching for my shoes when Sullivan
called back. "The game's still on."

"Are you crazy?"

"The chief talked to the mayor. The idea that it's the
game is completely conjecture."

"You want to wait for proof?"

"Even if it is the game, if we call it off, they'll know we're on to them. They'll disappear again, turn up somewhere else, somewhere no one's prepared. The chief wants to flush them out."

"Not *them*. Premador says he's alone. He made a point of telling Linus that."

"He also made a point of telling his mother he was going camping."

"This is insane, Sullivan. You can't let them play the game."

"That game," Sullivan said, "is the second-biggest thing that happens to this town, after the play-offs."

"Shit," I said. "This isn't about flushing him out, is it? Letourneau can't call this game off. Not even with a threat like this."

"Vague postings on the Net, Smith. He never said there, he never said Warrenstown. He didn't mention a game, Hamlin's, anything. It might not even be Paul."

"He said today."

"The mayor said, play the game. The Booster Club said, play the game. Al Macpherson said, play the game."

"You tell them who Hamlin is?"

A pause. "I told them. They wanted to know where I got that."

"And when you told them that, they said it was all bullshit. They'll have to deal with it sooner or later, Sullivan."

"But not before this game."

"Shit," I said. "What about Plaindale? It's their territory. They could close it down."

"Hamlin's generates a lot of jobs, pays a lot of taxes. We called Plaindale. They have a dog; they'll sweep for a bomb."

"Premador could see that."

"He won't risk being there this early, there's no place to hide."

"If the place is clean?"

"If the place is clean, the bus'll come, the parents, like normal. You've been there, Smith. It's a hard place to sneak up on, especially the football field. Plaindale can secure it, stay out of sight, and then we wait."

"When the bus arrives—"

"Plaindale can secure that," he said again. "And it won't be then. If it's today, because of the game, he won't be going for the team off the bus. He wants the headlines, Smith. No one's shot up a football game yet."

Sullivan had moved from *them* to *he*. That was to appease me, I knew, but it didn't work. "It's too risky," I said.

"The boys won't take the field unless it's safe."

"How will you know?"

"Either we'll have him, or he won't get close. He'll have to come around the back to get to the stadium, through those trees, it's the only way. Plaindale will be there, we'll be there."

"Warrenstown cops? You don't think that'll scare him off?"

"It's a big game. A couple of cars always escort the bus."

"Police cars? All the way the hell from Warrenstown to Plaindale?"

"This is Warrenstown," he said.

"What about you, Sullivan? What do you think?"

I heard him lighting a cigarette. "I'm a cop, Smith, and I was a marine. If this is the operation, I'll carry it out."

Different, Premador's post had said. *Bigger and better*. I had no arguments left for Sullivan and who the hell cared if I did? I didn't like it, but I wasn't a cop. I wasn't anybody, just the uncle of a fifteen-year-old boy who'd left home to go do something important. A boy tied somehow to another kid who'd been pushed over the edge. And now this other kid was ready for slaughter, and he said he was alone.

Lydia had called back just as I'd left the house. "Sorry," she said. "I was at the dojo, at the early class. What's up?"

I told her and I picked her up on the corner, grateful for the coffee she'd bought while she waited.

"They might not let us near the place when we get there," Lydia said now, sipping her tea as I moved up to seventy-five to pass an SUV.

"You think we should forget about it, go home?"

She looked at me sharply. "I think you should figure out exactly why we're going and what you're going to do when we get there and the police tell you to back off, besides punch somebody."

"Where's Gary?"

"Is that the question?"

"Goddamn right it is. Premador says he's alone."

She sipped again. "Listen to us. We're all afraid of him and we call him Premador. In real life he got stuffed in lockers and called a geek."

"This is real life, too."

She reached into the paper bag on her lap, pulled out two buttered rolls, handed one to me. I looked at her in surprise.

"You'll be even crabbier," she said, "if you don't eat."

I took the roll.

"If Gary's not with him," she said, "then maybe wherever he is, whatever he's doing, it has nothing to do with this."

"Unless," I said, "this is Gary."

"What?"

"Premador. It's just a screen name. What if Paul Niebuhr's camping at Bear Mountain, and Gary's planning to shoot up Hamlin's?"

She stared at me. *"Why?"*

"Who knows? None of these kids are sane, who do this."

"But they all have reasons. Gary has no reason."

"Tory Wesley?"

Lydia frowned, the way she does when she's thinking. "No," she finally said. "No, I don't buy it."

"Any reason?"

"I . . . nothing you've said about Gary, or that we've heard anywhere else . . . no, no reason. Just instinct. But I'm sure."

Until we reached Plaindale, we didn't speak again.

• • •

It was half past nine when I turned onto the long drive into
Hamlin's. The sky was a flat heavy gray above the playing
fields. Sprinkles of rain had started and stopped twice on
the drive out. Right now the rain wasn't falling and the
winds were still, but above us the clouds were moving and
this storm wouldn't hold off forever.

A Plaindale cop stood a few feet down from the road, by
the big sign: BUILDING MEN BY BUILDING CHARACTER
THROUGH COMPETITIVE SPORTS. When he waved me to stop
I punched the button to roll down the window; before I
could say anything Lydia leaned across me and smiled. With
a hand on my arm to keep me quiet she told the cop we
were here for the Warrenstown game. He nodded and directed me to a parking spot, as though this were his regular
job, organizing the parking for Hamlin's Saturday games. I
thanked him, gave Lydia a nod of thanks, too, and pulled
the car over where he'd waved me.

As Lydia and I got out of the car I looked around. I
spotted sharpshooters on the roofs of Hamlin's buildings, as
they had been on the roofs of the diner, the garage, the
warehouse across the street. We walked down the drive to
the smaller lot in front of the barracks entrance. A Plaindale
police car sat in that lot. Next to it stood a broad-shouldered
cop with gold bars on his uniform jacket. He was carrying
maybe fifteen pounds more than he needed and he smiled
at us pleasantly. "You folks are early."

"Wanted to be sure to get parking. Place fills up for the
big game."

"Uh-huh. You're Smith. Jim Sullivan said you'd show."

I shrugged. "Trouble with this modern world, no one has
secrets anymore."

"I'm Chief McFall. Sullivan's on his way. He said if I
told you to get lost I'd be wasting my time, said as long as
you behaved I didn't need to arrest you. On that assault
complaint from the other day."

"Macpherson," I said. "I forgot about that."

"Sure you did. I don't have time to bother with it right now, but that could change."

"I'll keep that in mind."

"Just do me a favor? Stay where I can see you until he gets here."

It was another half hour before Sullivan arrived, in an unmarked Caprice with Jersey plates. In that time the sky darkened and rain flew briefly as though in practice. It stopped again, an athlete satisfied with timing and agility, saving strength for later, when it would be needed. Lydia and I waited with the Plaindale chief, standing off a ways while he talked to other cops by two-way and sometimes in person, someone coming up to coordinate something, walking off again. Plaindale had brought in a handheld metal detector, was methodically sweeping the kids, their gear, Hamlin's staff, the furniture and equipment. The dogs—Plaindale had two—had come and gone by the time Sullivan got there. They'd covered the buildings, the playing fields, the bleachers in the baseball and football stadiums, and come up with nothing.

"You must have flown under the radar to get here this fast," I greeted Sullivan as he stepped from his car.

"I am the radar. This your partner you told me about?"

"Lydia Chin. Lydia, Jim Sullivan."

"You have your work cut out for you," Sullivan said to her, nodding toward me.

"But I get to meet such interesting people," she said, and Sullivan gave her a small smile as they shook hands.

Sullivan turned to the Plaindale chief. "Joe. Everything under control?"

"Everything. You in command for Warrenstown?"

"My chief's coming, with the bus. It's me until he gets here. But we're observers. It's your show." Sullivan, I noticed, was not wearing his gun. I was, under my jacket, but if he noticed that, he didn't show it. "How's Hamlin taking this?"

"Told me we could knock ourselves out, just keep out of his fucking way. Excuse me, ma'am," he added, to Lydia.

"Guy seems to be getting some weird kick out of this. It was me, I'd be having a cow. He's walking around with a shit-eating grin. Excuse me, ma'am," he said again.

"You searched him?" Sullivan asked, surprising me.

"Searched everyone, everywhere. Fuck me if there's a cap gun in this camp. Excuse me, ma'am."

"No sign of those kids? You've been through the woods?"

"With the dogs. It's not really woods back here, y'know, more like a fucking swamp. Excuse—"

"Oh, forget it," Lydia said.

Sullivan headed around the back, to the football stadium, and Lydia and I went with him, all of us silent. We stopped to survey the field, white lines freshly painted, goalposts pale against the darkening sky.

"Will they play in the rain?" Lydia asked.

Sullivan said, "Warrenstown?"

As we circled along the track to the bleachers, Sullivan said, "Got the coroner's report on Tory Wesley."

"And?" I said.

"Ready for this? Kid died of a stroke."

"What?"

"Crystal meth. It can happen, you snort too much."

"But the bruises—"

"Oh, someone beat on her, all right. Someone was pissed, or maybe it really was rough sex, like the Macpherson kid said. That's why the report took so long. I wanted everything checked, and they checked everything. But she died of a stroke. So the thing is," he said, "no one killed her."

"Then . . ." I stopped, not knowing what this meant. "Gary?" I said. "Paul?"

Sullivan shrugged.

I looked at the heavy black clouds and didn't know why they didn't break under their own weight, send the rain crashing down. I didn't know why the lines on the field glowed so white when there was no sun to shine on them.

We walked the area under under the bleachers, then along

the length of the fence on that side that separated the field from the marshy woods behind it.

"You think he's planning to come from there, shoot through the fence?" I asked.

"There's nowhere else."

I peered through the trees, nearly leafless now, and the shadowy scrub. Dark clouds pushed across the sky, a wet wind gusted, and deep in the undergrowth something moved. "Sullivan, *there*." I reached into my jacket for my .38.

Sullivan stayed completely still except for the hand that flashed out to clamp onto my wrist. "A Plaindale cop," he said calmly. "In plainclothes, with one of the dogs. He'll be working the area all day. I assume you two have permits for those?"

Lydia's gun was already in her hand. I could see the two figures now, man and dog. "Yes," I said.

"Good. If I see them again I'll take them anyway."

"Aren't you out of your jurisdiction?"

"Joe McFall deputized me, to act for Plaindale."

"I must've missed it."

"Yeah," Sullivan said, "you missed it."

The sky lowered and the wind blew more steadily but still the rain held off. Cars started to arrive and park on the stubbly field. These were parents from Warrenstown come all this way to watch their sons play, and other people too, local football fans coming early for a good seat. The Saturday games at Hamlin's were one of the few times the public was allowed into camp, and the Warrenstown game seemed to be legendary. The scouts would come later, Sullivan told us, closer to game time. Their seats were reserved.

The mothers and fathers of the Warrenstown seniors needled the underclassmen's parents, and the juniors' and sophomores' parents warned them to look out, this was going to be the first year in Warrenstown history when the underclass team won—and big, too. Parents with sons on both teams walked around with shamefaced smiles. They had no team to root for, only individual kids, and their cheering would be an affront to Hamlin's, and Warrenstown's, fiction that it was the team that mattered, that we don't do this for ourselves, but for each other.

Tailgate parties started, coffee and sandwiches, burgers and franks on portable grills that emerged from SUVs, and, even though it was long before noon, six-packs and whiskey flasks. Noon was when the bus was expected, and the game was set for one.

Cops in street clothes wandered among the crowd, along the fences, by the road, looking for two faces, two teenage boys far from welcome here, at this place where people lined up to send their teenage boys. According to Sullivan, Plaindale cops and state police were working the town, showing photos of Paul and of Gary, hoping to locate them and head off whatever "bigger and better" meant.

Lydia and I walked the grounds, too, with Sullivan's and McFall's permission. "He'll recognize Gary Russell," Sullivan said. "And she'll keep him from shooting anyone." About eleven we saw Macpherson's Mercedes SUV drive up. He ignored the cop directing traffic, swerved into a prime space by the edge of the drive, a place where cars coming later would have to maneuver around him, but he'd have an easy time getting out when he wanted to leave. The cop shouted to him to move the car, but Macpherson strode off toward Hamlin's door as though no one else were here.

"Where was Macpherson going?" I asked Sullivan when we ran into him again. "He went inside."

"Coffee and doughnuts in one of the trainer's rooms. Hamlin's answer to skyboxes. For the VIPs."

"Last time I saw Macpherson here he was about to strangle Hamlin."

"They made up since Hamlin took the boys back."

"The ones you arrested?"

"Had to. Without them, even with the fill-ins from Westbury, the seniors might actually have lost."

Another arrival, a few minutes later, was my brother-in-law. He parked where he was told, slammed his door when he got out of the car, but made no move to go anywhere, just stood and looked.

"Why is he here?" Lydia asked. We were a hundred yards away across a crowded parking lot; Scott hadn't seen us, and maybe he wouldn't.

"I'd have come," I said. "If it were my son. Gary was excited about this game."

"He can't be thinking Gary might just walk in, ready to play? As though everything was okay?"

"He's thinking he's got nothing else."

A little later I saw Sullivan heading in our direction, his eyes moving, scanning the crowd, but his path straight. We stopped, waited for him to reach us.

"Looks like you might be right," he said to me.

"You realize you said that in front of a witness?" I said. "Right about what?"

"The steroids. I just got a call. We found clembuterol, Primobolan, and Anavar in Ryder's office, in quantity, in zip-lock bags."

I stared. "You picked him up? Before this game?"

"No," Sullivan said easily. "The bus left Warrenstown at ten. I had a search warrant and a team waiting to go in as soon as he was gone."

"There's a judge in Warrenstown who'd give you a search warrant for the coach's office?"

"Judge Wright," he said. "Three daughters, no sons."

"I thought you said forget it, you can't touch Ryder at all until tomorrow."

"No, I said I couldn't pick him up unless I had something solid. I said I'd investigate."

Our eyes met, his cool and steady. I said, "I'm sorry."

He looked out over the parking lot. "I'll take him aside when the bus gets here, but I'm telling you now I won't be able to arrest him, I'll have to let him coach the game. But I'll try your ecstasy theory on him, see where it gets me. Tonight, when he gets back to Warrenstown, I'll arrest him. Then," he said, a corner of his mouth turning up, "I think I'll retire."

The Warrenstown bus rolled in, to cheers from the crowd. The seniors were already here, of course, had been here all week, but this was Hamlin's and they'd see their parents later, when their week was over. Right now they were in the field house running sprints, loosening up, going over new formations, plays they'd just learned. Some of them might have been wondering why they were inside, not out on the field under the weighted sky, but they were football players and they did what their coaches told them to do.

Coach Ryder climbed down off the bus, shouted for the boys to move it. The juniors and sophomores, tough-faced and serious, filed off. The crowd, though still applauding, knew not to approach its sons, who pulled their gear from the baggage hold without looking around. They headed, for their first time, through Hamlin's doors.

"Do you think," Lydia asked, watching them, "that Hamlin could be right? That once these people know who he is, they'll still send their kids?"

I thought of the skateboarder at the bottom of the ramp, last night. "Yes," I said.

The sky began to spit rain. Slickers and ponchos came out, men held umbrellas over sizzling grills, people shrieked and ducked with their sandwiches into their cars, and the party went on. Lydia and I zipped our jackets; she pulled a baseball cap out of a pocket, gray with red Chinese characters on it.

"What does it say?" I asked.

" 'Truth is one, paths are many,' " she told me. "My cousin Doreen makes them."

At noon one of Hamlin's trainers opened the chain-link gates to the stadium, and the crowd lined up. The stands filled more slowly than usual, because Plaindale police were checking hampers, coolers, and backpacks as people carried them in. The fans kidded the cops, rolled their eyes at each other, said, well, but security's high everywhere these days, and Hamlin, you know, sure, maybe the guy could lighten up a little, but a hell of a coach, right? Finally inside the gates, they settled, bright with rain-slick umbrellas and ponchos, to see what their sons could do.

And when Paul Niebuhr was finally found, it was, as it had always been for him, far from the center of things, and in a place where he could see no help, no way out.

twenty-seven

About twenty minutes after the gates were opened, I felt Lydia's light touch on my arm. "Something's happened," she said. I followed her eyes. Three cops were converging on Joe McFall, the Plaindale chief. He spoke into his radio, then to them; one of them stayed with him and the other two jogged back through the worsening rain to their cars.

"Sullivan," I said, pointing. He had pushed through Hamlin's doors, shouted something to McFall from thirty feet away. He got an answer, waved and headed at a rapid walk to the Caprice. Reaching it, he stopped briefly to talk to a Plaindale cop, then yanked open the car door.

Lydia and I, running across the muddy lot, had reached him by then.

Sullivan slid into the car, started it up. I put my hand on the door, didn't let him close it. He looked up at me. After a beat he said, "They're together. Will he talk to you?"

"What?"

"Gary and Paul. They're together. *Will he talk to you?*"

"Yes."

"Get in."

The sirens howled on the Plaindale cars and their lights spun, white and red. Sullivan wedged the Caprice between a squad car in front and McFall behind us, sped with them through the streets. "A motel," he said. "Two miles."

The miles were dreary, especially in the rain: an aging strip mall, a vocational training center, a plumbing supply yard. Wooden houses that had needed a coat of paint for too long. I said to Sullivan, "You get this from Coach Ryder?"

"Ryder? What, you mean just now? No, Ryder told me to go to hell. Doesn't know anything about the steroids, the ecstasy, Paul and Gary. All he knows is that if I think I can get him rattled so he can't coach, I'd better think again, and however much money I have on the seniors today, I can kiss it good-bye."

"How much of that is true?"

Sullivan glanced into the mirror. "My money's on the underclass team. The odds were longer."

The Halfmoon Motel, when we got there, showed itself to be at home in the neighborhood around it: two dozen shabby rooms on three sides of a cracked asphalt parking lot; a one-story concrete office; pink neon buzzing from a dented sign. Two Plaindale cars were already in the lot, cops with guns drawn crouching behind them. Another car stood sideways, blocking the driveway. Three or four civilian cars were there also, parked at concrete bumpers in front of white-painted, numbered doors.

Sullivan pulled onto the sidewalk, next to the Plaindale car we'd been trailing. Red and white lights pulsed from all the Plaindale cars, and I heard the distant sirens of more approaching fast. McFall left his car on the street, climbed out. A short, dark woman in a navy slicker with POLICE in white across the back approached him.

"Unit Six, Chief," we heard her say as we joined them. Rain dripped from the bill of her cap as she nodded at one of the rooms across the way. "Niebuhr's been here for two days. Went out early this morning. Came back about an hour ago with the other kid."

"Who saw?"

"The manager. Spano was showing the pictures around.

He thought this place was a long shot, but the manager recognized Niebuhr right away."

"Any contact?"

"No, sir. Secured the area per your orders."

"Other units all evacuated?"

The cop allowed herself a small smile. "Not that many of them were occupied, sir."

"Good work, Hayden. Sure they're still in there? The room's dark."

"Someone keeps moving the curtain aside, sir."

McFall moved his gaze to the pink-painted concrete building. "Who's in the office?"

"Gardino. The manager showed him how everything worked, then beat it."

McFall nodded. He looked at Lydia and me, pointed a thumb at us, said to Sullivan, "You want them here?"

"He's Russell's uncle. The kid might talk to him."

"Didn't you say the father's at Hamlin's?"

"We're finding him. He'll be here."

"Niebuhr's folks?"

"In Warrenstown. I sent somebody over."

"Can we get them on the phone if we need them?"

Sullivan shrugged. "We'll set it up."

"Where's your chief?"

"He was in the stands. He's on his way."

I wiped water from my face as Hayden pointed to the street behind. "Tech van's coming, sir."

An anonymous blue Econoline pulled up hard beside us. Before it stopped the back doors flew open. A blond young man in a Hawaiian shirt sat back there, surrounded by shelves of electronic equipment. Cords draped over boxes and speakers and screens. Red numbers glowed on dials and buttons.

"Chief." The man grinned at McFall. "What'll you have?"

"Phone hookup. Tape. Speaker in the van."

The young man jumped from the van with a handful of cords, crouched his way behind patrol cars to the office. He came back dripping wet, which he seemed not to notice. Back in the van, he turned some dials, punched some buttons. McFall asked, "Jesus, Hamilton, you got anything in there that can turn that shirt off?"

"Just trying to brighten your day, boss. Okay, got it." He pressed a button. We heard, "Gardino," echo through the van.

"It's McFall, Vince," said the chief, taking the receiver the guy in the Hawaiian shirt held out to him. "We're ready. You know how to put us through to six?"

"Sure." A hand waved from the motel office's window.

I heard tires hiss as two cars with spinning lights, a Warrenstown car and a Plaindale one, barrelled down the street toward us. At each end of the block I could see other patrol cars, setting the perimeter. Beyond them, a fire engine and an ambulance. Reporters, camera and sound people clambered out of the first TV vans to arrive, ran through the barricades on foot. At McFall's command two cops charged over to meet them, corralled them onto the sidewalk on the opposite side of the street.

Lydia said to me, "The Plaindale police. They do this as though they've done it before."

McFall caught that. He looked at us. "Training," he said. "Littleton PD was unprepared."

A sharpshooter jumped from the newly arrived Plaindale car, took off in a crouching run for the motel office. A young Warrenstown cop climbed from behind the wheel of the other car, Chief Letourneau from the shotgun seat. And from the back, my brother-in-law, and Al Macpherson.

"Chief," McFall greeted Letourneau. "Who the hell's all this?"

"The Russell kid's father." Letourneau pointed to Scott. He shrugged and said, "And Al Macpherson. Important man in our town."

McFall narrowed his eyes. Macpherson glowered but a glance from Letourneau kept him silent. Scott demanded, "What the hell shit is this? Where the hell's my boy?"

"Your boy's in there," McFall said. "Stay behind that car and out of the way until I tell you."

"Hey, don't you—"

"Scott," said Letourneau, and Scott clamped his jaw shut. His face was slick with rain and red with fury. He looked around then and he spotted me.

"What the fuck is he—"

"*Scott.*" Letourneau spoke again. "Shut up."

I met Scott's eyes, held them. I saw, as I had seen yesterday, the burning in them, felt the heat surge inside myself in answer. I turned away from him, stared through the cold rain at the window across the lot, at the room where his son was.

"We just got the phone hookup." McFall filled Letourneau in, then said, "You want to try it?"

Sullivan said, "Me, I think. They know me."

Letourneau nodded, Sullivan took the receiver. We all heard the phone ring, and ring. McFall leaned into his car, brought out a bullhorn. Sullivan took it, said calmly, "Paul. Gary." His words bounced off the buildings and the street, backed by the steady beat of the rain. "It's Detective Sullivan. Answer the phone." He stood, waited; the phone kept ringing. "Gary's father's here, and his uncle. Answer the phone."

The rain thinned; the phone rang. Sullivan lifted the bullhorn again. "Premador," he said. "If you won't talk to us, we're going to have to come in."

The curtain next to door number six moved, dropped back into place. Sullivan, McFall, and Letourneau exchanged a look. McFall turned to the sergeant, but before he spoke, the phone's ringing stopped. Everyone turned to the van except Sullivan, who picked up the receiver, faced the room, didn't move. A young voice filled the van. "It's Paul. Paul Niebuhr." As though, even in a situation like this, he was afraid of not being known. "I want to go to Mexico."

Sullivan, with no change in stance or expression, spoke. "Come out, Paul, we'll talk about it."

"No! Now! A helicopter to the airport and a plane to go there."

"We can talk about it, Paul."

"Talk! Bullshit! You think I'm stupid? You think I don't see you all hiding behind your stupid cars? You want me to come out so you can blow me away."

"No, so we can talk to you."

"You're so full of shit, Sullivan! You and everybody else. I want to go to Mexico."

"What does Gary want?"

"Gary?" A pause. The wind shifted, the rain began to pound again. "Who the fuck cares? Guys like him always get what they want. Guys like me have to have guns first. But I do now, Sullivan. Did you know that? I do."

"I know, Paul."

A mocking voice. " 'I know, Paul.' *Fuck you, Sullivan!*"

The whine of a bullet and the bright shattering of glass ripped through the rain. We dropped to the ground. Cops raised their guns but McFall's bullhorn boomed, *"Hold your fire!"*

For a moment, nothing but the rain. Crouching there behind the Plaindale car, my eyes met Lydia's; briefly, her hand covered mine. Cops checked with each other; the shot from the room had gone wild, hit no one. Jagged shards of glass reflected pink neon around the edge of the window where the drape had moved. Then Paul's voice again. "See? See what I mean? Now get me a fucking plane, Sullivan!"

Sullivan stood again, faced the room, as he had. "I want to talk to Gary," he said.

"I'll shoot Gary."

Wind blew the curtain back from the shattered window. I was frozen, unable to move.

"I hope not, Paul," Sullivan said calmly. "No one's been hurt yet. We can still work this out."

"No one's been hurt? What about Tory?" Paul's voice got faster, higher. "Or doesn't she count? She wasn't in the jock crowd, she wasn't pretty, so she doesn't count."

"She counts, Paul."

"She doesn't fucking count! You don't fucking give a shit. Except you think I killed her. That's fucking right, isn't it?"

"No one thinks that, Paul."

"You're a lying shit, Sullivan. Like that kid Jared, everyone said he raped that girl, and he kept saying he didn't, but no one believed him so he killed himself. And you think I killed Tory. I knew you would. I knew you'd think that."

"No one thinks that," Sullivan said again.

"Yes, you do! But I don't give a shit! Except I'm not going to kill myself, asshole. I'm going to kill Gary; then I'm going to kill you all!"

"Paul, nobody's going to kill anybody. Nobody killed Tory, she OD'ed by herself."

A pause, a silence filled only by the rain. Then, "Bullshit! That's bullshit and you think I'll believe it! You really think I'm that dumb!" A laugh burst from the speaker in the van, chilling my blood as a scream would have. "You lying dickheads—"

"No, it's true," Sullivan said. "Paul, you don't want to come out, all right, that's all right. I'll come in, we can talk there."

"No fucking way! You—" Paul's voice stopped abruptly. We heard rapid words, an argument inside the room, nothing we could make out. Then quiet: Maybe they were still talking, maybe not, but outside, with the pounding rain, the wind, we heard nothing.

Then Paul's voice, tight as a wire: "Gary's uncle. Bill Smith. You said he was there?"

"He's here."

"He can come in."

"Gary's dad is here."

Scott moved toward Sullivan, reached for the phone, but Paul said, "Fuck, no! His uncle."

Sullivan lowered the receiver, looked at me.

I nodded.

McFall said, "No. Only a cop."

"Forget it," I said. I took a step forward. McFall reached

for me. Lydia moved smoothly between us, cutting him off. If it had been Sullivan blocking him, McFall would have shoved him out of the way, punched him if he had to, but it was a small Chinese woman and McFall was flustered just long enough for me to make it around the car and out of his reach. I turned, looked back at him. He could have come after me. But I knew my eyes said I was ready for that, willing to risk what that might set off. He pressed his lips into a thin line and stayed where he was. I started across the lot.

"And you better not have a gun!" came from the speaker in the van behind me. "Don't think you can pull any bullshit on me! Don't try any shit!"

I stopped where I was, unzipped my jacket. Rain splattered my shirt. With my left hand I held my jacket wide so he could see what I was doing; with my right I very slowly lifted my .38 from my shoulder rig, laid it on the ground. I took off my jacket, so he could see I carried nothing else. I dropped that too. The cold rain drenched me as, hands away from my sides, I headed toward the room with the jagged glass in the window.

The door swung open when I got to it. It was Gary who opened it, Gary who was briefly visible to the cops behind the cars, to the sharpshooter on the office roof. I stepped inside, blinking in the dimness: No lights were on. The cold wind blowing through the broken window couldn't chase the smells of mold and McDonald's from the damp air.

Gary shut the door behind me. Only then did Paul Niebuhr rise from cover, a thin young boy in ragged-cuffed cargo pants and a filthy black tee shirt. He trained a rifle on me as he stepped from the other side of an upturned mattress.

"Paul," I said.

"It's cool, Paul," said Gary. He looked like hell, his skin gray under dirt and sweat, his eyes rimmed with the black of exhaustion. He was still wearing the shirt and jeans I'd given him four days ago. "This is my uncle Bill," he said. "He'll help."

"Yeah, just like you." Paul's voice was acid with contempt and he did not lower the gun.

"I wanted to. I'm sorry."

"You're fucking right you're sorry. *I'm* sorry I ever called you. Jock asshole. I should have let you play the fucking game and fucking blown you away like everyone else." Paul's eyes were red, his lips cracked and dry. He held the gun up, but its aim wasn't steady, and he couldn't keep his feet still.

Gary looked at me. His eyes were the eyes of a child alone and far from home.

"Paul," I said, "I don't know what this is about. But you haven't done anything yet that can't be undone. Put down the gun."

"That's it? That's your help? I thought you were going to get me to Mexico! Get the fuck out!"

"You found Tory after the party, didn't you?" I spoke matter-of-factly, careful to keep out of my tone any sympathy, any softness that might be heard as patronizing. "You sat outside in your car and watched because you were afraid for her. Of what might happen when the jocks found out she didn't have the drugs they wanted. When you found her like that you were sure one of them had killed her."

"She didn't *get* it." Paul's voice cracked, his feet danced. "She thought they liked her because they bought her fucking acid! No one ever locked her in a locker or shoved her face in a toilet and now they were all her *friends*. She was so fucking sure her *friends* would never do that shit to *her*."

"Paul," I said, "they didn't. The coroner's report just came in. Tory was snorting crystal meth and she died of a stroke."

"A stroke? A fucking *stroke*? My fucking *grandfather* died of a stroke! How dumb do you think I am?"

"I don't think you're dumb at all. You've avoided a two-state dragnet for days, you're armed, you made a plan and you've carried it out well so far." I spoke calmly, slowly, as Sullivan had, trying to give Paul a rhythm to counter his wild syncopation, a coolness to counter his heat. "But tell me something, about Tory and that night. Tell me where she was getting the ecstasy."

The wind shifted, blew rain hard against the shuddering curtain hanging in the window, forced the curtain back so it could splash water into the room, soak it into the shabby carpet. Paul's eyes flew there. He bit his lip, then burst out, "She didn't! That's the whole point, asshole, she couldn't get it!"

"I know. But where did she think she'd get it?"

He looked from me to Gary, licked his lips. Don't move, Gary, I thought, don't say anything, don't blink. Gary, maybe following my lead, maybe his own instincts, stood absolutely still. Finally, Paul said, "You'll say I'm a fucking liar."

I asked, "From Coach Ryder?"

His eyes flew wide. "You know? You fucking *know*?"

"We just found out about the steroids." Gary opened his mouth in protest; I glanced at him, and he stayed silent. I looked back to Paul. "How did she know? Tory, about the steroids?"

"Asshole here," said Paul, and I could see the pain in Gary's eyes. "Jock asshole. He told her. He was *upset*," Paul's voice became sarcastic, mocking, "he was upset, he needed someone to talk to. Poor baby jock asshole!"

"Upset about what?"

"Who the fuck knows?"

I turned to Gary.

"I . . . Coach wanted me to take steroids, Uncle Bill. He was kind of . . . leaning on me. In preseason practice. I needed to talk to someone about it."

"Your folks?"

He shook his head. "Coach could've—I mean, you can get fired for stuff like that, can't you?"

I looked at Gary a moment longer, then said to Paul, "And the ecstasy?"

"She was so dumb!" Paul wailed. "She thought all she had to do was tell him she knew."

"Blackmail?"

Paul swallowed, nodded. "She said she wouldn't tell
about what he did if he got her ecstasy for the party. The
guy she bought her acid from, he couldn't get ecstasy, but
she thought the coach'd be better connected."

What did Tory Wesley have? I thought. "What did she
say to him, Paul? Do you know exactly what she said?"

"Oh, she was all, like, mysterious! She said, people who
have guilty consciences, you just tell them you know, you
don't say *what* you know, so you can make them more nervous. She told Coach Ryder this jock she was dating, he
told her what he did. And she expected him to give a shit.
Like *Coach Ryder's* really going to care what some geeky
girl says."

But he did care, I thought. "Paul," I said carefully, "I
think there are some things Coach Ryder can get in serious
trouble for, if you can tell this story. Come with me now,
and I'll help you. I promise."

For a moment, I thought that that might work. Paul's feet
stopped shuffling, his eyes met mine and seemed to believe
what he found in them. He looked at Gary. Then his eyes
changed again, and his face darkened as though he'd suddenly remembered something. "Premador!" he screamed,
swinging the rifle to point at Gary. "How the fuck do they
know about Premador? You fucking told them, didn't you?
My friend! My friend, Gary!"

"No," I said. Paul's eyes snapped back to me, but the
gun didn't move. "Gary didn't tell anyone," I said. "Gary
never mentioned your name. When Gary disappeared I
started to look for him. I sent a hacker into his computer."
And into yours, I thought, but didn't say that to Paul. "My
guy found the name, knew what it meant. I went to your
house and saw your room."

"Oh, that's fucking great! You're looking for him, he's
looking for me, that's just fucking awesome!"

I glanced at Gary. "That's what you were doing? Looking
for Paul?"

Gary nodded.

"Why?" Paul howled, a child's cry. "Both of you, why couldn't you just leave me alone?"

I said to Gary, "You wanted to be part of this?"

"Part of it?" He stared blankly. "Shit, no. I wanted to stop him."

"You knew?"

He shook his head. "I guessed. I mean, not really, but something. Sunday night, Paul called me. He told me not to play the game at Hamlin's."

"Jock asshole!" Paul hissed. "He's a jock asshole now," he said to me, with a distorted grin. "But he was cool for a while. He used to hang out with me. Before he knew."

"Knew what?"

"Oh, fuck you!" He danced around, calmed down. "Everyone knows you don't hang out with me. I'm a geeky little nerd. Out on the court you peg basketballs at me and in the lunchroom you need to dump Coke on my head."

"Did you do that?" I asked Gary.

Paul answered: "He never did that shit. That's why I warned him. We were, like, cool once, when Gary first came. We used to hang. Those days, some shit, he was the only guy I told."

Gary said nothing. His hands moved, trying to speak for him.

"Sting Ray?" I asked. "One of the things you told Gary was about him?"

"How do you fucking know about him?"

"He was arrested the other day," I said, careful to try to make it sound like coincidence. "He said he'd sold guns to a guy named Premador." To Gary I said, "You were seen near there."

"I was looking for Paul. That's where I was trying to get to when I . . . when the cops picked me up, and you came and got me. But I didn't really know where to go. Just, like, the neighborhood. I never found the guy." He looked at Paul. "I just wanted to, like, talk about shit."

"You mean, like we used to? You mean, like until football practice started, and you found out who was who, and you fucking forgot my phone number?"

I looked at Gary. He looked down at the carpet, up to me again. He said, "I was new."

"But I thought, he never did the really bad shit," Paul said. "And he brought my board back." Tears formed in his eyes; he shook them away. "So I thought, I'll give him one fucking break! And now look at this shit!" He waved the gun at the room, the broken glass, the red and white lights beating beyond the curtain.

I said to Gary, "Why didn't you tell me? Why didn't you let me help you find Paul?"

"If I told you," he said, "if I told anyone, Paul would get in trouble. And it was . . . I knew it was part my fault, what he wanted to do. I thought, if I could find him, I could, like, talk to him, because I couldn't, I just couldn't rat him out. My dad . . . that's like, the worst. He always told me, ratting guys out, that's the worst."

Paul shook his head, rapidly, maybe more tears, maybe something else. Gary said to him, pleading, "And see, they were all waiting for you! They knew! If I didn't find you this morning, they were going to shoot you!"

"Yeah?" Paul's face was damp with tears; he gave up trying to stop them. "Yeah? And now? Now they're not going to shoot me?"

"No," I said. "Not if we leave now."

"That's such bullshit!" Paul yelled. "They're all out there—"

"*Paul,*" I said, my tone hard. "Paul. Put the gun down, come with me. I'll tell them we're coming, I'll tell them not to shoot. I'll go out first. They don't want to shoot you, Paul. They don't want to."

Paul looked from me to Gary, around the room, at the pulsing lights outside the curtain. He was all bones, his ribs outlined under his tee shirt, his elbows sharp as he held the rifle. I could see his arms trembling a little; the gun was heavy, and he'd been holding it a long time.

"Who's out there?" he said.

"Jim Sullivan. Chief Letourneau. The Plaindale chief, a man named Joe McFall. Most of the cops are Plaindale cops."

"Are reporters here?"

"Some. You want to make a statement?"

He looked at me a long time. He swallowed, and he nodded.

"Okay," I said. "We'll go out, you can talk to the reporters, then to Sullivan or Letourneau. Or McFall if you want. I'll stay with you, Paul, I'll be there the whole time."

He nodded again.

I said. "Let me call out and tell them what we're doing."

"I'm not putting my rifle down," he said. "I'm keeping it until after I talk to the reporters."

"Paul—"

"After!"

"All right." I walked slowly to the desk, picked up the phone. "Sullivan?"

"Here," I heard immediately. "What the hell's going on in there?"

"It's okay. We're coming out." Through the phone I heard my own voice echoing from the van's speaker. "Paul wants to make a statement to the press. He'll talk to you after that."

"This is straight or it's bullshit for him?"

"No, it's straight. But Paul's got a rifle and he's going to keep it until after he talks to the press."

"Christ, Smith, they've got to come out without weapons."

"Gary's unarmed. But Paul's rifle's not negotiable."

A pause. "He holds it in one hand. It points at the ground."

I relayed that to Paul. Slowly, he nodded, lowered the gun.

"All right," I said to Sullivan. "I'm coming first. The boys will be behind me."

Another brief pause, then Sullivan said, "Any time."

I put down the phone, opened the door. I looked back.

Both boys seemed, for a moment, unable to move, the way a child freezes when he's startled by a big dog or a loud noise. Then Gary shook his head once and started toward me, and Paul did, too, and we left the room, walked into the pounding rain.

There are times, now, when I replay what happened next, when I look for my mistake, the thing I should have done, or shouldn't. It wasn't that I didn't see: a flash of red and silver as Al Macpherson, standing behind everyone else, yanked a pistol from his jacket. The silver was the gun, the red a circling light glinting off it as he lifted it over his head; and as I knew that I heard two sharp bangs, two shots fired into the air. It wasn't that I was too slow: I lunged for Paul as he swung the rifle up, looking around wildly for his enemies. I knocked him off balance so that his shot blasted only asphalt. And I was loud, roaring, *"No!"* across the lot. But the answering shots had started already, gunfire whining through the rain. It came from everywhere, and it came in startling, beautiful slow motion. I heard each crashing report separately, distinctly, saw each shooter aim, squeeze off every shot, saw each crouching cop, the sniper on the office roof. Macpherson stood unmoving, did not shoot again. I reached for Paul, my slow hand closing only on rain and air as Paul, with all the time in the world, sidestepped me, threw his skinny body into Gary with more power than I knew he had. Gary twisted and went down, still in this extraordinary, leisurely dance. Paul stumbled and stayed on his feet.

I dived, floated toward Paul, hanging in the air forever, as though I could fly. I clutched him and we drifted to the ground together. I tried to hold him, but he lifted the rifle butt, swung it at my head.

For a moment, all I knew was bursting lights and pain. When I forced my eyes to focus, time had snapped back into place.

Paul had rolled away. He fired, lying on the asphalt like a sniper, and fired again. His shot blew out the window of a Plaindale car, glass like diamonds flying in all directions.

I reached for him. He threw the rifle at me, jumped to his feet.

"Assholes!" he shrieked, his voice carried on the howling wind. "Fucking assholes, I'm *Premador*! You can't defeat me!" A percussion of gunshots, and he staggered back but did not fall. He shoved a hand into the cargo pocket of his soaking pants, came out with a grenade. He got one, I marveled, someone sold him one, as I stretched toward him, fell short. He dropped to one knee, used his teeth to pull the pin, sent the grenade soaring in a perfect arc across the lot. It flew far, much farther than I'd thought those skinny arms could throw. Cops dived for cover. The same car he'd shot the window out of exploded in a deafening blast. Flames thrust skyward. Rain, splashing onto suddenly searing metal, turned to rolling clouds of steam as Paul collapsed onto the asphalt and didn't move again.

twenty-eight

The pounding of the rain kept up but the gunfire stopped. I heard running feet slam the ground, men shouting, sirens. I lifted myself on one elbow. "Gary? *Gary.*"

"Yeah." The word was tight, forced through clenched teeth. "Yeah. Uncle Bill—" Curled on the pavement just beyond my reach, Gary had his arms wrapped around his right knee, pulling it close to himself.

"All right, Gary," I said. "It's all right."

I pushed myself to sit, scrambled over to him. I saw red and orange flames reflected in the water that sheeted the lot. Paul Niebuhr lay sprawled a few yards away, surrounded by cops training guns on his unmoving form. His eyes and mouth were open. His torn flesh lay exposed where his shirt had been shredded by bullets. The rain, falling hard, swept across the black asphalt and across us all, and the blood that should have been pooling beneath him was washed away as fast as it flowed.

I bent over Gary, tried to shield his pain-contorted face from the rain. Across the lot the Plaindale car was burning. Fire hissed and spat, throwing great arms of orange flame skyward. The wind tried to wrap sheets of water around the fire. The flames changed direction, danced away, reached high again. White steam hissed through roiling black smoke.

Medics reached us, me and Paul and Gary, and Lydia

was there, and Scott, bending over Gary. The young men trying to help Gary had to order Scott back. I pushed away the medic kneeling beside me.

"Don't try to stand," he said.

"Fuck you." I climbed to my feet. Sullivan stood in front of me. "Why did you shoot?" I asked, my voice hoarse but loud, pounding like the rain. "Why did you have to shoot?"

"He was firing at us." Sullivan's tone was quiet, calm as before.

"He was a kid! He was scared shitless."

"He was firing."

"At Macpherson's shots! He was answering fire! What the hell was that?"

"Macpherson?"

"The first two shots. They were Macpherson's!"

Sullivan shook his head. I shoved him away, staggered past. "That's a bad gash," he said, reaching for me. "You should—"

"Fuck yourself, Sullivan." I yanked my arm away, kept walking.

Lydia was beside me, striding with me through the rain. "You're hurt," she said.

"Leave me alone." She didn't, though, but stayed with me as I crossed the lot, cut around the cars to where, out of the way so he wouldn't interfere, Al Macpherson stood beside the tech van.

"You set him up!" I shouted.

"Back the fuck off." A Warriors cap kept the rain from his face, kept his eyes in shadow.

"You knew he'd shoot, and all this firepower would answer! *Why*, Macpherson? Why?"

"You're insane. Maybe it's the head injury. You should have that looked at." He took a step away.

"You bastard—"

"Smith!" A hand grabbed roughly at my arm; it was Letourneau, beside me. "Enough. I have enough ambulances here. Get your head looked at. We'll be taking your statement. You have anything to say, say it then." His eyes were

hard, commanding. Macpherson's eyes glittered, the eyes of
a winner. I turned and walked off through the rain.

I spent the rest of that day, into the evening, at Plaindale
General. Not because the gash on my head was bad: Three
stitches took care of that. But Gary was in surgery.

While we waited for the surgeon's news, Joe McFall took
over a corner of the cafeteria for an impromptu interview
room, to take statements from the civilians: me, Scott, and
Lydia, because it was clear none of us was leaving the hospital until Gary was out of the operating room; and Macpherson, who was offered the choice of this place or the
station house. Letourneau's statement, and Sullivan's,
McFall would get later, down at the station, where each
Plaindale cop who had fired a weapon was writing a detailed
account of the circumstances and outcome.

Gary's statement would have to wait, until tomorrow.

When I'd sat with McFall it was right after Gary had
gone into the operating room. Letourneau and Sullivan were
there as a courtesy, Plaindale to Warrenstown. I answered
what they asked me, surprised at the effort it took. These
cops are talking to you, Smith, I had to keep telling myself;
but I found my eyes following the movements of people I
didn't know as they came and went across the room, and
some questions had to be asked twice.

In the end, though, I told them about it all: the dim motel
room, Paul's dancing feet, the important thing Gary had
come to do.

"He knew what the Niebuhr kid was planning?" McFall
asked, glancing at the tape recorder he'd set up on the plastic
tabletop, making sure the thing was running.

"Not knew, guessed. He was looking for him to stop
him." I sipped hospital coffee, but I didn't expect it to warm
me and it didn't.

"How do you know he wasn't in on it?"

"He said he wasn't." I raised my eyes to McFall's. My
voice sounded toneless to me, but something in it, or maybe
in my eyes, ended that line of questioning.

"Macpherson," Sullivan said.

I nodded. "He fired the first two shots. Over his head, as we were coming out."

Sullivan said carefully, "Why?"

"Ask him."

"He says he didn't shoot until Paul started firing."

My head was pounding dully, my forehead swollen under the bandage. "Why the hell was he there, Sullivan? Why was he armed?"

"He has a New York carry permit," McFall said. "We checked it, it's good. He's had it for years. Seems he's been threatened by clients' wives before."

"Scott was there because it was his son. Why was Macpherson there?" No one answered. I looked at Letourneau. All I got was a shrug.

We have a mayor and everything, I heard Stacie's voice in my head. *But Randy's father is who really runs this town.*

"He fired those shots," I said.

"He says he didn't."

"He's lying."

"It was pouring rain," McFall said. "Everyone was tense—you included, for Christ's sake, Smith. Some of my people say Paul fired first. Some heard shots before his. But it could have been any one of them. I hoped I had them better trained than that, but it was probably a cop."

"It wasn't a cop."

"The rain—"

"Fuck the rain, McFall. Macpherson fired because he knew Paul would shoot back and he knew what that would start."

"Why would he do that?" McFall asked.

I looked from Letourneau to Sullivan; neither of them spoke.

"Shit," I said, rubbing my eyes. "There was a girl in Warrenstown who was blackmailing Coach Ryder." I realized how exhausted I was, and how cold. McFall gestured to a young cop across the room, turned back to me. "She knew he deals drugs," I said, "and she wanted him to get ecstasy for her."

McFall shot a look at Sullivan; Sullivan shrugged.

"But the blackmail," I said, "she told him she 'knew about him' but not what she knew. She thought that was clever. She told him a jock she was dating told her."

The young cop from across the room came over, put another cup of coffee in front of me. I looked at him, surprised; McFall nodded his thanks. The coffee was hot and freshly made. I drank almost half of it before I went on.

"She thought he'd have a bad conscience about the drugs—steroids, McFall, for the boys—and get her what she wanted. But he doesn't. He doesn't care who knows. No one in Warrenstown would give a shit. In Warrenstown you could put that on the front page of the paper and people would come up and thank him for helping their boys get big."

I drank more coffee; I was desperate for a cigarette. "He does have a bad conscience, though, about something else. A crime Al Macpherson committed years ago, that Ryder framed another kid for. That might be too much even for Warrenstown to swallow."

Letourneau looked away. Sullivan didn't, but he didn't speak.

I said, "He found out which jock she'd been dating: Gary Russell. The son of one of the only other people in Warrenstown who knew about the details of the old crime, the cover-up, the frame. He thought that's what Gary told her, that that was what she knew. He talked to Macpherson about it. The two of them think I know, too, and Paul, and another Warrenstown kid who had the shit beat out of her the day before yesterday by someone trying to find out what she knows."

"Stacie Phillips?" Sullivan interrupted. "You're telling me one of them beat up Stacie Phillips?"

"Ryder, probably, but you'll never prove it," I said. I saw Sullivan's mouth set into a hard line, but I didn't care. "When the three of us came out together Macpherson must have thought it was Christmas. All he had to do was get a firefight started and the Plaindale PD would take care of the rest. He didn't know," I said to McFall, "what a tight operation you run here. Most small-town departments, trying to deal with something like this, every weapon in that lot would have been emptied, and Gary and I would be dead now, too. But your people are trained better than that. They stopped firing as soon as they could and *it wasn't them who fired first*."

McFall exchanged a look with Sullivan and Letourneau. "I'll talk to Macpherson again," he said.

"Yeah," I said, "you do that. It'll get you fucking nowhere, but if it makes you feel better, McFall."

"Wait," Sullivan said. "You're saying Gary was Macpherson's target?"

"All of us. Gary first, but Macpherson thinks we all knew."

"If the that were true, why wouldn't he—"

"He will. Put a guard on Gary's room."

Sullivan looked at the other two cops. "Joe can do that as long as Gary's here. But eventually he'll go home."

"Pick up Macpherson before that."

"For what?"

He caught my eyes; I looked away, watched the steam rise from my coffee.

"A twenty-three year old crime," Sullivan said. "Victim who doesn't remember. Witness who may have seen, what, an argument? No physical evidence. Confession and suicide at the time, for Christ's sake. You want me to find a DA who'll indict a guy like Macpherson on that? Where would you suggest I look?"

He was right. Of the whole thing—the rape, the frame, the suicide, even the shots today—the only crime was the rape. New Jersey has no statute of limitations on rape, so technically Macpherson could be prosecuted, even after all this time; but he wouldn't be. He might be willing to see people die to avoid the embarassment of it all coming out, but he wasn't about to be arrested, and he knew it.

"And what about you?" Sullivan said. "A guard on Gary's room, but what about you?"

"I'll take care of myself."

"Don't go near him," said Letourneau.

"What?"

"I think this is crazy, Smith, and I can see it could lead to trouble."

"Lead—"

"Stay away from Macpherson."

I stood. "Yeah," I said. "Because if you catch me near him you'll throw me in the can. Because if you don't, Al Macpherson'll be pissed off, and in Warrenstown, that's a disaster."

I'd walked away then and no one had stopped me. I went outside, had a cigarette. Once I was beyond the doors I wanted to keep going, through the lot, to the sidewalk, onto the suburban streets. I didn't give a damn about the rain, the wind; all I wanted was to *move*. But I stayed by the door. The media, barred from the hospital, had set up at the edge of the parking lot, and the place was thick with broadcast vans and slicker-wrapped reporters. Stacie Phillips's dream, to be out there with them. Right now I'd have killed the first one who shoved a microphone in my face.

When my cigarette was gone I had another, standing under the hospital canopy, watching the streetlights glitter in the rain that crashed across the cars, the pavement, the hunched-over people hurrying to shelter. It wasn't night, not yet, but the rain made the day dark. Behind the streetlights hung a featureless iron sky, no depth or distance or sense that anything but this violent and lasting storm could ever come out of it. But of course sometime—tonight, tomorrow—the rain would stop. Days would be sunny, either mild or cold, but beautiful; nights would be clear. And then, other storms.

I asked a man arriving with flowers and a stork balloon if the game was over at Hamlin's. It was, he grinned, and though the seniors had won, as expected, the coach called some spectacular new plays for the Warrenstown underclass team, and they came within six. Closer than ever before, he said. A victory for both sides. I thanked him and congratulated him on the new baby. "It's a boy," he said. "Ryan. Eleven pounds, three ounces. Huge. And strong. Helluva kick, already."

"Great," I said. I watched him walk inside, then went back to my cigarette, and the rain.

twenty-nine

It was two hours after that that the surgeon came into the waiting room. Four hours altogether from when the ambulances had come screaming in, from when Paul had been pronounced dead in the emergency room and a resident, smiling reassuringly, had moved close to look at my forehead, and Gary had been rushed into surgery. The doctor reported: A bullet had cut through the flesh of Gary's left arm, but that was easily dealt with, nothing serious. But another had shattered his kneecap, ricocheted and damaged the bone below. The orthopedic surgeon was called, and he assembled his team and did what he could. "Although essentially," he said, "really, what I did was stabilize. The reconstruction will have to be done by a specialist. There's some terrific work being done in that field right now, really kind of miraculous." My sister had arrived by then, passing by me with a long look and no words, crossing the room to sit with Scott, speaking softly to him in the waiting hours that followed. The surgeon gave them an encouraging smile and the name of one of the miraculous specialists, promised to call him, discuss Gary's case. Helen, with Scott's arm protectively around her, thanked him.

When the doctor left the room I followed. I had been in and out of the waiting room all afternoon, unable to sit there long with Scott, later with Scott and Helen, unable to trust myself. Lydia had been there, too, sometimes sitting beside me, sometimes pacing, as she does. I had felt Scott's eyes, full of venom, burning through me all afternoon, but he never spoke. Lydia's pacing, though, was more than he could take. Late in the day, he exploded at her to fucking sit down or get out. She stopped, met his eyes, turned and left. I had to leave then, too, or I would have laid Scott out right there.

Lydia and I had gone to the cafeteria then, had coffee and tea, blankly watched McFall still questioning people, and then come back upstairs to wait for Gary. Now we left the room again, after the doctor; we stopped him in the hall.

"I'm the boy's uncle," I said, and the surgeon, a thin man younger than I, said nothing, just nodded and waited. "His parents want the sugar coating; I don't."

"As I said, he's doing well—"

"Will he lose the leg?"

"Oh, good God, no. There's no danger of that."

"Will he walk?"

He gave me a long look. "He's young. There are break-throughs in rehabilitative medicine all the time. We can do things now that were impossible five years ago. A year, two years from now—"

"He's an athlete. Football, baseball, track."

To that he said nothing. He met my eyes, then turned away, walked down the bright corridor shaking his head.

Across the street from the hospital, neon beer signs glowed in the windows of a bar called the Recovery Room. Lydia and I spent the next hour there, the hour we waited for Gary to be brought from his own recovery room to a place where we could see him. We took the long way around, leaving the hospital by a rear door to avoid the press. As we walked through the cold, sharp rain I said to her, "You don't have to stay."

"Is it easier for you if I do?" she asked. "Or if I leave?"

I didn't know the answer to that, so she stayed.

I had bourbon while Lydia drank more tea. We didn't speak much. She ordered food for us after a while, grilled

cheese for her, a burger for me, though I said I wasn't interested. The burger, when it came, smelled surprisingly
good, and I ate it, watched the young doctors and nurses,
orderlies and lab techs drink and flirt and pretend to themselves and each other that they just had regular jobs like
other people, jobs you could leave behind at the end of the
day. When the burger was gone I had a second drink, and
when that was gone Lydia called the hospital. Folding her
cell phone, she said, "He's in room two-oh-three."

I left two twenties on the table, a huge tip, because the
waitress did have the kind of job you could leave behind at
the end of the day.

Back at the hospital we picked up visitor's passes and
headed to Gary's room. A cop sat in the corridor outside.
Maybe that meant McFall believed me about Macpherson, or
maybe he just wanted his own ass covered in the unlikely
event I might be right. As Lydia and I approached we could
see the door was open, Helen and Scott sitting by the bed.
The cop asked for ID, we showed him some, and he went
back to staring at the ceiling.

"I'll wait for you," Lydia said to me softly. "He doesn't
know me."

I realized with a shock that that was true: all this time,
all this pain, and Lydia and Gary had never even met.

She stayed in the corridor, I entered the room alone. The
three of them turned to me. Gary's blue eyes, exhausted
though they were, lit when he saw me. Helen blinked; her
lip trembled. Scott heaved himself out of his chair.

"Get the fuck out of here," he snarled through clenched
teeth. I couldn't speak, but I didn't move.

"Dad?" Gary's voice was weak. I looked at him; Scott's
eyes stayed on me. "Dad? Can I just talk to Uncle Bill a
minute?"

"I don't want him here." Scott did not look at his son.
"Christ," he said to me, "you've been drinking. I can smell
it on you."

I still said nothing, focused on the hot, tight place inside
me, focused on forcing the fire to stay locked there.

"Just for a minute?" Gary said.

Helen stood, silently took Scott's hand, looked in his eyes. Color rose in his face, his own fire. "All right," he finally said, in a voice like sandpaper. "A minute." He moved aside so I could reach the bed.

"Alone?" said Gary.

"God*damn*—" Scott began, but Helen squeezed his hand again. I didn't know how far this would go, didn't have any sense at all of what I was prepared to do. All sound vanished, all sights except Scott's burning eyes.

Then he turned and left the room. Helen, with a look at me I had to turn away from, followed, and I was alone with Gary.

I sat in the chair my sister had been in, by the side of the bed.

"You okay?" Gary asked, his eyes taking in the bandage on my forehead.

"I'm fine," I said.

"I fucked up, huh?" He looked small to me, young.

"No," I said. "You did the right thing. The stand-up thing."

"I should have told you. What I needed to do."

"It might have come out the same."

"Paul's dead."

"He wanted to die."

"No, he didn't." He opened his eyes wider, anxious to correct me. "He only wanted things not to be the way they were, anymore."

I nodded. We were silent for a while, together. Gary's left arm was bandaged near the shoulder, where the bullet had cut through. An intravenous drip was needled into his other arm. He gestured to his right leg, immobile inside a thick cast under the blanket. He began to speak, stopped, swallowed, started again. "It's bad, huh?"

"Yes."

"Mom and Dad, they say everything'll be okay, but I can tell it's real bad."

"It's bad, Gary."

He tried a grin. "Out for the season, huh?"

I couldn't answer.

"Shit," he said, looked away. "Worse than that?"

"Yes." My voice was a whisper.

"Are they gonna—are they gonna cut it off?"

"No."

"Okay," he said, and he was whispering too. "Okay, that's good then."

I looked at him; his eyes were damp. He saw me see that, raised a quick hand, wiped the tears away.

I stood, bent by the bed, put an arm around him. It was an awkward embrace, because of the needle and the bandage, because of the cast, because we were both men, because of so many things.

His tears didn't last long. When his hold loosened, so did mine. I gave him a damp cloth for his face, took it from him when he was through.

"I'd better go," I said. "Your mother . . ."

He nodded. "Uncle Bill?" he said rapidly, as I turned.

I turned back, waited.

"Will you come see me?"

"Whenever you want," I said. "Nothing will stop me."

I passed by my sister and Scott in the hall, didn't look at them, didn't stop. Lydia was leaning on the wall a few doors down. We fell into step as we walked. When we reached the elevator she took my hand. We said nothing.

Lydia and I headed for the rear door again. As soon as we were outside I lit a cigarette. We walked through the rain to my car. The wind had gone elsewhere, leaving the rain behind, and the rain fell vertically now, steadily, without fury but not letting up, doing the job though it had forgotten just why.

As I took out my car keys a voice called my name.

"Smith!"

I drew a breath, turned. Scott stalked through the rain, headed toward us.

"Smith! What the fuck did you say to him?"

I spoke quietly. "I told him he's a brave, tough kid. I told him I was sorry."

"Bullshit! The kid's been crying. He—"

"Christ, Scott! He's crippled, a friend of his is dead. How is he supposed to feel?"

"There's more. You told him some other bullshit—"

"There is more," I said. I dragged deep on my cigarette, then tossed it down. Its burning tip glowed briefly through the rain, vanished as the water won. Scott stood close to me, rain running down his face. All his muscles seemed taut, working, as though he were pulling against invisible restraints. "But I didn't tell him."

"What do you mean, more?" Scott's voice was low now, dangerous. "You told him some bullshit, some lying shit, and now he—"

"No, Scott." I felt my own fists tighten, my face begin to burn. "Not bullshit. I saw it happen and so did you or you wouldn't be out here now. But I didn't tell him."

He took a step in. "You lying sack of shit—"

"Tell him what?" Lydia asked, and I think it was just to try to bring us down, to move the fire away from the fuse.

"Nothing!" Scott shouted. "It's bullshit. He told him bullshit because he fucked up so bad. Because he went in there to be a hero but that other kid's dead and Gary— Gary—"

I should have had the strength to do nothing, to turn and walk away. But the old fire swept through me, bursting from where I had tried to keep it, and fire weakens what it burns. "Gary's crippled," I said. "Because your friend Macpherson wanted him dead, Scott."

"You—"

"I saw every shot," I said. "Like when I played, like being in the zone. Everything was clear, everything was slow." It was that same way now, I realized: Scott before me, his face tight with rage; Lydia, motionless; the sound of each raindrop hitting the pavement, sharp and distinct. I had time to choose my words, time to do or say whatever I wanted. "Your pal Al," I said. "He fired the first two shots because he knew what that would start. He thought we'd all end up dead. The way he wanted."

"It's bullshit." Scott forced out rough words. "Pure fucking crap!"

I shook my head. "You hid what Al did before, twenty-three years ago, hid it from the town, hid it from yourself. You want to try to hide this, too?"

Scott, trembling, said nothing, but it hadn't really been a question and I couldn't stop now.

"It was because of what Macpherson thought Gary knew. What he thought you'd told him, about that time. But I didn't tell Gary. You know why?"

Still nothing; and I knew that was because any move Scott made now would trigger the explosion. "If Gary knew," I said slowly, "he'd hate Macpherson, and he might start hating you. That would make things worse for him, and right now things are about as bad as he can handle. So I didn't tell him. He thinks it was just bad luck, some cop's bullet that blew his leg away. He thinks he can trust you, and he does, and he loves you. And you're going to have to look at him for the rest of your life, and know that."

Each raindrop, pounding as it fell; each streetlight, each taillight on each passing car glowing completely alone, separately in the night. I didn't know if Scott heard them, saw them all, the way I did, didn't know how my words, intended as blows, fell on him. I waited, and then it came. With a wordless roar Scott leaped at me, fingers spread on hands that reached for my throat. He was powerful, stocky and muscular and full of fury; but I had all the time in the world.

I moved fluidly aside, clamped his wrist, yanked him toward me. His own forward force made him stumble and he crashed across the hood of my car. I hauled him up, threw a hard fist into his face, another into his chest, wanting his heart. He bent, staggered back, came up out of that with a punch that caught my jaw, snapped my head around.

I felt no pain; I felt nothing but the fire, sweeping me.

devouring. I reached for Scott, grabbed his arm. I twisted it high, pulled him in by it. He tried a roundhouse but I moved my head aside; he didn't even clip me. I was in the zone. I could do anything, land any blow, duck any punch. I hooked my ankle behind Scott's, sliced his leg from under him. He hit the ground with a howl. His face knotted, but this time with pain. He clutched his left arm. I stood over him, and when his eyes met mine, his widened, maybe with hate, though I hoped it was fear. He scrambled to stand, his left arm angling oddly, but he slipped on the slick pavement, moaned in pain as he landed. I dived for him, but Lydia shoved me from the side, and I crashed down onto the wet asphalt, too.

I jumped to my feet, still burning, ready, saw Lydia now standing in front of me, between me and Scott. I shouted, "Move!"

"No," she said.

"Get the fuck out of my way!"

"No."

"This isn't your fight! I'm going to kill that bastard!"

She said nothing and she didn't move. Rain fell like a curtain between us.

Scott lay moaning, clutching his arm. He stared at me, made no move to rise. It would have been so easy, and so final, to let it happen, let the fire consume us both.

But Lydia stood, feet spread, hands open, still and quiet, in the rain.

"Goddammit!" I roared. "You think you can stop me? You think you can take me?"

"No," she said. "I know I can't. But you'll have to go through me."

The fire raged everywhere now, in my skin, in my blood, in my heart. I saw it reflected in Lydia's eyes, heard it crackle in the crashing of the rain. It shook me, tore at me. I couldn't look at Lydia. I raised my fists, but everything was gone, the fluid grace, the timing and the strength. I couldn't move. I stood another moment, burning, then wheeled and took off through the storm.

· · ·

The streets of Plaindale: homes with yellow windows glowing in the night; blocks of stores, all closed now, except for
the bars. Streetlights defying the weight of the rain and the
darkness. I blundered, running, walking, stumbling. I
stopped in one of the bars, or two, choked on their smoke,
drowned in their tinny jukebox music, the repetitive idiotic
melodies and the words about nothing that mattered at all.
I walked past the grade school, through a park, and along
the edge of the highway. I stood and watched the cars stream
by: white lights racing at me, hulking bodies passing, red
lights vanishing, over and over. At a 7-Eleven I bought a
six-pack. Sometime, somewhere else, I found myself sitting
in a doorway, a can in my hand, one in my pocket; the
others were gone. Later, I was walking again, through a
ghost area of high fences topped with razor wire. I couldn't
make out, through the steady rain, much of what was behind
the fences: low buildings, trucks, piles of whatever needed
to be protected. I smoked until my cigarettes were gone,
looked for someplace to buy more but everything was
closed. I was soaked but I didn't care; I may have been cold
but I didn't feel it. The sky had begun to lighten, or maybe
I was crazy, when I found myself at the 7-Eleven again. A
young kid, maybe eighteen, sold me more cigarettes, but
said sorry man, no beer, it's Sunday. He paled when I began
to laugh, and he slid his hand slowly beneath the counter.
As though in a mirror, or standing beside him, I saw myself
as he did: sodden, bandaged, unshaven, unsteady. I backed
off, said hey man, no problem, left his store before he had
to take out whatever weapon he kept there, learn something
about himself he didn't need to know yet. I smoked, and
walked, and sat and stood and walked some more, and the
sky went to gray. The rain thinned, finally stopped. A guy
in a white apron was unlocking the door of a bakery as I
passed, so I waited until he was set, bought a cup of coffee.
At a doughnut shop, later, I bought another. I heard church

bells ring across a distance as I turned a corner, cut from the sidewalk into the hospital lot.

The lot wasn't empty, but my car sat by itself, nothing near it but glossy flat puddles and dull, rough asphalt. The streetlights had gone out, though cold blue flourescents still burned in the hospital windows like a sharp reproach. As I unlocked the car, the hospital doors slid open. Someone walked toward me: Lydia. I waited, watched her. Her skin was dull; dark crescents hung below her eyes. When she reached me we both stood, neither of us speaking. When I got in, she did, too.

I started the car, steered out of the lot. I drove through Plaindale, headed for the highway. Waves crested out of puddles as cars sliced through them. Horns blew, lights changed, people walked and stopped. All that was outside: in the car, only silence, solid and hard.

"What you did," I said finally, hoping to find the control to speak. "That was crazy." We were moving steadily back toward the city by then, the Sunday morning traffic flowing. They were the first words from either of us.

She turned her head to me, said nothing.

"I could have gone through you," I said. "However good you are, you couldn't have stopped me."

"I know."

"I could have hurt you badly, to get to Scott."

"You would have killed Scott."

"No loss."

"No."

I looked over at her. "Then why?"

"Why?"

"That kind of risk, for a bastard like him?"

"Him?" She said the word as though she didn't understand it. "You think I did that for him?"

"To keep me from killing him."

"For *him*?" She kept her eyes on me for a moment, then turned, clamp-jawed, to stare out the windshield at the other cars.

I lit a cigarette; Lydia rolled her window down.

I said, "I didn't ask you for help."

"I'm your partner."

"When did that make you my conscience?"

"You can be wrong," she said.

"So can you."

"But last night," she said, "I wasn't."

A long time later, not looking at me, she said, "Scott has a broken elbow."

"You expect me to be sorry?"

Staring out the window, she said, "I talked to him, while they were setting it. I told him Gary will never be safe as long as Macpherson thinks he knows his secret. As long as he thinks that without Gary it can stay a secret."

"What did—?"

"I don't know. But it might start Scott thinking." She turned to me. "It might make him useful. Killing him, that's useless."

That was all; I dropped her home in Chinatown, put the car away, walked back to my place. It's quiet in my neighborhood on Sunday morning, empty, especially on a morning like this, dull and gray and cold. Cold; I realized as I unlocked the street door, climbed the stairs, how cold I was.

thirty

I poured some bourbon as soon as I got upstairs, stripped off my wet clothes, and wrapped myself in a blanket on the sofa, thinking to sleep; but though sleep came, it wasn't deep and it was not peaceful. I kept waking to the light, to the sounds from the street, to the blanket's roughness and the pounding in my head; and I kept falling back into a restless state where vague ghostly shapes moved in dark waters of fear and longing. A dream finally came where the images were clear: my daughter Annie, alive as she always is in my dreams, ran beside Gary through the mist on a forest trail at the edge of a stream. They were fleet and strong; they were laughing and beautiful. I stood on the opposite bank, called to them, but my words had no sound, no strength to rise above the tumbling water. They ran on. Lydia walked out of the mist to stand on the path and face me. "You can ford it here," she said, but I couldn't move. The water flowed harder, swirled and crashed. Lydia pointed again at the place where the stream could be crossed, then turned and walked on. She went in the direction Annie and Gary had gone; I lost them in the shadows.

I woke violently, covered with sweat, heart pounding, mouth dry. I threw the blanket off, staggered to the bathroom.

Standing for a long time under the shower, I tried to let the real water, hot and steaming, erase the rushing stream I couldn't cross.

Finally I emerged, toweled off, shaved. I replaced the now-useless bandage on my forehead with gauze and adhesive tape. I did a good job on it, and it didn't take long. This was something I knew how to do, clean up after the damage was done.

I made coffee, stood at the front window and drank it. A truck sat in the loading dock across the street. The dock was shuttered, the truck all closed up. No one was around.

When the coffee was gone I had a cigarette, and then another. After a while I just stood at the window, looking through my own reflection at the empty street, the shadowed loading dock, the silent truck.

When the phone on the desk rang I turned to it, stared. It stopped after five rings; the voice mail had gotten it. I turned back to the window, and the same the second time, but the third time I walked over to the desk and picked it up.

"Smith."

"Sullivan. Jesus, you're a hard man to get a hold of."

I picked the cell phone up from the desk where I'd left it; it showed eleven messages, four from Sullivan's number. "Maybe I don't want to talk."

"Then listen. I thought you'd want to know Coach Ryder's retiring after this season."

"What does that mean?"

"They worked out a deal."

"Who?"

"Ryder and my chief. Brokered by Macpherson. Ryder quits, leaves town, we don't bring charges."

"On the steroids?"

"He says they were planted in his office. We have nothing else, and we won't unless we can get some of the boys to talk."

"And for that you'd have to lean on them."

"I tried this morning, with Randy Macpherson."

"They let you? I'd have thought he'd be off limits." I heard the meanness in my voice, but I didn't care. "Especially after yesterday. Must have been traumatic for all those kids, to hear about what happened, huh? Of course, Paul was just a geek, and Gary's new. But still."

"Warrenstown has counselors at the high school all day today and tomorrow." His voice expressed nothing.

"Gee, that's great. I hope the kids can get their heads screwed back on straight. Next season's sooner than you think."

"About Randy," Sullivan said mildly, ignoring my tone. "When Macpherson didn't stop me I knew it was a setup. Randy said yeah, he took clembuterol, but probably wasn't going to take it anymore, because he used to get it from Tory Wesley."

"That's shit."

"If I asked, that would be their story, all of them."

I waited for the fire, the anger, but all I felt was empty and cold. Tired beyond words. "Yeah, well, thanks for the news, Sullivan. See you around."

"Jesus Christ, will you hold on?"

"Why? It sounds over to me. Two kids dead, one crippled, but it's never too early to start getting ready for a new season in Warrenstown. It's only too bad you have to get a new coach. Hey, but maybe Tom Hamlin's available."

"Goddamn, you give up easily."

"I've been told my problem is I don't know when to quit."

"That's true, too," he said. "Here's what we have: I can't get at Ryder. ME says no one killed Tory Wesley. Even if you're right about Macpherson firing those shots—"

"I'm right."

"—even if you are, there's no crime. And you're the only one who tells it that way."

"Did you talk to Gary?"

"He doesn't know. He just remembers a lot of gunshots, and then he went down."

I saw, suddenly, rain, the circling lights on patrol cars, a wide stretch of water-sheeted asphalt. I heard gunfire and the howling wind. I lifted my eyes to the room: chairs, books, my piano, hard objects that I knew.

"Smith?" Sullivan said. "You still there?"

"What do you want?" I asked him.

"What do you want?"

Nothing, I thought, there's nothing I want, just go to hell, leave me alone. But I heard myself say, "Ryder and Macpherson."

"There was never anything I could have charged Macpherson with."

"You've made that point, Sullivan."

"And Ryder, like I said, they made a deal on the drugs."

"What about Stacie Phillips?"

"The attack? Without a positive ID from her that would never get off the ground. You said that yesterday."

"So what's your goddamn point, Sullivan? You trying to make sure I get it that I'm supposed to lay off these guys? *I get it.*"

"It was never me they were afraid of," he said, as if I hadn't spoken. "It was never about the law, never about the steroids. It was about something that happened twenty-three years ago that wasn't prosecutable."

"So?"

"Well, Al Macpherson and Coach Ryder still went to a lot of trouble."

"Sure," I said. "Macpherson's King Shit in Warrenstown and Ryder's the god of war. Who'd want to lose jobs like that? But if it came out what they did back then—they must have been afraid there are things even Warrenstown can't stomach. But so what? You heard your chief yesterday: 'All conjecture, no proof.' Conjecture like that from Gary Russell's uncle? What the hell good would it do for me to bang on people's doors to get them to listen? It would just make things harder for my sister's family."

"I thought making things hard for your brother-in-law was what you lived for."

"I'm out of that business."

"That a fact? Well, I don't know what your partner was whispering in his ear after you broke his arm last night, but I thought the guy was going to crap his pants."

"Scott? He was scared?"

"Maybe a little, yeah."

It might make him think, I heard Lydia say. *It might make him useful.*

Exhaustion flooded me with the suddenness of a cloudburst. I reached for my coffee cup; empty. I wanted nothing more than to end this conversation, hang up, to be alone, in silence and stillness.

"So what?" I said.

"So what, what?"

"All of this. What the hell difference does it make now?"

"I don't know," he said. "But you're the one that brought up Stacie Phillips."

"Stacie?"

"And you're not from around here. Maybe you don't know the *Tri-Town Gazette* isn't published in Warrenstown. It comes out of Greenmeadow."

"I did know that."

"What the hell else," he asked, "do you need to know?"

After we hung up I had more coffee, walked around the apartment, until I realized I was pacing, like Lydia. I sat on the sofa, thought about Scott in the Plaindale emergency room, about Macpherson's eyes under the Warriors cap. I thought about boys playing football in slanted fall sunlight, and about the tug streaming up the black Hudson in the middle of the night.

Goddamn that tug, I thought. Goddamn it.

I went to the desk, picked up the phone, dialed Linus Kwong.

"Yo, speak to me."

"Linus, it's Bill Smith."

"Dude! I've been calling you!"

"I know. I saw your number on my phone. I'm sorry it took me this long—"

"Hey, dude, it's cool! I mean, I saw that shit on the news last night! That was him, right?"

"That was him."

"What was his deal?"

"A football game," I said. "His high school seniors playing their own juniors and sophomores."

"Wow." Linus was silent for a moment, in awe. " 'Bigger and better,' that's what he said. Like, wow." After another silence: "But, dude. That whole thing I saw, that was like, some motel or something. Nobody said anything about a game."

"He never got near it. You stopped him, Linus. You and another fifteen-year-old kid. I want to thank you."

"Oh, hey, dude. Oh, hey. He was scary. He needed someone to stop him. Just . . ."

"Just what?"

"Nothing. The news. They showed the pictures, all you guys. Him being, like, shot. And it was like, I mean, I *talked* to the guy. I almost knew him."

"Yeah," I said. "I know, Linus. Listen, I'm sending you a check."

"Oh, hey, forget about it."

"No, I hired you."

"No, man. This was like . . . like, I don't want to be paid for it, you know?"

"I do know," I said. "Okay, Linus. And can I ask you something? I have a question I need to ask someone young."

"Sure, dude. What's up?"

"You could have gotten in trouble for some of the things you did for me, but you did them anyway."

"Well, yeah."

"Because you figured I could get you out of trouble, if it came?"

"Not really."

"Because you thought it was important enough to be worth the risk?"

"Sort of like that."

"What else?"

"Well, because," he said. "I mean, this is what I do."

"Okay, Linus. Thanks."

"For what? What's the question?"

"That was it, and you answered it. I'll see you, Linus." I added, "Stay out of trouble, okay?"

"Sure, dude." I heard a smile; I realized I didn't know what that looked like, on him. I'd never met Linus, never seen his smile myself. "Later," he said.

I hung up, lit another cigarette, made another call.

"Stacie Phillips."

"You ever just say hello?"

"Are you kidding? What if it's a source?" she demanded. "Or, say, someone involved in like the story of the year, calling to give me an exclusive?"

"How do you feel?"

"Who *cares*? I called you four times already! Come on, what happened out there? Wait, let me get my pad."

"I care, but I assume you're much better or I wouldn't be hearing this level of enthusiasm."

"For a story this big? I'd write it from a body cast."

I took a drag off my cigarette and went ahead. "I'll tell you everything that went on. And yes, it's an exclusive. I'm not talking to any other media."

"Cool!"

"It's the least I can do."

"That's true. So, spill it!"

"First I need to ask you something."

"After!"

"No, first. You know the story about the time the first mate was drunk?"

"If this is a corny joke," she said dubiously, "maybe you want to talk to my dad."

"No, I want to talk to you, and I want you to listen. The first mate was drunk, and the captain wrote in the log, 'First mate drunk today.' The mate begged him to take it out, because it could mess up his career, but the captain said any true event of unusual interest had to be entered. So the next day it was the mate's turn to keep the log. He wrote, 'Captain sober today.' "

"Is this a reporter joke?"

"It's a parable," I said. "About the uses of truth."

I spent an hour on the phone with Stacie, detailing everything I knew and thought, every theory and every fact, very careful to point out the differences between the two.

"That was the coach? Who beat me up?" she shouted, when I got to that part of the story.

"You just melted my telephone."

"I'll kill him! My dad will kill him! I—"

"No, Stacie, that's the point. You can't. You couldn't ID him then and you can't now. He'd deny it and he'd call you a hormone-crazed schoolgirl."

"*Hormones?* What do my hormones have to do with it?"

"Nothing. I'm just telling you how it works. The only thing you can do—the only thing *anyone* can do—is what we're doing now."

"That can't be true. You mean he can just get away with it?"

"People get away with things all the time."

"Is that what being a grownup is about?"

"It depends who you are."

"What do you mean?"

"You," I said, "are a reporter."

I finished the story, all the details. I asked, "You understand I'm the first mate here?"

"You're drunk?"

"Besides that. I'm the guy you quote, attributed or not. Then you say, there's no proof. No evidence of truth to the rumor. You interview Tom Hamlin, publish whatever he says, all in quotes. The army can do a positive ID for you, by the way. You interview Chief Letourneau. He'll probably talk to you, but he won't be happy about it. Do you care?"

"No, but I'll tell my dad to watch out for parking tickets."

"That's a point to remember, Stacie. Your folks could catch some heat over this, from other kids' folks."

"My dad and mom are expecting to retire to Tahiti after

I win my Pulitzer and can support them. I don't think I can do that if I let stories like this get away."

"Tahiti," I said. "I like it there."

"You've really been there?"

"I can tell your folks where to get breakfast."

"I'm sure they can't wait."

"Stacie? You'll need to talk to my brother-in-law."

"He'll talk to me?"

"He's your only real witness."

"But after all these years?"

"I think he understands now," I said slowly, "that the only way to protect his son from Macpherson is to stop protecting Macpherson's secret." And you had nothing to do with that, Smith, I reminded myself. All you wanted was to kill him, to make your sister a widow and Gary a killer's nephew. Lydia did it: found a way to use Scott's fear for his family—Scott's love, goddammit, because that's what we were talking about, love—found a way to use that, while you were desperate to use hate to destroy everything.

"Hel-*lo*?" I heard in my ear. "Earth to detective. Come in, detective."

"Sorry," I said. "Did you say something?"

"The Gettysburg Address. Your phone run out of batteries?"

"No, I did."

"Well, welcome back. The question was, do you think I can talk to Gary?"

"I . . . that's your call, Stacie."

"Okay," she said, and for a moment neither of us said anything else.

"And then," I started again, "you call Macpherson and let him deny it all, and publish whatever *he* says."

"Can he do anything to you?" she asked, sounding a worried note. "Get you in trouble?"

"Let him try. But he could sue the paper, so you have to be really careful how you write it. You and Stuart."

"Stuart?"

"Isn't that his name? Your rival at the *Gazette*?"

"Stuart Early? You think I'm giving any of this to him?"

"You have to. Most of it. The byline, if he'll take it."

"What?"

"You're the one who got beat up. This can't read like some wild revenge fantasy. It's got to look like you're trying to help out Ryder and Macpherson by giving them a chance to deny all these rumors, going back years."

"My story!" she wailed.

"Justice," I said.

"Not really," she said. "So we embarrass them. So what? It's not enough."

"You don't know what'll come of it. For one thing, if enough people believe the coach beat you up and Macpherson started that firefight, it'll ruin them. For another, you don't know who'll remember what from those days, stop telling himself he didn't know. This could change your town, Stacie."

"Is that what we're hoping for?"

"I am."

"It's still not enough. I don't see how you can call it justice."

"That's the problem with justice. There's no such thing."

We talked for a little longer, going over facts, times, dates. Then she hung up; she had a story to write.

I lit a cigarette, leaned back in the chair, shut my eyes. A few minutes later I sat up again, killed the cigarette, checked the voice mail. I listened to Sullivan's messages, and Linus's, and Stacie's. I erased them.

And there was one from Lydia: "Call me."

I stared at the phone, then walked over to the piano, lifted the lid off the keyboard. I didn't sit down. I fingered the keys, a few tentative chords. I used no strength, no serious muscle, but still the sound was too strident, the harmonies false and the notes unsustainable.

I closed the keyboard, stood looking around this place where I'd lived for so long. Outside, I heard a man shout to another. The steel shutter of the loading dock groaned and clanked as it lifted, ready to begin another day.

I picked up my jacket, went out to walk along the river.